I0761028

THE CAPTIVE MISSING

Book Two In The Captive Series

LK MAGILL

First Hale Press

This book is a work of fiction. Any references to historical events, real people, or real places are used fictitiously. Other names, characters, places and events are products of the author's imagination, and any resemblance to actual events or persons, living or dead, is entirely coincidental.

The Captive Missing/ LK Magill – 2nd ed.

ISBN Paperback - 978-1-7336155-2-5

ISBN Ebook - 978-1-7336155-3-2

ISBN Hardcover - 978-1-950928-04-0

DEDICATION

For every person who read ***The Captive Born*** *and asked me…*
Will there be another?

This one's for you.

ACKNOWLEDGMENTS

To God, the original author of life's many stories.

To my mother, Jan Koury-Hale, I could not have come this far without you.

To my early readers, Jenna, Krystal and Sara. These stories are only good because of your honest feedback. Your contributions are invaluable.

To the rest of my support system: Daddy and Kathy for your unending love. Jack and Molly for living with a writer in the midst of my artistic chaos. Cindy for babysitting and laundry. Lots of laundry.

To all of you… I thank you. I thank you. I thank you.

PREFACE

Stop right there.

Have you read *The Captive Born*, yet?

Because to understand the complex world that Val lives in…

You've simply got to read Book One in The Captive Series first.

Otherwise… Enjoy.

CHAPTER 1

Her heart was going to explode. The way it hammered in her chest she couldn't hardly breathe. Clutching at her seatbelt with one hand, Val braced herself against the inside of the rear door with the other. The driver's heavy foot pressed steadily down on the gas pedal, causing the Bentley's engine to rev and strain.

How long had it been since she felt this type of fear? Four years. Four peaceful years living under the radar in the south of France and in only a moment, it all came flying apart.

"My son?" Val managed to breathe out the question.

"We're on our way to his school now." The driver's hands twisted on the wheel, sending the car careening around a corner. "He should be fine."

"*Should* be?"

"Your husband's attorney already called. Jace is waiting for us."

Victor's words were calm, the way he himself always was.

He'd been her personal driver for as long as they'd been in the country and Jason trusted him. But this? Val hadn't even been at the stables an hour when Victor had come for her. Bracing both of his hands on her shoulders, he had steadied her before delivering the news.

Your husband has been placed under arrest.

She had merely blinked at him then. Her brain was so slow to catch up.

But then Victor had led her to the backseat of the shining silver car. With her horse still in the grooming racks and her saddle sitting on a post, they reversed down the brick driveway and out onto the asphalt road.

Her stomach lurched once more. Sweat came to tingle in her palms.

"What are the charges against him?" She asked.

The French police have taken Jason. But why? She had seen him just that morning. They'd been safe in their home with Jace rushing all about. His boyish energy was typical of any five-year-old at the start of a new day. Nothing was amiss. At least nothing on Jason's end.

Val had been forced to lie to him again, but that couldn't have anything to do with his arrest. She was certain.

"Some American problem." Victor answered, then braked hard before swerving to pass a slow moving van.

"What American problem?"

"I don't know."

Val exhaled, but the pit in her stomach did not ease. Outside her window, lavender fields whipped by. Row upon row of the romantically purple flower with its intoxicating scent blurred as they passed. They left her feeling slightly woozy.

It was beautiful here. Of course it was. It was beautiful everywhere Jason Riggs tried to blend in. Tilting her head up, Val examined her own reflection in the window. This area was expensive. The town car she was riding in was expensive. Jace's private school was expensive. In fact, all around her, luxury bloomed.

And she couldn't fault Jason, not really. Her husband just couldn't help himself. No matter what identity he used, or where he lived, the man turned everything he touched into mountains of money.

In fact, he had his fingers in half a dozen businesses now, the largest of which was still Riggs Oil. Despite the promise he'd once made to give it all up and disappear, Val's initial assessment had been correct. After the first few years, Jason's father had tracked him down. It wasn't long after that Jason stepped back in as CEO.

Just ahead, Val could see the heavy iron gates of Jace's school rapidly approaching. The sedan slowed before pulling carefully between the two pillars of stone flanking the entrance. Clinging ivy climbed the building beyond, adding charm to the blend of stone and plaster walls.

When Val twisted to unbuckle her seatbelt, Victor shook his head.

"Wait here," he instructed, as he put the car in park. "Jace will notice something is wrong if you go to collect him."

Ducking her head in acceptance, Val stilled her hand. He was right. And she didn't want to upset her son. But watching Victor move off toward the building alone was a challenge. As a mother, she wanted to run inside, flying down the corridors until she reached her son.

Only when he was with her would she begin to feel okay. Only then would she really be able to breathe again. Because if they could take Jason just like that, what was stopping them from taking Jace? From discovering he was truly a captive born?

Yes, they had done their best to kept his true circumstances a secret. On paper, he was the son of a free born woman named Kelly Martin. Later, that free born woman married Jason Riggs and became Kelly Riggs. And though Jason insisted on legally adopting his own son, Jace's birth certificate still listed his biological father as "unknown."

By fleeing the States and staying out of the lime light, their little family had been able to escape any real scrutiny. Tucked away on another continent, Val worked hard to avoid the media's eye. For all intents and purposes, she lived a good life as Kelly. The only time she even heard her old name was when she was at home with Jason. He just couldn't seem to kick the habit.

Squeezing her eyes shut a moment, Val inhaled deeply. Agency rhetoric sounded in her head. *Unwarranted emotion of any kind is intolerable.*

Deliberately she counted to four before releasing the air in her lungs with control. Composing her face in a relaxed sort of serenity, Val was soon worthy of any display box.

If Jason were here he would be frowning, she could see it. He hated her old training, the way she could pull down a mask and hide. But her husband wasn't here right now, and what

Jace needed was an unaffected mommy. And an unaffected mommy is what he would have.

So, the moment her boy appeared at the top of his school steps, Val was able to smile gently instead of cry.

"Mama, Mama!" Jace bounded through the car door, held open by Victor. "Why are you here? Mademoiselle said I had to leave early."

"Well, you've been such a good boy lately that Daddy wanted me to surprise you with a special treat." Val beamed into his blue eyes, laying an affectionate finger on the tip of his nose.

"What is it? Ice cream?!" Jace practically squealed.

"Does ice cream sound good to you, Victor?" Val called to the front seat, wondering if her driver would approve, he was often tasked with protecting her.

"It sounds more than good, Madame."

And so, for the next ten hours, the old agency Val went to work. She swallowed the bile that tumbled about in her belly and painted an easy smile on her face. She doted on her son while absently wiping the sweat from her palms on her riding breeches. She hadn't had time to change.

All day long, her ability to go through the motions without missing a beat served her well. At the outdoor cafe, Jace slurped up his double scoop of mint chocolate chip while Val sipped on an espresso. When they arrived back home, she folded her hands demurely in her lap and watched Victor and

Jace play soccer on the wide lawn beside their two-story Manor house.

Did she cringe just a little when the black and white ball barely missed shattering a window? No. Instead, she focused on the sound of Jace's laughter as it mixed with Victor's shouts in French. The noises lifted to curl in the thick canopy of trees that filled their garden.

On the surface, Val was picture perfect.

She sat at the outdoor dining table and watched them until evening fell. When the kitchen staff came to ask her about dinner, she requested a pizza, even though she knew the chef's lips would twist in disgust. It was Jace's favorite, and tonight, he would have it.

Running her manicured nails along the sleek wood of the table, Val glanced around at the pruned bushes and flowering plants. Anyone watching her would see an indulgent mother, or maybe a bored housewife. But no matter the outward composure she kept, the internal questions kept coming.

What was happening to Jason? Why was he in custody? Would they be coming for her next? For Jace? A sudden spike of panic threatened to undo her, so she clamped down on it… made it go away.

Thankfully, Jace carried on unawares. It wasn't until bedtime that her son began to notice his father's absence. In a normal week, Jason missed about half of their evening meals due to work so Jace hadn't questioned why he wasn't at dinner. No, it was bedtime when the fretting truly began.

"When's Daddy coming home?" Jace's little face was downcast as Val walked him slowly to his own room.

"Soon."

"Can I stay up until he gets here?"

"No, sweet boy." Val's heart twisted, she didn't know when Jason was coming home. Would it be tonight? Longer? She felt suddenly ill at the thought. "What about cuddling with me instead?"

"Really?" Jace's face lit with the invitation.

Before Val could even turn, Jace was backtracking down the hallway. He zoomed ahead of her, his little boy legs pumping like pistons as he slammed through the heavy carved wooden door to the master suite.

Normally, Val would scold him for it, but tonight she found she no longer cared. By the time she made it into the bedroom, Jace was in the center of their king-sized bed, rolling back and forth, causing pillows and blankets to tumble to the floor. Stopping for a moment on the threshold, Val watched him. His thick chestnut hair and bright blue eyes were a mirror image of his father. And the love she felt for him? There was no comparison.

After a beat, she moved forward to scoop and bend and pick up his never-ending mess. Jace merely giggled as Val tossed the discarded items back onto the bed before leaving him to go shower and change. When she returned, he was already asleep.

Settling down beside him, Val wrapped her arms around his lanky body, then blinked into the darkness. She had drawn all of the heavy curtains, which was unusual. Normally they slept with the moonlight streaking across the hardwood floor.

But tonight, she felt compelled to cover the wall of windows that overlooked the garden. As the silence engulfed her, Val did battle with herself. She was slipping. The fear had returned full force and it was suddenly so very hard to breathe.

A lifetime of terror was taking up all the room in her chest. And this was the exact reason she had been lying to Jason. This right here was the reason she was a sneak and a fraud.

Was it any consolation she'd been proven right? No. No it wasn't. Because apparently you can be right about something and still feel completely wrong. Val had discovered that little fact too many times to count.

CHAPTER 2

THE VOICES BEGAN SOMETIME AFTER MIDNIGHT. DRIFTING hauntingly up the stairs, the sounds snuck beneath her closed door, muted, but there. Mind groggy, Val registered male laughter. Could she be dreaming? Her body felt like a weight had sunk her down to the bottom of a pool. Beneath the water, she struggled against the slowness until panic had her sitting up, gasping for air.

Blackness permeated the bedroom. The curtains were still drawn against the moonlight that shone outside. Reaching out, Val laid her hand across Jace's back, drawing reassurance from his still steady breathing. He hadn't woken. So why had she?

The house was utterly silent for a few moments, making her question what had brought her around so abruptly. Maybe it was all just a bad dream. But then the distant deep murmurs resumed and a single set of footsteps began their ascent up the wooden stairs. Val's throat went completely dry.

The staff had already gone home and the security alarm

had been set. Victor was the only one staying the night and he never came up the stairs. Never.

Pressing one hand to her forehead, Val thought back. She was sure she'd turned the alarm system on.

Adrenaline began to course its way through her system as she swung her bare legs down from the bed. There was a pistol kept high in the closet where Jace couldn't reach.

Hands shaking, Val made a beeline for the gun, wishing all the while she had paid attention when Jason had shown her how to use it. Helpless. Why was she so helpless? Was the safety on? How could you tell?

"Val-" The whisper came from the other side of her bedroom door accompanied by the soft rap of knuckles against the old oak. "It's me."

"Jason?" Val's chest heaved, her hand still searching for the weapon hidden somewhere above her.

"Yes." Jason's voice was hushed.

Abandoning her quest for the weapon, Val raced to the door and wrenched it open. Jason stood in the doorway. He was all alone but his face had new lines of stress etched into it.

The moment he saw her, his hands snaked out to grab her waist and gather her close. Clinging to him, Val buried her face in his collared shirt, the one she herself had buttoned at the start of the day.

Jason shushed her quietly before walking them both back into the bedroom. He did not loosen his grip, but instead held her tight. After shutting the door firmly, he flipped the latch and stepped back. His hands ran up her arms, but his eyes were darting over her face.

"Where's Jace?" He whispered. "He's not in his room."

"He's in here." Val gestured to the bed and watched her husband's shoulders go slack with the relief of it. "What's going on?"

Exhaling, Jason ran his fingers through his crop of brown hair. He seemed to gather his thoughts, pacing away in the dark to stand over his son's sleeping form. When he returned, he drew her into the closet and began throwing his clothes into a bag.

"The gendarmes came to my office this morning," he began, trying his best not to let the empty hangers click in the quiet.

"Gendarmes?"

"Policemen," he supplied, not willing to meet her gaze. "But a kind of military police. Things in this country are not the same as back home."

"What do they want? Who's downstairs?"

"I spent all day going around with them and my attorney. When I agreed not to fight the extradition order, they became more… amenable."

"Extradition?"

Val grabbed at his wrist, causing Jason to meet her eyes. Even in the darkness, she could tell he was holding back.

"I'm a wanted man back home. Charges have been brought against me and I have to face them."

"What charges? Is this about Jace? Your businesses? What?" Val worked to keep her voice low, trying not to draw notice from their son.

"It's not about Jace. They can't possibly know about him. It's a bogus charge but I have to be there in person to fight it. The political climate has grown… more heated, since we left.

I've drawn the attention of some powerful people and this is just a play in a larger game. That's all."

"That's all? You make it seem like it's no big deal. Like you aren't packing your clothes in the middle of the night," Val hissed.

"The men downstairs are waiting for me." Jason put a hand on Val's shoulder, gave it a little shake. "I'm going to give them some expensive wine. Maybe a box of cigars, possibly with money in it. They're going to escort me to a plane and send me back to the US."

"What am I supposed to tell Jace? When will you be back?"

"As soon as I leave you're going to pack your own things and wake Jace up. *Do not* wait until morning. Victor will drive you to the airport where the jet will be waiting. While everyone is watching me get transported back home, you're going to fly to the Maldives."

"To Gabe and Bee?" Val's face filled with confusion.

"Yes, but more importantly, where there is no extradition to the States."

"What have they charged you with?"

"When you get there, I want you to stay. Do not leave the islands under any circumstance unless I tell you it's safe. Okay?"

"*What* are your charges?" Val's question became a demand.

"Promise me that you will take Jace and stay there."

"What are the charges?!" Her voice escalated along with her panic, causing both of them to glance towards the bed.

Jace shifted, but still slept.

"Harboring a captive," Jason admitted finally.

"Jason." Val's insides flipped. "How is this not about our son?"

"Trust me," Jason reached out, ran his thumb down the side of her cheek. "I'll take care of it."

There was no time to give her details. At least that's what he said before gathering her to him. When he brushed his lips against hers, ran his fingers through her hair, the gesture left a lingering sweetness of which she could still feel.

It wasn't until after he had gone, taking the policemen with their wine and their money with him, that Val wanted to collapse. She *wanted* to. And maybe for just a second, she let herself sag against his clothes hanging so still in their closet. But it was only a momentary slip.

Straightening her spine, she wiped the damp tears from her cheeks and quickly went to work. She had to get Jace out of the country and she had to do it now.

Victor was already in the hallway when she stepped out. They stood there staring at one another, Val's fingers wrapping the wrought iron railing that stretched to the staircase. Without a word, he brushed by her and entered her bedroom. As she watched, he scooped up her son and carried him carefully back down the winding staircase.

Jace's small legs dangled with each step, but thankfully he remained sleeping. Val followed close behind. His eyes fluttered briefly as he was lowered into the backseat of the town car. Quickly, Val wrapped him in a blanket and watched as her son succumbed to the heaviness of his eyelids once more.

With Val's two small bags stuffed in the trunk, Victor slid into the front seat and drove the car out into the night.

Absently, Val stroked along Jace's hair. Even though they were safely underway, a sick sort of dread filled her. She stuffed one hand into her oversized purse and clutched at the passports that lay inside. *Running. They were running again.* Tilting her head to the side, she felt the cold of the window glass soak into her hair. Would she ever be able to stop running?

The drive from Provence to the airport in Nice took a little over two hours but it felt like an eternity. Other headlights on the roadway were rare, but whenever they appeared, Val's pulse jumped. As the city loomed in the distance, the flash of headlights became more frequent, increasing until she had to shut her eyes against the pervasive glare.

Entering the airport took Val to a whole new level of anxiety. Despite the odd hour, it bustled with activity. And with activity came people, and with people, eyes.

It wasn't that she thought they were all looking at her, because they weren't. Some stood in line, walked the terminals distractedly or slept hunched in the rows of fixed plastic chairs. But all it would take was the wrong person to notice her. To notice her son and snap a photo.

Cambric Agency had been disbanded, Sharon Baine was locked in a prison cell, but still, someone was pressing captive charges against Jason. And that someone was too close for comfort. Ducking her head, Val held Jace's little hand tightly and walked close behind Victor. He led the way calmly, as if this were all normal, rolling her bags alongside him.

Together they navigated security and customs without incident. Victor did all the talking while Val soothed Jace's groggy protests. In silence, she watched her driver pass a few discreet envelopes to certain people and the way ahead of them was cleared. Jason's money. It was Jason's money saving them all over again.

Not until the final boarding gate did Victor finally stop and dip his head in farewell. He would be staying behind in France; his life was here. Val thanked him and she hugged him and he smiled at her before he left. They didn't have captives in France, so she didn't think he knew anything about them. Fleetingly, she wondered what that was like.

By the time Val settled into the wide white leather seats of the jet, Jace had fallen back to sleep. His small figure was curled up beneath his blanket, the seat reclined to almost horizontal.

Pressing the heels of her hands to her eyes, Val exhaled shakily. She should use this time to rest, try to get some sleep herself. But the flight promised to be a long one. It would be almost fourteen hours before their landing gear reconnected with runway, and so she knew there would be time.

Out the window, she watched as the jet pulled back from the terminal. Its wing tips flashed in the dark. Rotating ever so slowly, they pivoted until the whir of engines had them inching forward. Her fingertips dug into the armrests. The thrust of propulsion pressed her back into the seat. Faster and faster they went.

She held her breath, panic tightening her chest, heart pumping painfully in protest. At any moment she felt it all would end. At any moment they would be called back to the airport, asked to disembark, brought into custody. It wasn't until the plane lifted into the air, that Val was actually able to take in a fresh breath.

They made it out of France. Jace was safe.

CHAPTER 3

Out the tiny oval window, a vast sparkling ocean spread itself in every direction. They were somewhere high above the Pacific, and their final destination wasn't too far off. Tracing her fingertips over the thick glass, Val's eye caught on the far promise of islands. She could see their flash of browns and greens dotting the cerulean blue water.

An entire day spent on board an airplane would have been grueling for most. And in all honesty, Val was bone tired. Thanks to the luxury of a private jet, however, Jace had been able to pass the time well. With no other passengers, he stretched and jumped about, working out the jitters that youthful bodies seemed bound to contain.

Despite the threat of an impending sugar crash, Val indulged him. He watched movies, played video games, and ate junk food to his heart's content. Really, she was just putting off the inevitable.

When Jace questioned her about his father and their

sudden trip, she told him only that Jason had been called away on business. Her boy had frowned at the simple explanation until she mentioned visiting Bee and Gabe. The little boy simply adored his Auntie and Uncle, so he swallowed that bit of information happily.

Throughout the years they had traveled to the Maldives a number of times. It was always a comfort to reconnect with her old friends in their tropical hideaway. Although, only Bee had ever reciprocated by coming to France. Since landing in the islands after Sharon's trial, Gabe had never left.

As Jace continued to rush about the cabin, the jet began its descent. The sun was just setting over the water now, making the light from the runway and collection of nearby buildings seem small and isolated. Reaching out a hand, Val finally snagged her son's wrist and pulled him onto her lap. She pointed out the window, redirecting his attention to the lone airstrip below. It occupied an entire small island by itself.

Wriggling excitedly, Jace pressed his face against the glass for a better view. Somewhere down there, Gabe was waiting.

During the flight Val placed a call to Bee who set everything up. They weren't able to speak openly with Jace listening, but oddly Bee seemed to already know what was going on. A strange sense of foreboding pricked at the back of Val's mind ever since. Though she tried to push the feeling aside, it continued to spring up again and again, blending itself with worry over Jason's arrest.

Purposefully now, Val shook her head. The strip of asphalt was rushing up to meet them and Jace's eyes had grown to the size of saucers. Squeezing his little body tight, Val whispered to him until the bump of landing gear signaled they were safe.

Beyond the window, the promise of tropical heat hung heavily in the air.

Gabe was waiting for them, as promised.

His golden-blonde hair stood out amongst the crowd in the terminal, though his tan skin had grown even darker with all the days spent in the sun. Island life made this already gorgeous man more so, if that was possible.

Val flashed him one of her winning smiles before wondering at how effective it was. Gabe's brown eyes were filled with concern and didn't waver at her reassuring expression. It was easy to fool most people, but a fellow captive… that was a different matter.

Upon spying Jace though, Gabe produced a brilliant smile of his own. Faker, Val thought ruefully, as they stopped beside him.

"Uncle Gabe!" The boy cried, before flinging himself up to be caught in Gabe's strong arms.

"It's my favorite guy!" Gabe hoisted the boy easily onto his shoulders, where Jace grinned triumphantly. "Ready for some man time? Fishing? Snorkeling?"

"Oh yeah." Jace bobbed his head.

"What about your Mama?" Gabe reached for Val, pulling her in close with one arm. "How's she doing?"

"She's fine." Jace dismissed the question.

"Fine is good." Gabe gave Val a knowing look before lowering the boy and grabbing their luggage.

Out on the docks, the wooden platforms shifted with each step they took. Dusk had settled in, filling the ocean with uncertain shadows. There were no roads or bridges connecting the airport to the rest of the islands, not even the capital city of Male. To get to the house, they would have to take a ride in Gabe's speedboat.

Val's stomach twisted uncomfortably as she stood back, watching. Gabe loaded first Jace and then their bags. He was being too quiet, his eyes glancing at her every so often. Something was definitely up. But then his hand was bracing her waist and she was stepping inside. Normally, the two of them would have traded jabs by now, teasing each other as they always had. But instead, only the sound of Jace's excited banter filled the air.

Gabe stepped to the wheel of his sleek white boat, fired up the dual outboard engines and cut through the dark water without comment. Eager to catch the mist of salty spray, Jace leaned his face over the side, laughing. Val gripped the blue nylon straps of his lifejacket in both hands but did not stop him from experiencing the rush.

The truth was, she didn't want to hold him back from anything. She wanted him to be as free as free could possibly be. Feel the wind in his face, taste the salt of the water, laugh in the night. Everything she had never been allowed to do, she wanted Jace to have.

Soon, a massive two-story home appeared in the distance. It was built up on stilts over the water, a lone structure poised at the end of a winding wooden dock. Just like in all of Gabe's daydreams, the tiny island was mostly empty. There was even a white sandy shore with a scattering of palm trees. He had come a long way from the windowless bedrooms of Cambric and Val was proud. It was everything he had ever described, and maybe more.

Pulling up to the home now, Val marveled at its beauty. All lit up in the night, the in-deck pool and jacuzzi glowed, throwing light against the face of the house. Its windows poured forth with illumination. The slim figure of a woman could be seen standing still as a silhouette in one. Bee. Here, waiting for her. Even after all these years, it made Val's heart heave with relief.

Angling the bow of the boat towards the dock, Gabe cut the engines and let them coast until they bumped lightly against several large buoys. In a heartbeat, he was throwing ropes and hopping out after them. Before he even had a chance to secure the boat, Val heard Bee's cry.

"Val!" Bee jogged towards them along the dock. "I'm so glad you're both here."

"Me too." Stepping out, Val let herself be wrapped up in Bee's embrace, rocking together slightly. "Sorry about the late notice."

"You're sorry? We're the ones who are sorry." Bee took a step back, holding Val at arm's length. The worry in her eyes could be seen clearly in the cast-off light from the house. "This is all our fault."

"Your fault? What are you talking about?" Val's eyes traveled away from Bee to land on Gabe. He looked down, rubbing at the back of his neck with one hand.

"You mean you don't know?"

"Don't know what?"

"The charges against Jason-" Bee swallowed, squeezing Val's hands in her own. "They're because of us."

"I don't understand."

"It's Gabe. The captive that Jason is charged with harboring is Gabe."

CHAPTER 4

"This doesn't make any sense." Val drank deeply from the glass of Merlot that Bee had poured for her. "Gabe made a deal with the FBI, he's free."

Val's oldest friends shared a meaningful glance, the likes of which had her heart descending into her stomach. They were situated in the living room, Jace playing distractedly with new toys on the wood floor. Before long he would need a bath and then bed, but she couldn't bring herself to face the chore at the moment.

Shoving up from the turquoise cushions on the sofa, Gabe walked to the open doors that led out onto the deck. For several moments, he faced the water. Its gentle lapping was a constant background noise, soothing any sharpness.

"The deal I made was unprecedented," Gabe spoke finally. "It had never been done before and Sharon has contested its validity."

"She's in prison," Val stated flatly. "Can she even do that?"

"Yes, apparently," Bee supplied. Her bare legs, tan from the sun, were folded beneath her on the couch.

"I told you Sharon is dangerous." Gabe rotated to face them before leaning his shoulder against the doorframe, his arms crossed over his chest. "Maybe Agent Finn and Jason didn't realize just how dangerous. Cambric floundered for a while after her conviction, but I'm guessing that was only because it took her time to settle into her new surroundings."

"I thought Cambric was being disbanded." Val frowned.

"It was one suggestion," Gabe supplied. "But before that could take place it was purchased by a shell corporation. No one knows who the owner actually is but The Agency is back and fully functioning. Sound familiar?"

"You think Sharon owns it again?"

"I know she does." Gabe blew out a breath, head tilted towards the ceiling. "I know because she transferred ownership of me back to Cambric and they have legal standing enough to contest my freedom. Their argument is that I had no right as a citizen to negotiate my own release. I would have needed Sharon to sign off on the original agreement for it to be valid. She never freed me and she was the only one who could."

"When did all of this take place?" Val questioned.

"Cambric filed a lawsuit two years ago against the Feds, Riggs Oil and Jason personally." Gabe's face remained serious as he watched the information wash over Val. "I'm sorry, but at the time we all agreed you shouldn't be burdened with the details."

"*Burdened with the details*?" Val was incredulous, she could hear her husband's voice in those words. "Give me a break Gabe, you're even beginning to sound like him."

"Don't start." Gabe held his voice in check, gesturing towards Jace who had ceased playing to listen. "The three of us took a vote on it. The decision was unanimous."

"You kept this from me?" Val turned on Bee, emerald eyes glistening.

Leaning closer, her friend placed a warm hand over Val's knee and gave it a light squeeze. Bee wouldn't respond with words, but instead simply ducked her head once before pursing her lips and letting go. Sitting back in awe, Val's mouth hung open as she watched the woman she had once called her sister unfold her legs from the couch and stand.

"I've got some new bath toys waiting for you Jace," Bee said, extending a hand towards the boy. "Want to check them out?"

"Sure!" Jace scurried away to follow a departing Bee, not bothering to look back over his shoulder.

Alone now, Gabe's face folded into a deep frown. There had been a time when he had raged against Jason and all that he stood for. He hated the money, the power, the cocky surety and careful calculation. Accusing him of not only siding with the man, but sounding like him, had Gabe's back up, if only for the moment.

Over the past years though, the two of them had formed a relationship of sorts. A trust had grown, and so yes, maybe things had changed and Gabe was beginning to see Jason differently.

Pushing off the threshold of the door, he stalked to the kitchen and began opening the white lacquer cabinets. Val refused to turn her head to watch but she heard him remove a glass. The tap of it striking the stone countertop was loud in the large space.

Out past the wide doors, the moon had risen over the ocean. The rolling murmur of the waves glimmered in the distance. The beauty, like the betrayal, felt solemn.

"What would you have done differently had you known?" Gabe crept up behind her, the ice in his glass clinked lightly just behind her ear.

She took her time thinking about it. The question rolled over in her mind, already cloudy with the events of the past twenty-four hours. Two years ago Jace would've only been three. He had been home with her all the time then, and even with his nanny's help, Val had been overwhelmed. If Jason had told her about the lawsuit, about Gabe and Sharon and Cambric, what would she have done?

"Nothing," Val admitted at last. "I would've been scared out of my mind, but I don't know what I would've done about it."

"For what it's worth-" Gabe leaned over the back of the sofa, forearms braced next to Val's head. "I'm sorry."

Staring down at her wine glass, Val took a moment to study the last of the ruby-colored dregs. All this time she thought they were safe. That Jace was safe.

Swirling the tiny bit of liquid twice, she brought the glass to her lips and downed what remained. The truth was, as a captive born, there was no such thing. Taking her cue, Gabe raised his tumbler of whiskey and swallowed it down.

After a moment, Val looked up and over her shoulder. His eyes full of apology, Gabe bobbed his head once before retreating up the far staircase, leaving her all alone.

CHAPTER 5

THAT NIGHT VAL SLEPT CURLED UP WITH HER SON, WINDOWS open wide to the melody of the sea. She didn't recall what it was that filled her dreams, but upon waking, she was left feeling drained. Sitting up on the queen-sized mattress, Val drew her knees to her chest and sighed. Worrying would do nothing to fix the unfairness of the world.

Eyes drifting out the window, she took in the winding wooden dock as it snaked its way toward the shoreline. This bedroom faced the island, with its pristine white sand beach and clusters of inviting palms. Their radiant green leaves fanned out to drift in a mild breeze. It was going to be an absolutely perfect day.

But almost every day here was an absolutely perfect day. Because Gabe had been right about one thing. All those nights the three of them sat huddled together at Cambric, hiding his forbidden presence in their room, they had talked of where he would go. *If* he could go. And this place was indeed paradise.

Jace stirred beside her. His mouth, which hung open slightly in his sleep, snapped shut as he arched his back to stretch. The space rocket pajamas he loved so much were twisted about his body, causing his small hands to clutch and grasp at the cotton fabric. He often tossed and turned in his sleep.

Down below, the sound of breakfast could be heard. Soon the smell of bacon began to creep up the stairs.

"Good morning," Val said.

Standing up to stretch, she straightened her own oversized shirt. It was one of Jason's. She loved that it captured his smell. Murmuring sleepily under his breath, Jace took a few seconds to come fully awake. The moment he remembered where he was, his energy flooded back full force.

Eyes bright, he practically bounced his way off the bed before disappearing down hall. The pounding of his footsteps on the staircase sent shivers to echo throughout the quiet house. Val smiled. At least one of them was still blissfully unaware. Absently, she ran a hand back through her tangled locks before following her son's path down and into the kitchen. Time to face her friends. The ones who knew danger was coming, but hadn't warned her.

Bee was already up and dressed. Holding a frying pan poised in one hand and a mug of coffee in the other, she leaned in to press her lips to the top of Jace's head. Her son was balanced on a stool standing off to one side, waiting to crack the eggs necessary to make pancakes. Bee always let him do it, even though egg yolk ended up everywhere.

When Bee glanced over her shoulder and spied Val, her expression was one of tentative appeal. She wondered if she would be forgiven. And of course she already was. Grudges were particularly hard for Val to keep, there just didn't seem enough time to hold onto them. And time was one commodity captives valued most.

Walking up next to her friend, Val leaned in to give Bee a peck on the cheek. It was meant as a gesture of peace between them and ended in a tight hug.

"Alright, which one of you two ladies is my woman?" Gabe boomed from just behind them. "I don't want to get in trouble for pinching the wrong behind."

"The one that's cooking," Bee giggled, grabbing up a spatula. "And I have a weapon so be warned!"

This sent Jace into a fit of laughter as Gabe backed away, both his hands raised in surrender. Avoiding his questioning eyes, Val grabbed her own cup of coffee before retreating to the center island bar and settling on a stool.

Gabe did the same. He wouldn't let her get away so easily.

After a few moments of perching there quietly together, the upset between them began to fade.

Over the next several weeks, each day was more beautiful and peaceful than the last. They explored the island, went fishing off the dock, took turns driving Gabe's boat and marveled at the vibrantly colored fish while snorkeling. At first, Val had been concerned about being surrounded by water. Not only was the entire ocean wrapped around the house, but the deck itself had a pool and spa.

But Gabe was a watchful uncle, keeping Jace always within

his line of sight. Even so, he still worked with the boy every day, teaching him how to swim. Val made Jace wear his life-jacket while riding in the boat or playing on the dock, but her instinctual fear eventually waned. Gabe had her son swimming like a fish, even Val had to admit it.

Every evening at six o'clock, Jace and Val would wait for a phone call from Jason. By the time the sun was setting in the Maldives, it was cresting the eastern sky in Texas. The arrangement actually ended up working well. The morning was always the best time to catch Jason before he began his day.

Nestled next to his mother on the couch, Jace and his father would discuss the day's adventures. After they were finished, Val peppered her husband with questions about his court case, then rolled her eyes as he danced around providing any real answers. Although frustrated that he was holding back, the sound of his voice and charm of his smile melted any real anger that wanted to form.

It was the nights the internet dipped out on them that were hard. When they couldn't see Jason, or hear his voice, then both Jace and herself dropped into a sort of melancholy. Jace missed him. She missed him.

"Uh-" Val huffed one evening, tapping her finger angrily on the screen of the tablet. "Is the internet not working?"

"Should be!" Gabe called from the front deck. He and Jace were busy cleaning the fish they caught for supper. "I'll check in a second, okay?"

"Okay," Val echoed before she tossed the tablet onto the sofa.

She had spoken with Jason only the day before, but he

mentioned having to attend another court hearing in New York and she wanted to know the results. So far, his attorney was able to get the charges against Riggs Oil dismissed by proving that their funds were not used in the five million dollar payout to Gabe. Despite this bit of good news, Jason and the Feds were still defendants.

"Worried?" Bee lowered a glass of wine down in front of Val's face, then waved it slowly side to side.

"No, just helpless." Val took the offering, shifting her body to make room as Bee settled down beside her.

"Why so?"

"Because I've tried to look up the court case online and the website is impossible. I can't get any real information out of Jason, and all the articles I've seen are just sensational fluff pieces. I have no idea what's really going on and it's driving me crazy."

"Maybe I can help with that." Gabe strode through the door, fish filets piled across a cutting board. Jace zoomed behind him, proudly carrying his own catch.

"Do you know something we don't?" Bee twisted her head, following Gabe's progress to the kitchen.

"No, but we're running short on supplies and I was thinking of making a run into the city. I can pick up a few newspapers while I'm there."

"Do they even have newspapers anymore?" Val joked.

"In Male? Yes." Gabe washed his hands in the sink. "I was thinking I'd take Jace, too. It'd be good for him to have a change of scene."

Bee and Val eyed one another, communicating in silence while Jace raced around to start the process of begging. On the one hand, the idea of letting Jace leave her sight made Val sort of queasy. On the other, it would be awfully nice to have a bit of peace and quiet. They wouldn't technically be leaving the islands, just going to the capital, and Gabe would take care of him, no doubt.

As the seconds ticked by, Jace hopped on his tip toes, clasping desperate hands together in prayerful hope. Male was a bustling city, surprisingly filled with high-rise towers, restaurants and various shops. The ride by boat wouldn't take them long, and the break in routine would probably do everyone good.

"There's an arcade..." Gabe hummed from the kitchen, sending Jace's puppy-dog eyes to pout even further.

"How could I say no to an arcade?" Val sighed, then clutched at her wine glass as Jace threw himself gratefully into her arms.

"We'll leave tomorrow morning and be back sometime in the afternoon." Gabe informed them before striding back out to the barbecue.

That night, despite the fact that Jason did not call, Jace was able to drift off to sleep happily. He was distracted by the promise of an adventure with Gabe and it made Val even more certain she made the right decision.

When the morning came and Gabe loaded Jace into the boat, Val and Bee stood on the dock waving as the they reversed into the open ocean. Jace's innocent face radiated his pride as he sat in the shotgun seat. The attention from his uncle had done wonders to lighten the child's spirit.

Little did he know; the women were possibly just as pleased to see them go. No more mess, no more yelling and splashing. Peace, at last. Well, for half a day at least.

"Pina Coladas on the beach?" Bee squealed.

"Yes please!" Val smiled.

Back in the kitchen, the blender whirred as Bee dumped in rum, coconut cream and pineapple juice along with a hefty scoop of ice. Val changed into a black bikini and fetched an armful of oversized towels, the heavenly blue colors of which matched the intensity of the water.

Arm in arm, the two of them strode down the dock until they felt the hot sand simmering beneath their bare feet. A few hundred yards down the strip of land there was a small wooden structure with palm fronds draped over its slanted roof.

Bee and Gabe's home was not the only one on the tiny island. There were two more homes of a slightly smaller size but they were vacation rentals and remained uninhabited for most of the year. During the travel season, when the homes were full, Bee and Gabe hosted outdoor parties using the shared building as a bar. Val had attended one such gathering, and recalled the fantastic spectacle of music, dancing and drinking that was involved.

But today it was all quiet. Today, they were all alone. The other houses stood empty and the small bar unused. Just past the building were a series of posts Gabe had installed to hang hammocks from. He even erected a shade cover to make them more inviting.

"Yessss." Bee exhaled her satisfaction, setting down the large thermos of booze and flopping face first onto one hammock.

"I can't even tell you how amazing this is right now." Val dropped the towels and laid back next to her, gingerly testing the extra wide swing before reclining fully.

For several minutes the two of them absorbed the warmth of the breeze and listened to the steady pulse of the ocean stroking the sandy shore. Val lay on her back, one foot dangling low enough to touch the ground. Slowly, she pushed them back and forth, back and forth.

Finally, Bee rolled over and sat up, adjusting her sunglasses.

"Ready for that drink?" Bee smiled.

"Lay it on me." Val cackled, then leaned over to retrieve the two cups they had brought.

Holding them steady, Val inhaled the scent of saltwater while Bee filled them with the candied concoction. The taste was enticing and sweet, hiding the shock of alcohol that promised a pleasant buzz. Together the women sank back into the folds of the hammock, shoulders touching, legs overlapping easily. Time like this had become increasingly rare. Who would have known there was something about Cambric they both would have missed?

"So, still no ring, huh?" Val began the familiar line of questioning.

"Nope." Bee groaned, then gulped at her drink.

"What's holding him back?" Val asked, staring up at the thatched shade above them. "You guys own this place together and the boat. You're practically married already."

"Again, nope." Bee let one leg dangle over the side of the

hammock. "This is Gabe's house and that is Gabe's boat. I didn't help him buy either."

"Oh." Val bit at her lip subconsciously. "I guess I just assumed."

"You know he was an initial investor in two of Jason's companies."

"Yeah, but I guess I just didn't think much of it."

Val sipped at her drink, remembering how Jason had gone to Gabe to pitch that startup. It was back when they first fled the country, back when he vowed to disappear, back when he promised to give up Riggs Oil.

"The investments have really paid off, Jason's a genius." Bee shifted to reach for the thermos and poured them both a refill. "Actually, Gabe has almost paid him back that five million from the FBI deal. Two more payments to go."

"Wow."

"Yeah, wow." Bee shifted to look over at Val. "You really don't have anything to do with his work, do you?"

"No, I guess I don't."

A few birds called from the tree line. Val watched the sway of the palms.

It was true, she had never shown an interest in how Jason made his money. Blame her agency training or the suppressive breeding that had surely gone into her existence. Or maybe in the end, Val simply trusted her husband. She did what he told her to, without much serious thought. And for that matter without many questions. On second thought, perhaps that hadn't been wise. Maybe she should have been more aware. Then perhaps she would've seen this court mess coming a lot sooner.

"I do have a theory," Bee said, breaking through Val's reverie.

"About?"

"Gabe and his inability to commit."

"What do you think it is?"

"Well, he never got to choose to be with a free woman. I think that maybe he still wants to experience that." Bee exhaled before holding out her cup for another dose.

"You think he's cheating?" Val picked up the thermos and topped them both off.

"I don't know."

"Come on, Bee. He *chose* you, didn't he? And he's been crazy about you since day one."

"I don't know if that's the same thing. We were sort of thrown together, he never got to date or anything. I just think maybe that's what's wrong."

"Have you talked to him about it?"

"We don't talk about that kind of stuff," Bee replied.

"Okay, have you had a fight about it?"

"Oh, yeah." Bee smiled ruefully.

The two of them were like lighting a match to a powder keg. All heat and spark and fire. They usually skipped normal discussion and went straight to argument.

"So, what about you?" Bee resumed. "Have you told Jason the truth yet?"

Val grimaced, thinking back to only last month when he had pressed her again about seeing a fertility specialist.

"I take that as a no."

"How about a *not yet*?" Val ventured.

"Come on, Val. Don't you think this has gone on long

enough? I mean, he's been wanting another baby for years. Why don't you just tell him?"

"You don't understand." Val sighed.

"How hard would it be to explain you don't want any more kids?" Bee pressed. "It's better than taking birth control behind his back."

"I *will* tell him." Val swallowed before adding. "Just not yet."

For a minute, maybe longer, they sat there in silence.

Guilt flooded her.

It was true, Jason wanted more children. And the thing about Jason was… he got *everything* he wanted. So even if Val had been up front in the beginning, she knew things wouldn't have gone her way. Even if she had explained about her fear and anxiety it wouldn't have stopped him. Even if she reminded him that each child she had would be vulnerable to the captive system, he would have dismissed her, convinced her, overruled her.

So yes, Val had lied to him. She had nodded her head and pretended to want a baby, too. She had kissed him and loved him and welcomed her into her bed time and again, pretending to try for one. But all the while, she had smuggled birth control pills down her throat. All the while she made *certain* what Jason wanted would never, ever happen.

"Enough with this serious stuff." Bee broke in again, giving Val a swift elbow to the side. "Let's go for a swim."

Running quickly down the beach, the two of them splashed into the sea at the same time. It was cool but not cold, with a gentle tidal flow that lapped about their legs. Sunshine beat down from high overhead.

Sitting in the shallows, they let the water drift about their waists until their feet were wrinkled prunes and the afternoon approached. Val could spend all day here, day-drinking in paradise with her best friend. But in the distance, the sound of a boat engine purred, signaling the return of Gabe and Jace. Adult fun time was at an end.

Begrudgingly, Val and Bee waded out of the sea. They gathered their things slowly, stifling drunken giggles before trudging back to the dock. It snaked back and forth, winding prettily back towards the imposing house.

Beneath her bare feet, the sand felt gritty as Val padded along the smooth wooden surface just behind Bee. When the white boat drew closer, her old friend lifted one hand to her brow, squinting her eyes against the glare on the water. Seeing Bee's scrutiny, Val did the same and stopped short.

Her boy wasn't in that boat.

No. In fact, it was occupied by three adults instead.

"Gabe is going to kill me," Bee whispered before raising her voice in a shout. "Mother! Mrs. Riggs! What brings you two way out here?"

CHAPTER 6

Bee's mother is here... along with Jason's. Great. That's just great. Careful not to show her immediate impulse of despair, Val composed her features in a welcoming smile and offered a wave. It was not returned. No wonder Jason hadn't phoned the night before, Val thought ruefully, he didn't want to tell her his mother was coming.

Undaunted by the rise in tension, Bee forged ahead and embraced her own plump mother in an *almost* natural hug. Almost. As the women said their hellos, a tall man hopped onto the dock and set about unloading their luggage. Leather satchels scattered with expensive logos began piling high, causing the floating dock to list to one side.

That's when Elaine Riggs stepped out. Tugging at her chartreuse linen dress, she sighed audibly. The heat caused it to cling to her slight figure. Her short black hair, which had previously held a curl, now frizzed unexpectedly at the ends.

Though these were tiny cracks in her usually impeccable image, they did nothing to squelch the vigor of her demeanor. She was a pint-sized stick of dynamite, oozing explosive command from every pore.

Val blinked once before giving her head a little shake to clear it. She wished half-heartedly she hadn't helped Bee polish off that batch of Pina Coladas.

"Veronica!" Elaine called, her wrist flicking around in the air. "Such a lovely vacation home you have here."

"Thank you, Mrs. Riggs." Bee ducked her head. The only people to call her by that name were her parents and the Riggs family, everyone else stuck with Bee.

"I am sorry not to have given you notice." Lillian Durand stood off to one side, allowing the boat's driver to carry their suitcases up to the house. "Your phone line seems to be down."

"We are having some trouble with it," Bee acknowledged, eyes scanning the belongings that still littered her dock. "To what do we owe this pleasure?"

Sticking her tongue in her cheek, it took everything Val had to keep from rolling her eyes. The tone of voice and cadence of speech that Bee was using were text book agency training. So polite. So formal. Enunciating each and every word. But even so, never in all their years there together had Bee been quite *this* polite.

"I'm afraid that Elaine is on a bit of a family errand." Lillian linked her arm with her daughter's before beginning a careful walk down the dock. "But seeing as we came all the way out here, I thought perhaps you'd be willing to entertain us for a few weeks."

"Of course, Mother," Bee responded, shoulders remaining relaxed. Any hesitancy she may have felt was well-concealed. "We have two additional guest rooms that you and Mrs. Riggs are more than welcome to occupy."

As the two women meandered toward the house, their voices were caught up by the wind and swirled away. Left alone now, an awkward silence filled the space between Val and Elaine, one which neither of them was tempted to break. The former for lack of having anything to say and the later for having too much.

It was no secret Elaine disapproved of Val from the start. She was a proud and highly moral woman who abhorred the idea of captivity, especially when her eldest son partook in the practice. Even when Jason's true motive for purchasing Val had been revealed, and his character eventually cleared, the initial distaste for Val had remained. She wasn't good enough for him. Not smart enough, ambitious enough, educated enough, wealthy enough.

When Jace was added to the deal, a truce of sorts had formed between them. Though Elaine could barely tolerate Val, there was nothing she wouldn't do for her grandchild. Their mutual love for Jace was probably the only thing the two women shared.

As the boat driver walked by, hauling with him another load of luggage, Elaine caught him by the sleeve and pressed a few folded green bills into his hand. He smiled and ducked his head before hurrying on. Elaine glanced once at Val, then headed towards the house.

Forced to trail doggedly at her mother-in-law's heels, Val

focused on the creak and sway of the wood beneath her feet. Lillian mentioned staying a few *weeks*. Val stifled a groan.

"Where is my handsome grandson?" Elaine asked finally. "I expected him to be rocketing about already."

"Gabe took him for a trip to Male," Val offered, hands clutching the empty cups and damp beach towel loosely. "They should be back any moment."

"Well, I do have some family business to discuss with you, but I'd rather wait until Jace is tucked up in bed tonight before going into detail."

"Of course."

Val fought the frown that threatened to crease her brow. It was like Elaine to dangle this tidbit of information over her head for an entire evening. Brushing it off, Val tried not to let the woman get to her. After all, the "family business" was likely some small announcement meant to torture her for a day. It was already working.

The wooden steps leading up to the deck of the house were narrow, so Val paused and watched Elaine go first. Head a little thick from the alcohol, Val felt her heart trip just a little in her chest. She rarely had to deal with Jason's mother without him and when she did, it was no easy task. Her husband did his best to protect her, always. Now the sting of his continued absence only sharpened further. How much longer would she have to wait until he came home?

When they entered the wide living room, Bee and Lillian were bustling about in the kitchen. The boat's driver swept past them all again heading one last time up the stairs with an armload of suitcases. On his way back out, Elaine stopped him with a small hand on his arm. She took the time to thank him again and request his contact information so she could be sure to recommend him in the future.

The small interaction had Val marveling. So, the woman was not *all* bad. In fact, Val realized, she was downright pleasant to just about everyone else. Everyone that wasn't a threat. Everyone that hadn't trapped her brilliant son in a hidden marriage with an unplanned pregnancy.

Standing off to one side, Bee rolled her eyes convincingly. Val was quick to make an answering silly face before both of them instantly sobered. *Best behavior girls*, Val could hear her old agency trainer murmur. *Always best behavior.*

"Can I offer either of you ladies a fresh drink?" Bee broke the silence.

"Do you have sweet tea?" Lillian asked, so formal. They were all so painfully formal.

"I can brew some," Bee responded, then glanced over her shoulder. "Val, why don't you take the first shower so you're fresh when Jace gets back?"

Val bobbed her head in acceptance before beating it up the stairs to her room. She owed Bee. Owed her big time. There was no greater gift than the offer to disappear. It was the only way they had been able to relieve stress back at Cambric. Melt away. Melt into the background, then hide. The shower was as good a place to disappear as any.

Making a brief stop in her bedroom, Val grabbed a beige sundress from a wooden hanger in the small closet. It was hot here, even at night. Tiptoeing along the hall, Val headed for the large guest bath. Unlike her own room, it was on the ocean side of the house and the view was… breathtaking.

An oversized white tub was positioned in the middle of the

far wall, which was actually a floor to ceiling window. The bather could lie back, caress its smooth porcelain surface and gaze out at the ocean for hours. If Val had more time, she would have definitely chosen to linger there. But she didn't. So instead, she ran her hand along the teakwood countertop and tossed her dress over the bowl sink.

On the opposite wall, the shower beckoned. Its oval-shaped tiles were made entirely of cerulean-blue glass. Letting out a long sigh, Val twisted on the water and shed her black bikini. At once, steam rose from the spray, obscuring the air.

She took her time, working the suds into her long hair before letting the water cascade down her back to rinse it. She stood still there, perhaps longer than she should, until the skin on her belly was a bright pink from the heat. Once she was done, she twisted the faucet off and stepped out, her bare feet dripping water on the cool tile floor.

Grabbing a plush towel, Val blotted at her hair and suppressed a smile. Rock music blasted from somewhere downstairs. That meant Gabe was home with her son. He was the only one that played that sort of music.

Dressed and ready, Val made the descent to the first floor and came upon an exasperated Bee chopping mushrooms in the kitchen. Her mother stood steadfastly beside her, filling a large pot with water, her thin lips pressed together in tolerable silence.

Clearing her throat, Val waited for someone to notice her, but no one did. They didn't notice because it was impossible to hear anything. Gabe's music blared uncontrollably from the speakers out on the deck and dominated every inch of space.

"Mommy! Mommy!" Jace wrapped his arms around Val's

legs, shouting at the top of his lungs to be heard. "Guess who's here! It's Gramma! Look, see?"

"I see," Val answered, though her voice barely registered in her own ears.

Swiveling her head to the side, she followed Jace's manic pointing to the living room where Elaine sat on the floor. Toy cars of all types and colors were scattered around her, they had clearly been deeply involved in a game of Jace's own invention. Releasing him to scurry back to his devoted gramma, Val strolled out the open French doors and onto the wide deck.

Gabe stood over the stainless-steel barbecue, his back to her. Smoke plumed over his shoulders as he poked at what appeared to be steaks with a giant set of tongs. He held an open can of beer loosely in one hand. Walking up behind him, Val purposefully placed both fingers in her ears and waited. After another moment of prodding the meat, Gabe slammed the lid of the barbecue and turned around.

"What?!" Gabe laughed down at her, still having to yell though they were only separated by a few inches.

Val blinked at him expectantly as the lead singer, or screamer rather, hit an impressive high note followed by a guitar rift that sent ripples out over the water. With a protesting eye roll, Gabe fished around in his pocket and used a slender black remote to dial everything down. For several moments after, the feeling of the music's vibration rang in her ears.

"I've seen you sweep a room full of women off their feet in less than half an hour," Val commented. "Is there a reason why you're determined to do the opposite here?"

"It was my job to sleep with half of them too, but you

don't see me doing that anymore." Gabe brushed by her, lifting the can of beer to his lips in frustration.

"This isn't the same thing," Val pressed, watching the shift of muscles in his back.

"Isn't it?" Gabe countered, turning suddenly, eyes bright with some unclear emotion. "They don't approve of you either, why are you protecting them?"

"I'm not protecting them." Val tried to soften her voice, knowing she was stepping on thin ice here and trying to figure out why. "I'm protecting Bee. That's her mother in there and both of them are really making an effort. Can't you support that?"

"They show up here at *my* house and act like they're doing me a favor," Gabe hissed.

"Because that's what free people do, Gabey." Val reached out a hand, rubbed at his shoulder comfortingly. "Can't you turn on the charm? Fake it?"

"No." Gabe was abrupt, stepping away from her reach purposefully. "When I landed on this island, I promised myself I would never do anything I didn't want to ever again. I would never have to smile when I didn't feel like it, or fetch drinks like a damn dog, or get on my knees for some bored housewife that I couldn't stand."

"Hey-" Val hadn't realized how much of captive life still haunted him. "I'm sorry, okay? I'm sorry."

"It's not your fault. And I know it's not their fault either." Gabe gestured to the house. "I'm just not that guy anymore and I never want to be him again. Not even for a little while."

Nodding, Val gave him one last pat before retreating inside. She could've told him she understood how he felt, but the truth was their experiences within the captive system hadn't been the same. Sure, Val had been required to suppress her emotions, give up her desires for those of others and perform physically when she hadn't wanted to.

But she hadn't been required to don a fake persona in order to seduce rooms full of people. Gabe had been so good at it, in fact, that even Val hadn't realized how much of it was an agonizing ruse. How could she not have seen? She felt suddenly ashamed.

Taking a seat on the sofa, Val scooped up a miniature toy car and zoomed it along Jace's back. He squealed in delight, turning to blink happy eyes at her before continuing his own game with Elaine. The two of them made engine noises, driving around a pretend track they had set up on the oval area rug.

In the kitchen, Lillian and Bee now chatted more easily. Many years of therapy had helped to smooth over some of the rough edges. Well, at least it gave them a fighting chance at developing some sort of relationship. Outside, Gabe lingered. Val watched his tense movements through the glass.

When the steaks came off the grill and the long teak table was set with china and candles, the six of them settled along it in relative peace. Gabe complimented the au gratin potatoes and Lillian exclaimed over the tenderness of the meat. Red wine was poured all around, excepting of course Jace, who wriggled and squirmed in his seat until Val pulled him onto her lap.

The gentle embrace of his mother worked to calm him along with a belly full of rich food.

Their conversation was guarded, as it usually was during the rare meals that brought them all together. The weather was fine, though tropical and hot. The stock market was high, except for when it wasn't. Hardly able to stand it much longer, Val finally broke through the politeness and inquired about Jason. How was his court case going? Why hadn't the internet been fixed yet? What newspaper articles had Gabe been able to secure?

The tense silence that followed grew more uncomfortable still as the face of every adult closed up. They all knew something. Something they didn't want to tell her.

"Why do I get the feeling you all know something I don't?" Val murmured almost to herself.

"I miss Daddy," Jace whined, tilting his little face up to peer at his mother.

"Me too, baby." Val kissed the top of his head, stomach churning at the continued quiet. "But I'm sure we'll get to talk to him again tomorrow. Let's go clean up for bed so the morning comes quicker. Race you?"

"Okay!" Jace brightened, then wriggled from her grasp. "But you'll never beat me!"

Laughing, he scurried towards the staircase but then slowed, glancing over his shoulder to make sure his mother gave chase. Val obliged him. Pushing away from the table, she made a show of running to catch him, making sure all the while that he kept the lead. By the time they crested the stairs and entered the bathroom, Jace was puffed up with pride at being first place.

Filling his bath with bubbles, Val worked to control her nerves. Downstairs, bad news awaited her, and she alternated between wanting to know everything and wanting to hide. Whatever was going on, Val knew one thing, she had absolutely no control. The feeling itself was not a new one. In fact, she had been conditioned to accept this particular state of her existence. Of course, that had been much easier when she wasn't a mother.

Despite the unease that now simmered within her, Val reminded herself that she actually could control one thing. She could protect her son. Jace was here. Happy, unaware and safe. And that's exactly how he would remain.

After his bath, Val wrestled her son into his green dinosaur pajamas and then coaxed him into bed. Laying down beside him, it didn't take more than a few minutes before his busy day overtook him. Mouth parting in release, his breathing evened out and he fell asleep. She didn't want to, but Val forced herself to get up and leave.

Pausing at the doorway, she hugged herself and turned to watch her son. The house was cooling down with the nighttime breeze, but it was in no way cold. Even so, she couldn't quite shake a chill.

On her way down the stairs, Val could hear harsh voices pitched against one another in debate. She hesitated, wanting to hear what they said, but the sound of her footfalls on the wooden steps had already given her away. Sighing, Val continued on, making her way back to the dining area where everyone still sat, plates piled with half eaten food.

Another wine bottle had been opened and placed alongside an empty one which already occupied center stage on the table.

"Alright-" Val resumed her seat, hands trembling in her lap. "He's asleep. What's going on?"

The four of them looked at each other, all reluctant to be the first one to speak. Finally, Elaine cleared her throat and shifted to address Val from her place across the table. Beneath the surface, Val felt Bee's hand move to clasp her own. The two held on tight.

"Jason was taken into custody two days ago." Elaine's face couldn't hide the strain. "He's currently being held without bail."

"I don't understand." Val's voice wavered.

"Jason is in jail." Elaine was blunt. For the first time in Val's memory, the woman appeared fragile.

"But I thought you said this was a civil lawsuit," Val clarified. "How could they put him in jail?"

Elaine opened her mouth to speak, but the words just wouldn't come. Tears filled her eyes, making them appear glassy, but no drops spilled over. She glanced at Lillian who scooted closer for comfort, then at Gabe who exhaled audibly and took over.

"The case was originally a civil suit brought by Cambric for harboring me, but that was years ago. Jason's attorney was able to get Riggs Oil dismissed, but both the FBI and Jason remained in the suit.

Recently Cambric made a backroom deal with the Feds. Cambric agreed to dismiss them from the lawsuit but only if the Attorney General would file criminal charges against Jason, thus applying leverage to get me back."

"I-" Val's hand shot to her throat.

"My son does not belong in prison," Elaine began, finding her voice along with her anger. "He's spent years of his life protecting you but this time it's gone too far. You have to turn yourself in, Gabe."

"He is *not* going to turn himself over to those monsters!" Bee jumped to Gabe's defense. Then turned quickly to Val. "I'm sorry. I'm so sorry, but I can't let him give himself up. Jason can get this bogus charge dropped with a trial."

"Every day that he waits for a trial, Jason is exposed to abuse in prison!" Elaine shouted, her little hands slamming down on the tabletop.

"If Gabe steps foot back on American soil, then he will never see freedom again." Bee released Val's hand to lean forward, willing Elaine to understand. "Cambric will use him and Sharon will control him. It's a prison sentence that will last for the rest of his life. Jason will eventually get out. Gabe never would."

Their voices swirled and raised in panic, then ebbed and flowed. All around, the argument raged. But none of it got through to Val. They couldn't touch her because she wasn't there anymore, not really. Like Alice, she had been sucked down the rabbit hole. Falling, falling, the bottom rushed up to meet her, but the impact never came.

Squeezing her eyes shut, Val tried not to imagine Jason locked up in a cell. She tried and immediately regretted what she saw. A sudden sickness formed like a pit in her stomach. Looking up finally, she dialed back in.

Both Elaine and Bee stood, shouting at one another. Dishes rattled as palms banged down in frustration and desperation. Because that was it above all else. Desperation. Elaine was desperate to free her son, and Bee was desperate to keep Gabe from entering his own sort of prison. Each one knew the point of the other. Each one understood the reasons, even agreed maybe, but emotion ruled on this one. Emotion and panic.

"He stood up for all of you but you don't have the decency to do the same." Elaine was shaking now. "You've left him with no witnesses! You've seen the subpoenas, but have failed to appear!"

"Wait." Val's voice was a tiny croak in her parched throat. "What subpoenas? What do you mean witnesses? What does he need?"

"You and Gabe are the only people that witnessed the five million dollar negotiation," Elaine explained. "The FBI agent wasn't present for it, so he can't testify to what actually occurred. The Attorney General is alleging that the price tag was suggested by Jason, not Gabe. They are alleging that Jason used it as a bribe to illegally buy Gabe through the Federal Witness Protection Program."

"But that's not true," Val protested.

"They only have Jason's word and that's not enough. He's failed to produce Gabe though everyone knows exactly where he is. And Jason continues to deny any contact with the captive formerly known as Val." Elaine looked pointedly at her.

"I don't understand."

"Jason claims he set you free, legally speaking, which is true. He then states you made your own deal with the FBI and are under witness protection, which they have stipulated is also true. The only problem is, no one has been able to track you down under your new identity. Even your case handler, who attempted to contact you with the subpoena, has been unable to find you."

"I didn't know." Val looked sadly into Elaine's drawn face. "He never told me."

"We all understand why he's willing to sacrifice everything to keep your whereabouts a secret." Elaine's eyes darted to Gabe. "But to rot in jail for another man who he has helped in so many ways…"

Elaine let the last sentence fade as Bee leapt again to Gabe's defense. As the two women resumed their heated battle, Val shifted to watch Gabe.

Through it all, he had remained silent. Sitting straight in his chair, his face was impassive. The only tell he provided was a slight tightening along his jaw.

Val flashed back to their earlier conversation, the things he said now had a new layer of meaning. Gabe had known the entire time what was going on with Jason. The loud music, the angry attitude, it was not so much in response to the arrival of Lillian and Elaine. It was the knowledge of a looming decision. The end of his free life. The beginning of more years spent at the mercy of Cambric, pleasing others, killing his true self.

Would he exchange his entire life to do the right thing by Jason? That is the question Gabe had been wrestling with. *That* is the horror he'd been remembering. The horror he experienced at the hands of Sharon.

Val's gaze was fixed on Gabe. She watched as he finally came to a decision. For the briefest moment, a crease of unending pain filled his face. But in a blink, it was gone, disappearing into a carefully blank expression. An expression that was well-practiced. An expression Val herself, knew all too well.

"I'll go." Val spoke out suddenly, causing all other voices to drop away. "I'll go instead of Gabe."

CHAPTER 7

"WHAT?" GABE SHIFTED TO STARE AT HER, HIS EYES narrowing.

"I'll answer the court's subpoena. I'm free. Cambric has no hold on me. I witnessed the agreement between you and Jason so I can testify on Jason's behalf. On top of that, he isn't harboring you anymore because you've almost paid him back right?"

"I can't let you do that." Gabe shook his head fiercely. "You can't risk Jace, the danger is too great."

"The summons is for Val," Elaine reasoned, her quick mind working ahead. "If she answers it as Val, then her identity as Kelly is still protected. Val has no children, no record of a birth, no nothing. Jace will be safe and so will she."

"No." Gabe stood, his broad shoulders tense, muscles shifting beneath his shirt. "I promised Jason that I'd keep her and Jace here."

"But that was before they put him in jail," Bee reasoned,

reaching out a hand to tug at his wrist. "It makes sense. They can't do anything to Val and if we keep Jace here, then no one can touch him."

"No!" Gabe jerked his arm from her grasp. "*I* will go. It's the right thing to do."

"It's the stupid thing to do." Bee's voice pitched in anguish. "Val going is a good solution!"

Gabe whirled away. Turning his back on all of them, he strode deliberately out of the room and onto the deck. The wide door slammed shut behind him, rattling the glass panes in its frame.

At the table, the four women looked at each other, but said nothing. The angry words that had been hurled between Elaine and Bee were now forgotten. The tide had suddenly shifted. Things were not the same.

All along the table, the array of candles flickered and withered, forming tiny pools of melted wax in their blue-tinged glass bowls. Hands wringing beneath the table, Val wondered how soon she could leave. How long would it take them to get a hearing? To get Jason released? God how she wished he was here to tell her she was making the right move. But he wasn't here and without her help, he wouldn't be for a very long time.

Lillian was the first to rise and begin clearing dishes. Stolidly she gripped glasses, plates and platters and made trip after trip to the kitchen. Val knew in her own home that this was likely a rare occurrence. The Durands kept a full staff, as did the Riggs, herself and Jason included. It was only Bee and Gabe that were the hold-outs.

They both seemed so determined to be alone together, or

maybe it was mostly Gabe who had refused to hire help. No servants, he had said once, but refused to elaborate.

"I didn't realize Gabe was paying Jason back." Elaine stood slowly and reached for the empty bottles of wine.

"Yes, he only has a handful of payments left," Bee confirmed.

"I'm not sure how far it will go," Elaine resumed. "But if he could pay if off entirely then maybe our lawyers can make the argument Jason no longer 'owns' Gabe. Does he have enough money?"

"I'm sure he does." Bee paused, gazing down into her own empty glass. "But I'm not sure he'll agree to make the final payments if we want Val to go in his place. He might hold out on us."

"Well, can't you pay it?" Elaine asked.

"I don't have any money," Bee replied, causing Elaine to huff indignantly.

"What about your settlement from Cambric?" Elaine was talking about the cool ten million that The Agency was forced to pay out for the illegal trafficking of Veronica Durand.

Bee bobbed her head, acknowledging that the money had existed, then shoved her glass away before answering.

"I gave it away," she said.

"You gave-" Elaine let her mouth drop open for a few moments before shooting a look at Lillian who rolled her eyes.

"I don't want any of their blood money." Bee smirked at the reaction she was drawing, always having enjoyed getting a rise. "I donated it to the Freed Captives Transition Fund. They help captives who are released to start a new life."

"I am familiar with the fund, Dear," Elaine scoffed, before switching tactics. "What about your trust? Lillian?"

"She has not been willing to draw from it so far," Lillian supplied, while loading dishes into the washer. "But she has access to it at any time."

"How have you been living all these years?" Elaine asked.

"Gabe's been supporting us."

"Of all the stubborn-" Elaine stopped, thinking. "Well, this might be the time to draw on that trust, Veronica. Will you make the final payment if he refuses?"

"I will." Bee didn't hesitate.

"But that might mean you are harboring him instead of Jason," Val pointed out.

"I don't care."

Bee stood and smoothed at the fabric of her cotton dress before following Gabe's path out onto the deck. Val ventured a look across the space to where Elaine still stood, staring down into her own crystal goblet.

The inky red contents streaked down the inside of the glass where she had drained it only seconds before. The moment Val heard of Jason's incarceration, the contents of her own stomach had soured. But the rest of them had already gone through that initial stage of fear. Passing through the wave of denial, they had moved on to drowning the reality along with the pain.

Out on the deck, raised voices could be heard filtering through the closed doors. Although Val couldn't hear the words they said, Bee's tone was pleading. Gabe's was one of steadfast denial. They had always been fire and fire, Val thought, and some things never change.

Rising to clear the remains of the meal, Val stepped up alongside Lillian and began scrubbing at the dishes that were too large for the washer. All the while, the argument outside escalated.

"Why do they yell like that?" Lillian asked, clearly uncomfortable.

"Because they can." Val sighed. "At The Agency, all of their fights were in whispers. If they attracted too much attention, then we would all have been punished."

"Are you certain you want to go back?" Lillian glanced over at Val, who was taken aback by her look of genuine concern.

"I am." Val nodded, but couldn't stop her hands from trembling. "I can't let Jason sit in prison and I can't let Gabe turn himself in. Like Elaine said, I'm free. The worst that could happen is they somehow find out about Jace. Even then, he's here and they can't touch him."

"What if they won't release Jason?"

"Then at least I tried."

Elaine walked up behind them then and deposited the last of the mess on the counter. Taking a soapy sponge, Val traded her places and went to clean the dinner table.

Over and over she circled the wood, watching the tiny suds swirl. Somehow the work had a numbing effect, as if Val were wiping at the cluttered contents of her mind as well. Like a mantra, she allowed herself to repeat only a few ideas in her head. Jace was safe, she was free, and Jason would be released.

When the table was finished, her initial misgivings about whether she should go or not were gone. In their place was a steady resolve.

"Fine!" Bee slammed through the outer door and back into the space with Gabe close on her heels. "It's like you want to go back to them! If you wanted out of this relationship, then why not just tell me? You don't have to become a captive again just to escape me."

"Woman, you are crazy!" Gabe was incredulous, standing at the bottom of the staircase as Bee jogged up alone. "You're going to stay here and take care of that boy whether you like it or not!"

Chest heaving, he waited for a response.

The sound of Bee's stomping could be heard all the way to her bedroom where she slammed yet another door. Shaking his head in exasperation, Gabe rotated around to find all three remaining women staring at him.

"Val stays. I go. That's the end of it."

This time Gabe didn't wait for a response. Instead, he strode into the kitchen and grabbed down an entire bottle of whiskey. Not bothering with a glass, he turned on his heel and walked back out onto the deck. The door clicked quietly closed behind him.

At Cambric, Val had always played the peacemaker between Bee and Gabe. And her role had served their little family well. The fighters would fight, retreat to their corners, and the enabler would come to each of them in turn.

Normally, Val would have gone to Bee first, as was their custom, but that somehow seemed an unnecessary move here. It was Gabe that she needed to sway. So she rinsed her hands calmly in the sink as the two mother's murmured together. Drying her hands on a nearby towel, Val left it folded neatly on the marble countertop before departing.

At the row of wide French doors, she hesitated, but only for a moment. The deck was all dark, save for the pool which glistened in the caress of the moonlight. The water of the sea rippled just beyond.

Inhaling a great big breath, Val held it. Willing her hands to stop in their tingling, she reached for one silver doorknob and twisted it sharply. Without looking back, Val stepped into the night and shut the door firmly behind her.

The air was cool, a pleasant contrast to the damp sweat that now covered her body. How had she not noticed the suppressing heat that simmered inside that house? Or perhaps it wasn't actually hot in there at all, but just inside of her.

Gabe was nowhere to be seen. Illumination from inside the home shone out onto the deck, but revealed no figure.

Circling the pool and passing the spa, Val approached the railing. Her palms spread over the smooth wood as her eyes darted to the boat. It still bobbed softly in its mooring. She exhaled. The fear of him already leaving was now gone.

For a moment, she let her eyes adjust to the darkness. Up above, a million stars seemed so close that she could reach up and grab a handful. They sparkled and glittered, giving up light like a million diamonds. It made her think of Jason, and the necklace she had so foolishly forgotten back in France. How she missed him, the way he looped the strand around her neck, the gentle caress of his breath on her skin.

Giving her head a little shake, Val spied Gabe walking along the dock. The glint of the bottle in his hand gave away his position.

Taking the steps two at a time, she had no regard for her bare feet on the planks, or the sway of the wood as it moved under her. By the time she reached him, Gabe had flopped down on the edge of the dock, his legs dangling in the ocean.

All the while she had hurried, as if there was actually a way for him to escape. But now that he sat in surrender, one hand propped up behind him, the other clutching the whiskey, she slowed her pace.

He acknowledged her presence with a bob of his head, but didn't glance her way. Getting down beside him, Val too lowered her feet over the edge until her ankles were surrounded by the salty kiss of water.

Together, they sat in silence, listening to the creak of the dock beneath them and the constant rumble of the waves lapping delicately at the shoreline. Eventually he offered her the bottle, but she declined, not sure her stomach could withstand the hit.

"So," Val began. "You're going back."

"I'm going back."

"Cambric will conscript you, whether Jason and his lawyers fight it or not."

"I know what conscription is."

Gabe swigged at the bottle, smacking his lips when done. The law concerning captives had been written in favor of the agencies so many centuries before. Conscription was the right an agency had to its captive. If there was any question, the agency involved would maintain possession of said captive until a judgment was entered by a court.

If Gabe returned, even though his freedom was in dispute, he would be taken back by Cambric; conscripted into their service until such a time as a judge or a jury set him free. It could last years, or forever.

"Is Bee right?"

"About what?"

"Does some part of you want to go back?"

"How can you even ask me that?!" Gabe whirled on her, his expression a mix of anger and hurt.

"She thinks you feel trapped by her," Val explained. "That you didn't get a chance to choose a free woman. That it's holding you back from committing to her."

"Committing?!" Gabe gestured over his shoulder to the house. "I bought us a house, pay for everything, support her. What isn't committing in that?"

"You aren't married."

"No." Gabe sighed, letting his gaze drift out over the water. "We're not married."

"Because part of you doesn't want her?"

"Is that what she thinks?" Gabe asked, taking another shot from the bottle.

"Isn't that why?" Val watched the side of his face, searching for a tell in the moonlight.

"No, that's not why."

"Then what is it?"

"I got fixed." Gabe let out a rueful laugh before tilting his face up to stare at the sky.

"You did what?"

"As soon as I could, I went to a doctor and got a vasectomy. I just don't know how to tell her."

"Why? Why would you do that?" Val reached for the bottle and choked down a shot of whiskey.

"I have over thirty children out there that I've left unprotected and without a father." Gabe closed his eyes. "How could I bring any more into the world?"

"But Bee doesn't have any," Val snapped. "You didn't even talk to her about it. You've taken away that possibility for her."

"No, I've taken away the possibility that she would have one with me."

"Of course she wants one with you. Who else would she be with?"

"Hence why I haven't trapped *her* in a marriage." Gabe's voice tinged with sadness, but no regret. "It's my body. Well, at least for now it still is. I do *not* want any more children. How could I face the ones that I've abandoned while giving a free life to more? It's not right."

"You didn't abandon them," Val protested. "They've been kept from you, and you have no legal right to them. You're still fighting for a legal right to yourself."

"I haven't even tried to fight for them," Gabe countered. "I've been too busy running scared. Now it's time to face it. At least Cambric won't get any more out of me."

"Can't they reverse the procedure?"

"The doctor prescribed me a round of medication to help with that," Gabe said. "I shouldn't have any swimmers left to swim."

"And you expect me to keep this from Bee?" Val caught his gaze, held it.

"I *will* tell her." Gabe nodded, expression steady. "But until then, yeah, I want you to keep it to yourself."

"You know I can't do that."

"If you can tell me honestly that you've never prevented a

pregnancy that Jason wanted, then you can go ahead and tell Bee."

For a moment, Val's heart stopped. Had Bee told him? She had sworn that she wouldn't. She *promised.* But how else would he know?

"That's what I thought," he said, responding to her silence.

Sighing, Gabe grabbed the bottle back and tilted it up for another swig. When he was done, he passed it over. Val yanked it from his hand before downing a few more gulps. This time the taste had a warming effect.

"How did you know?"

"Jason and I talk a lot these days because of business and such." Gabe shrugged. "He mentioned you were having fertility issues. You and I both know that Cambric screens for that type of thing and if you actually had any problems then they would've dealt with it a long time ago. I know you have a clean bill of health and you had Jace. So…"

"You didn't say anything did you?" Val's voice hitched.

"No, I didn't," Gabe assured her. "Because I'm a good friend that happens to share the same problem."

"Except we don't have the same problem," Val corrected. "I don't want any more children because each one that I have is not safe. It doesn't matter what order they're born in, if Cambric can't get at the first one, then they'll conscript the second or the third."

"You and I both don't want any more kids and we are both actively preventing it behind our partner's back. If that's not the same problem then I don't know what is."

Silence ensued.

The lights from the house were switched off, throwing

them into further darkness. After several minutes, the stars seemed to come out all the more. High above them, a vast glittering swath populated the heavens. It was so beautiful that even sitting here, amidst the fear and uncertainty, they grabbed at her attention, reached somewhere deep inside.

But there were no stars on the inside of a prison cell. And there were no stars on the ceiling of the rooms at Cambric. Couldn't both of these men have stars? Did one have to give them up for the other?

"Don't go," Val whispered. "If you go, then you're giving up any future of fighting for your kids. You'll never be able to get them out."

"What about you? What about your kid? I love him too you know."

"I know." Val laid her hand over Gabe's on the dock. "But getting yourself conscripted isn't going to help Jace. I can go do the work for both of us and stay free. What's the harm in me trying?"

"And if you go and they won't release Jason?"

"Then you can come." Val gave his hand a last pat before reaching for the bottle and downing yet another shot. Her head began to spin, the alcohol working to both ease and blur. "But not before you tell Bee."

"I'll tell Bee about the vasectomy," Gabe qualified. "When you tell Jason about the birth control."

"And I go to court first?" Val asked.

"And you go to court first." Gabe paused, eyes darting over her face in the moonlight. "But if you're really going back, then I think there's one last thing we need to do."

CHAPTER 8

It took three days. Three more days of running into Male on Gabe's boat, arranging for money transfers, notarizing documents and talking endlessly with any number of attorneys. Finally, Val was settled on the Riggs private jet, lifting up into the blinding blue of a tropical sky.

Her destination was set for New York and it would take over twenty hours to get there. The hardest part of leaving, by far, was her goodbye to Jace. His little arctic eyes, so piercing like his father's, hadn't understood why he was being left behind. It was no matter that Uncle Gabe would be there to play with, or that Gramma Elaine was staying to help keep him content.

He was just a boy, like any other. One whose beloved daddy hadn't made an appearance in almost two months. The idea of letting his mommy leave too had been overwhelming.

On her knees on the dock, wooden planks rubbing her bare skin, Val held him tight. She rocked his body back and forth, kissed the tears that fell onto his cheeks and tried like hell to prevent any of her own. Apart from the brief weekend of testimony at Sharon Baine's trial, Val hadn't spent one night apart from her son in all his life.

This separation would be hard, but hopefully brief. She would testify for Jason, get him released and then be back in a few days. Maybe a week at the most.

Looking out the oval window now, Val could see the dotting green islands below her. Their white sand beaches and array of custom villas were soon invisible though, as the jet soared, gaining in altitude with its nose pointed heavenward.

Nervous palms spread themselves out over her simple sundress. It was summer on the East Coast, but Val's outfit wouldn't be appropriate for the task at hand. By the time the plane touched down she would have to make the complete transition back to being captive Val.

Hairstyle, clothing, shoes, nails. Everything needed to be on point. There could be no more casual sundresses. No more bare feet or tousled hair.

Before Val's departure, Bee had rummaged through her own closet and selected a few outfits that might fit the old captive Val's persona. They hung in the cabin now, swaying slightly as the jet cut through the air.

For her part, Elaine ordered Val a new array of clothes and had them sent straight to her husband's penthouse in the city. Once Jason had been taken into custody, the entire family had moved to New York and set up a home base of sorts there. That's where Val was headed now.

The stewardess, her platinum hair pulled back into a tight bun, worked her way back through the small cabin, bringing a mixed drink and soft blanket along with her. Accepting both items gratefully, Val tucked her legs beneath her and leaned back in the wide leather seat.

At first, she attempted to watch an array of mind-numbing movies. But try as she might, they failed to keep her full attention. Often, she found herself drifting, thinking of what lay ahead or worrying over what she had left behind. The stewardess served her meals which Val picked at broodily. Her appetite was off. Her stomach left twisted and sour.

Several times she got up to pace the aisle, running her hands over the collection of empty seats before moving to sit at the tiny table in the rear corner. More than once, she tried to write a letter to her son, but always ended up scratching at the silly words that took up residence on the paper.

Nighttime came and went. They made a brief stop in Moscow, but Val knew better than to leave the safety of the plane. For now, her whereabouts were still unknown to the media, though Elaine had warned her they were aware she would be returning stateside. In order to get another hearing so soon in Jason's case, their attorneys had to petition the court with new evidence. That evidence of course centered around Val answering a long ago summons. It was public record, and the news had spread like wildfire.

With any luck, her arrival at the airport would go unnoticed but the hotel that Jason's father was holed up in was already swamped with reporters and cameramen. Although Val had been able to dodge them many years ago, it likely wouldn't be so easy this time.

Every move she made would be under intense scrutiny. After all, she was Jason Riggs' first and only captive. The one who went undercover for the FBI to unearth a human-trafficking ring. Val had been front page news for months. The fact that she promptly disappeared without offering a single television interview, well, that made her all the more desirable.

Overwrought and fatigued, she finally nodded off. Val's head tilted down onto the table, her arms spreading out over its cool surface.

Hours later the stewardess shook her awake. Val practically levitated out of her seat. She had been sucked down so deep in her slumber, that the simple touch of another person sent angry tingles coursing through her blood.

"I'm sorry Miss," the stewardess said. "But we're on track to land within the hour."

"Thank you." Val nodded, rubbing at the back of her neck, now pinched with strain.

Left alone in the cabin, she unzipped her garment bag and selected a short black dress that's skirt ended high up on her thighs. Setting it aside, she let it hang over the back of one wide leather chair while she removed a curling iron, hair spray, brush, and copious amounts of makeup.

Over the next hour, as their destination drew ever closer, Val transformed herself. Lush lips pouted behind crimson lipstick. Long chestnut locks flowed in careful waves down her back. The form-fitting dress showed off appealing curves with a plunging neckline.

By the time the stewardess reentered the cabin to warn of their descent, Val had resumed her seat a new woman. There was only the one remaining tell that needed removing. Twisting reluctantly at her diamond wedding ring, Val worked to pull it and its white gold band over her knuckle. Once they were off, she held the circles in her tightly closed fist.

For the last few minutes, her eyes shut against the rush outside her window, Val composed her face in mute serenity. It wasn't until the bump of landing gear skidding along runway that her eyes slowly opened.

Glancing out the window, Val's chest heaved once before she shut it down, closing her outward appearance until all of her body spoke only of alluring charm. Casually, she deposited the rings in her tiny black purse and stood. When she moved towards the exit, it was with confidence.

Leaving the jet, walking through the terminal and going through customs; those tasks were simple, straightforward and without fuss. She didn't have much luggage and what she did would be transported straight to the hotel via currier. It wasn't until the arrival gate loomed before her, that Val stilled in her steps.

Reporters. There was a swirling swarm of them hovering already.

Donning dark sunglasses, Val scanned the group of humanity, looking for Senior. She didn't see him anywhere but her eyes did fall on a familiar face. It was their former body-guard, CT, and he was hard to miss. The man's bulk stood head and shoulders above everyone around him. Senior must be tucked by him somewhere, Val thought.

Tipping her chin up, Val pressed forward towards the man who looked as if he had eaten a linebacker for breakfast. It didn't take long for him to zero in on her. The second she was spotted, the jig was up. Cameras flashed, questions were shouted, the throng surged forward like a wave approaching the shore.

CT easily outdistanced them all, coming to shelter her in the looming shadow of his presence.

"Hello, CT." Val smiled into his face. She hadn't seen him in years.

"Miss Val." He bobbed his head once in acknowledgement before taking her by the arm and bulldozing a path towards the exit.

They hadn't moved more than a few steps before Senior appeared on her other side, holding up a briefcase to help part the reporters blocking their way. It was loud and Val's body was knocked against CT and Senior repeatedly.

By the time they maneuvered through the outer doors and into the waiting town car, her lungs felt tight, as if they had shrunk inside her body. She hated crowds. Hated the smothering volatility of them. Beside her, Senior's face was a mix of worry and relief. He had aged since she had seen him last. The stress of having a child in jail forced lines into his handsome complexion that didn't belong there.

Side by side in the backseat, Val did battle for her self-composure while Senior fanned her face with a stack of papers from his case. While they drove, he attempted to distract her with small talk. Jeremy was doing well in college and on track to graduate next spring. Though he still dreamed of a career in baseball, a torn rotator cuff didn't speak highly of that coming to pass. He had a head for business, thankfully, so would likely wind up at Riggs Oil. They would be glad to have him.

Angela's pregnancy was going well, the baby was due within the next few months. A girl. Though she wanted to be present at all of the court hearings, her husband managed to convince her that the stress was too much. With pressure, she had agreed to stay home.

Theresa's internship in New Zealand was already set to expire this month, so she was able to stop work early. She arrived in New York last night.

With the air conditioning set to full blast and CT's broad shoulders filling the front seat, Val's pulse began to even out. The burn of oxygen inside her chest lessened. Despite the tension with Elaine, Val got along well with Jason's father and siblings. They typically made a visit to France once a year and stayed for about a month over the holiday season.

"Val-" Senior cleared his throat. "I know you don't like the media, and after what happened to Jason in the past, I don't blame you. It's just that they are almost like a member of the jury right now. The court of public opinion could go a long way to help Jason in his case."

"How is he?" Val smoothed at her hair before reapplying lipstick from her clutch, remembering Elaine's instruction about keeping up appearances.

"I haven't seen him since his arraignment, but our attorneys assure me he's doing fine." Senior paused, then pressed on. "If we can get the media on our side, then they can put constant pressure on the prosecutor, the judge, and other powerful people that might be able to make this mess go away."

"How can we get them on our side?" Val asked, glancing out the window.

"You could make a statement. Get them to like you, feel sorry for Jason, explain how he's being treated unfairly."

"But I'm not good at that."

"I know you don't think that you are, but I saw you in that courtroom at Sharon's trial and I've seen you take on Elaine when you disagree over Jace. You speak well, you're an intelligent woman. All you lack is confidence about it. And with your ability to fake it… no one would ever know how unsure you are."

"You want me to talk to them."

"I want you to give them some of your attention for just a few minutes before we go into the hotel."

"I don't know what to say, Jason always handles that part." Val's stomach churned at the memories.

"Make them think you like them. Say you've been forced into hiding and you've only returned to help an innocent man escape injustice. Can you do that? For Jason?"

"Yes," Val whispered. Ducking her head, she looked down at her hands. They had resumed their trembling.

When the sedan pulled to a stop in front of the hotel, Val narrowed her eyes at the group of people already waiting there. Had this collection of cameramen jockeying for position also been at the airport? If so, how had they returned to the hotel so quickly?

Then it dawned on her. These were secondary crews. One team was dispatched here and the other back there in anticipation of her every move. She was like a tiny bird trapped at the corner of a metal cage. The cats were meowing their pleasure all around.

"Are you okay?" Senior laid a hand on her shoulder. "It's only for a few minutes."

Sucking in a breath, Val squeezed her eyes shut before purposefully opening them wide. Agency training flooded her brain.

She would choose an older man in the crowd, there had to be at least one. She would speak to him as she had been taught so long ago. Winning him over, throwing him off balance, leaving him feeling unsure. The camera behind him would hopefully get the same impression.

Clearing her throat, Val swept back her hair and pursed her lips together in one final check for a glossy shine.

"I'm ready," she said.

CT and Senior exited first, leaving the driver to sit quietly in the front seat of the car. The man was not familiar to her but he made no remarks. She expected his time of service with the Riggs family was a long one.

Straightening her sunglasses, Val flashed a brilliant smile as her door opened. Deliberately, she placed her small hand in CT's large one. As soon as her high heel touched the gray cement of sidewalk, cameras clicked and voices rose in conflict. All of them wanted to be heard, so hearing any of them was impossible.

Scanning the press of faces, Val found the one that she wanted and walked confidently towards him. As his eyes zeroed in on her, she tugged at her dress in a way that had his attention shifting to her exposed length of leg. CT helped to clear her path. Senior stepped back to watch.

Stopping just a hair too close for comfort, Val opened her mouth to speak and all other voices fell away.

"I feel so fortunate to be here with you." Val directed her gaze into the surprised eyes of the seasoned reporter, his suit jacket and tie looked uncomfortably hot in the midst of summer. "With all of you."

For a moment, the man's mouth hung slack. The crews had prepared for many things, but none of them included Val submitting so willingly to an interview. She had never done so in the past, so the man was at a loss for words now.

In the brief lull that followed, Val let a knowing smile play across her lips which further drained the color from the reporter's face. Those who were positioned behind her, jogged around to get a better angle.

"Yes." The reporter finally found his voice, his finger hooking subconsciously in his collar. "What brings you back to New York, Val? Do you still go by Val?"

"As you all know, even though I have been given my freedom, my safety in this country is very much in question. That is why I have never been able to spend time with you, though I have wanted to many times in the past."

"Where have you been hiding?"

"Do you still have a relationship with Jason Riggs?"

"Do you ever see Veronica Durand?"

"Are you having an affair with-"

The questions began in earnest, each one coming from a different mouth. Before long, they overwhelmed the air, making the space feel tight, claustrophobic. Despite a sheen of sweat that broke out on her lower back, Val kept her face easy and accepting.

Finally cutting through the volley without effort, Val spoke once more.

"I am here because a dear friend and champion of the weak has been incarcerated on a false charge. I know all of you admire Jason Riggs for what he has done to root out injustice. Like you, I simply cannot stand idle while an innocent man is forced to endure a similar fate."

"And that's all the time we have for today." Senior swooped in, setting firm hands on Val's shoulders. "I trust you will attend the court hearing in two days. We will see you then."

The reporters' voices rose in earnest, but the two men guided Val quickly away towards the hotel. Its great glittering awning was made of black iron and shining glass. Once they passed under it and through a revolving door, Val exhaled in relief. The lobby was safe and serene. Free of cameras and questions.

White marble flooring stretched out beneath her high-heels until it met with black marble inlay. A geometric design formed at the center of the space. Above her head, heavy chandeliers gave off romantic light, complimenting the subtlety of classical music that played.

Senior didn't bother to stop at the check-in desk. Its attendants stood calmly behind a long stretch of marble counter. Instead, he directed their small group towards a bank of hidden elevators. Depressing a round button, they waited in un-accosted silence.

Upon entering the golden-hued box, they were transported up and up and up. When the ding of arrival finally sounded they were released onto a floor all their own. Two security guards, gun holsters barely hidden beneath smart suit coats, nodded recognition of Senior as he punched in a code and beeped their way into the hotel suite.

The space before them showcased a sweeping view of the city through a far wall of windows, its high-rise neighbors glinted in the midday sun. Shoes echoing against the travertine marble floor, Val noted a baby-grand piano tucked in one corner and an unlit fireplace along the opposite wall. In the center, two long sofas were arranged around a glass top coffee table. The two occupants that had been sitting only moments before sprang into action.

"Oh, Kelly!" Theresa exclaimed, throwing her arms around Val's shoulders. "How are you?"

Returning her sister-in-law's embrace, Val closed her eyes against the anxious look that clouded their younger brother's face. Jeremy hovered just to one side, looking slightly stricken. He loved Jason to distraction, having always idolized him as a boy.

"I'm alright," Val whispered. "It's Val again, remember?"

"Right," Theresa responded. "I just got so used to it back in France."

For the rest of the day Val's nerves were on edge. The lengthy flight combined with jet lag had her struggling to focus when Theresa detailed her itinerary or when Senior reviewed their trial strategy. Sagging finally against the back of the sofa, Val sipped on an offered cocktail and let her emerald eyes stare at the darkness that had overtaken the city skyline.

It was eleven o'clock at night and they were all huddled

around Senior's laptop, awaiting a call from the Maldives. It was eight in the morning in the islands and Jace should just be getting up. Val held her breath, hoping that the internet had been fixed so she could see her son.

As the minutes ticked by with no flash of life across the screen, Val began to wring her hands. She knew logically that everything was fine, but it wasn't logic that ruled her now. Strung out on lack of sleep, she willed her mind not to fly in a million different directions collecting fears as it went.

Suddenly the ding of an incoming call had Theresa clapping her hands and Val blowing out a breath. Senior reached forward and tapped the keyboard in acceptance.

"Mommy!" Jace's enormous grin spread from one side of the screen to the other.

"Hey baby!" Val had to put her hand over her mouth, working hard to keep the shiver of tears from her voice. "I miss you so, so much."

"I miss you, too. Where's Daddy?"

The question had everyone in the room shifting uncomfortably. Val gulped, eyes darting to Senior who took over the conversation. He explained that Jace's daddy would be coming to visit very soon, then promptly changed the subject. The two talked about fishing, driving the speed boat and hunting for crabs on the island.

Sitting back, Val held Theresa's hand as Elaine made an appearance, then Bee and Lillian, and finally Gabe. Each adult peered over Jace's shoulder, competing with the little boy for screen space. Val watched them all, but wondered especially about Gabe.

She wondered if he felt the guilt the way she did. If he had reservations, or regrets. But his handsome face showed only casual interest. If what they had done that last day in Male bothered him, he didn't let it show.

When the call ended, and the screen cut abruptly to black, Val lifted her drink to Jeremy, who went obligingly to fetch the vodka.

The entire family had agreed to keep Jace's true identity a secret, even from their own lawyers. The less people who knew that Jace was born to a captive, the better. So, for the sake of her son, Val would have to appear as her former self in court.

She was not married to Jason. She did not have a child. These were hard concepts to wrap her mind around but Val tried nonetheless.

CHAPTER 9

She woke up on the morning of the court hearing to see that the sun had already risen high in the eastern sky. Nights had been hard since Jason's arrest. Though utterly exhausted by the end of each day, Val would flop heavily into the hotel bed only to find that sleep would not come.

Alone in the center of the king-sized mattress, curtains left open to reveal the glow of city lights, she would twist and turn uncomfortably. Sometimes for hours on end. By the time unconsciousness took over, dawn was often just over the horizon.

And this day was no different, other than it was *the* day they had all been working towards. The hearing was scheduled for one-thirty that afternoon, just after the court returned from lunch. Shoving back the covers, Val glanced at the bedside clock and noted the time was already half past nine. She straightened her night shirt, still one of Jason's, and rubbed at the ache that spread over her lower back.

The room was beautiful, with an attached sitting area, wide-screen television and ensuite bath. Since Val's arrival two days before, she had not left the comfort of the hotel suite. She took her meals here, met with the Riggs legal team here, and wished she didn't have to leave here in order to free Jason.

Pacing to the long window, Val pressed her fingers against the glass and looked down. Asphalt streets could hardly be seen through the crowd of cars that filled each lane. People, small as ants, scurried in groups, rushing down sidewalks that hugged gleaming glass buildings. In the distance, she glimpsed the park, its empty patch of green so incongruous amidst all the humanity. It was a far cry from the breathtaking ocean of the Maldives.

"Val?" Theresa knocked at her bedroom door, lifting her voice to be heard through the thick wood. "Are you up?"

"Come in," Val responded.

"Our nail appointment is at ten, then lunch is at eleven-thirty," Theresa reminded her. "We need to leave here by twelve-thirty to make it to the courthouse in time."

"I thought I set the alarm on the clock," Val explained, brushing past her sister-in-law to enter the bathroom. "I guess it didn't go off."

"Well, it helps if you have a phone." Theresa leaned against the doorframe, crossing her arms over her body.

Without further comment, she watched as Val turned on the shower then held her hand under the spray until the temperature was just right. Although Val had been offered a cell phone time and again, she was still adamant in her decision against them. She saw what it did to everyone who held it, and she simply refused to give herself away to the tiny electronic device.

Stripping down, Val hopped into the shower and began a thorough wash of her hair. All the while, Theresa talked. She questioned Val about the notarized bank statements from Gabe, and about the night of the original negotiation for the five million dollar payout. When each of Val's answers were exactly as they had rehearsed, she departed, leaving Val alone to complete her ritual.

Legs shaved, body scrubbed and hair dripping from the spray, Val turned off the water and stepped out. In the central living area, she could hear the arrival of the nail technicians. The foreign cadence of their speech reminded her of life abroad. Running short on time, she wrapped her hair in a towel, threw on a tank top and pair of cotton shorts and hustled into the shared space.

For the next hour she submitted to the relaxing process that is your typical manicure and pedicure. Well, at any other time in her life Val would have considered it relaxing. Not today, however. Today she sat stiffly, eyes focused on the puff of clouds that passed outside the bank of windows.

Part of her tingled in anticipation. She would see Jason again. He would be only a few feet away. The other part filled with a sickly dread. How was he really doing? Would the evidence she presented today be enough to get him out?

After the nail techs had gone, Val picked over her salad for several minutes before excusing herself to the bathroom. She blew out her hair, curled it in soft waves, and applied a reserved palette of makeup. Today she must look professional, believable, but still alluring. The combination was not an easy balance to strike.

Stepping into the closet, she perused the options that Elaine had sent over. There was a smart pant suit but she thought it was a touch too conservative. Plucking a navy pencil skirt from the rack she paired it with a cream-colored blouse whose material was just thin enough to make out her lace bra.

Checking herself in the full length mirror, Val completed the outfit with a pair of four-inch black patent heels. The skirt hugged her in all the right ways, but wasn't too short. The top had long sleeves and a conservative neckline, but the opaque material revealed more than a hint of the sexy undergarment just beneath.

Stylish, expensive, distracting.

Perfect.

Senior, Jeremy and Theresa waited for her on the sofa. CT stood by the front door, ever vigilant, even when locked safely inside the suite. All eyes tracked her as she entered the room and gave them a slight nod. She was ready.

Down the elevator they went, through the lobby and into the heat of another July day. Dodging cameras, they fled single file, not offering any comments this time as they loaded into the limousine that was necessary to transport them all.

The team of lawyers employed by Riggs Oil was already at the courthouse, monitoring Jason's transfer from jail. The judge was allowing Jason to change out of his orange prison jumpsuit for the purpose of the hearing, so Senior had sent over a brand new suit instead.

Traffic was bad and the mood inside the limo was worse.

No one spoke. Any attempt at small talk seemed trite and they'd been over the details of the case a thousand times. Rocking with the stop and go of the vehicle, Val braced her hands beside her on the long bench seat. She gazed out the window, but her eyes didn't see. Her focus was very much internal.

Fighting the knot that had formed in her stomach, she felt the presence of Cambric all around her. They were inside her head, always. Their words ran like ticker tape through her brain until they further affected her body. Soon Cambric would be standing in the same building with her, then the same room. Legally free or not, fear threatened to destroy her.

When they arrived at the courthouse, its massive stone columns cast a much desired shade over the front steps. The pack of reporters that waited there was triple the size of anything Val had encountered before. Microphones were set up on a wooden podium in anticipation of a promised interview with the legal team.

Two of Jason's attorneys stood waiting at the curb. A man and a woman, both of whom Val had spoken to the day before. They seemed sharp and confident, but wasn't that what attorneys were paid for?

CT exited the front passenger seat first along with the limo driver. As they walked around to the rear door, Val watched CT button his sport coat, and in that brief moment, recognized the outline of a handgun positioned neatly at his back. Trying to swallow, she found that she had no saliva left. CT had a permit to carry, she remembered from before, but up until this moment the reality of it hadn't registered.

Before she could think further, the door swung open and Senior stepped out. He was followed closely by Theresa, leaving Val to go next. Sensing her hesitation, Jeremy gave her a firm nod, willing her to steal some of his resolve. She ducked her head in response, then sucked in a breath before relaxing her expression and stepping out.

Sunlight hit her face, cameras clicked, voices shouted, people swarmed. The smell of their bodies in the heat permeated the air.

Keeping her head down, Val paced closely behind Theresa. They walked purposefully into the shade of the wide stone steps and up through the protective doors of the courthouse. Once through security, their group was guided down corridors, up elevators and along hallways until they arrived at the courtroom of the Honorable Judge Allen.

He had sat the bench for over twenty years and had a reputation as a no-nonsense jurist who loved procedure and order of above all else. *But is he fair?* Jeremy had questioned his father. Val recalled Senior's smirk and non-committal answer. *Depends on which side you're on, Son.*

Heavy doors made up of a dark wood were opened to reveal a room filled with more of the same rich material. Wood spanned the length of benches, lined the walls, curved around the jury box and witness stand. Deep burnt-red carpeting covered the floors. Its thin threads showed the wear of well-trafficked areas down the center aisle and in front of the judge.

More bodies filled the space. Curious on-lookers, who had waited for hours in line to get a seat in the audience, along with a few hand selected news crews, turned to watch.

Val did her best to keep a straight face, though she couldn't stop her eyes from darting about. She was desperately tracking for some sign of Jason but he hadn't been brought in yet. The defendant's table sat empty.

Following Senior and Theresa, Val glanced sideways at the plaintiff's table and spied the prosecutor. This was not your typical District Attorney. Senior had explained that due to the notoriety of the case, it had been referred to the Attorney General herself. She had been the top of her class in law school and it wasn't for nothing. She was highly intelligent, calculating and patient. She did her job, and she did it well.

Seeming to sense eyes resting upon her, Attorney General Collins glanced over her shoulder and locked onto Val. Dark eyes appraising, the woman's expression gave the impression of unhindered confidence and strength. Her jet-black hair was styled neatly in a bob which showed off her high cheek bones and the smooth brown tone of her skin. She appeared neither menacing, nor amenable. But rather gave the air of someone who wanted above all else to *win*.

Just as Val felt the need to look away, a familiar figure stepped in front of her, effectively blocking her from AG Collins' view. Serious brown eyes frowned down into her face, the look of intense concern that filled them was palpable.

He had the same crop of short black hair, chiseled jaw and reserved demeanor that he always had. For a moment, a genuine smile creased Val's lips. It had been many years since they had last seen one another. And after all, in the end it was Agent John Finn who had protected her, hiding her precious secret from all the world.

"Agent Finn," Val breathed, her voice was barely audible over the noisy din of the packed room.

Continuing behind Theresa in their slow walk down the aisle, Val's progress was impeded by the press of people shifting all around. Eyes intense, Agent Finn did not respond to her verbally. In silence, he deliberately placed one foot in her path, causing her to stumble forward. Swiftly, he then shifted his body to catch her fall. His mouth brushed close to her ear and he whispered a few words before setting her back to rights and walking away.

Anyone watching would have thought she simply tripped of her own accord, and then he braced her, as any person would. But the hushed words he had just spoken echoed loudly inside her head.

Stunned, Val stood still in the aisle.

A quick nudge from Jeremy got her moving again.

Senior led the way to the first row and stood aside to allow Theresa down first, followed by Val. After seeing them safely tucked in, Senior sat and slid along the bench until Jeremey joined them. Everyone was seated directly behind the defendant's table.

Glancing sideways, Val saw Agent Finn take a seat on the side of the prosecution. Her gut churned. What was he doing over there? She had been told a representative from the FBI would be present to ensure the integrity of her witness protection identity, but she hadn't expected it to be Agent Finn. And she certainly hadn't expected him to be sitting across the aisle.

Before she could analyze the implications further, a side door at the front of the courtroom opened and in walked Jason.

She gasped. They had shaved his head.

Where a thick crop of chestnut locks had been, a short bristle poked up instead. It was almost blonde in the glint of the overhead lights. Senior took one of her hands in his and held on tight. The courtroom fell into a ghostly silence.

"I'm sorry I didn't warn you," Senior whispered, leaning close. "But I knew it would only make you upset."

For the first time since Sharon's trial, anger brewed deep down somewhere. Well, Val thought the feeling must be anger, for it tasted like bile stuck burning inside her throat. Not able to rip her gaze away from Jason, Val saw the moment he spotted her. Those arctic eyes that had always pierced her so deeply, registered with shock, then a slice of fear before he purposefully blinked the emotions away.

Wedged between two large bailiffs, Jason's hands were bound in metal cuffs. A chain dropped from his wrists down to his ankles, where the iron wrapped itself around first one and then the other leg. Even with the fancy suit and tie, the combination of haircut and restraints screamed criminal.

A rumbling murmur worked its way through the room. Everyone present was wondering the same thing, was this really necessary?

"Remember," Senior spoke quietly next to her ear. "You aren't married, you haven't seen one another in years."

"You didn't tell him I would be here?" Val asked. They watched as the bailiffs took out their keys and began the process of removing the cuffs.

"No," Senior admitted, keeping his voice low. "I wanted it to seem real when he walked in and saw you. I wanted the cameras to believe he hasn't seen you in a long time."

Val nodded at that, her eyes fixed on Jason who kept looking over his shoulder, trying to catch a glimpse of her. All these years, Val had thought Elaine was the calculating one. Now it seemed it was really Senior you had to watch out for.

When the last metal chain lay loosely on the floor, Jason stepped out and was greeted by his lead attorney. The short man was heavy set, with silver rimmed glasses and a great booming voice. He was the best that money could buy, and he clapped a hand heartily on Jason's shoulder as they walked the short distance to the defendant's table and sat down.

"What are you doing here?" Jason hissed. Turning around in his seat, his hands reached impulsively over the side of the partition.

"Uh-uh." Senior gave a slight shake of his head, before laying a protective arm across Val. "I know you haven't seen her in *years,* Son, but Val has agreed to come out of hiding to testify on your behalf. Eyes forward. If you please."

Taking the hint, Jason rotated back around to face front, but not before giving them both an exasperated glare. Tilting towards his attorney, Jason spoke quietly, obviously trying to get as much information on Val's involvement as possible.

Up at the front of the courtroom, things were happening. The clerk came to standing along with the court reporter and other staff. The buzzing and rumbling of the packed space rose ever higher, until one tall bailiff cried out, causing silence to fall like a blanket, smothering them all.

"All rise. The Court of New York is now in session, the Honorable Judge Allen presiding."

In unison every single person rose to attention. Chairs

rolled back from both the prosecution and defense tables, attorneys tucked ties and straightened skirts. The audience rustled papers, set down purses, shifted briefcases to make room. Val held her breath as Judge Allen swept inside.

His long black robe hung off of his slight frame. He was slender and short, maybe five-foot-eight at the most. Once dark hair had turned silver-grey, and a matching short beard graced his chin. Intelligent, almond-shaped brown eyes surveyed the room, taking in the respect he knew he deserved.

"You may be seated." The bailiff announced, after Judge Allen had assumed his throne.

For the first several minutes the judge verified the case number, title and other various procedural issues with his clerk. No one dared to speak a word. The attorneys waited patiently and everyone else took their cues from them.

Val stared at the back of Jason's neck, eyes cruising up and over his newly buzzed head. How she longed to wrap her arms around his shoulders, to kiss him, and feel the reassurance of his presence. Ruefully she thought that Jace would want to cut his hair now to match. Then abruptly she shoved the image of her son from her mind. She was not a mother here. If she wanted to save his life, then she must remember *that* above all else.

"This is a specialty hearing granted to the defendant based on the presentation of new evidence as well as the answering of a summons by a formerly absent witness." Judge Allen spoke with command, eyes focused on Jason's attorney. "Is that correct?"

"It is, your Honor." The lead attorney stood, bracing his

plump hands across the wide wooden table. "We thank you for granting us this hearing on such short notice. As you know it was necessary due to the difficulty in tracking down this witness and assuring her continued presence for testimony."

"Well, as you know this is a criminal case concerning Captive Law, so we have our own set of rules and procedures. The trial date has not been set and we have not yet selected a jury. Is it your request that we proceed today without a jury present?"

"It is, your Honor." The lead attorney bade Jason stand. "My client waives his right to a jury trial and requests a bench trial in this matter."

"Do you understand the implication of that choice Mr. Riggs?" The judge leaned forward, looking critically at Jason.

"I do, your Honor." Jason's voice was steady, he did not look away.

"Then you may proceed."

Over the next hour the notarized documents obtained by Val in the Maldives were presented to the judge as well as the prosecution. The lawyers argued back and forth about the manner of evidence, but the documents were not new to the judge nor were they new to AG Collins.

In order to get the hearing, Jason's attorneys had submitted the packet of papers already, and everyone knew they would be accepted by the court today. This part of practicing law was just heavy-handed posturing. But the longer it dragged on, the more nervous Val became.

Wringing her hands together in her lap, Val did her best not to look at the Cambric representatives that sat calmly in the audience. Their upright demeanor, clean appearance and pleasant expressions belied the command and control that was exercised in private. She recognized one. Shane.

He had been the head of the training program in which Val had been raised. He was an overseer, not an instructor, but he often waited at the back of the room, observing. Average height, fit, but not overly so, his blonde hair and light eyes gave off a cold appearance. Or maybe that was just how Val saw him, because he was present at each disciplinary session, seeming to take great pleasure in the handing down of punishment.

When the court finally called her name, Val jumped visibly. Theresa and Senior exchanged a look, but the matter was out of their hands, now.

Biting at the inside of her cheek, Val rose as gracefully as possible and made her way to the witness box. They went through the familiar routine of swearing her in, stating her name and leading her through the events of that night on the yacht. The night where Jason had walked in on her and Gabe wrapped up together in an embrace.

She testified that Gabe had been the one to demand the five million dollar pay out, not Jason. She swore he came up with the idea alone, and that he also came up with the amount.

Then Jason's attorney walked her through the notarized statement signed by Gabe in the Maldives. It corroborated her testimony, confirming that Gabe was not beholden to Jason. That Jason did not own him, support him or control him, and that in fact Gabe had officially reimbursed Jason for every dollar paid out. In effect, Gabe was now the harborer of his own self, technically speaking.

"Thank you, those are all the questions that we have for this witness, your Honor." The defense attorney gave Val an encouraging smile before resuming his seat.

Blowing out a breath, Val let herself lock eyes with Jason. He gave her the slightest of smiles. It was everything she could do not to smile back. Even here in this room full of people, he had the ability to make her feel as if they were in a world all their own. Throughout her testimony, she had sensed his stare, but remembered Senior's warning well.

She was not here as Kelly, she was here as Val. The last time that the public had seen her, she was sitting in this very courthouse, offering testimony against Sharon Baine. At that time, she no longer belonged to Jason and their separation was well televised for months afterward.

"Miss Val, is it?" AG Collins stepped into her line of sight, and gestured over her shoulder. "How well do you know the defendant?"

"I was owned by him for a little less than a year." Val refocused her attention on the imposing woman.

"And in that time did he ever lie?"

"Lie?"

"That's right. Have you ever known the defendant to tell a lie."

Val thought for a moment, knowing that she was under oath and trying to make certain of her answer. The AG stood patiently, letting the silence fill the court with its own weight.

The longer she let this go on, the more uncertain it would make her answer seem.

"I don't remember specifically," Val said finally.

"When is the last time you had sexual relations with Jason Riggs?"

"Objection!" Jason's attorney shot to his feet. "Relevance? Your Honor, this is a highly inappropriate line of questioning."

"He's right, Counselor. Sustained."

"I'll move on." AG Collins ducked her head in apology. "Were you aware that Jason Riggs is married?"

"Yes."

An undercurrent of murmuring flowed through the gallery as news of this secret washed over the crowd. Jason Riggs was married? To whom? When? The hushed questions built in momentum until Judge Allen rapped heavily with his gavel, calling for order and threatening to drain the courtroom if silence wasn't maintained.

You could hear a pin drop.

"Were you aware that Jason adopted his wife's young son?" AG Collins held a piece of paper in her hand, but Val could not make out what it was.

"Yes," she answered.

Val's heart pounded hard against the inside of her chest. This wasn't a line of questioning they had prepared for because Jason's attorneys did not know she was actually his wife. They were aware he was married and had adopted a son, but not that it was with her. As a captive born, she knew she could not risk perjuring herself. Any infraction of the law could cost her free status, sending her right back down to where she had begun.

"May I approach, your Honor?"

AG Collins waited for Judge Allen to nod his acceptance before she walked up to Val and handed her the sheet of paper. It was a picture of Jace, his school photo from France. They must have dug up the records somehow, or paid someone off. Val struggled to maintain an expression clear of emotion.

Agency rhetoric sounded in her head, helping her to separate her outward shell from her inner desperation. For what right did a captive have to feel anything for her child? None, because no children belonged to her.

"This is a photo of Jace Riggs." AG Collins shifted her body to let the gallery see her speak. "He is the son of Kelly Riggs, formerly Kelly Martin before she married the defendant."

"Objection!" Jason's attorney leapt again to his feet. "Is there a question in there somewhere?"

"Sustained."

"I'll rephrase. Is this your son, Val? Are you Kelly Martin?"

The court erupted with sound as the gallery took in the allegation. AG Collins turned and gave the cameras her best triumphant smile. Jason blanched. His attorneys leaned in to whisper furiously in his face. No doubt they were desperate to know if this was the truth. Senior reached over the partition and did his best to intervene while Judge Allen banged his gavel, shouting for order.

And while chaos reigned around her, Val sought her former protector once more. The words that he had whispered in her ear hours earlier came back to echo in her mind over and over. Agent Finn caught her eye, and in that moment gave the most imperceptible of nods. Now, he seemed to say, use it now.

"I plead the Fifth Amendment," Val spoke up, causing AG Collins to whirl back. "I am taking the Fifth."

CHAPTER 10

"ORDER! I SAID ORDER!" JUDGE ALLEN BANGED AGAIN WITH his gavel but to no avail. Gesturing to the bailiff, he ordered the audience on their feet. Slowly, they all stood and shuffled begrudgingly out the far doors. Val sat stiffly in the witness box, forgotten in all the confusion.

As the courtroom drained, only the hushed discussions between attorneys and clients remained. Jason's family had been allowed to stay, along with Agent Finn and the representatives from Cambric. Now alone in the expanse of gallery, Val was able to pick out two security contractors as well. Their dark tailored suits fit snugly over broad shoulders. CT towered over them all.

"Your Honor, if I may." Jason's attorney stood once more and waited for the go ahead from the judge. "We would like to move for a directed verdict in my client's case at this time."

"Are you certain?" The judge lifted his eyebrows.

"We are, your Honor. The defendant has been charged

with harboring the captive, Gabe, and we believe we have proven he is not guilty of that crime. The identity of his wife and child are of no significance in the matter."

"So noted." Judge Allen gave a curt nod before turning to Val. "Is it your intention to invoke the Fifth Amendment?"

"It is, your Honor." Val studied the man that held the fate of her husband in his hands.

"Then you may step down."

"Objection, your Honor, if I may." AG Collins shot to her feet. "We are not done with this witness."

"Not so fast, Counselor." Judge Allen frowned. "You forget whose courtroom you are standing in."

"Yes, your Honor."

AG Collins sat, but glanced quickly over her shoulder. By the time Val had stepped from the box and walked back to the safety of her seat, the AG had checked the far door twice more. She was waiting for something, or someone.

Jason twisted in his chair, resting one arm along the wooden partition that separated them. Despite the disapproving look from Senior, he grabbed at a loose strand of Val's hair, tugging gently on the ends. He was playing it cool, trying to reassure her, and the intimate gesture filled her with a dull ache. She bit subconsciously at her lip and saw the wanting response that filled his eyes.

"I have taken all evidence into account in the matter of the State of New York vs. Jason Riggs Junior and have reached a verdict," Judge Allen announced, causing Jason to whip back around and tense in his chair.

"The facts of this case have proven extremely troubling to me. In particular it seems that the defendant acted in good faith at the bequest of the FBI to negotiate a deal with an informant who happened to also be a classified captive.

Though this sort of deal had never come to pass before, that did not mean the burden was on the defendant to legally vet the circumstances. On top of this, the defendant apparently financed the operation, thereby saving the tax payers large sums of money.

And how has he been repaid for answering his country's call for assistance? This is the most troubling aspect of all, and I fear it has the ability to set a dangerous precedence. How many other good citizens will think twice before assisting in an investigation? More than one, I fear. More than one.

Therefore, I hereby find the defendant, Jason Riggs Junior, not guilty on all counts and order him released, effective immediately."

Jason exhaled and leaned forward over the defendant's table, hands splayed against its flat surface. His lawyers clapped him on the back, then turned to shake hands with Senior who stood, an expression of immense relief filling his face.

Theresa and Jeremy too were rising, incredulous laughter spilling from their lips. Val sat still, holding back tears. He was acquitted, they couldn't come after him anymore. Her thoughts flew all around. She wanted to throw her arms around him. She wanted to rush home, to bring Jace his beloved father and see the happy way they would cling to each other.

But then the far doors of the courtroom banged open and a courier dashed inside. Down the aisle he came, clutching a stack of papers in one hand. Breathless, he made it to AG

Collins and handed them over before falling heavily into a nearby seat.

Scanning the documents quickly, AG Collins shot to her feet and drew a disapproving frown from Judge Allen.

"Your Honor, we request the court's leave to serve a Writ of Conscription against former captive Val, here and present in this very courtroom."

"What?!" Jason jumped up, whirling on AG Collins.

The color drained from Val's face. The announcement rocked her. Cambric sought to conscript her back into their service.

Suddenly, she couldn't move. She couldn't speak. Numbness took hold of her body as she sensed the security contractors move towards her. Jason's face twisted at once in confusion and then in horror. CT shifted his bulk closer, positioning himself firmly in the aisle.

"Order!" Judge Allen called again, and huffed angrily. "AG Collins you cannot simply conscript any captive you like in place of another. The law might be construed in favor of agencies but there are some rules."

"Your Honor, if I may explain." AG Collins waited for the nod from the judge before proceeding. "We do not seek to conscript the former captive Val in place of the captive Gabe. We seek to conscript her per the purchase contract signed by Jason Riggs Junior which specifically gives Cambric the right to exchange her for any child she may have conceived if said child has not been turned over."

"No!" Jason shouted, causing Judge Allen's frown to deepen. "I didn't know what I was signing, your Honor. It's a standard form contract and I wasn't given the proper amount of time to review it."

"You expect me to believe that the CEO of Riggs Oil signed a contract and didn't review each and every line?" Judge Allen shook his head slowly. "That is a hard pill to swallow. AG Collins, please hand the documents over so that I may review them."

"Yes, your Honor."

In the ensuing silence, the shock that had frozen Val in place began to wear off. Jason kept shaking his head, murmuring to his attorneys. His face was contorted with dread, his movements jerky and harsh. They did their best to keep him quiet.

Painful tingles crept up Val's legs and arms working their way to her chest. It felt as if she were being held in a vice, the tightness around her ribcage constricted her breathing. As she worked for air, she began to rasp. Theresa glanced worriedly into her face.

"I think she's going to pass out," she said.

"Look at me, Baby, look at me." Jason reached for her, his pleading eyes searching her own.

"Damn it, Jason," Senior hissed, pushing his son away. "If you don't want these people to think she's your wife, then stop acting like it."

"I have had a chance to review the contract in question along with the Writ of Conscription," Judge Allen announced, drawing all eyes back to the front. "Captive Law is very clear, and so it appears that the former captive Val would be subject to conscription in place of any child she may have conceived and not turned over to Cambric."

"Thank you, your Honor." AG Collins beamed, then gestured to Cambric security who stepped up to CT. He did not blink. He did not move.

"Not so fast, Counselor," Judge Allen admonished, with something of a smile working into his face. "As you know, the rule of law only works because it is based on strict procedure. This Writ was not filed correctly, nor was this purchase contract. On top of that, the underlying case still contains many holes.

There is no proof that the former captive Val has produced any child. No birth certificate, no witnesses, nothing. I hereby refuse to acknowledge service of this Writ of Conscription and caution you to be more thorough in your application in the future."

"Get up." Jason turned, grabbing for Val. "Get her out of here *now*. Let's go."

Senior and Theresa each took an arm, propping Val between them. Everyone in the courtroom was standing. Cambric's security contractors stood toe to toe with CT, who was still a head taller than either of them. Jason pushed past his attorneys, trying to skirt the partition that separated them, eyes tracking Val the entire time.

She wanted to speak, wanted to walk, wanted to stand on her own, but her brain had stopped sending signals to her body. Cambric would get to her. She knew it better than anyone. It may not be today, or even tomorrow, but The Agency would file the documents properly. They would be granted the Writ and she would become their property once more.

Absently, she looked down at her right forearm. Under her

shirt, the place where her tracker had been removed was forever marked by a vertical scar. Somethings never heal.

"Your Honor," AG Collins pressed on. "The court case Havana Agency v. Perkins ruled that if a captive is seen as a flight risk, then the Writ of Conscription is not required to follow application protocol. As you know this particular captive is an extreme flight risk. For the past several years neither the court nor the FBI has been able to locate her."

"I am familiar with the case," Judge Allen conceded. "But Val is legally a former captive, not current. We both know that the law is on the side of The Agency in this matter, but this particular case has a lot of uncharted territory. I must admit it would make for a very interesting trial. However, this is still *my* courtroom. And therefore, I have the final say. My decision stands."

"But, your Honor-" AG Collins voice raised with her plea.

"That being said-" Judge Allen nodded to his bailiffs, who moved quickly to stop Jason in his tracks. "I agree that Val is a flight risk, and would not want to be accused of bias in the matter. As a compromise, I will select a third party and designate them the job of maintaining her residence in the state of New York until you've had the chance to seek the Writ's approval through the proper channels."

"Who would that person be, your Honor?" Jason's lead attorney spoke up.

"I believe FBI Agent John Finn is present in court today. He has been charged with the protection of Val's witness identity and is familiar to both sides of the aisle. It is my understanding that his reputation for law and order are beyond dispute and so in that vein I hereby charge him with the responsibility for daily check-ins with Val until such a time as the Writ can be filed. Agent Finn, are you up to the task? It is on your honor that Val not leave the state."

"Yes, Judge Allen." Agent Finn nodded, face devoid of any emotion.

"AG Collins?" Judge Allen lifted his eyebrows. "Do you so stipulate?"

"So, stipulated, your Honor."

"What in the hell just happened?" Jeremy asked.

They were all packed into a tiny meeting room located down the hall from Judge Allen's court. Jason's legal team was in a heated discussion with Senior, who nodded solemnly from time to time. Theresa paced like a cat, her high heels tapping along the thin red carpet while CT stood resolutely at the door.

"The Judge gave us a reprieve," Jason explained to his brother, all the while keeping his arms wrapped around his wife. "We have a few days before they'll get the Writ approved, then they'll come get her."

Val kept her face buried in Jason's neck. The smell of his skin was a comfort amidst the turmoil that threatened to overtake her. She felt his strong hands stroke her arms, then move to tighten around her waist.

If this was it, if this was all the rest of him that she got, then she wanted to embrace it. She didn't want to let Cambric steal these last few days along with the rest of her life. For deep down, though she quaked at the thought, she would gladly give her life for her son. If they conscripted her in his place, then they could never touch him.

"I want you to go to Jace." Val lay her head on Jason's chest, listened to the tripping beat of his heart. "Give him a good life with his father. Don't spend your days here, fighting for me."

"Stop." Jason pressed his lips to the top of her head. "I'm not going to let them take you."

A knock at the door had them all turning. Before anyone could answer, it swung inward. Agent Finn stood on the threshold, his arms were crossed formally in front of his body. Again, his face gave away nothing. The serious countenance that had so often covered it, remained there still.

"Everything's set up," Agent Finn said. "Have you decided where Val will be staying tonight?"

"We're going back to the hotel," Jason responded. "Is your escort really necessary?"

"Yes, it is." Agent Finn shifted his weight, but didn't look away. "They're even placing agents at your door overnight."

"All this over one captive?" Jason squeezed Val tighter. "Who's paying for it? You and I both know your boss is too cheap."

Agent Finn remained silent, letting the question hang in the air. Cambric was paying for it. Of course they were, Val thought. She wasn't just one captive and they weren't just proving a point. The Agency only did things that made financial sense. If they were willing to pursue Val this hard, that meant they had a plan in mind to profit off of her.

A shiver snaked its way up her spine. She couldn't help it.

Keeping her thoughts to herself, she knew that sharing them would do no one any good.

"What about the press conference?" Senior spoke up, indicating Jason and Val. "One of you has to speak."

"She's not talking to anyone and I'm not leaving her. You'll have to do it."

For a moment, Senior looked as if he would argue, but then he noted the array of defeated faces that were strewn about the room. They may have vindicated Jason, clearing his name and gaining his freedom, but they had lost an entirely different battle. One they hadn't been prepared to fight. Eventually he dropped his head in acceptance. They agreed to meet back at the hotel.

CT, Jason, Val and Agent Finn fled through the halls of the courthouse together. While the rest of the Riggs family and their brilliant legal team stood at a podium on the front steps of the building, the real object of the media's desire was being whisked away in a nondescript town car.

Agent Finn led the way down into the belly of the courthouse. They would exit the same way that he and Val had so many years ago, through a prisoner's entrance. It was the same way Jason had arrived just that morning.

The plan went off without a hitch and soon they were tucked inside the black vehicle, stuck in evening traffic on the streets of New York. Val sat nestled up against Jason in the rear seat, his arm was draped protectively over her shoulder, his other hand rubbed at her palm. She could sense something building within him.

Jaw clenching, Jason's eyes focused on the rearview mirror. He stared at Agent Finn, who drove with both hands flexed on the steering wheel. CT was quiet in the front passenger seat, poised, as he always was, but saying nothing.

"Is this the part where she disappears?" Jason asked quietly.

"No." Agent Finn held up a hand, tapping twice on his ear as if to say, *they're listening.*

As soon as he was able, he pulled to the right and stopped the car at the curb. Fishing around in the pocket of his slacks, he produced his cell phone and handed it over to CT. With a nod to the big man, he indicated the passenger door.

CT twisted to look back at Jason, who patted him on the shoulder and released him to go. Taking Finn's cell phone along with him, CT stepped out onto the busy sidewalk and shut the door. Left alone in the car, Agent Finn faced forward, but began to speak.

"Tell me you left the kid where he was." Finn's knuckles whitened over the steering wheel.

"Yes." Val sat up straighter, staring at Finn's dark eyes in the rearview mirror.

"Why did you come back? Why didn't you stay where you were? They would've gotten him off eventually."

"I didn't realize-"

"Don't blame this on her." Jason jumped in. "Just tell us what we need to do to get her out of here."

"Damn it, Jason, a lot has changed in four years. We have

a new President, new members of congress, and I've got a new boss. Things aren't the way they were before."

"But you made her disappear back then. Her and the baby."

"I still followed the law." Agent Finn glared. "Now a court full of people heard me swear that she wouldn't leave the state. I can't *not* deliver her. Take the days you have left, then turn your legal team loose and build a case. You just might get her out."

"After everything we've done together. You and me." Jason pursed his lips, his face tight. "The years of searching… building the case. All the things that I gave up to see it through to the end. Because it was the *right thing* to do, remember? You and I both know what's going to happen to her in there. And you're just going to hand her over like this?"

"It's not my choice to make. You knew the risks. It was your job to protect them."

"But is it the right thing, John? Are you doing the right thing?"

"There's more at play here than either of you realize. If I let her go now, then I'll lose my job. People other than you depend on me. I'm sorry." Agent Finn shifted his eyes to look directly at Val. "She's been trained for this. She can handle it. Don't make it harder on her, Jason."

Leaning over, Agent Finn pulled at the passenger door handle and let the door swing wide. CT slid back inside, handed over the silver cell phone and shut the door behind him. Before anyone else could speak, the car shifted into drive and eased back into the flow of traffic.

CHAPTER 11

The remainder of the car ride with Agent Finn was silent. Silent and tense. And that tension seemed to follow them back to the hotel and up the elevator, even though no reporters swarmed. When they arrived at the double doors of the suite, Jason hesitated at the keypad. He didn't know the code and Senior was still miles away.

Although the armed security guards standing nearby recognized Jason and Val, they simply shook their heads. They didn't have the code either and were unable to open the door. After a beat, Jason tilted his face up to analyze CT.

"Open it," he commanded. "I know everyone thinks you're dumb as rocks but you and I both know that's not the case. You've seen him punch the code."

Shrugging, CT stepped to the door and let his large fingers pass over the keypad. Within seconds the door clicked open and Jason shoved inside.

The space was clean and peaceful, just as they had left it

hours before. Only, it seemed a world away now. Regardless, Jason refused to stop, refused to take it in. Hand wrapped firmly around Val's wrist, he asked which bedroom belonged to them, then dragged her inside and locked the door.

"I won't let them take you." His arctic eyes darted across her face. "You know that, right?"

"I know," she assured him. "I know."

Reaching up, she let her fingertips trace the side of his face. She knew that he wouldn't stop fighting. It wasn't in Jason's nature to back down, or give in. It wasn't in his nature to accept the hand dealt to him. But it *was* in hers. It was bred into her parents, whoever they were, and it flowed through her blood like a richly laced drug. As soon as stress came, squeezing her into a corner, The Agency had trained her to submit.

Drawing his face down to hers, Val pressed her lips against his, ran her hands over the soft stubble where his thick hair had been. For the first few moments, their kiss was sweet, flowing with the months of separation and the heartache that had overtaken the day. But then a sharp desperation came forward and she felt him gathering her body against his, greedy in the use of his hands.

His mouth became hot as it passed over hers, nipping along her jaw before seeking the tender skin of her neck. With a groan he backed her against the closed bedroom door.

She felt the hard surface against her back as his hands hiked up her skirt, roamed to her panties, yanked at her blouse. He was everywhere at once, as if he couldn't get enough.

Eyes closed against the skyline of the city, she felt him

ignite a fire within her. Biting at her lip, she used her hands to push his suit jacket off of his shoulders before working nimble fingers down the front of his shirt, undoing buttons as she went.

"I love you. I love you." His voice was thick as he whispered the words, all the while working her lace thong down over her hips.

By the time his shirt fell to the floor, more than half of her clothes drifted down to follow. Lifting her up, he wrapped her legs around his waist, then bent his head to kiss and fondle each breast. She gasped, eyes opening wide, hands clutching at his bare shoulders.

Before long, he had her shifting her hips against him, a quiet moan forming in her throat. He groaned in response.

Reaching down, he fumbled with his belt. She could hear the snap of metal and leather as he jerked to free himself. Arms still wrapped around his shoulders, she licked and sucked the skin just beneath his jaw.

Cursing softly, he pivoted around and carried her towards the freshly made bed. In his rush, he stumbled just a bit and they landed together on the mattress, still wrapped up in each other's arms. His mouth covered hers then, and he entered her.

His breathing came harsh and panting as he worked on top of her, his thick strokes growing faster as he went. Arching beneath him, she whimpered and clenched. Over and over he moved between her thighs until she was crying out, tightening around him, raking her nails down the length of his back.

He didn't last long after that.

~

Still wrapped in his heavy arms, she lay on her back and blinked up at the ceiling. She was warm. *He* kept her warm. The tangle of their naked bodies radiated heat as they lounged together on the wide bed.

Eyes flicking to study the rise and fall of his chest, Val's heart began to beat in trepidation. This may be her last chance and she needed to say something. Something she had kept hidden from him for too long.

"I don't want another baby," she whispered.

"I should've thought about that." Jason sighed. "I didn't use protection."

"No." Val sucked in a breath, knowing he thought only of tonight. "I mean, I haven't wanted another baby at all."

Raising his head, Jason looked down his nose at her, trying to get a better view of her face. Abruptly she sat upright and turned towards him. He gave her a quizzical look, but she shut her eyes and willed herself to confess the whole story.

"I've been taking birth control." She spit the words out before she could change her mind. "For years."

He blew out a long breath, then his arms came to circle her waist. Deliberately, he collected her back down beside him. Stroking along her skin, he kissed her forehead tenderly.

"Why didn't you just tell me?"

"I don't know. Because you wanted it so badly and I couldn't risk you convincing me otherwise. Are you mad?"

"I wish you would've trusted me at least to talk about it, but no, I'm not mad."

Shifting in silence, they lay still. Her thoughts drifted to

Jace and the Maldives. Would she ever see her son again? Tuck him into bed? Scold him for all of his boisterous mess?

Throat constricting, streaming tears stung at her eyes. She had never felt such utter devastation in all her life. Sensing her despair, Jason sat up and pulled her onto his lap.

"I won't let them take you," he repeated, rocking her slowly.

"Promise me you'll go to Jace right away," Val choked, but managed to get the words out clearly. "Promise me you'll take care of our son. He needs you *every* day."

"Hey-" Jason's voice cracked under the strain. "I promise we will go see him, the both of us. We'll be on a plane by tomorrow at the latest."

"What are you talking about?"

"I've got a plan." Jason gave her a last kiss before scooting away. Rising off the bed he went to fetch his clothes. "But first, let's take care of this pregnancy thing. I'll send someone out for the morning after pill."

"That's not necessary," Val stated, twisting her fingers together nervously. "I-"

"You… what?" Jason stepped into his slacks, then paused to watch her.

"Well you see, Gabe and I-" Val hesitated, wondering just what to say without breaking her friend's confidence. "He took me to see this doctor in Male. I got a shot that should last me about three months."

"You and Gabe." Jason shrugged into his shirt, then worked purposeful fingers over the buttons. He was angry. "You can trust him, but not me. You tell him, but not me."

From her position on the bed she watched Jason struggle.

He zipped up his pants and buckled his belt, tugged at his collar and avoided her eyes. Ever since that first day when Jason caught Gabe with his hand spread across her thigh, he had fought off his own jealously. Despite the fact he knew nothing had gone on between them, and the fact he knew how Gabe felt about Bee, it was a natural reaction that he just couldn't seem to shake.

Any time she confided in Gabe or turned to her friend instead of Jason, it triggered a spark in him that he had to work hard to put out. Going behind his back and taking birth control for years was one thing, but Gabe offering his assistance in the matter was another.

Val twisted her fingers in her lap, watching how he tightened his jaw. She could almost hear his teeth grinding. That night on the dock, alone with Gabe, Val knew this exact scenario would play out. She knew if she accepted Gabe's offer of help, that it would hurt her husband in ways she couldn't easily repair. But she had done it anyway. She wasn't willing to risk the alternative.

Guilt flooded her, but she knew better than to approach Jason just now. Instead, she let him walk out the door, trying not to let it sting that he didn't look back.

Flopping back on the mattress, Val resumed staring at the ceiling. The sun was setting, casting an array of shadows that played in the constantly dimming light. Not having slept well the night before, her eyelids felt heavy and her thoughts blurred.

With the last of her strength, she crawled beneath the covers and rolled onto her belly. Jason was free and he had a plan. She would see her son again. She had to have faith in that. Closing her eyes, her breathing evened out until she spiraled down into the waiting abyss.

In the far reaches of her dreams she heard his voice. The sound of his delightful giggle was a million miles away. Still, it made her smile. A big wide grin, the kind that makes your cheeks hurt, that's what spread across her face.

Then someone was pulling her and she felt sucked through a swamp. The muggy thickness was all around her and she had her arms outstretched grasping in the direction of her little boy. But she was being tugged away. Tugged up into the light.

"Babe, wake up." Jason was standing over her in the darkened bedroom. "Come see this."

"Hmmm?" Val rubbed at her eyes, trying to shake the raw feeling of the dream.

"Come on, you'll like it. I promise."

Then she heard the sound again. Jace's undeniable laughter lilting from the living room. Springing up suddenly, she made a dash for the bedroom door. The crack of light that seeped through left a long line on the plush carpet. Jason grabbed her around the waist easily, stopping her progress.

"Hey-" he chuckled. "You're still naked."

"Oh!" Val blushed before retreating to the closet to throw on some clothes.

Out in the living area, Jeremy sat on the sofa, hands wrapped around the laptop. He was making silly faces into the screen, and each time he would change expressions, Jace's laughter would tumble from the speakers. Glancing at the clock that hung on the wall, Val saw that the time was a quarter past eleven. The internet was still working in the Maldives. Thank God.

As she crossed the room, Senior and Theresa glanced up. They were seated at a nearby table, picking through Chinese takeout boxes. The smell of the spice-laden food filled the space.

"I think there's someone else here you'll want to talk to Jacey." Jeremy slid to the side, making room for Val next to him on the couch.

"Really?" Jace's small voice squeaked. "Who is it?"

"It's me!" Val peeked around the edge of the screen, causing Jace's eyes to grow wide with excitement.

"Mommy!" He sang it out. "I got to see Daddy, too. Did you know?"

"Yeah, I know. Isn't that awesome?"

"Did you see his haircut? I'm gonna have the same haircut. I better get the same thing."

"Ugh." Val kept a fake smile plastered across her face. "You sure about that? It's pretty short already."

"I'm sure." Jace bobbed his head in confident determination.

The rest of the conversation centered around his latest exploits on the island. Gabe and he were officially building a fort. With real walls and a real ladder and everything. Jace beamed. Val reached out to stroke his little face, but felt the slick screen's surface instead. Soon, she consoled herself, soon.

Jason strolled over and wedged himself down next to her. They chatted happily for a time, but before long their little boy became bored. It was the beginning of his day on the other side of the world and sitting still was not on his itinerary.

When the call clicked off, Val felt renewed. She lay her head on Jason's shoulder, and he drew her in closer, pressing a kiss into her hair. The incident between them had been forgiven, or at least put on the back burner until a much later date. She could live with that, feeling content just to be close to him.

But Jason, like his son, was not a body that could remain seated for long. The intensity with which he lived each moment, propelled him forward, and he soon shifted, calling for everyone to gather round.

"So, did everyone get what they needed?" Jason asked.

Senior, Theresa, Jeremy and CT all nodded. Val looked perplexed.

"What's going on?" She asked.

"While you were resting-" Jason motioned CT toward the doors. "We were preparing for tonight."

"What's tonight?"

"Your escape." Jason paused as CT called the two security guards into the suite and shut the door. The men came over to stand behind the couch and listen. "I figure that tonight will be the best time to make a move. It's late, and the Feds that have been stationed outside are new to the schedule. Likely they're feeling a bit tired."

"What are we going to do?" Val leaned forward.

"Theresa, did you get it?" Jason asked.

"Yup."

"Alright, good." Jason gave his sister a nod. "So, Theresa went out today and bought herself a long brown wig. She's about the same height and weight as Val, and with a jacket and hood on, I think she could pass for her."

"Jason-" Val frowned.

"Jeremy is going to put on my suit from today, and unfortunately for him, we're going to buzz his head."

"Damn it," Jeremy groaned, but cracked a sly grin.

"Jason, stop." Val locked eyes with him. "What's going on?"

"We need to create a diversion." Jason spread his palm over her knee reassuringly. "Jeremy and Theresa are going to dress like us. Dad, CT, and these two security guards are going to rush them from the hotel and make it seem like we're trying to escape.

We booked the jet for a flight out tonight, so the Feds are already on notice that we're going to try to do something. If the agents here are a touch tired, then they won't hesitate just to follow the first person that looks like you."

"But that still leaves us here, right?" Val pointed out.

"After the Feds follow Theresa, then you and I will sneak out using the stairs. There's an exit off the side of the hotel that opens out onto the street. We'll walk a few blocks and hail a cab. I've got a car parked just outside the city and we can take it out of the country."

"Wow." Val blew out a breath. "Do you think it'll work?"

"I hope so."

Theresa and Val stood side by side, surveying the collection of clothing strewn across the bed. In the background, the sound of hair clippers whirred. Jeremy's new look was coming along nicely.

Eyeing each piece critically, Val selected a tiny jade-green dress with stiletto heels and a short black coat, it had a hood lined with satin. Holding them up against Theresa, she tilted her head to the side and figured the fit would be just about right.

"Well." Theresa changed into the outfit quickly. "It will certainly attract attention."

"That's the idea," Val reminded her, knowing that Theresa had never been the kind to show off so much leg.

"How do I look?"

"Just right." Val ran her fingers through the long chestnut wig, then pulled up the hood and adjusted the fit. "Just keep your head tilted down, let Jeremy lead you along. Maybe cover half your face with your hand."

"Okay." Theresa nodded. "Your turn."

Reaching for a pair designer jeans that fit low on the hip and wrapped tightly at the ankle, Theresa handed them over. Then came a pair of brown leather flats, a short-sleeve blouse and finally a cashmere sweater. Val wriggled into the clothes, then allowed Theresa to bind back her hair and tuck it into a ball cap.

"You look… casual." Theresa grinned. "How do you feel?"

"Terrified," Val admitted, then examined both of their reflections in the full length mirror.

Standing side by side in the dim light, Val saw herself in the style of Theresa and vice versa. This just might work, she thought.

When Jason appeared, he was wearing his younger brother's clothes. Black t-shirt, blue jeans and navy-colored hoodie. Wrapping her arms around him, Val felt a bulge just under one arm. Sucking in a breath, she glanced up into his face.

"I've got a permit for it," Jason murmured, then drew her against him, offering her what comfort he could.

At two in the morning, the group was assembled and ready. The men shook hands and the women embraced. They all hoped that by this same time tomorrow, Jason and Val would be far north of here, having crossed the border into Canada.

Standing in the foyer, all the lights in the suite had been flicked off. Jason glanced at his phone before giving his father a final nod. The security guards shoved through the door first with Jeremy dragging Theresa along at his back. CT and Senior followed.

As the doors swung shut, Val could hear shouts ring out from the FBI agents. Then came the pounding of feet, the shuffle of bodies and the sound of elevator doors dinging. Jason clutched her tightly to him, she could hear the sound of his breathing. Please let this work, she thought. Please.

Through the doors they heard one agent radio for backup, then race by on his way to the end of the hall. When the far door to the stairs slammed shut, Jason dared to look through the peep hole.

"All clear," he whispered.

Turning to face her, Jason adjusted her ball cap and then pulled up his hood, cinching it down to cover his forehead. Quickly, she rose up to kiss him, balancing on her toes to reach. It was just a peck, a fast brush of trust that passed between them before it was gone, replaced by the pounding of blood that pumped in her ears.

Taking her firmly in hand, Jason quietly opened the door and set a fast pace for the opposite set of stairs. No one at all was left on their floor.

The eerie sound of their steps echoed in the emptiness as they breached the stairwell. It was a long, long, long way down. By the time they reached the bottom, Val's head was spinning and her lungs burned. She wasn't sure if it was the carousel of their descent or the fear of their flight that had her short of breath.

At the bottom, Jason hesitated for only a second. His chest heaved and his eyes sought hers in the garish light. Swallowing hard, she gave him a slight nod before he opened the exit door and stepped outside.

It was the middle of the night in the city, but the sidewalks still had pedestrians and the streets still spilled with cars. Light from the towering buildings, overhead lamps and headlights forced odd pools of shadows to collect next to the hotel.

Glancing first one way and then the other, Jason stepped as casually as possible into the open. He pulled Val along next to him and they managed to walk a few yards before the first body leapt at them from the darkness.

"Stop! FBI!" The man in the suit shouted, gun drawn to point directly in Jason's face.

Val's heart stopped beating in that moment.

Jason released his hold on her and she backed a few steps away. Just as she considered turning to run, she saw her husband lunge forward to attack the agent. Faster than she had ever seen him move, Jason ducked to the side before knocking the weapon from the man's hand. Then without hesitation, he pushed in closer, striking the agent in the throat with his clenched fist. Val could hear the gurgle as the agent collapsed onto the sidewalk, clutching at his neck, working for air.

"That will be enough."

The voice that growled just behind her was familiar, making her jump. One large arm snaked its way around her shoulders, while the other leveled a gun at Jason. Agent Finn held her body firmly against his. She could hear the sound of his breath exhaling through his nostrils.

"Don't-" Agent Finn's voice rose as Jason reached beneath his hoodie. "Even think about it."

Val wrapped both hands around Finn's forearm where he held it pressed just beneath her neck. Wide eyes reeling she wanted to beg her husband to surrender. This wasn't worth dying over. But she couldn't get any words to pass from her throat.

Slowly, Jason raised his hands, palms out, but kept his gaze locked on Agent Finn.

"You couldn't just chase the car out front?" Jason's voice was tight.

"No." Agent Finn shifted, adjusting the aim of his weapon. "Been doing a little training?"

"Being jumped by a crowd of people will teach you a few things." Jason's eyes darted to Val, then back to Finn. "Like you can't trust another person to save you. Like sometimes you get fed to the wolves. Sound familiar? Johnny?"

Traffic whizzed past, other pedestrians gave them a wide

berth, but no one stopped, no one attempted to interfere. The other agent regained his feet and, swearing to himself, came up behind Jason to disarm him. Tossing the gun a few feet away, he yanked down on Jason's wrists and secured him with a set of shining handcuffs. Val could hear the ratcheting click as they tightened.

"Put him on the ground," Agent Finn instructed.

The other agent forced Jason onto his belly, then knelt down on top of him, one large knee pressing into his back. It was then that Jason completely lost it.

"Fuck! You! John!" Jason screamed, picking up his head from the sidewalk in order to yell. "You're a fucking traitor! You're a fucking snake! How could you?! How could you?!"

Holstering his weapon, Agent Finn slid his hand into his waistband and produced another set of cuffs. He pulled Val's arms around to the small of her back, then fastened them snugly around her wrists. Unceremoniously, he turned her around, then marched her away from Jason. Away down the sidewalk, where a black sedan sat purring at the curb.

Jason's screams followed them. Haunting their steps all the way to the car before following them inside of it. The echo of his words didn't stop until the doors slammed shut and together they drove away.

CHAPTER 12

Sitting in the rear of the vehicle, the scene was all too familiar. Agent Finn drove in silence, the radio switched off, concentrating on the road. Wrists bound awkwardly behind her, Val twisted to the side in her seat, watching the buildings pass in the darkness beyond her window.

She didn't know the procedure. She wasn't sure of the exact timing. But she knew that she was on her way back to Cambric. They had a conscription intake protocol which she was vaguely familiar with, having heard stories about it from back in the day.

Unbidden, her mind traveled to Bee. For some reason she was inundated with flashes of her old friend. They were young and in training, Bee's smile was bright, always filled with a mischievous tilt.

This was the part where she would say something sarcastic to break the mood. This was the part where she would make a face behind an instructor's back, or spill her water in front of her trainer's feet, causing him to slip and fall. *Why, Bee? Why are you here with me now?*

The car made a turn and Agent Finn shifted around in the front seat. Val glanced over and watched him. His eyes flicked to the rearview mirror, then away. Reaching into his pocket, he produced his silver cell phone, pulled up a contact, then held it to one ear.

"Alright," Agent Finn spoke into the phone. "Release him. No. No report, no paperwork, just let him go. Keep the gun though."

After listening for a beat, Agent Finn ended the call, then tossed his phone down onto the center console. The silence that had occupied the cab before, resumed.

At least Jason wouldn't be brought up on more charges, Val thought. Assaulting a federal agent, violating a court order, assisting in the flight of a conscript. Agent Finn could have made things worse for him, but in the end, he made it go away. What he could anyway, she corrected, as the vehicle headed for the highway and what lay ahead in Upstate New York.

The drive took a little over three hours between stopping for fuel, bathroom breaks and fast-food. During that time, they didn't share a single word. Laying low in the backseat, Val wedged herself into a ball. Occasionally, she shifted her head, craning her neck to check the windows for signs of where they were.

The area just outside of Albany was thick with Balsam Fir, Scotch Pine and Norway Spruce. The old growth trees stacked up one against another, forming a forest of overlapping needles that prevented you from seeing more than ten feet. She hadn't missed them. She hadn't missed them at all.

When the vehicle slowed and she heard the crunch of gravel beneath the tires, Val's stomach began to twist. They had driven through the night and the sun had just risen into the sky. Sitting up straight, she spied the enormous red brick building.

It was half-hidden under decades worth of clinging ivy. Behind it, stretched the sprawling Cambric estate. Gardens, a pool, a gym, and two towers that stretched towards the heavens. Those were the dorm rooms in which thousands of captives were housed. Home sweet home. The sight of it made her break out in a cold sweat.

Shifting the car into park, Agent Finn unlocked the doors and got out. Val waited in the backseat, covering her face with both hands. About an hour into their drive, Finn had removed the handcuffs, but as he opened her door, she could see he had them ready once more.

Sucking in a ragged breath, she let him help her from the car, then studied the ground as he bound her wrists together in front of her. He wrapped one large hand around her right elbow and urged her forward. He was more gentle than she had expected.

Together, they walked up the stone steps and pushed through the wide double doors into the lobby. A Cambric receptionist sat tidily behind a desk along one wall. Chairs meant for waiting were positioned along the other. No one occupied them.

Walking up to the woman, Agent Finn explained that he was turning over a flight risk conscript and had called ahead. Little mouth forming an "o" in surprise, the woman tapped at her keyboard and then picked up a phone.

"Doesn't look so bad here," Agent Finn spoke to Val under his breath, eyes scanning the expensive furnishings and clean space. "Jason's lawyers should have you out in no time."

Val took one look at Agent Finn and laughed.

It was a rueful one, full of shock and malice and spite. The tone of it had his eyes narrowing. She could see the calculations running through his head. Before he had a chance to speak, the receptionist stood and directed them down the far corridor.

"Follow the hall to the end and then make a right," she said, smiling easily. "The door should be marked *Conscription.*"

Taking her again by the elbow, Agent Finn followed the path indicated. When they reached the heavy metal door, he frowned. It had a reinforced glass window just at eye level so he peered through it while laying one hand on the doorknob.

Briefly, he tried the handle, but it was locked. After a beat they heard the sound of a buzzer and a metallic click. The door swung slowly inward of its own accord.

Beyond the threshold was a wide blank room. It had a long metal bench that ran the length of one wall and every few feet there was a metal ring bolted to the floor. This was where captives were chained if Cambric had to deal with more than one at once.

Standing in the far corner, hand braced on a padded table, the other holding a clipboard, was Shane. Another man, clad in light blue medical scrubs, was adjusting instruments off to one side.

Val managed two steps inside before her stomach revolted. Dropping to her knees, she retched violently all over the linoleum floor.

"Ah, Agent Finn, right?" Shane spoke casually, as if the stench of vomit hadn't taken over the room. "I see you've returned one of my favorite girls."

Agent Finn made no reply, only frowned deeply and bent to check on Val. Looping one arm around her waist, he used the other to brush at her hair, still mussed from their long trip. She could feel his gaze on her, feel the worry that suddenly flooded his system. But she wouldn't give him the satisfaction of eye contact, so she turned away.

"She's fine." Shane chuckled. "Aren't you, Val?"

"Yes, Sir."

"We see this a lot during intake, the time on the outside doesn't sit well."

Shane made a few notes on his clipboard, then took out his cell phone and placed a call. They heard him order a cleanup kit before he hung up. The male orderly finished arranging his tools and turned to watch them. His face was passive, clouded with disinterest and the repetition of routine. Nothing here was shocking to him.

"You can remove the restraints, I think the two of us can manage her well enough," Shane instructed, eyes enjoying the reluctance that played out clearly in Finn.

The way his hands hesitated in searching for his keys. The way he glanced into her face as he removed the binds. It was obvious in the silence that Agent Finn had concerns about leaving her here with these men. But it was too late to change his mind. It was too late for different choices, different actions and consequences. It was never too late for regret, though, and it oozed out of his pores. Even Shane could sense it.

With the handcuffs off, Val wanted to rub at her wrists, but knew better than to do so. Shane motioned for her to come to him, and she kept her eyes averted, but followed his orders.

When she was within his reach he placed both hands on her shoulders and peered into her face with a triumphant grin. This was the man who had stood in the corner when they removed Bee. This was the man who had refused her food while urging Gabe to eat. This was the man who had told her trainer he wasn't being brutal enough when they were trying to get Gabe to submit, so he made him turn around and try her again.

Body trembling beneath his touch, Val couldn't stop the shaking that moved through her limbs. Her reaction was visible, causing her to jerk slightly. Shane's eyebrows raised in delight. Glancing over Val's shoulder, he noticed Agent Finn hadn't left.

"You can go now," Shane called. "Thank you for your service."

When Agent Finn didn't move, Shane's expression changed to one of cold calculation. Turning Val to face Finn, he wrapped one hand around her throat, then let his fingers play along her jaw. He didn't squeeze, didn't grab her or hold on tight, but the implication was clear. Shane had the power here. Agent Finn did not.

And that was all that Shane really wanted. He was never the one to actually hit, never the one to force, or to shout. His pleasure derived from something else entirely. He liked to dominate, to strike fear, to feel other people's submission. It didn't matter who it was, or even what it was.

"Did you want something?" Shane asked calmly, eyes locked on Agent Finn. "I know you've worked closely with Val in the past. She's a real beauty, isn't she?"

Again, Agent Finn did not respond, but merely shifted on his feet. Val could see a new knowledge filling his eyes. It had taken coming here and experiencing it for himself for the reality of captive life to sink in. Through all of the fear and the trembling, the knot in her stomach and ache in her limbs, Val took a moment's pity for Finn. He really hadn't understood what he was doing.

"I'd offer you an hour with her, but we've got a waiting list a mile long stacked up already. Our clients just can't get enough." Shane sucked in a breath at the desperation that flitted across Finn's face. This is exactly the reaction he wanted.

"It's alright, John." Val's voice came out steadier than she felt. "This is what I've been trained for. Remember?"

The slap of his own words coming back to taunt him hit Agent Finn full in the face. She watched his expression shift between misery and guilt until he turned his back on her and fled the room.

After he left, Shane dropped his hands from her neck and resumed scribbling on his clipboard. For him, it had only ever been about getting a Federal Agent to submit. Once the object of his desire had left, so had the nastiness.

The process of intake was a slow and methodical one, filled with procedure. She was made to strip and change into a Cambric uniform. The slate grey dress with its numerous black buttons stopped just above her knees. It was form fitting, but not overly tight, and the stiff cotton fabric had been ironed free of any creases.

The male orderly performed a medical check. They documented her weight, height, blood pressure, temperature and listened to her breathing. He inserted a new tracker in her right forearm, careful to use the same line of scarring as the last one. They didn't want any additional marks on her body. She was given a cup of water and made to swallow a tiny orange pill. Shane looked in her mouth after, making her lift her tongue to show it was gone.

By the time they were finished with her, Val felt completely numb.

She was escorted to an isolation room and locked inside. There was a thin mattress in one corner with a pillow and wool blanket. Her mind flashed back to her weeks spent here with Gabe. She wondered when she would be transferred to a dorm, or if they planned on keeping her set apart forever.

Suddenly, her knees buckled and she dropped heavily to the hard floor. Whatever drug they had given her was potent. Mouth dry, eyes starting to blur, she crawled on her hands and knees until she reached the bed. The last thing she remembered was feeling the blanket scrunched up in her palms. After that, it was all black.

When she woke, it was to the piercing pain of a needle being slipped beneath her skin. Val cried out and struggled briefly to sit up, but the male orderly pushed her back down.

"Easy," he said quietly. "It's just some fluids."

Groaning she blinked her foggy eyes, trying to get the room to come into focus. How long had she been out? What time was it? What day was it? There were no windows in the narrow room, only the bed and the toilet. The far door had a single square of glass with which to see through, but it only led out onto a hallway. She knew from experience, remembering her weeks of confinement from years before.

"How long will they keep me here?" She rasped, her throat was so dry.

"Most conscription captives are kept in Isolation for a period of ten days." The man didn't make eye contact with her, instead focusing on the flow of fluid through her IV. "Then they're slowly reintroduced. The transition back can be a hard one."

She nodded at that, feeling the cold shock of the liquid entering her veins. It flowed along with her blood, pumping through her entire system until it eventually overtook her. Despite her best efforts, the blackness came again, and quickly.

By the time it was all said and done, Val would be revived and put under another three times. The purpose, she later found out, was to recalibrate her system, shrink her stomach, and leave her feeling weak.

Cambric found that conscripted captives often have an unnatural sense of themselves. They're used to eating more, making choices, defying authority. In order to shape them back into the proper mold of a captive, it helped to break them all the way down first. She was in the beginning stages of that process, now.

Somewhere around the morning of the fifth day, Val was revived and kept awake. Her knees quivered when she tried to stand, muscles trembling after such a long time without use. The male orderly from before had not returned.

Instead there was a woman, a free woman named Tracy who had spiked auburn hair and a round face. A black folding chair had been brought into the room. Tracy sat on it, legs crossed casually as she swiped and tapped at a tablet.

"I'm going to ask you a series of questions and I need your honest answers."

"May I have a sip of water?" Val's words scratched inside her mouth.

"After you answer the questions."

"Okay."

"Have you given birth since leaving Cambric?"

"No." Val's stomach clenched, but she kept her face downcast.

"Were you ever pregnant?"

"No."

"I'm going to show you a photo and I want you to tell me if you recognize the person." The woman flipped the tablet around and shoved it close to Val's face. "Who is he?"

"I don't know."

Val's eyes passed over the photo of her own son. Jace's school picture again, with his bright smiling expression. She denied knowing him. It made her at once dizzy and sick.

"Are you certain? Look again."

"I've never seen him before in my life." The words were some of the hardest she'd ever spoken, but she said them clearly while managing to hold Tracy's appraising stare. "May I please have a drink of water?"

Tracy frowned, but nodded once before rising to leave. She fetched a paper cup half-filled with lukewarm liquid and watched as Val gulped at it greedily. The contents were gone in a split second, and though Val's mouth longed for more, she knew she wouldn't get any.

Round and round they went for the rest of the day. After each line of questioning, Val was offered a bit of water or a scrap of food. They kept her strung out. Weak, hungry and thirsty. On the edge is where you get people to confess. On the edge is where people get sloppy.

They asked about Jason, about witness protection, about Kelly Martin. They demanded to know about Gabe and Veronica Durand and pressured her over her interactions with the FBI.

By the time she was allowed to lay back down in bed, she fell asleep quickly. The next day was the same, and the day after that. Through it all, Val stuck to the same story. She never saw Jason after the trial. She wasn't Kelly Martin, didn't know who that was. She'd never been pregnant, didn't have a son, and knew nothing of the FBI.

Most certainly, Cambric knew she was lying. But what else could they do?

Though they didn't get the confession they sought, their methods were effective. By the time they were finished, their point had been made. They left her needing them, depending on them. She was entirely at their mercy for food, water and comfort.

Val's personality had never been the first to rebel anyway, so obtaining physical submission from her was not hard. When they told her to get up, she got up. When they told her to sit, she sat. When they bade her get on her knees and stare at the wall, she did so until a tap on her shoulder released her back to her bed.

Finally seeming to find satisfaction, Tracy and her beloved tablet changed up the routine. One morning, Val was allowed to follow her out the door and down the hall. Slightly wobbly, Val teetered close behind Tracy, keeping her eyes focused on the slick cement floor. At the end of the hallway was a door which led to a group shower facility. No one else was around.

Stripping out of her uniform, Val bathed under the cold spray. She washed her hair and body, shaved with a disposable razor then twisted the water off when instructed. Her head spun and her hands trembled with all the activity but Val managed to button herself into a clean grey uniform in silence.

When they left the bathroom, her soaking wet hair dripped a trail along the floor.

Instead of making a left towards her room, Tracy veered right. Without a word, the other woman pushed out of the building and into a wide open courtyard. Reaching up reflexively, Val shaded her eyes. The sun was blinding after so many days inside and the air felt hot as it wrapped around her legs. There were other captives all around, so Val quickly ducked her head. She wasn't ready to see them. Not yet.

Pacing demurely behind Tracy, Val listened to the gasps

and whispers as they passed. She didn't lift her head even though the murmuring seemed to follow them all the way to the cafeteria. Val's feet were bare, her hair left unkempt in an effort to make her feel vulnerable.

This tactic was often used in discipline and isolation captives. It was effective. If you were barefoot and damp, then other captives knew not to approach you. They knew you were under discipline and it wasn't allowed. For the first time in her life Val was grateful for this rule. She couldn't imagine wanting to speak to anyone.

At Cambric, meals were given in shifts due to the volume of captives that needed to be fed. For the most part the process was extremely casual. Captives came and went at their designated times, laughed, talked, and interacted without much interference from The Agency. As long as they all followed the rules, everything was okay.

Today, Tracy directed Val to a lone table in the middle of the room. It had a red plastic placard that was marked *Discipline.* An empty plate was positioned along the center of the picnic-style table and Val sat in front of it. She knew from experience that the plate would not be filled.

The idea behind this spectacle was just that, to be a spectacle. Others around you are eating, the smell of food is swirling through the air, but you, bad you, will not be allowed to partake.

It was a good deterrent actually. And in the past Val had only found herself there once. For most captives, this step was enough to guarantee their total compliance.

As Tracy stood watch, the rumbling of voices died away.

The clatter of plates and utensils, the peals of laughter and shuffle of steps were all gone. It was an unusual silence.

For a beat, Val thought perhaps she had gone deaf. Maybe a side effect of the drugs they had given her. Tentatively, she reached up to cover both of her ears. But she could still hear the sound of her own breathing and so she lowered them again. Out of the corner of her eye, a person approached.

"This captive is in isolation, do not speak to her," Tracy commanded.

Despite the order, the set of footsteps continued, drawing steadily closer to the table. Val was weak and hungry, her stomach churned and her body trembled, but her mind still managed to be curious. Instinct had her looking up, trying to steal a glance at the person who dared to defy Tracy.

And in that moment, Val's eyes widened. Because it wasn't one person. It wasn't one captive. It was all of them. The whole room was standing, the whole room had gathered, and one by one they walked past Val's table.

Tracy pointed her finger, she shouted and threatened. Cambric security rushed in, but what were they against three hundred bodies?

Over and over Val's fellow captives placed pieces of food on her plate. They placed biscuits and bacon, strawberries and toast. They piled on sausage, pancakes, blueberry muffins, bowls of cereal, cups of juice until it overflowed her plate. Until it overflowed the table and the benches.

And all of it was done in utter silence. In this way, none of them could be accused of breaking Tracy's command. They did not speak to her. But they did give up their food, the only commodity worth having on the inside.

She recognized many faces, absorbed the reverent looks from people she had known throughout her childhood. They were giving her their respect with each offering. And they gave it up again, and again, and again. Tears rolled down Val's cheeks until Tracy stepped in and had two guards haul her away.

CHAPTER 13

THE OTHERS MAY OR MAY NOT HAVE SUFFERED BECAUSE OF THE display in the cafeteria, but Val most certainly did. Waking in the morning, or whatever time it was, she would stare at her empty ceiling. Its harsh whiteness seemed as unfeeling as the guard that occasionally passed by her door. Inset into one wall of her narrow room was a wide plexiglass window. Unlike before, the other room remained empty.

Memories of Gabe on the other side flooded her. The way he sat with his back to the wall, refusing to eat. The sound of his shoulder impacting the glass as he tried again and again to break it. But it was thick, maybe two inches even, and he hadn't managed the slightest crack. Then there was the way he buried his face in his hands, crying. Crying over Bee and Val, crying over himself. How defeated he looked in the fluorescent lights.

She had teased him then, about the crying. It was an attempt to lift his spirits and at the time he had cracked a sad sort of smile. It dawned on her now that he knew things back then. Things that she didn't. About loving someone and losing them. But Gabe wasn't here to see her through now, and she was the one left crying.

Tracy made an appearance exactly three times a day. She arrived with a few select items for breakfast, then again for lunch and once more for dinner. It was not a lot of food, but Val was allowed all the water she could drink.

At first, Tracy carried the food in on a red tray, setting it down just inside the door before leaving. Val wanted to eat it. Her stomach grumbled and saliva flowed, urging her forward to crouch on the floor by the door.

But after a few bites of bagel, or eggs, or toast, something inside of her turned. The rumbling of her stomach morphed into a sour warning. The saliva that had flooded her mouth before, now tasted of sickness and bile. Reluctantly almost, she would replace the half-eaten item and sip at the water instead.

When it became clear she wasn't going to finish the meager portions provided, Cambric resorted to more drastic measures. They wanted to break her down, yes, but they wanted to build her back, too. She was of no use to them half-starved and sick. That meant Tracy could no longer simply leave the tray by the door.

Each and every day for each and every meal, the other woman dragged the black folding chair inside the chamber and sat. Keeping the tray poised on her lap, Tracy would patiently, deliberately, hand-feed her charge.

"Take another bite."

Tracy would blink down, fork in hand. And Val, for all of her training, was not able to refuse. Opening her mouth, she would take that bite, then chew and chew and chew. She fought like hell to keep it down. Tracy would exhale in disgust before turning her face away.

Deep down, Val lost the ability to care. She lost all manner of feeling, in fact. She felt it slip away from her along with that human portion of herself. After denying her own son, what did any of it matter anymore?

And thoughts of Jace were… all consuming. Isolation itself could make a person crazy. But add in the loss of a child and well, with no one else to talk to, you begin seeing things. Things that aren't really there.

Lying on the mattress, curled up in a tight ball, Val would stare off at the faces. She saw Jason sitting at their dining room table in France, his brow furrowed over some bit of news that played over his tablet. Sometimes he would glance up at her, a smile playing across his lips, sometimes he wouldn't look up at all.

Then there was Bee, legs covered in white sand from her beach, singing up into the palm trees, having consumed that last Pina Colada.

And Jace.

Always the visions ended with Jace.

Leaping onto her bed in the morning, he would toss pillows aside and laugh. God. It was his laugh. His laugh and his sweet little face. What she wouldn't give for just one more chance.

After seeing him… Val would break. Face pressed into the corner where the wall met the bed, she would lose all control, sobbing until she had no breath left. She would choke and sputter and retch up what little she had eaten in the first place.

When they caught her at this, the pills started. Oval-shaped white pills.

First thing in the morning, Tracy would enter with her tray and one solitary pill. Val was made to swallow it right away, so that any other bites she took would be sure to carry it down along with them. They didn't want her avoiding the medication.

But that step was unnecessary because Val didn't care what they gave her. She would take it. She would take all of it.

Within the week, her appetite returned, followed by an increase in energy and the ability to sleep soundly. She was no longer plagued by memories or dreams, but instead was left wrapped up in some sort of haze.

Her thoughts were cloudy. She felt neither intense sadness, nor any other form of intensity. The pills, whatever they were, had evened her out, but in a slow, dispassionate sort of way.

One morning after breakfast, Tracy led Val out the door and down a familiar hallway. The shower facility at the end had other women in it this time, some that Val recognized and some that she didn't. They were all in various stages of bathing.

Positioning herself in the far corner, Tracy swiped over her tablet, eyes focusing on emails, or charts, or appointments elsewhere. With no further instruction, Val shed her clothing and dropped it in a basket marked *Laundry*.

Stepping into an empty stall, she twisted on the silver faucet and stared at the tiny white tiles lining the wall. The cement flooring was cold and wet on her dirty feet, but the tepid water felt good. This must have been one of the new government regulations at work, Val thought absently.

Cambric was no longer allowed to keep the water frigid, though it wasn't warm by any means.

Eyes blinking slowly, Val let the water soak her tangled mass of hair. Why hadn't they cut it all off, as they had with Bee? Did it really matter? Val tilted her head to one side and tried to sharpen her mind on the thoughts, but they slipped slowly away from her. She couldn't hardly focus with the medication. Maybe that was a good thing.

Inside the stall sat three opaque plastic bottles. Each one had a pump on top and faint cursive writing. *Shampoo. Conditioner. Body Wash.*

Holding her palm beneath one spout, the exact amount allowed to her was automatically dispensed into her hand. Waste not, want not. Val sighed, then scrubbed at her hair, taking the time to work the suds deep into her scalp. Everything she did now seemed drawn out, like she was a fish swimming in a great round bowl.

By the time she was done, most of the other women had left. None of them spoke to her, though more than a few flicked their questioning eyes in her direction. Their expressions shifted between appraisal and concern. Did she look all that bad?

Twisting off the flow of water, Val walked to the cupboard marked *Towels* and wrapped herself in one threadbare white sheet. Over her shoulder, she threw Tracy a questioning look but the woman was consumed by other things and didn't seem to notice.

Crossing to the long sink, Val caught the first glimpse of herself in the wide mirror. If she hadn't felt so out of sorts, she might have let out a tiny gasp. She was thin, gaunt even, her hair a wild knot that hung down her back. Dark circles marked the skin beneath her eyes. Vacant, frosty eyes.

Giving her head a little shake, Val reached for a brush that lay in a basket marked *Combs.* It took a long time to free her hair of its dread-locked tangles. She had no strength, no energy. By the time it was all straight, Val was panting, palms spread over the Formica countertop, face downcast, arms aching.

Seeming to clue back in, Tracy marched up behind her and barked out a series of orders. She was to brush her teeth, bind her hair in a braid and change into a set of workout clothes. Val followed these instructions, stepping into a pair of fresh underwear, grey spandex shorts and matching sports bra.

On the way out of the room, Tracy handed her a protein bar which Val quickly devoured. Like that day so many weeks before, they walked out of the building and into the midday sun. It was the height of summer with not a cloud in the ultra-blue sky. Val blinked her eyes, raising one hand to shield them. Everything felt exactly the same, like she was living a dream.

A high brick wall ran from building to building, enclosing the lush green of the courtyard, effectively trapping its occupants inside. The space was dotted with picnic tables and covered mostly with thick grass. In their youth, the area had been a source of great release. When their behavior was good, they were allowed free time here and Val had many fond memories of rolling around on the lawn with Bee.

As she passed through the space now, the murmuring from before was less so. People looked up, but then away, returning to their activities without incident. Tracy led Val into a low building on the far left. Val knew that just past it was an outdoor pool.

Before walking through the door, Val could hear the laughter of children. Instantly her heart squeezed in on itself, but then just as quickly it evened out. The drug successfully dampened the flood of emotion.

Inside the building, the light was dim. They traveled down a wide hall which skirted a gymnasium. There was a basketball court just beyond a set of double doors where she had watched other children play games in school. Memories of all kinds haunted her. At the end of the hall there were a bunch of classrooms, then beyond that, a playground. The distant sounds of shouting and sneakers squeaking along the linoleum floor caught her attention. The kids were in between classes. A bell would sound soon.

At the end of the hall Tracy veered right instead of left and soon Val found herself in a workout room instead of the school. It was large, with a wall of windows that looked out over the pool. Various treadmills, elliptical machines and stair climbers faced out. Val counted over fifteen lined up side by side.

Along one wall was a set of weights on a low stand. The middle of the room was covered with a blue padded mat. Around it were a series of exercise machines. One for legs, one for arms, one worked out your core, another strengthened your back.

Twenty or so captives occupied the space. They didn't pause in their conditioning when Tracy and Val walked in, but instead maintained their focus. She could hear the puff of their breathing, smell the mix of sweat and skin. Val's stomach growled, it wanted another protein bar. She wouldn't get it.

Tracy beckoned to the lone security guard who quickly hopped over to her side. She gestured to Val, then drew his attention to her tablet and then the clock on the wall. He nodded acceptance, then stood quietly as Tracy addressed her charge.

"You will begin a daily exercise regimen. Until you are familiar with the routine, a trainer will be provided to instruct you. Though he is not Cambric staff, you are expected to follow his commands explicitly. Is that clear?"

"Yes, Ma'am." Val ducked her head.

"I will return for you within the hour."

Tracy spoke to the guard once more before reaching into her pocket and producing a thin black wand. She passed it over Val's forearm until it gave up its customary beep. That sound. She'd never escape it now.

Once Tracy left, the security guard visibly relaxed. The workout room was a cushy job. The captives here were of the highest quality. On the whole, they never had discipline issues, were obedient and quiet. If they kept their heads down, they got to exercise in relative freedom. So that's exactly what they did.

"Charlie! Your appointment's here," the guard called over his shoulder. Not giving Val more than a second's glance, he retreated to his chair by the door and resumed reading a thick book.

"Charlie?" Val whispered it, feeling the once familiar name roll around in her mouth.

Eyes traveling the room, Val cleared her throat and

watched the figure that approached. He was taller than she, but not more than six-foot. Well-muscled shoulders shifted beneath his tight gray shirt as he walked. His dark hair was styled short and stood out against the light tint of his skin.

As he came to a stop in front of her, his hazel eyes slid over her body once before settling on her face. It was him. There was no mistaking it. Gabe's old roommate. The quiet, reserved, ever-focused yin to Gabe's outlandish, attention-seeking yang.

"They worked you over good." Charlie exhaled through his nostrils, surveying her with another glance downward. "I'll have to request an increase in your calorie allowance."

"Charlie?" Val repeated herself, eyes searching his.

"Hey, Val." He glanced over at the guard before returning his gaze to her. "It's me. Ready to get started?"

"Yes." Val bobbed her head, knowing that was the correct answer, whether it felt true or not.

Following Charlie's purposeful lead, Val listened as he pointed out equipment, explained what it was for, and outlined how she'd be using it in the future. When the small tour was complete, he stopped on the large blue mat and began guiding her in a series of warm-up stretches. Conversation was non-existent as other captives came and went in a rotation around them. Occasionally, one would stop to stare, but never for more than a few seconds.

Charlie acted like nothing was amiss. He was, as he always had been, the picture of cool. Nothing ruffled him, nothing reached past his facade or stirred a reaction. Hands spread over Val's ankles, he applied pressure to her feet as she panted through a set of sit-ups. He counted them aloud, encouraging her for just one more, then gave her time to catch her breath.

Easing back to sit, he watched her flop onto her back, gasping for air on the mat.

"How's Gabe?" He asked finally, eyes shifting to the clock on the wall.

"He's Gabe." Val wheezed, lungs burning. "Same… pain… in… the ass."

"Huh." Charlie let a small smile cross his face. "He still getting you in trouble? Is that how you got back in this mess?"

"Uh-uh." Val propped herself up on her elbows, and tapped her chest. "This one's on me."

"So, I've heard," Charlie acknowledged, then leaned against her ankles once more. "Give me another fifteen."

Val only had time to shoot him a puzzled look before she folded her arms across her body and resumed the crunches. What exactly had he heard? And from whom? The questions were soon forgotten, however, as the pain in her muscles dominated her brain.

When their hour was up, Tracy returned. Again, the black wand passed over Val's forearm and gave up a piercing beep. Val stiffened, but felt nothing further than complete and utter exhaustion.

Over the next week, Val remained in Isolation with the daily exception of her appointment with Charlie. She took her meals alone, showered under the supervision of Tracy and swallowed the powdery white pill without incident. Per Charlie's request, Val's calorie allowance was increased. Her portions expanded to accommodate the physical exertion of her workout and her strength gradually returned.

At night, when the lights were switched off and the black nothingness filled her room, Val thought about her son. Even with the medication, a deep abiding sadness had settled itself somewhere in her chest. It burrowed down deep, making a sort of hollow place. But that was as far as it went. She didn't choke and sputter. She didn't throw up anymore. The heavy misery that had once threatened to demolish her, was gone.

A part of her wished she could still feel it. That intensity and great stabbing pain that went along with Jace. But the other part of her knew the drugs were for the best. If she let herself spiral down the hole inside of her, she knew she'd never make it back out.

"Where were you just then?" Charlie asked.

He had her on her hands and knees, one leg stretched behind her on the blue mat. Holding his hand above her foot, Charlie encouraged her to lift her leg to touch his arm before curling it back down underneath her. The process was repeated again and again.

"Nowhere," Val grunted. Her butt burned and her stomach quivered, but she pressed on, delivering the reps he required.

"You were definitely somewhere." Charlie's voice was easy and quiet. "Two more, then you can take a break."

"What's their plan for me?" Val pushed through the pain before collapsing onto her stomach. She shifted her face to the side to watch his expression.

"You really want to know?" Charlie grimaced, hazel eyes flicking away.

"I do."

Rolling his shoulders, he pushed up to standing and walked casually away from her. Val lay still, watching him.

He stopped at a small table that was pushed up against one wall and grabbed two water bottles off its surface. Twisting the caps to loosen them, he glanced over at the guard. The man sat as he always did, nose poked in a book, legs crossed at the ankle in front of him.

After taking a sip, Charlie recapped his bottle and walked back over to Val.

"It's treadmill time," he announced.

Looking down at her, Charlie extended a hand and waited. Val analyzed his face, wondering at the careful patience that seemed to dominate every move he made. Reaching up, she placed her hand in his and felt him lift her easily to her feet. They walked together over to the line of running machines where four other captives jogged along, shoes slapping at pedals, arms pumping in a disjointed dance.

Charlie chose two treadmills at the far end, away from any listening ears. Stepping up on the first one, he punched at a series of buttons, then leaned over and set up the same program for Val. She took her place beside him as the wide black tread began to rotate.

It was a slow pace, as if they were going out for a casual stroll. Through the wall of windows, they could see the pool. Kids screamed and ran, splashing together in the blue water. If Val craned her neck to the left, she could just make out the edge of the elementary school playground. Small children sat in a sandbox, or rolled around on a patch of grass.

"Cambric's been advertising something they call *The Val Experience*." Charlie's voice was low. "As far as I can tell, they plan on renting you out for a day at a time. It's set up for high-rollers only. The price is substantial."

"How do you know that?" Val's stomach twisted, but any fear was dampened by the drugs in her system.

"I have my sources," Charlie supplied, then seeing her face, he added. "If I tell you how, and you rat me out, then I'm done for."

"I won't tell," Val assured him. "No matter what they do to me."

They walked in silence for a while. Both of them watched the goings on outside the window. A little boy ran across the wet cement and just made it to the edge before launching his flailing body high over the water. Instinctively, Val had held her breath, waiting any moment for the child to slip and fall. But he didn't. Instead, he soared in an arc that ended in a glorious splash. When he surfaced, his friends clapped him on the back, encouraging him for more.

"I have a monthly client list," Charlie began finally. "Three of the women I've seen for years."

"I thought you were permanent placement?" Val interrupted.

"I was marketed that way at first but after Gabe sold, Cambric decided to keep me."

"Why?"

"Does it matter?"

"I guess not."

"Anyway, my regulars are sympathetic to my situation. One is a widow and the other two are married. The whole arrangement is really discreet, but that's beside the point."

Charlie paused to look quickly around the room before resuming. "They have me for an entire day, but mostly they just want attention. We watch television, I get to read anything I want and I get unrestricted access to the internet. They like to talk a lot. So, I mostly listen."

"And you get some news from the outside."

"I get *all* the news from the outside."

"Do you share it?"

"I tell certain people, and they tell their people and so on. The information gets around. So far no one's gotten busted for it."

"So…" Val sucked in a breath. "*The Val Experience* is all over the internet?"

"It's everywhere." Charlie's frown eased. "And so is your scary screaming husband."

Val looked sideways at Charlie who flashed her an uncharacteristic grin before composing his features once more. *Husband.* Captive Val did not have a husband, she reminded herself.

Her brain tried to rush forward with the information, but the words she wanted to say, the questions she wanted to ask, wouldn't form coherently in her mind. Instead, she put the heel of one hand to her forehead and rubbed hard.

"You've got to stop taking the pills," Charlie whispered. "And yes, there isn't a television program around that hasn't had Mr. Jason Riggs himself on it yelling about Cambric and yelling about you. Lawsuits are flying all over the place.

People are getting stirred up. It's almost like it was right before-"

Val waited, but Charlie didn't go on.

"Right before what?" She asked finally.

"Right before they tried to dismantle Cambric. If your husband keeps going like he is now, then there's still hope."

"He was my owner, I was never married to him," Val corrected, her heart taking one gigantic leap in her chest before it quieted.

"That's a good story to stick to." Charlie bobbed his head, perfectly serious. "But we all know it's not the truth."

"When will they start booking me clients?"

"I don't know." Charlie adjusted his machine up before reaching over to increase Val's alongside. "Best guess? A few more weeks. Your color has come back, your body is close to perfect. All they need is to re-train and submit you."

As the treadmill picked up speed, Val was forced into a jog. *Submit.* The word kept echoing around in her mind. Her chest grew tight. Clients after submission, of course.

Despite the foggy haze of medication, she knew what lay ahead of her. And suddenly, the surrounding air was hard to suck into her lungs. She gasped once, legs stumbling and tripping beneath her. Charlie snaked out a hand and grabbed her upper arm, holding her upright as he ran.

"Pick up your feet," he hissed. "Run through it, or run away from it. Doesn't matter which but you've got to keep running."

Val ducked her head and did as she was told. Charlie let go of her, then mumbled the next few words under his breath.

"And stop swallowing that damn pill."

CHAPTER 14

It wasn't long after that they moved Val out of Isolation. Tracy entered her room one morning without the customary plastic food tray. With a flick of her wand, she beeped Val back into dorm life.

Across the green expanse of courtyard, two red brick dormitory towers loomed tall, casting long shadows as the sun moved. One was set aside for adult captives, the other for children. She had lived in both, at one time or another, but always with Bee.

Riding up the elevator now, Val stared at the electronic numbers as they counted up, up, up. In front of her, Tracy tapped her foot impatiently against the metal flooring. This was an industrial sized elevator and it moved rather slowly. At any given time, it could fit up to forty people, though Tracy had waited for an empty one before boarding.

The floors themselves were separated according to training level and work designation. Hourly and party captives came first. They required more transportation, oversight and scheduling, so Cambric kept them on the lowest levels. Their floors were noisy, busy and crowded. Hourly captives were constantly being moved, driven to different locations and brought back, not to mention there were simply more of them. It took Cambric staff less time to move them through the stairwells or on the elevators if they only had a few floors to go.

As the elevator continued its rise inside the building, the designations, along with the atmosphere, changed. The next block of floors was occupied by trainees. These were high school graduates just entering the final phase of their classification.

Here they would be trained sexually for the first time, sit in class, observe demonstrations and get used to the feel of D2 life. Although security had once been fairly lax in this section, since the incident with Bee and Gabe, it had been tightened considerably. Still, everyone was young, had enthusiasm and wanted to have a good time. The daily grind of actually being a D2 captive hadn't yet sunk in.

Riding past those floors, Val could hear faint music thrumming from the trainee section. She remembered it well, though it was censored and the broken words didn't make much sense. That didn't matter of course to someone who had never heard real music before. None of the trainees had set foot outside of Cambric. None of them had listened to a full song.

Soon the vibrations settled into silence and the elevator doors opened onto one of the monthly subscription floors. These captives were in it for the long haul. They had set schedules and could develop a rhythm and routine. Most were experts in their line of work. To get here they all underwent a series of personality screenings.

As a result, they often had demure, accepting dispositions. Life on these floors was slow, gentle, calm. A monthly D2 didn't need as much oversight, nor security, and there weren't as many of them. The permanent placement captives that hadn't sold yet, were housed alongside.

With a huff of breath, Tracy stepped out first. The hallway was long and narrow. Every so often a fluorescent bulb could be seen inset deep in the ceiling overhead. Val watched the confidence in Tracy's walk, the way her sensible heels tapped along the worn grey carpet. About midway down the hall, Val spied an open door. Not able to help herself, she glanced in as she passed. There was a young woman draped across a single bed, flipping distractedly through an old magazine.

After that, it seemed almost every door was propped open. She noted both women and men, reclining by themselves, or chatting in small groups. As Tracy appeared, conversations ceased. When they caught a glimpse of Val, the voices resumed.

Abruptly Tracy came to halt and stepped off to one side. Val pulled up short in front of a closed door with the number nineteen displayed beneath its viewing window. Each door had a single square of glass through which a guard could monitor them. There were no video cameras in their rooms, only one at each end of the hall.

"Here we are." Tracy pulled out her wand and passed it over Val's arm until it beeped. "On this floor we expect you to adhere to a particular schedule. If you are unable to stick to it, then certain privileges will be revoked.

You have set times for meals which are listed on the inside of your door. If you miss a meal time, then you miss the meal, same as always. Any appointments booked for you will show up on the screen fastened to your desk. You are expected to check it when you get up in the morning and before you go to bed.

Showers are down the hall. You must beep in and out of all activities. Any questions?"

"No, Ma'am."

"Medications are dispensed by the morning shift guard. You are not allowed to leave your room until he provides it to you."

"Yes, Ma'am."

With a final curt nod, Tracy strode away. Val stood statue still, watching the other woman's progress out of her peripheral vision. Not until Tracy returned to the far elevator and disappeared out of sight, did Val exhale. Smoothing at the stiff fabric of her uniform, Val twisted the handle and pushed the door open.

The room was small. A twin size mattress on a wooden platform was shoved into one corner, a desk and single wooden chair were situated along the opposite wall. A closet, no deeper than the door was wide, was situated off to the left.

Three uniforms hung neatly from plastic hangers inside of it. On the floor were three pair of shoes. One pair of heels, one pair of rain boots and one pair of athletic shoes. All of them were black.

Stepping into the space, Val ran her hands up her arms to hug herself. She had expected to share the room with someone else, as she had with Bee. But there was only the one bed in here, and thinking back, the other rooms she had passed all seemed to be set up for a single occupant as well.

Moving over to the desk, she examined the small black screen fastened to it. She placed one finger onto its dark surface and felt it come alive beneath her touch. No appointments today.

"They'll give you time to settle in." Charlie's voice had her jumping. She had forgotten this was the section he lived in. "Looks like you missed breakfast already."

"Oh." Val subconsciously grabbed at her stomach. "I guess I'll have to wait until lunch."

"I have a stock pile, I'll grab you something."

Charlie gave her a small smile before disappearing out of sight. When he returned it was with a miniature box of cereal. The bright red cartoon of a bird was plastered across the side.

"You have kid's cereal," Val corrected, her lips twisted up just slightly. "You're a physical trainer but you eat junk food."

"Hey, hey." Charlie held the box just beyond her grasp. "If you don't want it, I can keep it."

"I'll take it." Val had to give him a full smile as Charlie taunted her with the cereal. "I'll take it."

Finally handing it over, he took a quick glance around before sitting on the edge of her bed. His long legs barely reached the floor. Ripping open the cereal, Val inhaled the scent of processed sugar and popped a few brightly colored loops into her mouth. They crunched with a delightful rush of energy. It was an unusual treat. She wondered just how he'd come by it.

"So, no workout today?" Val asked between bites.

"I have a client," Charlie explained, leaning his back

against the wall. "But don't let that stop you. There's nothing preventing you from using the gym."

"What about tomorrow? The computer only shows today."

"They like to keep you guessing," Charlie acknowledged. "It's not like training, with class schedules and all that. Though when you get a few regular bookings then things seem to get fairly predictable."

"Do you know who you're going to see?"

"Yeah, I do." Charlie eyed her closely. "It's an overnight thing but I'll be back in a few days."

"Alright." Val didn't know why, but she felt concern at his leaving.

"Keep at the gym while I'm gone, eat good meals, and maybe try to make some friends. I'm sure you'll recognize a few of the faces in here."

"Thanks, Charlie." Val waved the cereal box in the air. "For everything."

Bobbing his head once, he shoved off the bed and out of her room. He didn't look back. Instead, he cruised away with the same confident control that marked everything Charlie did. And Val watched him, one hand tucked into the pocket of his slate-gray slacks. The uniform fit him well. She nibbled at her lower lip. Where was he going?

It could be considered greedy of her, but Val hoped he would do some more fact finding and report back. Since his confession about Jason being on the news, Val had battled with a mix of hope and determination. Both feelings were dangerous on the inside and expressly forbidden.

When she had last seen her husband, she had been confident he wouldn't stop fighting to free her. But since that time the blend of medication and psychological reconditioning had done something to her mind. Whenever Jason or Jace came to swirl in her thoughts, she banished them. Quickly. Completely. Was this a good thing? She didn't know. And just like that, they were gone again.

Wrapped up in her own thoughts, Val didn't notice the new woman who had come to lean against her doorframe. It took the clicking of nails along one metal hinge to jerk her back to the present. Val blinked. The woman was pretty. A stunner even, though every captive on this floor would be.

Sensational curves marked every aspect of her figure from the fullness of her chest to the way her uniform drew tight across her hips. Layered strawberry blonde hair was silky as it fell around a porcelain smooth face. She was impressive, Val thought, and also vaguely familiar.

"Val, right?" The woman purred.

"Yes. I should know you… but I'm sorry, I can't seem to remember your name." Val stuck out her hand.

The other woman let it hang there for a beat. Eyes dropping to the space between them, she seemed to think. Val waited. Her flush of embarrassment was dampened, as were all of her immediate reactions. In the end, the other woman clasped it briefly in her own.

"I'm Mandy," she said. "I didn't think you'd remember me."

"Mandy, that's right." Val's mind focused on a memory of a gawky girl four years her junior. "You looked different back then."

"All knees and elbows, right?"

"Right."

An awkward silence filled the small space as Val blinked at Mandy, and Mandy just blinked right back. Suddenly remembering her manners, Val stepped aside and gestured for the other woman to sit. Ducking her head prettily, Mandy hopped onto the bed and let her legs dangle over the side.

"I can see why they talk about you." Mandy crossed her legs before shifting back to get a more comfortable position.

"They?"

"Charlie and all his little *freedom* buddies." Mandy huffed a breath, but kept a placid smile on her face. "Practically everyone here at Cambric thinks you're their savior."

"Oh."

"You should have seen this place after Sharon's conviction. No rules, everything in chaos. People just waltzed right out the door."

"Did you?"

"No." Mandy gave a quick shake of her head. "Most of us stayed. Nowhere else to go. But in the end, it didn't matter which way you went, the mighty hand of Cambric gathered them all back."

"I'm sorry, I don't know what to say."

"Exactly." Mandy's eyes narrowed. "They think now that you're back, you're going to bring the captive industry down once and for all. But you and I both know the truth."

"I'm sorry, I don't-"

"You aren't anything special." Mandy cut her off. "You do what you're told, when you're told to do it, same as everyone else. Charlie thinks you're here to save everyone, that you're part of some undercover investigation to track down the missing."

"Missing…" Val frowned. "What missing?"

"You don't even know?"

"Know what?"

"Unbelievable." Mandy was smug now, her chin tilting up. "A lot of bad things can happen in here, we all know that. But before *your* testimony and *your* government regulations, no one ever died."

"Died?"

"Yeah, died. Poof. Gone," Mandy sneered. "Too many times on discipline? Too many days in Isolation? Refusing too many clients? You go to sleep one night and the next morning… your bed is empty. Don't suppose they just release the troublemakers into the street, do you?"

"How many? How many have disappeared like that?"

"Four or five a month, every month, for the past three years."

"That's what?" Val tried to do the math in her head, but her mind was still slow, she hadn't been able to avoid the medication. "Over a hundred people?"

"One-hundred and sixty-two, exactly."

"You've seen the bodies? You *know* they're dead?"

"I *know* they aren't here anymore. Where else would they be?" Mandy's eyes scanned Val's face a moment before continuing. "You're bad news, not good, and whatever reason you're really back here I just want to tell you one thing. Stay. Away. From. Charlie."

Hopping off the bed, Mandy sauntered out of the room.

Val's mouth hung slack. Sitting heavily in her small wooden chair, her head began a steady pounding. Cambric was killing its captives? And no one on the outside knew about it?

In all her decades of living at The Agency, Val had never heard of a single captive being murdered, nor of any going missing for that matter. The ones who couldn't conform, like Bee, were eventually transferred to different work. They were sold to other agencies or trained as D1s. What happened to them after that was anyone's guess. But the transfers were widely known and well documented. Val had seen the transportation vans herself.

Shifting in her chair, she ran absent fingers over the black screen on her desk. It flickered to life. Peering once more into it, she noted the time. Over an hour had passed already. Rising from her chair, Val went to inspect the meal schedule listed on the back of her door. It seemed all of her meals were slated early. Breakfast was at seven, lunch at eleven, and dinner at four-thirty.

Almost automatically she moved to the small closet and pulled down one of two sets of workout clothes. Each one was identical to the next. Cambric wanted them to look the same, feel the same, think the same. But they didn't. Even with all of the training and breeding and manipulation. At their core, each captive was still persistently different. Would the next step to conformity be eliminating the outliers?

Giving her head a slight shake, Val changed into the clothes and stepped out of her black heels. Kneeling down, she laced up her running shoes and headed out. At the end of the hall she held her arm under the scanner fastened next to the elevator. The doors dinged open.

When she got to the gym, she presented her forearm to the

guard who swiped a black wand over her tracker until it too gave up a beep. This routine of tracking and beeping would repeat everywhere she went. It would happen in the cafeteria, in the showers, in every elevator and at all entrances to every building. Though the sound still caused her stomach to clench, she knew that in time she wouldn't notice it at all.

Even without Charlie present, Val followed the routine he had mapped out for her. She stretched on the mat, did crunches and leg lifts, worked with two separate machines and then finished on the treadmill. Out the window, the children swam in the pool.

It was the boys turn again, and that same brazen kid was running around on the wet cement. His golden locks curled a bit at the ends, someone at Cambric had let it grow to just below his ears.

Squinting, Val judged him to be about eight or nine-years-old, with a Cheshire Cat grin and personality to spare. Already, his good looks made him stand out. She could tell by the way the other boys laughed at the things he said that they liked him.

Frowning now, Val studied his features and fought the familiarity that played there.

"Hey, Val-" A female voice had her looking back. "Long time no see."

"Oh! Amber!" Val felt a genuine smile fill her face as she stepped down from the treadmill.

When the two women embraced, it was a heartfelt hug. They rocked to and fro for a minute, tears collecting at the backs of their eyes. Sniffling, Val held her old classmate at arm's length. Amber gave her a grin filled with perfect white teeth. Her tightly curled black hair sprang out all over her head, so much so that a slate-gray bandana hardly kept it out of her mocha-brown face.

"Where have you been?" Val asked. "I haven't caught even a glimpse of you."

"Were you worried?" Amber laughed.

"Not at first, but then I've been hearing things…"

"Ahh." Amber glanced over her shoulder. The guard was watching. "Shall we go for a run?"

"Sure."

Calm as you please they stepped up side by side and adjusted their treadmill controls to match. Picking up to a light jog, they paced in silence for what seemed a long time. Val studied the guard's reflection in the window pane, and when he buried his nose safely back in his book, she felt a flood of relief.

As her gaze drifted back out the window, she tracked to that boy again, following his movements around the pool.

"Notice anyone familiar?" Amber panted quietly.

"That boy," Val admitted, inclining her head.

"He's one of Gabe's."

Val grimaced, letting the fleeting slice of emotion work itself against the dullness of her brain. Gabe had well over thirty children… that he *knew* of. Had he ever come to the workout room and watched them? Had he ever wondered which was his? No. Val shook her head. He had never been on good enough behavior to earn a workout here.

For another few minutes they ran. They ran until perspiration rolled down Val's forehead, and she had to swipe it out of her eyes. In that time, she counted four more boys that had his same coloring, same characteristics and features. The youngest appeared to be about five and the eldest about ten.

Punching abruptly at the machine, Val switched it off and stepped back. Her legs were wobbly. Her lungs heaved as she tried to walk away from *that* feeling. That angry, consuming feeling. The one that wasn't something she was used to. It was a fresh, new type of torrent that filled her blood. And though the drug worked to dull it, the effect only went so far. Placing her hands on top of her head, Val cruised dizzy circles around the room, trying to cool down.

Amber maintained her position on the treadmill. Lowering her speed gradually over time, she was walking comfortably by the time Val had collected herself. Though she shouldn't have had to collect herself at all. She had overdone today. That's why the flood of hot energy had consumed her just then.

Between the move into the dorm and the visit from Mandy, it was too much change. Too many new faces and things to take in. Val stopped at the table with the bottles of water. Twisting off a cap, she held the liquid to her lips and gulped it down. The water felt soothing as it coated her throat and wound around the inside of her belly. Quietly, Amber crept up beside her and did the same.

"When's your lunch?" She asked.

"Eleven."

"Mine, too." Amber glanced at the clock. "We don't have time for a shower."

Val nodded her head in acceptance. If you don't make the time, then you don't eat. And if you want a hot shower, then too bad because the water here runs cold. And if you want another blanket, or an extra pillow, or a window, or any control whatsoever, then the answer is no. You just better give that idea up right away. There's no room at Cambric for choices. There's no room at Cambric for thinking or feeling.

As Val followed Amber out the door, she fought a constricting sort of panic that threatened to overtake all the air in her chest. This was her forever. It was where she was born and where she would die.

And to survive the in between, she was going to have to learn not to feel it. She had been that way before and without a doubt she could do it again. She could last.

Because at least in all her wasted years of freedom, she had done one thing right. Jace. Her Jace would never, *ever* see this.

CHAPTER 15

He was running down a wooden dock. Dark ocean water surrounded them. It was still as still could be.

Stop, baby. Just wait. Val called out but Jace didn't look back. He wouldn't listen. Then she was chasing him. Running as hard and as fast as she could. He was just ahead of her. Until he wasn't.

Skidding to a stop at the end of the lone dock, Val looked frantically down into the water. There wasn't a ripple. Not a splash. But somehow, she knew he was under there. Suffocating. Drowning.

Coming awake, Val sprang to her feet. Her covers were all tangled around her legs, causing her to fall to the floor. It was everything she could do not to scream. On her hands and knees in the dark, Val sucked in oxygen until her head swirled and she passed out.

When she woke in the morning, it was to the customary beep of the automatic alarm. She was still on the floor. Her back ached and her hip felt bruised. Since she had stopped taking the pill issued to her, sleep was once again hard to come by. Shutting her eyes, Val would toss and turn for what felt like forever. Then pushing up to sit in the dark, she would rub at her temples.

Eventually sleep would come for her but even then she found no rest in it. The hours that unconsciousness took her were spent twisting inside larger than life dreams. They were so vivid without the meds to erase them. It all felt too real.

Groaning now, Val pushed up to standing and braced herself against her desk. Without much thought, she swiped her finger over the black surface. What she saw there had her doing a double-take.

Rubbing her hand over her face, she stared. She had an appointment for nine a.m. Frowning, Val read through a few sentences that accompanied the booking. She must report to Room 115 having been freshly showered, though her hair need not be dry. Taking a step back, Val leaned against her bed, hands tingling with nerves. That was a prep room, she knew it well.

Closing her eyes, Val tilted her head back and worked to tamp down on the flood of feeling. Since stopping the medication, her emotions had come charging back and often threatened to give her away. She couldn't let them catch her crying, or shaking in fear, or having any other type of outburst.

Inhaling, Val held her breath and fought to replace her rampant thoughts with a serene inner screen of gray. Maybe that's why it was Cambric's color of choice. The lack of color and the lack of feeling combined into a welcome nothingness.

An hour later, Val listened to Amber talk over breakfast.

The cafeteria was bustling with its first phase of captives, so the tables were crowded with bodies and sound. Sitting across from one another on the far end of a packed bench, Amber assured her that the dreams were only withdrawals from the drug. Everyone who avoided the meds experienced it for a few days, up to a week at the most.

Val poked at her scrambled eggs and hoped that her friend was right. Half of the captives at Cambric were prescribed medication in some form. Either they treated you for depression, gave you pills to help you relax, or gave you drugs to make you lose all inhibition. The last category was what Bee had been hooked on. The uppers that made you want to party all night long were used widely, but in very strict amounts. You only got them before seeing clients.

Stopping medication the way Val was doing was not a choice that Cambric allowed its captives to make. If you wanted to get off the drugs, then you had to pretend to take them and later dispose of the pills. This task was a lot more difficult depending on where you were housed and what guard oversaw your dosing. In Isolation, it was nearly impossible to pull off, but up in the quiet halls of monthly subscription things were a lot more lax.

The morning guard walked the hall, handing out pills, but he didn't bother to check if you swallowed them before moving on to the next captive. Val hid her pills under her mattress, as instructed by Amber. Later, another captive would come around and collect them all. He or she would trade them for extra food or favors on the floors far below, where pills of any sort were in high demand.

Val didn't know which captive was the one dealing and

frankly she didn't want to know. If that captive were ever caught, then it would look better for Val to seem truly surprised. The word on everyone's lips would suddenly be deny, deny, deny.

"So, they've booked me into Room 115," Val said, glancing up at the clock on the wall.

"Prep?"

"Yeah."

"Do you have any idea what for?"

"No."

"Maybe they've booked you a client, finally." Amber was unperturbed, for her this was a weekly occurrence.

"Charlie mentioned I would have to be re-trained and then submitted. That hasn't happened yet." Val leaned back and took a quick survey of the room. "Where is he by the way? I haven't seen him for days."

"I think he's down in breeding." Amber sipped at her orange juice casually. "His clients only ever keep him for one night."

"He's in the breeding program?" Val choked on her last bite.

"Yeah." Amber frowned at Val's reaction. "After Gabe was sold, Cambric's birth rate took a dive. They decided to move Charlie there instead."

"I guess I just didn't think about it."

"Well." Amber smirked ruefully. "We're all going to end up there eventually right?"

Val nodded, trying to seem casual, but inside her brain screamed and screamed and screamed. For a split second, she thought she might be sick but then she shoved the feeling away.

It was true that most monthly subscription girls ended up in the program. Cambric wanted more of them. They were beautiful, highly skilled, compliant, successful, money-making machines. Why not have them duplicate as many times as possible? And you didn't need a lot of males if you could get one or two that were capable of outperforming the rest.

"Listen-" Amber's chocolate-brown eyes softened in their close examination of Val. "Maybe you should get back on the meds for a while. You were out longer than any of us and you haven't been back all that long. The first couple of months is the worst."

"You were out?"

"For a whole glorious year before Cambric started up again." A look of joy crossed Amber's face before she hid it away. "But we don't talk about that here, it's dangerous. And not just because Cambric might hear you, but because it makes living like this impossible. Those who can't forget, can't conform. And those who can't conform…"

Val waited for Amber to finish her sentence, but the rest didn't come. Instead, Amber stood abruptly and grabbed her red tray. Looking down at Val she addressed her with almost sad eyes.

"You better get moving." Amber blinked. "You don't want to be late."

Room 115 was located on the ground floor of a single story building that connected the two apartment towers. Hair dripping down the back of her uniform, Val beeped her way into the section that had been so familiar to her as a trainee. Inside these rooms is where she had been trained, groomed, educated and awakened to the demands of D2 service.

This is where she had lost her innocence, if she ever truly had some to claim. This is where she took classes with Bee and watched her fall for Gabe. In fact, in a room just down the hall, Val had been outfitted and styled for that trade show in the city. The one where Jason had seen her for the first time.

Sucking in a breath, Val stomped at the longing that leapt inside her at the thought of her husband. Purposefully she shoved him from her mind, knowing that having him present with her here would only bring on more weakness.

Coming to a stop in front of one tall door, Val held her right forearm beneath the scanner that hung on the wall. The beep came, and then the click, and a gentle opening as the door swung silently inward. A blank expression fixed itself over her features as she crossed the metal threshold.

"Val-" Shane's voice sliced at her from across the room. "Right on time, that's good. Please, have a seat."

He gestured to a black stool positioned at the front of the room. Ducking her head, Val did as instructed, eyes darting all around, trying to gauge her surroundings.

It was a standard sized room with closets that ran the length of each wall. The white doors were all closed, but Val knew that inside them were a myriad of outfits in all sizes and colors. Cambric never sent captives to see clients in their uniforms, not even by request.

As she took her place on the stool, she noted a small table covered in makeup with a variety of brushes, a curling iron and a hair dryer.

"Let's start with the red silk dress and move on from there." Shane spoke to a person positioned just over Val's shoulder.

Shifting around to look, Val spied a long-faced woman with shaggy red hair who refused to make eye contact. It was Alicia. The same Corporate Captive that had prepped her in the city. The same one who had once passed a message along to Bee. It would be best for both of them if Shane didn't know the connection. Val focused her eyes on the floor.

Over the next hour, Alicia worked her magic. Running her fingers through Val's hair, she applied product before slowly blowing the full length dry. Taking a curling iron, she methodically twisted the ends into sections, then wound them around, spraying them before letting a chestnut ringlet fall.

When she had finished with Val's hair, she moved on to makeup. First there was a creamy thick foundation, followed by powder, bronzer, blush and lip stain. Eye color would be next, along with lashes.

All the while, Shane paced the room behind her. Val could hear the shuffle of his steps. Occasionally he would murmur to himself, though not explicitly about her. He seemed to be working on something. Despite not being able to see him, Val sensed that he clutched a tablet in his hands.

When Alicia was finally done, she held up a small mirror.

The reflection that stared back was one so intensely familiar that it was slightly unnerving. Val had seen herself look this exact way before, but she couldn't quite place it. It was like looking at an old photograph.

"All done?" Shane came around to stand before the two women, eyes appraising. "You really are good, Alicia. She looks just the same."

"Thank you, Sir." Alicia's voice was whisper quiet.

"Why don't you stay in case we need a touch up," Shane said. It was not a question.

"Of course, Sir." Alicia faded into the far corner.

"I'm sure you're wondering why you're here." Shane smiled down at Val but she knew better than to take the bait.

"No, Sir."

"Ah." Shane nodded acceptance of her answer, then bade her stand up. "Do you recognize this dress?"

"Yes, Sir."

Val followed him like a dog at his heel toward a metal rack where a tiny silk dress hung. It was a dress she had worn before, on a dinner date with Jason. The same dinner that had ended with them surrounded by protestors and paparazzi. The one that had them fleeing to the car where a rock had broken the rear glass.

Reaching out a hand, Val traced light fingertips over the fabric. Without thinking, she checked the label. It was the same designer and everything. Glancing down, she noticed the matching heels. Cambric hadn't missed a beat.

"Ever since Jason purchased you, we have been inundated with requests," Shane explained. "Do you have another Val? Can you dress her up to look like Val? Will you put her in the little red number when they ran from the restaurant? Will you put her in the skirt that she wore at the airport? You can imagine the things poor Bee had to do."

Val's throat went dry as she listened, but she managed to keep her expression plain, unmoved. Shane was a frightening creature, but above all else he was an obedient arm of Cambric. And Cambric never did anything that didn't make them money. There was a strategy here, and if she could wait long enough, Shane wouldn't be able to keep himself from confessing it.

"We've done our best in the past several years to meet with this demand. We've purchased an increase of brunettes, trained them in the way you carry yourself and put them in your clothes. But it's not just that these men want to be with someone like you, per se.

It's that they really want to be Jason. They want to be rich and young, with the attention and the power. Being with a woman that looks like you is one thing, but to actually *be* with you. To actually have sex with Jason Riggs' wife. Wow. Now that is worth something."

"I'm not his wife," Val corrected.

"The hell you're not," Shane whispered just next to her ear. "Anyway, as soon as word got out that we'd reacquired you, our demand tripled. We've booked you solid for months."

Val held her breath, willing the trembling of her knees to go unnoticed. Shane chuckled, lifting the dress off the rack, he handed it to her. She took it quickly then averted her gaze to focus on the far wall.

"The biggest problem we have is that there's only one of you. And the men willing to pay top dollar for a night with Val aren't the kind of men that like to be kept waiting. So, to appease them, you will be filming a series of personalized videos to help lead them along. Get changed. Now."

Laying the silk dress over the black stool, Val stepped out of the high heels of Cambric and began unbuttoning the front of her uniform. Her fingers shook ever so slightly, but Shane's attention had been diverted elsewhere. He could care less what she looked like naked. He'd seen her that way hundreds of times.

While she shed her gray dress in exchange for the red one, Shane wheeled over a large camera and set up a black screen just beyond it. Heart pounding inside her chest, Val replaced the uniform on the empty hanger and slipped on the new pair of heels. When she was finished, Shane positioned her on the edge of the stool, then continued to adjust the camera.

He made her cross her legs, then uncross them. He had her lean forward towards the lens, then away. Quietly, he ran his fingers through her hair, pulled some to hang over one shoulder, let his fingers trace down her bare skin. She shivered.

Glancing up into his face, she saw a look of primal fascination hanging there. He liked that she was afraid of him. He liked it more than anything.

Stepping away, he grabbed a sheet of paper, then came back and dangled it in front of her face.

"We've had twenty-eight individual requests for the red dress. You'll be reading this script tailored to each and every one of those twenty-eight men. I will give you a different name each time and you'll need to memorize the lines and then speak into the camera as if you're talking only to them. Do you understand?"

"Yes, Sir." Val swallowed hard.

For the next six hours, she read the lines. They worked through lunch without pausing for food. Alicia adjusted her hair and makeup half a dozen times, dabbing at the perspiration that seemed to collect nervously on her brow. All the while, Shane paced and prodded, demanded and stared.

She wasn't being alluring enough, then she seemed too eager. She sounded strained, then too upbeat. At first, nothing she did pleased him. But eventually, he began to interrupt less, complain less, and nod more.

If she felt fear in the beginning, or disgust at the things she had to say, then it slowly ebbed away under a steady stream of frustration. And perhaps that had been Shane's angle all along. If he could pick at her long enough, make her re-do the same sentence over and over, reposition her for the millionth time, then it brought her out of the reality of what she was doing. After a while, it became a performance. It no longer felt real.

When she smiled into the camera, biting her lip and promising a night to remember, it wasn't Val herself who said it. It was another woman, the one she had been raised to be, the D2 captive. Unfeeling numb nothingness overtook her.

She performed and performed and performed until Shane was smiling and clapping his hands. Until the last of the twenty-eight names had been read. By the time he released her to go, Val stripped out of the red silk and left it to pool on the floor. Let Alicia pick it up, she thought, that's her job anyway.

Back in her uniform, Val beeped her way out of Room

115, but didn't even hear the sound. She coasted along in the steady stream of traffic heading for the cafeteria. It was the early dinner phase and hundreds of bodies were shifting to line up to eat. Val recognized a few faces, gave a little wave or stopped to chat for a moment when beckoned. All the while, a solid close-lipped smile had settled into her vacant face.

Tonight's dinner consisted of cauliflower mashed potatoes, that actually contained no potato, baked fish, green beans and a slice of lemon. There was no salt, no pepper, no butter and certainly no sauce. Carrying her full tray with one hand, Val stepped to the drink station and filled an opaque plastic cup with water. There was no ice and no soda. She could have tea, but fearing it would keep her awake, she passed it over.

Rotating around, Val's eyes swept over the crowded tables, seeking an empty spot to sit. At the far end, she spied a few benches that had not yet been filled and headed for them. Eyes straight ahead, she didn't glance down at the people as she passed so was surprised when she heard her name called.

Looking to her right, she saw Charlie waving her over. Mandy sat beside him, arms wrapped around his shoulders, chest pressed against his side. Hesitating a moment, Val was reluctant to join them. She had missed Charlie well enough, but Mandy's sharp tongue was not easily forgotten. When Amber came up behind her and gave her a friendly nudge, the decision was made.

"Don't you look fancy," Charlie commented as Val and Amber wedged themselves down at the table. Mandy made a sour face.

"Thank you kindly," Amber answered him with a knowing wink that made him laugh.

"Is that a southern drawl I detect?" Charlie shifted a little, trying to gain a bit of space.

"Hmmm, yes." Amber picked at her fish with her fork. "New client."

"Oh, I hate fantasy clients," Mandy piped up. "I have one that makes me dress like a maid."

"I'll bet you make a pretty cute maid." Charlie flashed a smile before picking up his glass. "Oh, man I'm out of water. Excuse me ladies-"

"I'll get it." Mandy shot up and snatched at his nearly empty glass.

When she was gone, Charlie rolled his eyes and sighed. Amber shook her head and looked conspiratorially at Val.

"That's what the man gets for going there."

"Except I didn't," Charlie corrected, shoveling in a bite of green beans. "I'm trying to be nice and everything, but a guy can't hardly breathe when she's around."

"Well then that might be the problem. She wants what she can't have. Maybe give her a little taste and see if she goes away."

"I thought you just said she was clingy because I *went there*."

For the entire time it took Mandy to refill the glass, Amber and Charlie debated the predicament at hand. He wasn't interested, but Mandy was. They all had to live together, like it or not, so what should he do?

Val listened disinterestedly for a beat before tuning them out completely. These sort of relationship problems were common among captives, especially long-term agency owned ones. Sleep with enough people and eventually everyone you lived with was your ex.

The second Mandy returned, the conversation died.

"So, how did your first appointment go then?" Amber addressed Val in an attempt to break the awkward silence.

"You saw a client today?" Charlie's eyes narrowed.

"Not exactly."

Val shoveled in her food with impolite abandon. Skipping lunch had made her ravenous. Not only that but the portions were much smaller to begin with so any bite you missed made a significant impact.

"Well don't tell us all at once," Amber complained.

"I guess I just don't know what to say." Val paused to take a sip of water, noted Amber's frown and the worry that played in Charlie's eyes.

"Because you only say what you're told to by someone else," Mandy supplied, anxious to make a point. "If you're not Jason Riggs' personal puppet, then you're Cambric's."

"That's not fair." Charlie leaned away from Mandy with a scowl.

"But it's the truth. You just can't seem to see it." Mandy pointed to Val. "She's not here to help you get out. She's not here to help anyone, or find the missing. She didn't even know about them. She's *just* here."

"Mandy. Shut. Up." Charlie's voice rose, drawing the attention of a few tables around them.

"Why are you defending her? Is it because you want her? Do you have feelings for her or something?"

"Well… I don't have feelings for you," Charlie snapped.

The last sentence fell heavily. Mandy sat stunned for several seconds, her chest heaving as it filled with embarrassment and hurt. Suddenly she pushed back to standing, her cheeks flushed pink, and stormed away.

Murmurs followed her rushing figure out the door and spread amongst the captives. Amber set down her fork and folded her hands demurely in her lap, eyes downcast. Charlie pressed the heels of both hands into his closed eyes and leaned forward over the table.

Val overflowed with guilt. They thought because she had testified against Sharon, and worked with the FBI on that investigation, that she was some type of operative. They didn't understand how right Mandy actually was. Val only did what Jason told her to do, nothing more. She owed it to all of them to clear things up.

"She's right, though," Val began. "I am what she says."

"Don't." Charlie lifted his head, eyes blazing. "Just don't."

With that, he too got up and walked away.

CHAPTER 16

THE FOLLOWING DAY ROOM 115 WAS RIGHT BACK ON VAL'S schedule. Things with Charlie were tense, Mandy pretended like she didn't exist and Amber faked her way through a solitary breakfast with Val.

By the time she had showered and returned to Prep, Val's heart had filled with a lonely deadness. All night long she had battled thoughts of her son and Jason. She could hear their voices in her dreams and woke bitter at the realization of where she was. More than once she considered starting back on the medication.

Now, sitting once more on the edge of the solitary black stool in Room 115, Val banished all feelings from her mind. As Alicia ran a brush through her hair, she focused on nothing and worked hard to keep it that way. By the time her makeup was complete, Shane's taunting banter had little to no effect.

Today Val was dressed in a tight blue skirt and billowing white peasant top that you could practically see through. It had been the outfit she was wearing when the press first discovered her with Jason. She had worn it while he dragged her through a bustling LA airport on their way back to Texas. She could almost feel the warmth of his palm as it wrapped around hers. It seemed a lifetime ago.

"There are thirty-four requests for the blue skirt," Shane began. "I've tailored this message a little differently so you'll need to memorize a few new lines."

"Yes, Sir," Val intoned, furrowing her brow in concentration.

Eyes darting across the script, Val saw where he was going with this one. She would need to be a bit more submissive, less seductress and more youthful nervousness. In the photos of her dodging cameras at the airport, she had looked surprised.

Shane showed her the one he wanted her most to emulate. You could see Jason's back as he pulled her along by the hand. She had on large sunglasses, but had just glanced over her shoulder as they pushed through the airport doors. Her mouth hung ever so slightly in a tiny "o" shape. Her hair was wild and makeup mussed.

For the rest of the day, Shane drilled her. It took a lot longer for her to strike just the right pose and use the correct tone of voice. At times Val forgot the lines completely, or repeated the wrong name from the video just before.

Surprisingly though, this time Shane was patient. He didn't yell or berate her. Instead, he took his time and coaxed. He encouraged her, giving her breaks and having lunch brought in. Whatever had prompted his change in treatment only served to make Val more wary. He could change in an instant. She had seen it before.

There were more names this time and the script was longer. Dinner came and went without the offer of food or a break. Alicia sat in the corner, stomach rumbling, but wisely said nothing. Even Shane began to look frazzled, but was insistent on completing the entire list. He didn't want to make her up in the same outfit again for only a handful of men.

By the time she was finished, her limbs felt weak and her face hurt from all the smiling. She changed back into her uniform and left the room, beeping her way back to her bed in dazed silence.

Hours of pretending to be captive Val for the videos had taken their toll. Her body was heavy with exhaustion and her overwrought mind had gone numb. For the first time since she had been reacquired by Cambric, she dropped easily into a sound sleep. No dreams came to plague her, only much welcome blackness.

When she woke, she repeated the same process. Then again, and then again. She repeated it until there were no names left. Until all of the outfits had been worn and hundreds of promises had been made. She repeated it until the words became a part of her, filling her brain, overlaying the last four years of her life.

For what woman could march steadily towards the end that awaited her and keep hold of herself? What woman could face the inevitability of submission that played along the horizon, while still calling herself a wife and a mother?

It was just as Amber had told her before. You have to let go of the free life that you experienced if you're going to survive. You have to shove it from your mind, like it never happened, like it was a distant fantasy that you didn't have any right to experience. So that is just what Val did.

Then there came a morning when her schedule changed. The flat screen attached to her desk no longer flashed the booking in Room 115. Val blinked once, then rubbed at her eyes in an effort to confirm what she saw was true. She had an eight-thirty appointment in Training 106, then a gym workout scheduled for two-thirty in the afternoon.

Straightening, Val sighed audibly. Things were moving right along.

A knock on her door had her moving to open it. The meds guard stood there, offering her a little white pill and a paper cup filled with water. Val hesitated for the briefest of moments before taking what he offered and swallowing it down. She no longer felt upset over Bee's long ago drug habit. If anything, she understood it more perfectly. With any luck, the fog would settle in soon enough.

Passing Mandy on her way to the shower, Val felt the hatred that resonated in the young woman's eyes. But tilting her head to one side, she realized she no longer cared.

Over breakfast with Amber, Val listened to her half-hearted complaints about the food, lack of coffee and simmering hot weather. Though Val ducked her head and offered the occasional *uh-huh* and *I know*, the truth was that she no longer cared about that either.

When Charlie came to settle next to the two women, Val studied her food quietly. She could feel the search of his eyes upon her skin, but she didn't make contact and instead rose to leave. In time he would see that she wasn't his savior. In time they would all see just how right Mandy was.

Training 106 was just down the hall from Room 115. Val knew what likely awaited her there. She just didn't know who. Walking demurely along the crowded halls, Val's stomach did the tiniest of somersaults before settling back down. The door was just off to her left.

Training rooms were extremely small and outfitted sparsely. They needed only a bed and the occasional chair. In one corner would be a single metal sink with which to wash if the need should arise. She couldn't count the number of times she had used one, there had been so many.

Before she offered her forearm for scan, Val composed her face into uncaring blankness, knowing her insides would soon follow suit. The beep sounded. The door swung inward. Val's heart skipped a beat. He was already waiting.

Sitting on the bed, his salt and pepper hair looking slightly mussed, was her former trainer. His dark eyes warmed at the sight of her and he stood, smiling that crooked way he always had.

"Hey, Val." He waited for her to step inside. He was nothing if not patient.

"Hi, Ben."

Val inched across the threshold before stopping once more to stare. Behind her, the door swung shut of its own accord. She heard the faint click of the automatic lock in the background.

Before her sat the first man she had ever slept with. He was her first for everything, in fact. And on the whole, he had made those experiences pleasurable, light-hearted and fun even. There had only ever been that handful of times that were… unpleasant.

And they had been at the specific demand of Shane. It was when Cambric had been scrambling to force Gabe back into submission. In the end, their tactics had worked.

If Val felt a twinge of fear at knowing what Ben was capable of, it was dampened by his quiet study of her. She kept flashing back to all the other times they had shared and struggled to reconcile the one experience against all the others.

Twisting her fingers together in front of her belly, Val tried to look at Ben in a different light. He was a captive after all, just like Gabe or Charlie. He'd started out the same, doing monthly subscriptions, then the breeding program. As he aged, he'd been transitioned into training. She gauged him now to be about fifty, still handsome in that rogue way he had about him.

"We both know why you're here." Ben pushed off the bed and began to stalk towards her. "We need to refresh your training and complete each phase with a submission."

Val nodded, then backed a step. Nerves cruised through her system. She glanced to the side, then back up at him before retreating once more. There wasn't anywhere for her to go, however, and her back quickly came up against the closed door behind her. Ben's eyebrow raised but he kept on coming.

Tilting her chin up, Val pursed her lips and looked him straight in the eye. What she saw there gave her pause. His expression didn't track with his body language.

"You ready?" He asked.

"Yes." Val's voice was low, but steady.

Reaching over her head, Ben pushed a button that was attached to a panel in the wall. The camera positioned in the upper corner of the room switched off.

"Well, now that's done." Ben gave her a wink before shoving off the wall.

Turning his back on her, he crossed to the far bed and settled himself back onto it. With his long legs crossed at the ankle, he rested them against the floor and leaned back. For several minutes, they just blinked at one another.

Val wasn't sure what to make of him. Was this a test? A new phase of training? She stood rooted to her spot, palms pressed against the cool of the closed door.

"How're you adjusting?" Ben asked finally. "The first months back are the worst."

"I'm fine." Val was cautious, she wasn't sure if she could trust him.

"Have you considered ending it?" Ben raised both eyebrows, watching her face in earnest. "Because for me that was about month five. I got over it though, as you can see. The meds do have their purpose."

"Why are you telling me this?"

"You don't believe me." Ben rubbed his hands together and leaned forward. "After what happened down in Isolation, I can't blame you. I never did get a chance to tell you how sorry I was over it. I did my best not to actually hurt you, but it had to look that way or Shane wouldn't have stopped."

"You didn't hurt me physically," Val admitted, softening at the look on Ben's face. "Maybe just my feelings, I guess."

"But you ended up in a good spot, right?" Ben reclined once more against the wall, tucking his arms behind his head. "I think you've probably had the best life out of any captive in history. You're the most famous one, at least. And to think about being free for all those years, it's astounding."

"You were out? You walked free?"

"Hell yeah I was. They had to pull me back. Kicking *and* screaming." Ben gave up an ironic laugh. "I've got you to thank for all that."

"No." Val pushed herself off the wall and went to sit beside him on the bed. "It wasn't me. People need to stop thinking that I was the reason they were released. I just did what my owner told me to, that's all."

"Ah, now who's gotten into your head?" Ben reached out, gave her shoulder a little shake. "From what I read, you gave some pretty damning testimony at Sharon's trial. Doesn't that count for anything?"

"I did it because I had to."

"You could've run away before the trial." Ben pointed out, retracting his hand to rest in his lap. "And maybe it was Jason Riggs and the Feds that steered the ship, but can you honestly tell me they could've done it without you?"

"I don't know." Val nibbled at her lip. "It's just that people here think I'm back for some undercover investigation and I'm not. I don't want to give everyone hope when I'm just as helpless as they are."

"What would you be investigating, if you were undercover?"

"The missing." Val paused. "Is it true?"

"Ah, the missing." Ben nodded. "When I was at my lowest,

I thought the guards would come for me any day. They never did though. It was always someone else."

"What guards?"

"Cambric security. They take you out in the middle of the night and you never come back."

"You've seen it?"

"I've seen it."

Ben shifted his shoulders. Val plucked at the buttons on her uniform. Cambric guards were hauling off captives in the dead of night, only to have them never return. How was this happening without anyone on the outside knowing? What happened to all the new regulations? The government oversight? Ben glanced at the clock on the wall and cleared his throat.

"They only take the captives who are at their worst. The ones who refuse clients, get constant discipline, or weeks in Isolation. I've seen the plans they have for you, Val. I've seen the list. I'm afraid that if you can't conform, you could very easily disappear along with the rest."

"So, what should I do?"

"Well, we're going to re-train you but I'm going to leave out the submission part." Ben reached out, ran his thumb gently along her jawline. "We'll go through all the scenarios but I'll never push you past kissing me. Do you think you can handle that much?"

"I haven't kissed anyone since…" Val's eyes dropped to her hands, then fixed on her empty ring finger.

"If you don't follow through with your first client, then I'm a dead man." Ben tipped her chin up to look at him. "If you refuse to sleep with him, whoever he is, then Cambric will investigate the tapes we are about to make. They will question why there are so many holes in them."

"I understand."

"While we practice, I want you to visualize completing the act with someone else. *Not* Jason Riggs. Think about me or some random guy or whomever pops into your mind. Get yourself used to the idea that you've already crossed that line."

Val swallowed hard and nodded.

"In the end it's your choice. We can do this for real now, you and me. Or you can have a little while longer. Wait until your first client."

"Why are you doing this?" Val asked suddenly. "Why are you going easy on me?"

"Because I owe you." Ben stood up. "I owe you for the only free year of my life. It's a debt that can never fully be repaid."

Walking over to the control panel, Ben waited for Val's decision. Sucking in a breath, she glanced again at her ring finger before clearing her throat and giving him a nod. She would accept his offer of a reprieve.

After Ben switched the camera back on, he put Val through her paces. Running different scenarios together, he reminded her where to place her hands, when to shift her body, how to use her eyes, how to best accept cues.

Cambric had a planned reaction to every action and vice versa. It was a carefully regimented script that had to feel completely natural for the other person involved. Each time Ben would bring Val to the very edge before getting up to shut the camera off. Then for the next several minutes, instead of completing the act, they would recline and talk.

He told her about the day the guards didn't get paid and walked out of Cambric. How they left the doors open to swing in the wind. It was shortly after Sharon's conviction and the place quickly fell into chaos. Some others were unsure at first but Ben hadn't missed a beat. He simply packed up a few days' worth of food and a change of clothes before hitchhiking his way south.

Several long-haul truckers had taken him across state lines tucked in the back with their cargo. One old man hid him in the bed of his pick-up truck under a pile of loose hay. It was itchy and uncomfortable, but oh so worth it. Somewhere around Kentucky he stumbled across a hippy commune and never left.

He told her how it felt to sink his hands deep in the soil and grow his own food. He talked about picking apples in the large orchard that rolled away down one hillside and what it was like to sell the crates out of their shared van.

The look of profound peace that covered his face when he talked, sent a joyful sort of sadness to fill Val's heart. For in that brief snippet of Ben's life, he had heard music strum out of an acoustic guitar, danced with a woman *he* chose, and got drunk off moonshine brewed in a still.

"Have you ever tasted honeycomb straight from the hive?" Ben turned to her abruptly between sessions.

"No, I haven't," Val grinned at his expression. "And I can't imagine you keeping bees."

"They aren't so bad. You wear special clothes and use a little smoke and they calm right down. If you ever get back out, you should try it."

"I will," she promised him, seeing the memory dance at the back of his eyes.

Their training session took all afternoon. Ben called in for lunch and cancelled Val's workout appointment. They ate happily together, laughing and talking, sharing stories of the outside.

Val was careful about what she told him, but she gave him some of her memories anyway. She described the cold of an early morning in Wyoming, how the frost still covered the ground outside. And the feel of a horse underneath you, breath puffing out of large nostrils.

By the time they had worked through every submission, Val had just enough time to shower before dinner.

The cafeteria was only half full by the time she arrived and the line to get food was long. Val stood patiently, mind still floating back in that room with Ben.

When she stepped up to grab a plastic try, she felt a nudge just beside her. Turning to look, she saw Charlie swoop in and effectively cut in line. A few people grumbled, but no one challenged him outright, so he selected a tray and walked along with her.

"You missed our workout today," Charlie began, holding out his tray to catch a bowl of spaghetti. "Where were you?"

"In training," Val answered, keeping her eyes focused ahead of her.

"They submitted you today? Who was it?" Charlie frowned. "Are you okay?"

"I'm fine."

"You're fine?"

"Yes, Charlie, it's nothing I haven't done before."

Val kept her gaze averted, though she felt him continue to appraise her. Inching along side by side, they neared the middle of the buffet. Their trays slid along the counter.

Without warning, Charlie wrapped his hands around Val's hips and spun her around to face him. She threw up her hands in defense, pressing her palms firmly against his chest. But that, of course, was a mistake. It wasn't the proper response to the training request and by the time she realized it, it was too late. Charlie's hazel eyes flashed with knowledge.

"That's what I thought." Charlie hissed, before releasing her. Returning to his tray, he whispered. "He didn't submit you, not even once. Who was it?"

"It was Ben," she admitted, voice low.

"He's taking a pretty big risk," Charlie commented. "I was with a client yesterday and I saw the videos they made you do. Someone leaked them to the press. I'm sorry Val, for being short with you before."

"It's alright."

People shifted ahead of them. They were nearing the end of the line.

"All I know is, you better get your game face on. If they find out what's been going on, both of you are screwed."

"You won't say anything, will you?"

"Me? Hell no, you can trust me. The question is, can you trust Ben?"

Momentarily stunned, Val stood frozen, holding up the line. Her brain dialed back to review the past hours of her life.

What had made her trust Ben? What exactly had she told him? Was she sure the camera had been switched off at the correct times? Doubt bobbed up to the surface of her mind, leaving a long line tethered to a sickly raw fear.

Charlie grabbed at her elbow with one hand and his tray with the other.

"Get going," he hissed, glancing around.

Val picked up her tray and let him direct her. They weaved through the push of bodies shuffling towards open tables. It was thick today, she had timed the meal all wrong. But the thought was a drifting one, meaningless in a sea of denial and doubt.

Finally, a pocket opened and they were able to step through towards a few vacant benches. Val sat heavily on one, with Charlie landing right beside her.

"Did he leave for that year?" Val shifted her head to the side, watching his expression. "Did they have to bring him back, or did he stay?"

"Ben?"

"Yes."

"He was one of the first ones out the door."

"Then I can trust him."

For a few more moments they sat in silence. Val poked at her food, listened to the clatter of plates and trays all around them. A group of captives at a far off table burst into laughter. People swirled about, choosing seats, chatting with one another. It was just another day.

Then a rear door swung open. And a train of Cambric security filed in. As they strode by the tables, people's voices fell away. Like a drop of water falling into the stillness of a pond, Cambric's presence rippled through everyone they passed. All eyes shifted to watch their progress. They never disrupted a meal.

Val's heart beat louder and louder insider her chest. Under the table, Charlie gripped her hand and held on tight. They were heading straight for them.

"Don't say anything." Charlie bent to speak directly into her ear. She could barely hear him. "Act like you've done nothing wrong."

Straightening then, he released her hand and moved a few inches away. Security came to a stop at their table.

Hovering over Val, three uniformed men addressed her, their broad shoulders thrown back, their feet shifting side to side. The instant they grabbed her arms, Val felt bile rise in her throat but she swallowed it back down, forced it all away. There was only way to survive this.

Rising without protest, Val tilted her chin up and followed them willingly out the door.

CHAPTER 17

THEY LED HER OUT INTO THE COURTYARD, ITS EXPANSE OF LUSH grass shone under the rays of a late afternoon sun. Summer was almost at an end, but the days were still long and hot. Val wanted to raise her hand to her forehead. She wanted to shade her eyes from the instant glare, but instead she kept her arms swaying loosely at her sides.

It had been many years since she had to play in this game. Back then, she had been very good at it. Looking back over the past months, Val realized she had still been struggling lamely as a free person, raging against the restrictions and bonds of captivity. If she wanted to survive, if she ever wanted a chance at staying alive, then she had to become the player she once was.

Purposefully, she filled her body with the seductive energy that had once gotten her so far. As a trainee, she had the ability to make any security guard blush. She had been able to manipulate Cambric staff and other captives alike by making them want things from her that they didn't know they should want.

Whatever lay ahead of her in the brick building across the way, she would meet it with equal force. And given the opportunity, she would bend it to her side.

Slowing her steps just a fraction, Val let the heels of her shoes tap a beat along the cement path that skirted the lawn. Throwing a glance behind her, she caught one guard's eye, then let the look linger for a beat longer than is acceptable. When he gave her a frown, she bit at her lip. A faint heat painted his cheeks. She slowly smiled.

One down. Two more to go.

They beeped her into the building, then led her down a narrow hall. She increased her pace until the guard in front of her could feel her presence at his back. Keeping her eyes fixed on his neck, she saw him stiffen, then eventually turn around.

Glancing over his shoulder, the guard's eyes lit with surprise as she gave him a sly smile. She let one hand dart up to the top button of her dress and undid it before giving him a quick wink. He stumbled slightly, but caught himself, causing her to stifle a laugh.

By the time they reached their destination, Val was oozing confident pride, and all three guards were a bit unsteady. Offering her forearm to the wall scanner, she listened to its accepting beep before the tall white door swung slowly inward.

The room before her was full of men but her eyes caught on the first one she recognized and stayed. It was Shane. He stood closest to the door, his brow furrowed. When he saw her, he beckoned for her to come to him and she obeyed with the same confident energy with which she had just dominated the guards.

"Here she is now," Shane announced, letting his arm encircle her waist. His fingers traced signals along her lower back. "One of my favorite girls."

Remembering her encounter with Charlie, Val knew she couldn't let Shane see any hesitation. He had to believe she had been submitted by Ben or they were both at risk. So, rising up on her toes, she responded to the subtle cues as instructed. Pressing a single kiss to Shane's cheek, she slowly smiled then laid her face quietly on his chest.

It was only then that her eyes drifted over to the other men in the room. It was only then that the color drained from her face.

Jason stood stiffly. His father and a team of lawyers were ranged out along one side of a long table. Agent Finn, and what appeared to be a police officer, were situated along the other. There was also a collection of Cambric staff and an outside nurse with a medical bag tucked under one arm.

Val absorbed the scene quickly. Eyes darting about before landing once more on Jason. Her husband was here. At Cambric. And the look on his face as he watched her willingly embrace another man was pure and utter torture.

Closing her eyes against the pain, Val bit down hard on the inside of her cheek. She bit down until the welcome taste of blood passed over her tongue.

"So, you can see this silly court order is all for nothing," Shane spoke easily, rubbing at her shoulder. "There are no black eyes, no bruises, she hasn't been forced to do anything she hasn't wanted to do. Am I right, Val?"

Charlie's last words to her echoed now in her mind. *Don't say anything.* So that is exactly what Val did, she remained perfectly silent. Opening her eyes, she caught Jason's gaze briefly before re-focusing on the floor.

"Regardless of the circumstances, this nurse is here to perform a full examination." Jason's lead attorney spoke, his booming voice took up all the air in the meeting room. "And you can save your demonstrations for another crowd because we aren't buying it."

Shane waited quietly for a bit. His hand moved to her waist where his fingers traced taunting circles. She didn't have to look up at him to know the expression of cold pleasure that had taken up residence on his face. He wanted all of these people, but especially Jason, to feel the exact breadth of his power. He could touch where he wanted and no one could do anything about it.

For her part, Val kept her arms around Shane's body. He hadn't given her permission to let go yet, and that was a step she could no longer skip. Because if she did, then she would be responsible for what happened to Ben, a fellow captive who had given her his trust in return for her own. There wasn't anything more valuable a captive could trade than that.

"Come on, Val." Jason's voice cut right through her. "You can come over here. He can't hurt you. We're all watching."

But Val did not move. She kept her breath even and calm. The blood inside her mouth tasted of iron and salt. She focused on it.

Shane threw back his head then and laughed. In that instant, Val let her eyes shoot up to Agent Finn. He caught her gaze and held it. Ever so slightly, he shook his head to one side. No, he was saying, you aren't safe.

Whatever had passed between them before, whatever betrayal he had been party to, she *knew* he regretted delivering her to Shane. Agent Finn had witnessed what the man was really like and so she would listen to Finn now. She kept her arms wrapped around Shane's body and patiently waited to be released.

"Val dear," Shane said finally, tilting her chin up to peer into her face. "You have to let this nurse examine you. Go ahead and have a seat over there."

Dropping her arms, Val walked to the chair indicated and sat down. She crossed her legs, letting the line of her body hike up her gray dress to reveal the full length of her thigh.

Jason darted forward. Skirting the table, he came around to kneel beside her. Val avoided his eyes. If she looked at him now, she just might give herself away.

Keeping her face averted, she focused on the nurse instead. But out of her periphery, her husband lingered. His arctic eyes swept the side of her face, she could feel his gaze on her skin. Then his hands came up to cup her chin, and his touch almost undid her. Ever so slowly, he forced her to look at him.

"It's me, Val," he whispered, before pressing his lips against hers. "It's me."

Hot tears clenched at her throat, threatening to unleash themselves over her cheeks. It took everything she had, everything inside of her, not to break. It was the feel of Shane's calculating stare that prevented it. It gave her enough fear to grab on to. Because Jason might be in this room at the moment, but soon he would be gone. When he left, his attorneys and all their protection would go with him, leaving Val alone once more.

"Please-" Val closed her eyes, refused to kiss him back. "Please don't."

"You'll have to forgive her," Shane chimed. "She's just been re-trained today, so she's probably not up for another round."

"Trained?" Jason's voice was tight, but his thumbs smoothed gently over Val's skin.

Her eyes shot open then, the guilty misery overflowing from them. Heart breaking silently inside her chest, she wished she could tell him that nothing had happened. Wished she could explain that it was all a ruse, a scam, that Ben had helped her. But she couldn't. She couldn't say anything at all.

"Yes, she couldn't get enough of Ben." Shane smirked, letting the implication roll over Jason. "The session lasted well over six hours."

It was that final sentence. It did something to her husband. In a word, he snapped.

In a split second he was off the floor, lunging for Shane. Cambric security surged forward. Shane laughed. Agent Finn stepped between them with the police officer not far behind. Senior kept shouting while the attorneys punched furiously at their phones. The nurse covered her mouth with one hand.

In the midst of it all, Val sat perfectly still. Blinking and blinking at a blank wall, a solitary tear traced a wet path down her cheek. If she ever made it out of here, if Jason ever succeeded in freeing her, what exactly would she have left?

"Get your hands off me you son of a bitch!" Jason screamed at Finn who braced his shoulders, keeping him back.

"You! Out!" Agent Finn barked at Shane, angling his head towards the door.

"You have no right to-" Shane began, but was cut short by the police officer. He stepped forward, his baton slapping loudly against one open palm.

"I'm the court's hand in this matter." Finn continued to hold Jason. "And I say you're out."

"The judge will hear about this." Shane eyed the officer a moment longer before walking calmly from the room.

Once he was gone, Finn released Jason, who whirled away and slammed a fist into the wall. Senior came up behind him then, murmuring quietly as Jason shifted his weight from one foot to the other.

The attorneys were speaking loudly into their cell phones, demanding this and citing that. All of them were scrambling to make some sort of difference in this complex situation. But the truth of it was, none of them had any control.

With a tug on his jacket, Agent Finn dictated instructions to the police officer who then ushered the remaining guards out the door. The nurse, finally able to collect herself, pulled a chair up to face Val and sat. Methodically, she began removing equipment from her bag and arranging it in some sort of order on the table. Val watched her, eyes flicking around every so often. Where were the cameras? They were in here somewhere, most definitely.

When Jason had calmed down, he walked back over to Val's side and knelt once more. Glancing at him briefly, Val saw the redness of his eyes, the sharp helplessness that filled them. He had been crying. She looked away.

Shoving back from her, Jason paced about the room. A heavy tension rose into the air.

Ignoring it, the nurse began her procedure. She started with vitals, took Val's temperature, oxygen level, and blood pressure. From there she produced a portable scale. Val had lost fifteen pounds.

Occasionally, Jason would stalk over. Arms crossed over his chest, he would stare down at her, then bury his face in his hands and walk away. Taking out a syringe, the nurse cleaned a spot on Val's wrist and drew several vials of blood. After that, the questions began.

"Are you on any medication?" The nurse watched her carefully.

"Yes."

"Do you know what it is?"

"No."

"How does it make you feel?"

"Numb."

"Have they withheld meals from you?"

Val didn't answer.

"It's okay honey, you can be honest, they're gone."

"They're never gone," Val whispered.

The nurse glanced up at an attorney, who made notes. Agent Finn stood, leaning up against a wall, watching Val. He was in a spot where he could analyze her face and she could see him clearly, if she wanted.

Jason approached her again. Crouching down, he begged, eyes pleading.

"We need you to tell us the truth. *Please.*"

"You don't know what you're asking me to do," she hissed.

"We're filing an injunction to stop them from booking you clients. If it's granted by the judge, then they won't be able to touch you. It will prevent them from withholding meals, forcing medication, hurting you in any way. I'll make sure that it includes… *training*." Jason choked on the word before continuing. "But we need you to be honest with this nurse right here, right now."

Val looked over at Agent Finn. His eyes were steady. Following her gaze, Jason swiveled to see who she was looking at and lost it.

"Why are you looking at *him*? He's the one that delivered you to the devil! He's the reason why you're here!"

On their feet once more, Senior and the lead attorney strode over to intervene. Together they had to drag Jason into the far corner of the room. She could hear their calming voices and her husband's panicked responses. He was a man on the edge and she had put him there.

The nurse waited quietly, making no promises one way or the other. Val glanced up at her, then dropped her head in acceptance.

"Have they ever withheld meals?"

"Yes."

"Have you been confined to one room for more than twelve hours."

"Yes."

"Have you been forced into sexual relations with anyone?"

Val remained silent, eyes falling to the floor. The truthful answer was *not yet*. But if she admitted that, and Cambric was listening in, which surely they were, then Ben would be absolutely screwed. Maybe the injunction would protect Val, but it wouldn't apply to anyone who happened to help her.

Jason came back around once more. Getting down on the floor he buried his face in her lap. Val could feel him shaking. He was crying, though it was muffled.

Slowly, she placed one tentative hand on the top of his head, then ran her fingers through his short growth of dark hair. He stilled at her touch. Then his hands were reaching up, clutching at her waist. Straightening suddenly, he gathered her to his chest and pulled her down onto his lap. Rocking back and forth, lips tucked close to her ear, he whispered.

"I'm so sorry. This is all my fault."

"No," she whispered back, eyes squeezed shut against the flood of emotion. "It isn't."

"I failed you. I made you into Kelly Riggs when I should've been Jason Martin. If we'd stayed on that ranch..."

"Tell me about *him*." Val's voice cracked, and her chest heaved. Jace. She wanted to say his precious name but she couldn't allow herself even that.

"He's bright and wonderful and safe." Jason rushed in his words, barely audible. "He loves you so much. We both love you so much. Oh my God. I'm so sorry."

Agony opened inside her chest. Bending her face into Jason's neck, Val finally let herself cry. He clung to her, laying kisses along her neck and cheek as her shoulders shook with her silent pain. And she must stay silent, for it was dangerous to allow herself to cry at all. Jace's face pushed its way to the forefront of her mind and ruthlessly she forced him back.

Sucking in one ragged breath, she shook her head and

purposefully banished her son from her thoughts. If she went down that road, there would be no coming back.

Val held her mouth up to Jason's ear, so close she could feel his skin under her lips as she spoke. "I didn't have sex with Ben today. But you can't let them know it. They'll make him disappear for not forcing me."

"Disappear?" Jason whispered back.

She wanted to tell him. Had been about to even. If she'd been given more time, then she would've been able to explain. If the meeting room door hadn't flown open, admitting Shane and his collection of Cambric security, then Jason would've been able to hear her tell about the captives that were taken in the night.

But the instant Shane unleashed his horde, the melee that followed left any words stuffed hollowly inside her throat.

"Your court mandated time is up," Shane announced.

"The nurse hasn't completed her evaluation, yet." One attorney argued. "She hasn't performed the full physical."

"You'll have to petition the court for an extension."

Shane gestured towards Val and her heart skipped at the look of icy discernment she saw there. She'd been caught red-handed, confessing to her husband. Punishment was in order.

Eyes tracking, Shane instructed the guards to escort her away. Jason sprang to his feet. Stepping decidedly in front of Val he met them toe to toe, forcing Agent Finn to dive in once more. Senior was yelling, the police officer ducked in to assist, and so Shane skirted the other side of the table. Unhindered, he made his way steadily towards Val.

"Stand," he ordered and she obeyed.

Despite the madness that carried on around them, Shane

took his time, cold calculation dominating his agenda. He placed his hands on either side of Val's face and looked deeply into her eyes. She blinked demurely up at him, forcing herself to relax and comply. Raising her arms, she encircled his waist, responding to the cue without effort. After a few seconds, she even softened her mouth into a knowing smile.

Turning abruptly, he strode from the room, his fingers clenched around Val's wrist. She kept pace willingly at his heels. Though she didn't have the luxury of looking back as she crossed the threshold, she could hear the heavy door swing shut behind her, taking the sounds of fighting with it.

They walked down the hall and through a series of doors until they were alone in one tiny office. Shutting the door at his back, Shane whirled to face her, his eyes appraising.

"What did you tell him?"

"Nothing."

He took a step towards her, but Val knew better than to step back. Meeting his gaze with her own, she let him come on. He centered himself in front of her before placing both hands on her shoulders and shoving her to her knees. His fingers traced along the side of her face, then over her mouth. The request was clear.

Insides revolting, Val kept her composure and sent her mind to fly elsewhere. Reaching up to his pants, she undid the button and worked slowly at his zipper. Curling her fingers into the waistline at his hips, she began to work his pants down.

Just before she had exposed him, Shane placed a hand on the side of her face and shoved her away, causing her to sprawl backwards on the hard floor.

Stunned, Val lay curled defensively on her side, blinking up in bewilderment at him. He adjusted his pants then, working to fasten them back in place with a smug smile fixed to his face.

"And to think you had me worried back there," he murmured.

Gesturing for her to stand, Shane led her out of the room and out into the courtyard where he released her. Unceremoniously, she walked away from him, out over the green sea of grass.

CHAPTER 18

In the middle of the night, Val heard a muffled scratching. At first, she thought she was dreaming it, floating there somewhere between awake and asleep. But then the noise kept coming. Lifting her head off the pillow, she squinted at the solitary window inset into her door. Charlie's face was illuminated by the dim light from the hall.

Throwing back the covers, she pushed groggily up to sitting and waved him on. As quietly as possible he opened the door and slid inside. Holding the knob carefully in his hand he waited until the door resealed behind him before speaking.

"Hey," Charlie whispered, creeping over to sit beside her on the bed. "I brought you a little something."

"What is it?" Val took the bundle he offered and began to unwrap it.

"You didn't get to eat before they hauled you away," Charlie explained. "I would've come earlier, but they've had extra guards on the floor all night."

As Val stared down at the array of goodies Charlie had smuggled in, a wave of hunger hit her. There was a whole red apple, thick slices of cheddar cheese and a miniature box of crackers. Gratefully, she took a bite of the crisp fruit and let out a tiny groan. They didn't serve this stuff in the cafeteria. Where had he come by it?

"Thank you," she said between bites. "I didn't realize how hungry I was."

With a quick smile and duck of his head, Charlie leaned back to rest against the wall. Val sat cross-legged next to him, the warmth of her blankets radiating up from the mussed bed.

Every so often, she paused and explained what happened after she was taken from dinner. Jason had shown up with all his attorneys. A nurse had examined her. Shane put a stop to it. Cambric knew nothing of the fake submissions with Ben, and she would keep it that way.

Charlie contemplated the idea of a court ordered injunction and wondered aloud if it would work. He and Val debated back and forth for a time, neither of them having had much experience with the law. As he made to leave, Charlie paused at the door and turned back.

"How long does it take to get an injunction?" He asked.

"I don't know."

"Well, let's hope it's fast."

"Charlie-" Val tilted her head to one side, watching him carefully. "Where do you get all this extra food?"

"I don't steal it, if that's what you're wondering." Charlie gave her a wink just before sliding out the door.

The six o'clock alarm came too early for Val. After Charlie left her room, she had trouble getting back to sleep. Tossing and turning, thoughts of Jason and their son plagued her. When the screen on her desk sounded out, it rattled her already fried nerves.

Rubbing a hand down her face, Val groaned before flinging back the covers and tottering the few steps over to her desk. Plunking down in the wooden chair, she swiped a finger over the screen and blinked at the words that flashed there. Room 115 was back on her schedule, but that's not what made her stomach flip.

She had a client booking for four o'clock. It was offsite because they wanted her prepped well before transportation, which was listed at noon.

Shoving away from the computer, Val tripped backwards over her chair and tumbled to the ground. Her head just missed hitting the edge of the bed frame as she fell. She must've cried out, because her bedroom door opened abruptly and a passing captive glanced in. It was a familiar face, but the girl's name didn't spring to mind.

"You okay?" She asked.

"Yes," Val sputtered, then twisted to get up. "Thank you."

The girl leaned her head back out the door and gestured to someone who was out of Val's sight. Just as Val pushed to her knees, Amber appeared, eyes narrowing at the fallen furniture. Without a word, she came over and helped to hoist Val upright, then picked up the chair and ran her own finger across the screen.

"Four hour transport window." Amber spoke aloud.

"That's either in the city or Rochester. Could be Syracuse, but that's a little closer, so I don't think so."

Val bobbed her head, but didn't say anything.

"Well, you've got plenty of time for breakfast. Why don't we go grab some?"

"Sure," Val answered, but wasn't certain she'd be able to eat.

By the time noon rolled around, Val was a wreck. Her nerves only registered on the inside though. Anyone watching would think she was as unaffected by her impending appointment as Amber or any other lifetime captive.

Managing vacant eyes and a placid face, Val appeared bored while Alicia arranged her hair and perfected her makeup. The outfit the client selected was hung inside a black garment bag. She would change into it at the last moment.

Sky-high stiletto heels were already strapped to her carefully scrubbed feet. The shoes were a vibrant red, along with her nails. It didn't take a genius to guess at the dress she would be wearing that evening.

Shane was not present for her prep this time. Instead, he was standing by the door to the transport garage and gave her a final inspection. His eyes swept over her face and down the length of her body. He lifted the skirt of her uniform and brushed quickly at her thighs.

Giving a curt nod, he stepped aside and let the Cambric guard pass through the wide metal exit door. As Val followed behind, she held her forearm underneath the waiting scanner and listened absently to its beep.

Inside the garage were rows and rows of buses, limousines, vans, and cars. It was enormous, resembling an aircraft hangar with all the vehicles having blacked out windows and reinforced glass. Val had been inside the garage only a handful of times before, though she knew it was a heavily trafficked area by most others.

Hourly and party captives were brought in and out like a herd of cattle, while monthly subscription captives went out in groups of three or four. Cambric tried its best to schedule them in clustered locations and at similar times so they could benefit from using a single vehicle or single driver.

Today, Val would be the only one. She had a Cambric driver as well as a designated guard who would follow her to her client booking and wait outside the door. Most guards did not have to monitor their captives quite so closely, especially if they had worked with them before, but Val was considered a flight risk and so extra precautions had to be taken.

Looking at her personal guard now, Val wondered if he was related to CT. This was no ordinary Cambric security. This guy was about twice the size. He was a huge hulking machine with a thick neck and shoulders so broad his arms couldn't rest at his sides. Along those same lines, he didn't say much. She thought his name was Hugo, or Rafael, but admittedly, she couldn't be certain.

Stopping at a black town car, her guard leaned over to look in the driver side window. He grunted, then rapped one chunky knuckle against the glass before gesturing to the driver. Whomever sat inside turned over the engine.

Val listened as the doors were unlocked but waited, eyes glancing at the far wall. It was made entirely of sheet metal. She spied a few Cambric security standing at intervals, looking out of large windows that were cut into the building. Looking out. Not *in* at the captives, odd.

"Get in." Her guard spoke gruffly as he yanked open the rear passenger door with one hand, still clutching the garment bag in the other.

Obligingly, Val folded down gracefully onto the leather seat and just managed to tuck her legs inside before he slammed the door shut. Tucking a strand of hair behind one ear, she huffed a breath and watched him walk all the way around before taking his position in the shotgun seat. Twisting around, he hung the garment bag carefully in the back before securing his seatbelt.

The driver, both hands held loosely on the wheel, a black ball cap pulled low over his eyes, put the car in reverse and maneuvered out of the parking slot. At the end of the long aisle they turned left and followed the narrow lane until they reached a wide rolling door.

It was large enough for a bus to fit through and had a guard shack situated just in front of it. Her driver handed the guard in the shack an ID card which was swiped through a handheld reader. All of a sudden, the garage door began to lift and the guard returned the card without another glance.

The sun was bright and directly in their eyes, so Val turned her head to the side and looked away. The concrete flooring of the garage gave way to gravel which crunched slowly as it rolled beneath their tires. Val blinked through her heavily tinted window.

There was a narrow swath of green lawn off to her left. It wrapped from the far end of one of the apartment towers to the edge of the garage. As they approached the outer wall of the Cambric estate, Val watched a lone rabbit nibbling quietly on some clover. It was so peaceful in that instant, so unaware of what surrounded it.

In the next second, Val's eyes widened in shock. The car had passed through a heavy iron gate and an angry hand was slapping hard against the outside of her window. Val jumped back, hands clutching instinctively at her uniform.

A crowd of people swarmed just outside the Cambric gates. They pushed at the car, hitting and kicking the vehicle as it crawled by. The driver inched forward, unperturbed as other Cambric guards shoved people out of their path. Val's mouth hung slack as people yelled.

One man climbed on top of the slow moving sedan. Then another, then another. Before long Cambric security was overwhelmed, she couldn't see their uniforms in the mass of bodies. The roof began to sag and moan in places, and the driver began to tap the throttle impulsively. The car leapt forward a few feet, then stopped just before running over a person.

Fixing her eyes on the last bit of blue sky through the front windshield, Val's pulse spiked. They were going to be crushed. She broke out in a cold sweat. Leaning forward, Val gripped the massive body guard with one clenched hand and pulled his sleeve towards her, trying to peer into his face. He glanced at her once, before giving her a brisk nod and patting at her hand.

"There she is!" A voice screamed.

"She's in this one!" Then another.

The collection of bodies had migrated to the windshield. They were looking in and pointing. The bodyguard shoved Val further into the backseat until she could feel the rough carpeted floor on her cheek. Then he was yanking at the steering wheel and growling instructions to the driver.

Suddenly, cameras began to flash.

Then gunshots. Pop. Pop.

They made Val cringe and people shout. Again and again Val listened to the rapid release of bullets. The driver slammed his foot against the gas pedal and the car flew forward.

Still on the floor in the backseat, Val heard the sound of gravel fly from the wheels before they bumped up onto the highway and tore smoothly down the road. It took several minutes for her breathing to even out. During that time, no one in the car said a word.

The four hour drive was really more like three and a half. They didn't stop for lunch, but kept right on going. Rolling through towns and cities, merging with other traffic onto highways and off. Val reclined on the leather seats, running her hands distractedly over the smooth surface. How many men and women had been led to their fate in this car? She didn't know the answer.

Occasionally, the massive guard would change the channel on the radio. This happened whenever the music stopped and a news reporter began to speak.

Once or twice Val caught snippets of information. There

was intense debate over the state of the captive industry, an upcoming vote of some kind, and political posturing on either side. The driver, for his part, didn't say much of anything, save for announcing the need for a bathroom break somewhere around the halfway mark. The guard grumbled about being exposed, but what more could he say? Val too, needed to go.

At a small gas station just off the side of the freeway, the guard escorted Val to an outside bathroom located around the rear of the building. Its single door was inset into the concrete wall. While Val pulled up her uniform and balanced over the metal toilet in the corner, the guard stood waiting just outside.

It was a filthy stinking place. Without touching anything, Val bypassed the soiled sink and called through the door for the guard to open it. When he did, she saw another man standing at the far side of the asphalt parking lot. The man locked eyes with her before shoving his hands in his pockets and moving away.

"Keep your head down," the guard grumbled. "We never should've stopped here."

Back in the car, the three of them finished the drive without speaking. The thrum of music from the radio was switched off.

When they neared their destination, the guard had Val freshen up and change. She wriggled out of her uniform and into her outfit in the backseat, not caring who saw what anymore. There was a small bag of makeup, some hairspray and a brush. She smoothed at her hair, then applied a thick layer of crimson lipstick, smacking her lips loudly as she gazed into the rearview mirror. The driver glanced up at her, then away.

She knew that Cambric owned a series of homes in central hub areas where they arranged for discreet meetings between captives and clients. Val figured that's where they were headed now. Tossing the makeup bag aside, she sighed and looked out the window. It was likely that Charlie himself frequented several of these. But then again, he had never spoken of it before. Val felt there was a lot Charlie didn't say.

When the car pulled into a hotel parking lot, Val blinked in surprise. She hadn't expected her appointment to be at a place like this. Though, when she thought about it, a hotel made a lot of sense in her situation. If she was going to meet a different man each time, then she would probably be going to a different location, too.

The driver bypassed the valet drop off area in front and headed around back. Pointing to a rear emergency exit, the guard grunted and the driver stopped them at the curb.

"This is a high profile client who wishes to remain anonymous." The guard twisted to speak to Val. "You will remember his name for the duration of your appointment and then forget it the moment you're done. Are we clear?"

"Yes, Sir." Val nodded, then asked. "What is his name? Sir."

"Peter."

"Alright." Val gulped, palms sweating. "Peter."

Stepping out of the car, the guard glanced around before opening her door. The air was warm and mild. A soft breeze picked up the ends of Val's dress, tossing them lazily about her legs as she exited.

Following demurely behind her guard, they entered the hotel without incident. His massive hand wrapped carefully around her elbow as he guided her down a narrow hall and came to a stop at a bank of service elevators. It was quiet and dim, though the hotel itself appeared impeccably clean and fairly new.

When the doors of one elevator slid open, they revealed an extra wide space used mostly to haul furniture and equipment. The chamber itself was empty.

Closing her eyes, Val stepped into the box and worked hard to control her breathing. Whoever or whatever was waiting for her, she *would* submit. She would close off her mind and do what needed to be done. Not only for herself, but for Ben. So they'd never think to investigate him. So he wouldn't end up dead, like all the others.

The elevator jolted suddenly. Then stopped.

Val opened her eyes. The guard had pressed the red stop button. She saw him retract his hand from it before jamming it into his pocket where he continued to fish around for something.

"This isn't my normal gig," the guard admitted with a frown. "But money is money. And I need the damn money. That said, I expect you to do your job, so I can do mine."

"Okay." Val wasn't sure where this was going.

"I guess this client wants you sober, so I wasn't supposed to offer you any pills. But if I was you, then I'd want to be high as fuck." The guard held out his palm. In it rolled three round pills. One was white, the other two were red. "Reds make you go up, and the whites make you pass out. Which is it?"

"The white one I guess," Val took the pill and swallowed it down without a second thought. "How long do I have?"

"About an hour, maybe less." The guard punched at the elevator button and had it moving again.

"If I pass out, then they'll know I took something."

"I'll say you must have smuggled it from another captive. Happens all the time."

Just then the service elevator doors opened onto a well-lit hallway lined with carved wooden doors and the occasional wide window. Glancing out, Val realized this must be near the top of the hotel. From the location and decorations, she guessed this was a floor comprised only of expensive suites. In a lifetime long ago, she had frequented ones just like them with Jason. The pinch of his name in her head made her feel a bit sick. She blinked the feeling away.

They came to a stop at a door with a series of numbers fixed beside it. Room 17003. The guard located a small doorbell and pressed it with his index finger. On the inside, a bell could be heard.

Footsteps came towards them and the door swung inward. An unfamiliar man in a black suit eyed them for a moment before stepping aside to admit them. Val's guard produced a cell phone from his pocket and handed it to the man.

"Peter?"

"No, I'm his personal security."

"Is he here? He needs to sign this."

The man in the suit gestured over his shoulder and Val followed his line of sight. What she saw took her breath away.

He was tall, with dark brown skin and smiling brown eyes. His once black hair had a sprinkle of silver in it, but she knew he wasn't a year over forty-five. It was Representative Peter Higgins. Her savior. Her dear friend. She had carried his business card on her body for months, memorized his phone number, ran her fingers over the life-line scrawled on the back. He was here to save her.

Her face flushed with the relief of it.

"Peter!" Val called.

Running to him, she flung her arms around his waist. He laughed. Reaching over her head for the cell phone, he scrawled his signature half a dozen times. When the formalities were over, both of the other men exited the suite to wait outside.

No wonder he wanted to be anonymous, Val thought, here was her life-line in person, come to take her home. But then he was kissing her. His lips pressed against hers. His strong hands stroked up her back. One hand snaked around to cup her breast. The shock of it had her reeling. She stumbled back.

"Peter!" Val cried. "Your wife! What are you doing?"

"I know this must come as a bit of a shock." Peter's expression was a mix of desire and guilt. "Tawny left me. The political climate shifted after Sharon's conviction and I could no longer stay in power if I had to follow her standards."

"But… you wanted to release captives," Val sputtered, her confusion clear across her face.

"You know what they say about politicians." Peter took a step closer, ran his fingers through her hair. "Whatever they yell about the most, they're probably guilty of doing themselves."

Val gasped and her heart heaved at the sudden reversal of her circumstances. How had she gone from almost freedom to certain doom in a matter of seconds? She ran her hands up through her hair, eyes darting about the room, not able to quite focus on anything.

Peter drew her closer to him. Bending down, he kissed at her cheek and neck. Involuntarily, she stiffened, causing him to hold her at arm's length and appraise her.

"I settled for the red dress because they didn't have any of your outfits from our time together on the yacht." His eyes traveled the length of her body. "We had a moment, I thought, that night when I gave you my card. Ever since then, I haven't been able to completely forget it. I offered to buy you permanent placement but Cambric won't sell."

Val didn't know what to say. No words came to her mind. Peter ran a finger down her arm, causing a shiver to snake through her system. He smiled at that.

"I know you're used to nice things and I want you to see that I can give them to you here." Peter shifted away from her then and strode into the suite's small kitchen. "Would you like a glass of wine? Red or white?"

"Red," she called, anything to stall the inevitable.

He chatted easily while opening the bottle. There was an impending vote on the captive industry in Congress. After he and Tawny split, he ran a successful bid for Senate using the donated funds of pro-captive conglomerates. The lifestyle they afforded him was beyond anything he had seen, even though he had grown up an upper-class kid in a private school.

Chuckling to himself, he poured out the garnet liquid into two crystal glasses and handed her one.

"So, it's *Senator* Higgins now?" Val asked, sipping on the glass slowly, wondering how the alcohol would mix with the pill that swam in her stomach.

"Yes." Peter looped his arm around her waist and stood beside her at a wide window. "I like how it sounds on your lips."

Through the glass, Val looked down on the entrance to the hotel far below. She had been right about one thing; the suite was at the very top of the hotel. The furniture around them was sleek and modern, the art on the walls splashed with color. Peter talked. His voice was a constant buzzing.

Occasionally, he stopped long enough to kiss her shoulder, or run his hands over her hips. Val stood still. A haze had settled over her. In her. She knew all the while that he was speaking, but as she looked at him, the sound would come and go. Sometimes his mouth moved and nothing at all came out.

Blinking slowly, she felt everything fade into the distance. A few moments later it would come in extra sharp and close. The room spun on its axis, then righted itself. In the background, she heard a pounding at the front door.

Peter disappeared from her side and she swayed forward, bracing her hands against the window. Down below, several vans pulled to a stop in the round driveway. People with cameras were getting out and jogging towards the hotel. Val gave her head a little shake to clear it. The blur only increased.

"How'd they find us?" It was Peter's voice that shouted, and another man who spoke back.

"I don't know Senator, but if you want to remain anonymous, then we need to get you out now."

"I haven't had all my time yet," he protested. "The injunction could come down any day."

"It's your call."

Val heard the snippets of an argument, then dropped

unbidden to her knees. Her head was heavy, too heavy for her neck. Suddenly, her own guard was yanking her to her feet. He tossed her over his shoulder and she watched as the carpet from the hall passed under his expensive shoes.

The last thing she remembered was being flung into the backseat of a car. The driver asked what was wrong with her. People were shouting all around. Her own guard yelled for him to step on the gas. Then it was all gone. All gone away.

CHAPTER 19

THE FIRST THING SHE NOTICED WAS THE WINDOW. IT WAS WIDE, about five feet across and four feet high. It wasn't one that opened, she knew that instinctively by the way it was split into four equal parts by a white wooden frame. It was the frame itself that gave it an old-world type feel. The rolling hills of farmland that rose beyond it were simply serene.

Lying alone on the thick mattress, tangled up in smooth white sheets and soft blankets, Val blinked out into the sunshine. The view was just so beautiful.

After a few minutes, she ripped her eyes from the window long enough to take in the rest of the space. She was in a decent sized bedroom, with a large armoire in place of a dresser. The warm red hue of the wood made her think it was likely mahogany. Rotating her head to the side, she spied a matching bedside table with stainless steel lamp and cream-colored shade. There was another just like it on the other side.

Pushing up to sitting, her head gave a little throb, so she

placed the heel of one hand against it until the feeling passed. Where was she? Her eyes drifted down. She was still in the red silk dress from the day before.

Peeling back the covers, she slowly stood up and waited for her head to stop spinning before walking through the open bedroom door. On her right was a bathroom. Ducking her head inside, she flipped on the light switch and took in the granite countertop and massive clawfoot tub. A sigh of longing came unbidden from her lips. She would definitely be using that.

Flicking the light out, she resumed her search down the short hall which quickly gave way to a living room and kitchen. There was one long sofa that faced a tiny brick fireplace. Off to one side sat a tiny table with a pair of matching dining chairs.

Clearly it was meant for no more than two people. The kitchen was small as well, taking up one full wall with a center island dividing the space.

"Hello?" Val called, her voice scratchy but strong. "Anyone here?"

When she got no reply, she entered the kitchen and began opening cupboards. There was a small set of dishes, cups, utensils, pots and pans, but no dishwasher. The sink was clean, with soap and a sponge still in the wrapper settled on the granite counter top.

Not able to help herself, Val opened the white refrigerator and gasped. It was full. Completely full.

Milk, butter, cheese, vegetables, fruit, even beer. Reaching inside with one shaking hand, Val selected a ripe strawberry and bit into it. The explosion of flavor made her groan and roll her eyes.

Stepping back, she leaned against the counter and savored it. Oh, how she wanted to eat more. But she still didn't know where she was, or whose food this was, so she closed the fridge and ran her hands along the cherry-colored cabinets instead.

When she got to the end, she pulled open the pantry cupboard and almost cried. Again, it was full of food. Boxes of crackers, cereal, spaghetti noodles, rice, beans, cans of corn, the list went on and on. She ran delighted fingers over the labels, then stopped short before selecting one miniature box. A box of kid's cereal. With a bird on it.

Her stomach dipped as her mind began to race. Dropping the cereal on the floor, she ran back through the small house and into the bedroom. Approaching the window, she placed one tentative hand upon it. All the while her lips moved silently, willing it not to be true. But the moment she touched what was supposed to be glass, an image jumped slightly and that's when she knew.

It wasn't a window at all. It was a screen. A fancy, wonderful, false, lying screen. One that made you think you were looking out, when there wasn't any real *out* there at all.

Just as she was about to scream, the sound of the front door opening had her biting down hard on her lip. Carefully, she snuck back down the hall and watched as a man stepped into the living room.

"Charlie?" Val asked.

Walking into the open, Val fixed her eyes on her friend who did a double take when he saw her. The door had already swung shut behind him but at the sight of her, he whirled and tried the handle. It jiggled noisily, but held.

He slapped an open palm on the heavy door and called through the solid wood. "Hey, guys! I think you've made some sort of mistake here!"

He paused, but got no reply.

"Charlie." Val began to walk towards him. "What's going on? Where are we?"

Seeming to give up on the locked door, he rotated to face her, but leaned back heavily, hands braced against the smooth surface. His eyes held strain, and a touch of pity. For a few seconds he searched for the right words to say, then squeezed his eyes shut and replied.

"You wondered where I got all the food?"

"Yes." Val was tentative, studying his tight expression.

"I got it from the breeding program."

"What?"

"I get it from kitchens just like this, in apartments just like this, deep down in the belly of Cambric. I get it every time I have to-"

Eyes opening, Charlie looked at the ceiling instead of her.

"Every time you have to what, Charlie?"

"Don't you get it?" He was angry all of a sudden. Shoving off from the door, he stomped to the kitchen and flung open the cupboard. "Don't you recognize some of the food? I come down here and I try like hell to get someone pregnant, then I get to take some extra food when I leave."

The implication rung like a bell inside Val's head. She threw her hands over her ears, as if by refusing outside sound she could make what she just heard not true. She was in the breeding program. With Charlie. They wanted her to get pregnant. With Charlie's baby.

She took a step back. Then another and another until she bumped into the corner where the living room met with the hallway. Whirling to the side, she ran the few steps into the bedroom and slammed the door.

By the time Val was able to collect herself, several hours had passed. Charlie had not come to the door. He didn't knock or push his way in. He didn't even call out to see if she was alright. Tired of pacing in uneasy silence, Val returned to the living room and leaned for a moment against the wall.

Charlie was busy, his figure hunched over the stovetop. Smoke curled in the air, but was sucked up by a loud ventilation fan. His back was to her. His well-defined shoulders flexed beneath his white polo shirt as he poked at the thing he was apparently cooking.

Scooting to one side, he grabbed for a pair of gray-striped oven mitts, and slipped them onto his hands. So focused was he, that he didn't notice Val lingering, didn't feel the track of her eyes upon him. Bending low, he opened the oven and pulled out a pair of baked potatoes. He set them on the counter, then poked at one with a fork, testing to see if they were done.

Seeming to find satisfaction, he slid to the refrigerator and rummaged through it. Opening drawers and shoving items around, he fished noisily until he found what he was searching for. A head of lettuce and some dressing. Ranch dressing.

“Ranch.” The word tumbled unbidden from Val’s mouth as saliva began to flow. “They have Ranch dressing.”

“Jeez, you sacred me.” Charlie huffed a breath, jumping at the sound of her voice.

They eyed one another for a beat, Charlie clutching the dressing in one hand, the refrigerator door still hanging open behind him. Val twisted her fingers together at her waist, one bare foot tracing a nervous pattern along the plush carpeted floor.

“It’s still me, Val.” Charlie began finally, shifting to shut the door. “They’ve made me into a lot of things, but I’d never force you.”

Val bobbed her head, noting the faint sting of hurt that passed over Charlie’s face. He was bothered she would think that of him, even for a second.

Turning away from her, he resumed his hunt through the cupboards, opening them and pawing around before moving on. When he grabbed down a large mixing bowl, it dawned on her that he was preparing a salad. Tipping forward off her post at the wall, she padded to the kitchen and took the lettuce from the counter. Quietly, she set about rinsing it in the small sink.

“You cook?” She asked, glancing at him over her shoulder.

“I’ve picked up a few things.” He rewarded her with a soft smile. “You like steak?”

“Steak?” Val sniffed the air. “Is that what you’re burning?”

“Hey! Hey!” Charlie frowned. “It’s not as easy without a barbecue.”

They fell into a comfortable silence then. Charlie working at the stove top, and Val hunting down things to add to their salad. She sliced tomatoes and mushrooms then shredded some cheddar cheese. All the while she wondered when he had the opportunity to try a barbecue. Maybe one of his clients had one, she thought.

When they settled at the small table together, there wasn't an inch of empty wood to spare. Val had set it formally, like the staff had back in her free life. There were water glasses, wine glasses, plates, utensils they wouldn't even need, and napkins.

All of the fixings for the baked potatoes were in tiny little serving dishes. Bacon bits, sour cream, chives, and butter. She even dug up a small candle and lit it off the flame from the stove. A few drips of wax melted down its side.

Charlie clutched an open bottle of frosty beer in one hand and scooted a few things around to wedge it down onto the table.

"This is really nice," he commented, cutting into his steak. "Thank you."

"I should thank you. The steak is actually really tender. Almost as good as on a *barbecue*."

He winced at her use of the word, seeming to catch his earlier mistake. Glancing up quickly, Charlie eyed the corner of the room. Val followed his line of sight. There was a small black camera attached in the upper corner. A red dot blinked just beneath it. Cambric was watching.

"So, how does this work?" Val lowered her voice, and focused her attention on her plate.

"When they give me a new girl," Charlie murmured, eyes flicking up to her briefly. "We usually get a few days to get to know each other. Then we're supposed to sleep together at least once a day for about a week."

"You stay here?"

"I stay here, or I might come and go depending on the girl."

"Why all of this?" Val gestured to the apartment, to its luxuries. "It's not necessary."

"Ever heard the expression: you get more flies with honey than vinegar?"

Val paused, brow furrowed. Charlie huffed a laugh.

"Pregnancy is a tricky thing. Cambric found more women get pregnant when they're relaxed and happy than when they're locked up in Isolation. Imagine that."

"I see." Val picked up her glass of wine and sipped from it deliberately.

They resumed eating.

Despite her nerves, the rich food of a home-cooked meal took over Val's senses. Closing her eyes, her thoughts wandered to so many meals shared with Jason in this exact way. The quiet clinking of silverware, the slow progression of tastes and textures, the heat of alcohol as it flowed through her blood. After a while her stomach groaned in full complaint, and she regretted having consumed so much. She pushed her chair back from the table and sighed.

"Who does the dishes?" Val asked.

"We do."

Standing at the sink, Charlie scrubbed the dirty plates with soap, while Val rinsed and dried. With the water running on full, and the sound of the dishes clattering together, they whispered.

"What happens at the end of two or three days when we haven't slept together?" Val asked.

"I don't know, it's never happened." Charlie paused before adding. "But I can imagine it won't be pleasant."

"What are we going to do?"

"Well, I think we should try to stretch it out as long as possible."

"How do you suggest we do that?"

"Let me wine and dine you for a few days. Pretend like it's working. Maybe we'll get extra time because it's you."

"Then what?"

"Then I don't know. We'll just have to face it when it comes."

"Charlie-" Val lay her head on his shoulder, arms next to his in the sink. "I'm so sorry this is happening to you."

"It's happening to you too, Val. It's happening to you, too."

After the dishes had been put away, Charlie directed Val to the bathroom where he turned on the tub. The faucet flowed with hot water. Steam danced in the air. He kept adding bubbles until they overflowed down the sides and onto the white tile floor.

Val undressed and climbed in, then carefully sank down until her entire head was submerged. Pushing back up, she blew out a breath and reclined with her eyes closed. How long had it been since she had experienced such a pleasure? Hot water. She swore as long as she lived she'd never take it for granted again.

On a sigh she opened her eyes and turned her head to look out the open door. Charlie leaned against the frame, arms folded comfortably across his chest. He smiled at her easily, then rapped his knuckles on the doorframe before lifting a book in the air and waving it side to side. Val's eyes lit with a mixture of surprise and amusement. They even had books to read down here, amazing.

"They're still censored." Charlie walked over and handed her the paperback. "But it's better than nothing right?"

"Yeah." Val gripped the book with damp fingers. "You know, you're really good at this."

"Thank you." He winked playfully before turning to go, then hesitated at the doorway, his face turned to one side. "I'm glad I get to do it for you."

Before she could respond, he was gone, leaving her with a melancholy sort of sadness. She was sorry for Charlie. Sorry he had to pretend. Sorry he had to seduce not only free women but captive women as well. Then she was sorry for Gabe and all the others who had ever been forced into this strange fantasy life.

Gripping the sides of the tub, she frowned into her bath water. Millions of tiny bubbles floated along the surface, all of them sparkling. Charlie was right. They should try to forget. They should just live the next few days here and not worry over the impending punishments. Shoving the turmoil from her mind, Val opened the book and began to read.

Later that night they lay down next to one another in the full-sized bed. It wasn't large enough to avoid touching, so after a few attempts to keep to one side, they both gave up. Cambric did not provide pajamas in Breeding. They wanted to encourage nudity in all its forms so Val was left only with her red dress. It was tiny and uncomfortable. The fabric cinched tight around her ribcage, making it hard to breathe deeply.

Sensing her discomfort, Charlie offered her his shirt. For his own part, he wore boxer-briefs and nothing else. The skin of her arm rested up against his, their legs tangled. He complained about her cold feet. She pressed them further into the warmth of his calves. Both of them fell asleep with the hint of a smile tugging at their lips.

In the morning, Val woke first. Opening her eyes, she blinked at the slack sleeping face of the handsome man next to her. Her heart dipped because it wasn't her husband. In the unconsciousness of sleep, his arm had been thrown across her belly. She lay still for a minute, watching the steady rise and fall of his back. Oh, Charlie, she thought. What are they going to do to you? To me? Frowning at herself, she carefully slipped out of bed without waking him.

The window, that was not really a window, shone with an early morning sun. The computer program that controlled it mirrored an actual outdoor experience. The sun tracked throughout the day, rising high towards noon and settling behind distant mountains at sunset. Last night, there had even been stars.

Out in the kitchen, Val opened the pantry and tapped her foot lightly on the hardwood floor. When she was about half-way through making pancakes, Charlie stumbled out and flopped down on the couch. He rubbed at his messy dark hair and stretched his arms wide in a yawn. Not a morning person, apparently.

Val smirked at his grumpy face. Catching her drift, he rolled his eyes and reclined, pulling a soft knit blanket down over himself. She turned her back on him then and filled a mug with steaming hot coffee.

"Cream or sugar?" She asked.

"Black."

"I still can't believe all the food down here." Val brought the cup over to him before moving back to finish breakfast.

"If you really think about it, it makes a lot of sense. They want us to come back here willingly over and over. Sometimes it takes a few months to get pregnant. This is a perk job with perk benefits. If you never got a taste of free life, then this would be pure fantasy land."

"Why not just go artificial?" Val pondered, arranging pancakes and bacon on two large plates.

"The old fashioned way is still the cheapest," Charlie countered. "No fertility treatments, no frozen embryos or semen."

"Good point."

She took a seat at the small table and began eating without him. There was orange juice, fresh berries, even syrup. Val sipped and munched lazily. Still wearing Charlie's oversized shirt, she crossed her bare legs beneath the table.

Charlie shifted around on the couch to watch. When he was done with his coffee, he got up and plopped down across from her before digging in happily.

"So, what do we do all day?"

"I have a surprise." Charlie wiggled his eyebrows, face suddenly mischievous.

"I'm not sure I like the sound of that." Val commented, rising to wash her plate in the kitchen.

When he was done eating, Charlie shoved his plate to the side and stalked after her. Grabbing Val by the wrist, he led her reluctantly back to the bedroom where he teased and cajoled her onto the bed. She sat as instructed, drawing her knees up to her chest.

Leaving her there alone, he returned to the living room, then reappeared with a stack of pillows from the couch. He tossed them at her and she caught them, laughing at the look of conspiracy on his face. What was he up to?

"Ready?" He asked, standing beside the armoire.

"I don't know, am I?"

Stepping in front of it, Charlie pulled the doors open wide. Inside was a flat screen television. Val's mouth dropped.

"That's right," Charlie announced. Fishing through a drawer, he started throwing movies onto the bed. "What do you want to start with? We can watch them all."

"I'm speechless," Val sputtered, then crawled forward to sift through the options.

They were all censored, of course, but they were movies. Real live movies. Entertaining shows that splashed across the screen, promising to take them away from this place and deliver them somewhere else. Anywhere else.

"You've probably seen these a dozen times."

"More like a thousand." He came over and flopped face first on the bed. "But I don't care, I'll watch them all again."

So they did. And it took all day. There were chick flicks

and action movies, black and whites, and full color. Val couldn't remember the last time she had been so completely lazy. For lunch they brought heaping sandwiches with bags of crunchy chips right into the bed. By the time dinner rolled around, her eyes were strained from the effort of watching and her body ached from the lack of movement.

"I'm gonna hop in the shower," Charlie announced, and shoved off the bed.

Alone, Val wandered back out into the kitchen and sighed. Was it really time to cook another meal? She hadn't realized just how spoiled she was. Jason kept a full staff and Cambric had a cafeteria. Thinking back, the only time in her life where she had to cook was with Granny Ida back in Indiana, and then again at Javier's ranch.

Suddenly, Val's heart squeezed tightly inside her chest. She hadn't let herself think of Jace in a long time. Thinking of those places brought him fresh to her mind. What sort of mother did that make her? How could she be here and function without him? How could she go so long without saying his name?

"You alright?" Charlie padded quietly over, white towel wrapped around his waist, hair still wet from the shower.

"Yeah," Val croaked, then covered her face with both hands. "Just let myself think too much."

Charlie nodded somberly once before reaching behind her and yanking open the freezer. The push of cold air had Val stepping away, wiping tears from her eyes. He busied himself collecting bowls and spoons, then plunked an entire pint of ice cream down on the counter. It was double chocolate fudge.

"You can't be serious." Val huffed a bit, fighting a pitying smile that wanted to play on her lips.

"Don't make me eat this all by myself," Charlie chided.

Moving to the couch, they sat huddled together. The bowls, they decided, were unnecessary. Because… *ice cream.* As their spoons dipped over and over again, they talked quietly about their old friends. Their voices were low, barely audible, even to each other.

Val told him about the life Gabe led now. How he made it to that anonymous island somewhere in the vast ocean. How he caught fresh fish and lobster and barbecued it on his very own deck. They shared gossip about Bee and her antics back in the day. Charlie laughed about how Gabe used to sneak back in their room in the mornings. How worn out he had looked after a night in Bee's bed. How that had never stopped him.

Then they talked about Gabe's sons. The ones who played by the pool. Charlie said it was hard to keep track of just who belonged to who, but Gabe's boys resembled him so it made spotting them easier. Val asked for their names, hoping that someday she could share them with Gabe. If she ever made it out. If she ever made it back.

They talked that way together into the dark of night. They talked until every last bite of ice cream was gone and the fake window had a full moon shining brightly inside of it.

CHAPTER 20

THE FOLLOWING DAY, PLAYTIME WAS OVER. AFTER CHARLIE downed his first cup of coffee, and was actually able to speak without frowning, he put Val through her paces. According to him, they had eaten far too much and done far too little over the past two days. The calorie count alone had his inner fitness buff twitching.

Cambric still hadn't supplied Val with any additional clothing, so Charlie lent her his shirt and an extra pair of boxer-briefs. The underwear sagged just a bit, hanging low on her hips.

Breakfast was lean, scrambled eggs and toast. Then the stretching began. They jogged in place, did sit-ups, leg-lifts and various other cardio exercises that ended with Val sweating profusely and clutching at her side. Charlie was all on fire for it though, the sheen on his brow barely glistened.

When he released Val to stop, he just kept right on going.

She left him in the living room, doing push-ups between the sofa and the coffee table. Veering towards the bathroom, she turned on the shower and let the water run.

Everywhere else in Cambric, the showers were tepid at best. Even in the dead of winter they never raised the temperature above a miserable lukewarm. Down here in Breeding, however, the hot water flowed and flowed, seemingly without end.

Val was sticky and uncomfortable already, so she kept the water on the cool side and lingered under the spray. Halfway through her washing, she heard a gentle knock on the door. Charlie let himself in and Val raised her eyebrows at him through the glass partition. Angling her body slightly away, she continued to scrub shampoo into her hair. He came over to lean against the wall next to her, keeping his eyes focused on the wall.

As quietly as possible he murmured to her through the sound of the running water.

"They came in just after you left," Charlie said. "Looks like our time is running out."

Val's stomach dropped and her hands stilled a moment in their careful rinsing. She was afraid of what came next. Afraid because of what she had shared with Gabe. Afraid because of the new rumors of the missing. Swallowing down her fear, she dipped her head once in acknowledgement before continuing in her routine.

"They gave me pills to give you. They want me to offer them to you if I think you'll take them, or slip them in your drink if I think you won't. I'm not going to, obviously."

"What are we going to do?"

"I don't know, but at least we have one more night."

Reaching for the shower door, Charlie opened it a crack and held his hand under the spray. Val glanced down into his open palm and saw the tiny red pills cupped there. Eyes darting up to him once, she placed her hand in his and took what he offered. Down the shower drain they went, slipping away in the mix of steam and spray, unnoticed.

The whole rest of the afternoon was tense. Val tried to keep reading in her book, but struggled to focus. Her mind would drift off, forcing her to re-read the same page again and again. Finally giving up, she tossed the paperback down on the floor and sat up with a frustrated huff. Running her hands through her mass of hair, she let it fall around her shoulders to shield her face.

Charlie, for his part, was the picture of cool. Except for the flash of worry she saw in his hazel eyes, he kept his body relaxed, lounging on the other end of the sofa, sipping on another beer. Drunk might be the way to go, Val thought, analyzing his easy countenance.

Charlie suggested another movie session and they migrated back to the bedroom. Propped up together amongst the pillows, they watched a black and white love story. The music was soft. The character's faces shone in the brightness of the lights. There was a war and the lovers couldn't be together. It had a soft sadness about it that drifted off the screen and filled their bedroom.

When the credits ran, Charlie pulled her up to standing and took her in his arms.

"Let's dance," he suggested, taking her hand in his own.

They swayed quietly in the cramped space. She felt the spread of his palm against the small of her back, it was a comfort offered from a friend. Laying her head on his chest, she listened to the steady tap of his heart, the even expansion of his lungs. If she closed her eyes, she might just believe they were somewhere else entirely.

When the movie came to an end and the music cycled away, they stood there for a while longer, clinging to what remained of their humanity while they still could.

Dinner was rich and full and slow. Charlie made chicken Alfredo pasta with heaping helpings of salad and hot baked rolls. Val slathered on the butter and drunk heavily from her glass of wine. They talked of safe things this time. Of youth, of boarding school, and friends that had been sold away. But after that was all exhausted, they were left with nothing else to say.

Val had a million questions she wanted to ask of him but couldn't risk Cambric listening in. What had he done with his year of freedom? Had he stayed? She thought he had likely fled. But if so, to where?

In silence, they scrubbed up the dishes and tidied the kitchen before climbing into bed. The fake window radiated with moonlight, so it was easy to see that Charlie wasn't sleeping. He lay on his back, eyes blinking up into the ceiling. Val rolled onto her side to face him and ran a comforting hand over his chest. He gave her a quiet sigh, but nothing more.

An hour passed, and then another. Still, sleep did not

come. Val's stomach churned and she shifted restlessly. But all the while Charlie remained outwardly unperturbed. Finally, he rolled onto his side, eyes searching her own. Scooting in close, he pulled the blanket up and over their heads and began to talk.

"I think I have an idea," he whispered.

"What is it?"

"We can fake it."

"Fake what?"

"Having sex," Charlie became earnest. "We keep the covers up and pretend to do it, but don't actually do it."

"You think that'll work?"

"I don't know. But it's worth a shot, right?"

Val nodded, gulping nervously. Charlie pulled the blankets back down so that just their heads were poking out. He placed a wide palm across her hip and gently applied pressure until she lay on her back. Slowly, he maneuvered himself on top of her and spread her legs with his hips.

His body hovered barely an inch above hers. Tilting his head to one side, he exhaled against the tender skin of her neck. For a solid minute, he moved his hips up and down, making sure to shift the blankets but not touch his body to hers.

"You're going to have to play along," Charlie breathed finally. "If they're going to believe we're having sex, you're going to have to moan or something."

"You want me to moan?"

"Hey lady," he hissed. "If we were doing this for real, you'd definitely be moaning. I have a reputation you know."

"Moaning, right." Val swallowed hard.

Closing her eyes briefly, she worked to compose her features. *Fake it. Right.* Charlie brushed whisper kisses along the line of her throat. He didn't actually make contact with her skin, but his breath panted out against her. She could feel it. Ducking her head to the side, she wriggled, trying to avoid the tickling sensation he caused.

Charlie paused and frowned down at her.

"Stop giggling."

"I can't help it." Val's voice was tight in her struggle to keep quiet. "Your fake kisses are tickling my neck."

"Come on, Val." Charlie resumed his movements. "You're better than this."

Eyes locking, Charlie watched her battle to keep composure. She bit down on her lip. He was so serious just then and it struck her suddenly how ridiculous they looked. They were pretending to have sex while Cambric's cameras rolled. This was crazy. They were crazy.

A giggle formed in her throat. She kept it tight, struggling not to release it. Charlie narrowed his eyes. Right when it appeared she was losing the fight and a laugh played out on her lips, Charlie acted. He covered her mouth with his, kissing her into a subdued silence.

He did it to save her. To save them both, she knew.

But that kiss. It sucked the very breath from her lungs. The moment his lips parted hers, they transmitted an electric heat that tore unexpectedly through her system.

Pulling back, Charlie gasped for breath, eyes mirroring her own in momentary shock. Before she could think, she was lifting her head to meet him, kissing him back, wrapping her arms about his neck. Whatever innocent reason they had at the beginning evaporated, leaving nothing but a demanding ache.

He collapsed on top of her, groaning into her mouth. Everywhere their bodies touched seemed to vibrate with sensation. She nipped hurriedly under his chin as his hands smoothed over her hips and up her belly. A real moan, not a fake one, curled itself inside her. It drifted lowly out of her mouth to sweep and stroke at his senses until it shook him suddenly awake.

Shoving back, he sat up abruptly, panting down at her, eyes wide. The blanket fell forgotten behind him.

Subconsciously, he ran a hand over the back of his neck, mouth hanging slightly slack. Val watched him wrestle with something inside himself, watched his eyes take her in. A confusing mix of guilt and lust built within her.

"Charlie?" She raised up just to her elbows, eyes questioning.

His hands snaked down to yank her roughly up against him. Bodies pressed together, Charlie's arms encircled her waist in a possessive embrace. She lay her head on his shoulder, trying to slow the rapid pace of her breathing and wondered at how it matched his so well. Quietly, he kissed the top of her head before murmuring into her hair.

"Is it just me or did that start to feel real?" He paused, rubbing one hand firmly down her back. "Like on the outside real."

She squeezed her eyes shut as the flood of heartache hit her full force. She knew what he meant, knew exactly what he meant. Because the only other time she had ever felt desire like that was with Jason. And the betrayal of it all stung.

"Tell me that it's just me," Charlie whispered. "Tell me you don't feel anything, that you still want to pretend."

Part of her wanted to scream it. *Yes, I am not this person. I don't feel anything for you. I don't want you like that.* But the words caught in her throat. They caught there because they were all lies.

Excuses ran through her head, then. Desperately she tried to make sense of the blurred lines. But she couldn't deny the burn that simmered under her skin where his body met hers. She averted her eyes, but did not let go of him.

Gripping her shoulders in both hands, Charlie held her at arm's length. His eyes sought answers. Unable to give him any, Val traced sad fingers along his cheek. The pain that crossed his face had tears coming to her eyes.

"I can't do it," Charlie announced, scooting back until he stepped off the bed.

"Charlie." Val's eyes darted nervously to the camera up in the corner of their bedroom.

"Get me out of here!" Charlie yelled over his shoulder. "I'm not doing this."

"Please, Charlie," Val pleaded, fear starting to take over.

The front door snapped open and the sound of stomping boots could be heard making their way back to the bedroom. For a moment, Charlie stared at Val, a look of apology filling his face. She shook her head at him. What was he doing? It was going to work. If he just-

Three men entered the already small room, and Shane was among them. Of course he had been watching. He was always watching.

"What's the matter Charlie?" Shane's voice was light, teasing even.

"Just do whatever you have to, I'm not sleeping with her."

"Come on now, we've all seen you do this a hundred times over." Shane reached out to pat him on the shoulder but Charlie stepped quickly away. "Val seems ready, and by the looks of it, you are, too. What do you need? What can we get you?"

"You can get me out of here."

"Do you want something to take the edge off?" Shane motioned to a security guard who pulled a bottle of pills from his pocket.

"No."

"You want someone else to start? Maybe break the ice? I could get Ben-"

"You make me fucking sick," Charlie snapped before turning to Shane and spitting directly into his face.

The next moments had Val leaping down from the bed. She screamed for them to stop. But it was too late.

In an instant the guards had Charlie face down on the floor, jerking his arms up behind his back. Struggling in vain, he wrestled and struck out. One of them stomped at his legs, then started kicking his body. Val could hear Charlie grunt each time a blow landed, but he didn't call out.

Val was screaming and lunging for him, but Shane caught her easily about the waist. He reminded the guards not to do any serious damage, but his voice was monotone and low, only Val could hear it. Swiping the spit off his face, Shane held her tight until the guards dragged Charlie down the hall and out the front door.

"What did you say to him?" Shane jerked Val closer, his fingers digging viciously into one bare arm. "What could you possibly have done to turn him like this?"

"I didn't say anything," Val cried.

"You've done this to him," Shane accused. "Just remember *you* are the one responsible."

With that he released her. She melted into a pile on the floor as he strode out. Covering her face with her hands, Val wept quietly. What Shane said was true. Whatever they were going to do to Charlie, whatever he was about to suffer, it was all her fault.

Then the front door opened once again. Feet stomped in. Val jumped up, listening as cupboard doors popped open, then slammed shut. Things were breaking. Staggering to the end of the hall, Val blinked into the living room. Unbidden, her hands came up to cover her mouth.

Cambric staff was clearing out the kitchen. Every can of food, every box of cereal. The fresh fruit, the meat and the milk. It was all being tossed haphazardly into an array of cardboard boxes, then hauled systematically out the door. They were taking everything. Because one minute you were feasting on steak and wine and the next you were being beaten on the floor.

Shrinking back, Val retreated to the bedroom and buried herself in the blankets. Curling into the tiniest ball possible, she hugged her knees to her chest. The bed still smelled of Charlie, of her and him together. A torturous confusion of emotions spilled out, leaving her wrecked and rocking.

Cambric didn't return Charlie until late the following day. By that time, he was slick with sweat and could barely walk. While he was gone, Val hadn't been able to sleep. When they brought in a tray for her breakfast, she hadn't been able to eat, either. The only thing she was able to do was pace.

Back and forth. Back and forth, the same track was burned into the carpet of the living room. And that was what she was doing when the front door finally swung inward and they half-carried, half-dragged Charlie inside.

Leaving him in a heap on the sofa, the guards made sure to remove her food tray before they left. Val knelt beside him. Her tentative fingers reached out to brush over his drawn face.

Bruises had begun to bloom everywhere. They filled the side of his face, trailed down his body and wrapped around to his back. When she ducked her head to check how far they went, he stayed her hand. His eyes were open, but only partially. He was watching her, a crooked smile working its way onto his face.

"What did they do to you?" She demanded.

"They're running me out."

"What?"

"Running me out. Putting me on the treadmill until I fall down or fall off. Then making me get on again. No food, no water."

Charlie's face contracted in pain and he reached involuntarily for his legs, kneading lamely at the cramps that worked there. Val moved his hands away and began to rub hard with her own until the muscles stopped jumping and his face relaxed.

"You've been running all night long? Since you left here?"

He nodded, then made another attempt at a cocky grin. "It's nothing, I could do this all day."

"With food and water and rest," Val countered, knowing he was in shape, but also knowing that nobody could withstand the strain of such work for more than a few days. "What can I do? Give me something to do."

"Don't suppose you have anything to drink? Or eat?"

"There's water from the sink."

"That's good."

She rushed away from him to the kitchen. Throwing open cupboards, she found a glass and filled it. His hands shook as reached out to take it, spilling a little as he gulped greedily. Before he had downed the entire thing, she took it back. She didn't want to make him sick with the sudden flood all at once. He nodded in understanding and returned his trembling hands to his sides. This time he let her bring the cup to his lips. Slowly, she offered him the water in manageable sips.

"What now?" she asked.

"A cold bath."

Nodding, Val rocked back on her heels and watched while Charlie tried to sit up. His face bunched with the strain but his stomach muscles just wouldn't bring him all the way upright. Stepping to him, she helped roll him onto his side first. With her support, they were able to get him down the hall and into the tub.

She plugged the drain and ran the water all the way to cold. He groaned in protest at first as the water licked at his skin, but after the initial shock, he sighed. Val sat on the floor next to him and watched as he slowly wriggled out of his underwear. Tossing the soaked material over the opposite side, he sank down all the more.

"Why, Charlie?" She asked finally. "Why'd you stop?"

"Because I'm just like you."

Eyes opening to appraise her, he wiggled his left ring finger as it rested against the edge of the tub. She frowned at the implication and he motioned for her to come closer. Leaning over the side of the tub, she held her ear just in front of his lips.

"I'm married," he confessed. "It happened when I was on the outside, that year we were all free."

"Oh, Charlie."

"You know, all these years back here and I've never felt like I cheated on her. Not until last night. Not until I kissed you."

Sucking in a breath, Val tipped back and landed heavily on the floor. She pressed the heels of her hands against her closed eyes. The ache and pain, the desire and guilt, it all mixed to create an agonizing cocktail that permeated her blood.

"I think it would've been fine," Charlie continued quietly. "If I thought I was the only one, but-"

Tears leaked from her eyes, dripping down beneath her hands and tracing salty pathways over her cheeks. Charlie reached out, his hand tugging at her wrists, but she resisted his effort to unmask her. She loved her husband. She loved him so much. But she couldn't deny what had passed between her and Charlie. It hurt so bad. She hated herself.

"We didn't do anything," Charlie persuaded. "We stopped it before it really started. We didn't do anything."

"But now what?" Val sniffed. Dropping her hands, she

stared at him. "We let them run you into nothing? Starve you? Beat you? What's the cost Charlie?"

"You have to promise you won't try to convince me."

"Don't say that."

"You have to promise me."

"At what cost?"

"If I ever make it out of here, if I ever make it back to her, then I want to say I've been as faithful to her as a D2 possibly could. And you get to say that to Jason, right?"

"Charlie-"

"If you tell me that you want me, if you ask me to be with you, I'm not going to be able to say no."

"What will it matter if you're dead?!" She hissed, voice on the verge of shrieking. "What happens if you're the next one that gets hauled out and doesn't come back?"

Shoulders lifting in a casual shrug, he dismissed her. Like he didn't care if he lived or died. Like he didn't care if they came and took him away in the middle of the night, never to return.

The rage that filled her had her rising to her feet. Val paced angrily away from him, then back. The feeling shot out impulses that jerked to her extremities. Whirling on him, she stared at his pitiful form sunk in the water.

"You're trying to make me angry," she announced. "You're trying to make me mad at you. Well it's not going work. If it was me being tortured and you had to watch, then you'd already be kissing me."

His eyes flashed with the truth of what she said, and the memory from the night before lingered a moment too long. Turning his head away, he shifted uncomfortably in the tub.

"And maybe the awful truth is that I do care about you," she continued. "And I don't want to force you into being with me. But maybe I can even things out."

"What are you talking about?" His eyes snapped to hers.

"I'm not eating unless you eat. Whenever they take you out to run you, I won't have anything to drink. They want the process sped up, well let's see how long we both last like that."

CHAPTER 21

Three more days. They were able to last another three days with each getting progressively worse. Cambric ran Charlie at all hours. Whenever he was gone, the guards delivered Val a tray of food. Staunchly, she refused to eat. While he was away from their apartment, she refused to drink.

On Charlie's end, the exercise sped up his deterioration considerably. When they returned him to her, he was in turns delirious and non-responsive. His lips were dry and cracked, his joints achy and he was unsteady on his feet. More than once Val swore he simply passed out altogether, but she couldn't be sure because he would come back around so fast.

Val herself was dizzy and often times irritable. The pangs of hunger in her stomach were relentless. Each day that passed it became more of a challenge not to eat. After all, the meals were placed so easily before her. But she wouldn't do it. She wouldn't cave this time, not with Charlie suffering for her the way he was.

When he wasn't being run, they laid together in bed. In the background, they let the television play out all the old movies again. Charlie held her hand. Rubbing his thumb absently across her knuckles he kept the contact but did no more than that. If she was being honest with herself, even that steady touch now felt like a betrayal.

Shane began to make appearances. First, he demanded that Val eat. Then he demanded she persuade Charlie to have sex. On both counts, Val remained unmoved, even in the face of his fierce persistence and vague threats.

Early on, she realized something was holding him back. If he was running out Charlie, why not Val, too? Though Shane implied violence and often shoved her to her knees when they talked, he never followed through. In some way she seemed physically untouchable to him, like she had her own set of rules.

It didn't really make much of a difference if they hurt her or not though. The things they did to Charlie were punishment enough. It destroyed Val to see how he suffered. If she wanted to end it, she could do so with relative ease. All she had to do was seduce Charlie. And he had already admitted he would cave to her.

The only thing holding her back now was her respect for him. She didn't want to force him. Just like he hadn't been willing to force her. But between her own increasing weakness and his, the reasons not to give in were becoming increasingly less important.

Soon survival would take over, and keeping Charlie alive would mean more than respecting his feelings. It would mean more than the look of hate she feared would take over his face if she violated his trust. Hate at her for seducing him, hate at himself for wanting it.

That evening, Shane entered their apartment and found them listless together on the bed. Instead of removing Charlie, he motioned for security to take Val. As she walked demurely behind them, she could hear Charlie protest. But that was the most he could manage. Already, he was too far gone to do more than sit up in bed.

Out in the living room, she heard his attempt to stand. It ended in a few stumbling steps and a hollow thud as his body hit the floor. She winced.

"How long are you going to let him take the heat for you?"

Shane folded his arms in front of his chest and watched as she swayed slightly on her feet. Val raised a hand to her head in an attempt to stop the throbbing. She made no answer.

"You have an appointment tomorrow. We need you to eat and undergo a full prep. Do we need to tube you?"

"If you tube feed me, then it still won't help with the prep work."

"We can force you to dress. Do we need to strap you down?"

"I don't care what you do to me."

Shane exhaled in frustration before studying her closely. Val blinked vacantly, her mind struggling to focus. She didn't want to be tube fed. She didn't want it at all. But she'd have them do it to Charlie if she could. Thoughts were slow in coming. It was hard to make connections.

"I want something and you want something." Shane waited for Val to respond, then snapped his fingers in front of her face. "Seems we should be able to make some kind of a deal."

Val's brow furrowed. No words came to mind. Shane rolled his eyes.

"Val, what do you want?"

"I want you to feed Charlie."

"We want you to eat and undergo prep."

Her eyes brightened for a split second before narrowing up at him. Why would Shane agree to this? Tomorrow's appointment must be pretty important if they were willing to negotiate.

"You will feed Charlie today?"

Shane nodded solemnly.

"And stop the running?"

"You must eat and submit to prep. Go to this appointment tomorrow and Charlie gets food and rest. But you need to understand one thing. Eventually we'll get right back to this point.

When you return from your appointment, if you want to save him, then you need to convince him to have sex. Whatever war you two think you're waging, you're only hurting each other. I go home every night and I eat well."

"Now?" Val asked. "You'll bring us food right now?"

Shane nodded, then reached out a hand and ran it through the length of her dark hair. He rolled the soft strands between his fingers a moment before letting go. Spinning on his heel, he motioned towards the camera before leaving the apartment.

Within ten minutes two trays heaping with food were delivered straight to their bedroom. Val propped Charlie up with pillows and fed him bits of scrambled egg with a fork. He moaned and choked and sputtered in turn. Every other bite she gave him, she took one for herself.

For several minutes they soaked up the insane flood of energy that each bite gave. It was like a shot of adrenaline straight to the system. After days without food, their stomachs had shrunk and it didn't take much to leave them feeling queasy. Nevertheless, Val swore she could feel her body rushing to put the calories to work.

Setting the trays on the floor, Val crawled into bed and wrapped her arms around Charlie's waist. He covered her hand with his own, letting his chin rest near the top of her head. Both of them fell into a deep sleep.

She woke to the gentle stroke of his hand along her face. Opening her eyes, Val smiled at him. Charlie was sitting up in bed next to her, eating more food from one of the trays. Exhaling a breath of relief, she crept up beside him and picked over a muffin. For a long while, they didn't say anything at all. They just ate.

"What did you have to do to get this food?" He asked finally.

"I have an appointment tomorrow," Val explained. "We both eat and I submit to prep."

"What kind of appointment?"

"I don't know."

"You didn't promise we'd sleep together, did you?"

"I didn't promise it."

"You understand why we can't right?"

"You don't want to cheat. Neither do I."

"And I don't want to fall in love with you." Charlie tipped her chin towards him, searching her eyes. "You think it would be just once? You think we wouldn't have to sleep together over and over?"

"Charlie-"

"Listen." He was adamant. "If I had you once, then I'd want you again. And if I had you again, then it'd never be enough. What happens when you have my baby inside you? What happens when Jason wins this lawsuit and you go back to your husband? Or worse, what happens if he loses the lawsuit and you stay with Cambric forever? Then I'd have to watch every day they sent you to a client. I'd have to stand back and let other men, countless men, have you. I couldn't do it. Don't make me do it."

"Stop." Val's heart split. "Just stop."

"I'm sorry."

He gathered her onto his lap, then. She tucked her face against his chest and held back the tears that wanted so desperately to fall.

"Tell me about *her*," she whispered, and felt him soften. "Tell me all about her."

Keeping his voice low, he did.

He told her about making a break from Cambric, walking to a bus stop and begging for change until he had enough to board. There were kindhearted people who took pity at first, then odd jobs here and there. He worked for cash under the table; washing dishes in roadside cafes, picking fruit in vast farmer's fields, working construction in small lazy towns.

About three months in, he had stocked away enough money to afford a fake identity. He bought a dead man's social security number and was suddenly certifiably free. With legitimate papers, he found solid work. It paid more so he bought himself an old car. And that's how he met her.

The car quit on the side of a two-lane highway, and for all the skills he had picked up, mechanic work hadn't been one of them. She drove past him at first. He remembered her car because he glanced up from under the hood and noticed the music that pumped from the open windows.

"She must have liked what she saw." He chuckled to himself. "Because she turned right around and came back, offered me a ride. That was it."

"And you married her?"

"Oh yeah. And I would a thousand times over, given the chance."

"Does she know where you are?"

"No." Charlie stiffened a bit.

"You mean you didn't tell her? You mean she doesn't know you're a captive? A D2?"

"I wasn't any of those things, then. And I never wanted to be again. By the time Cambric began prosecuting people for harboring its old captives, it was already too late. I couldn't tell her."

"So where does she think you are?"

"She thinks that I'm a drifter who couldn't sit still another minute."

"You walked out."

"I protected her."

"She thinks you stopped loving her."

Charlie shrugged out from under Val's arms and scooted to the end of the bed. Without looking back, he rose to his feet and stomped his way into the bathroom. The door snapped shut and the shower flipped on.

For a while Val sat still and listened to him bathe. She could hear the random bump of his elbow against the stall, then the squeeze and tap of soap bottles being used.

All captives were affected by their condition differently, though most of them handled the confinement fairly well. Then again, Val thought, that might be a misconception. Maybe captives were just better at hiding things. They were able to distance themselves more quickly, but not necessarily more effectively.

Gabe had a secret vasectomy, Val lied about taking birth control, Charlie walked out on the love of his life, Bee gave away all of her money. They each did these things in secret, not wanting to draw attention. Each decision was a way to exert a measure of control in a life that had always been lived without any.

By the time Charlie got out of the shower, Val had snuggled back down in bed. He drank deeply from a glass of water. She could hear him sigh and gasp. Lifting the corner of the covers, he crawled in beside her and looped an arm around her waist. She let him pull her up against him, knowing they would never speak of his wife again.

For the first time in days, her belly was satisfied and her throat didn't ache from thirst. The sound of his even breathing lulled her, calming any looming thoughts that threatened. She dropped down into slumber with him, not caring what the next day would hold.

And the next day held plenty.

In the morning, Val refused to leave Charlie, so Cambric was forced to bring in food as well as her prep team. Grumbling under his breath, Shane stabbed at her with those cold eyes of his. He wasn't used to giving in to any type of demand and she would pay for this. She could recognize it again, now that her mind had enough food and rest to function properly.

Whatever the reason Shane was holding back, there would come a time when he would be loosed. Fear snaked itself once more in her system, but she fought it. She fought it so that Charlie could have breakfast *and* lunch. She fought it to make certain they wouldn't run him again. But in the end, she would be punished. There was no doubt about that.

For his part, Charlie lounged on the sofa and surveyed the spectacle. He had his own version of prep, but it wasn't nearly the production that a female D2 received. They bade her shower and wash her hair before they blew it dry and styled it down. Her nails were painted, lotion was applied to her skin and a copious amount of makeup was slathered across her face.

They were trying to cover the dark circles that hung under her eyes and distract from the odd color that lack of food will leave on your skin. With their infinite products and years of practice, they succeeded.

Val received a clean thong and matching lace bra. They outfitted her in a miniscule grey skirt and professional white blouse. The buttons were left undone near the top so as to accentuate her chest. Next, she slipped into sheer stockings that ended high on her thighs, the tops of which were secured to a garter.

Stepping into four-inch black patent heels, she locked eyes with Charlie who frowned in concern as they fluffed and sprayed her hair. Who was she being prepped for? What type of appointment was this? She looked like a business woman on her way to meet a lover.

With the transformation complete, the prep team departed, and Cambric security came to collect their charge. Val threw a last glance over her shoulder at Charlie, who closed his eyes and turned his face away. The door locked shut behind them.

It took four hours to get there. Four hours of silent driving in a tinted sedan before they made it into the city. Val's stomach had twisted itself into knots all the while because Shane sat like a stone in the front seat. She had one security guard on her right and another on her left. Cramped and uncomfortable, Val's pulse sky-rocketed as she recognized their route.

When they pulled up in front of the courthouse, she blanched. Sucking in a breath, she could only imagine who would be waiting for her inside.

And suddenly she realized why they wanted her to eat. Now she knew the reason Shane had agreed to stop running Charlie if she submitted to prep. It was the media. They were everywhere and they were hungry.

Outside her door, they swirled and swelled as the Cambric car idled at the curb. Val's makeup was thick and expertly done, her clothing was expensive and fit perfectly. No one would see what they had done to her. No one would ever know what they had done to Charlie.

As the first hulking security guard threw open the door, people began to rush and shout. He braced against the tide as Shane exited and came back to help Val from the car. Keeping his face full of smiles and charm, Shane hid the chill that so often clouded his eyes.

Val rose from the sedan when beckoned and walked obediently at his side. He held her hand loosely in his own, waving casually to his left, then over to his right. The other security guard brought up the rear.

Once inside the courthouse, the attention ceased. It was crowded, but in the way that courthouses always were. People were distracted, hurriedly going about their own business. They didn't care who was in line behind them, only what lay just ahead.

Instead of taking the elevator to the floors which housed the courtrooms, Shane directed them toward an administrative wing. Val listened to the click of her own heels as they cruised down the narrow hallways. At the end, they reached a receptionist desk.

A plump woman with spectacles on the end of her nose blinked up at them expectantly, then tapped at an old boxy computer. Shane explained they were checking in for a court supervised medical evaluation and she waved them through a heavy wooden door.

On the other side was yet another hallway with rooms off to the right and left. This place was a labyrinth within a labyrinth. Eventually they stopped at the numbered door indicated by the receptionist and one of the security guards knocked briefly before entering.

The room was large. Much larger than the meeting room at Cambric. It contained one long conference table with many matching black chairs lined up all around it. Perhaps there were twenty all together, Val thought. Her eyes avoided the other faces in the room. She didn't want to see them now. Not really.

And anyway, it was just a repeat from before. Agent Finn, a police officer, Jason, his father and attorneys, the same nurse, they were all sitting. Sitting and staring. Well… except for Jason. Jason was standing.

She couldn't bring herself to look him in the eye. How could she after the things she had done? The things she was going to do?

"Val-" Agent Finn cleared his throat and gestured to a chair across from him. "Please have a seat."

Val kept her eyes focused on the toes of her impossibly shiny shoes. She could almost see her own reflection in them. Shane continued to hold her hand and she did not tug it away.

There was a hushed whispering, fierce in its intensity, and Val knew in her gut that it was Jason. Flicking her eyes up briefly, she watched him sit down hard next to Agent Finn and lean in close, hissing. Agent Finn merely held up a hand to gain instant silence.

"Release her." Agent Finn gritted his teeth on the words. "And play by the rules set forth by the court, or so help me I will kick you out of this session, too."

Letting go of her hand, Shane stepped forward and pulled out the chair indicated by Agent Finn. After a moment's hesitation, Val smoothed at her skirt and sat. She kept her hands folded together in her lap. Stomach churning with guilt, she wished more than anything to flee this room. The heat of her husband's gaze was upon her. She could feel his eyes as if they touched her very skin.

Swallowing hard, she shoved back the emotions that wanted to erupt. Shane took a seat next to her, with Cambric security remaining standing just behind.

"Do you know why you're here?" Agent Finn spoke to Val, and the others listened.

Pursing her lips together, Val tilted her head to one side and sought Shane's approval. It was a movement not lost on the rest of the room. An undercurrent of murmuring broke out, then fell away.

Shane was a lot of things, but he was not a stupid man. He didn't give her an answer. He didn't give her any indication either way. For this question, she was on her own.

"No," Val whispered it, so used to whispering these days with Charlie. The sudden thought of him made her want to throw up.

"Have you been made aware of any of the proceedings regarding your status as a conscription captive?" Finn again.

"No."

"So you were never told that an injunction filed by Jason Riggs on your behalf was granted by the court?"

"No."

"It was never a requirement of the court that she be notified." Shane cut in, drawing a warning glare from Finn.

"Were you told that you did not have to see clients?"

Val twisted her fingers together in her lap. They just didn't understand, and how could they? It didn't matter what court order was granted, or what posturing went on here today. She would leave in the custody of Shane. And Shane would make her pay for every question she answered.

It wasn't worth it anymore. She no longer cared about the truth, or what they knew or didn't know. The thought of admitting to what had gone on over the past week alone had her throat growing tight. So she turned her face to Shane and reached for his hand.

"Can you take me home?" She asked.

Shane rewarded her with an expansive smile.

Shoving back from his chair, Jason tried to stand up, but Senior managed to grab him and yank him back down. Agent Finn's face hardened, his broad shoulders tensing underneath his jacket. The nurse and a few attorneys began to scribble notes.

"I wish I could," Shane told her. "But this is a court mandated examination and you must participate until Agent Finn releases you."

"You. Out." Finn pointed to the two security guards, then lowered his finger to zero in on Shane. "You, too. Wait in the hall."

"I've broken none of the stipulations!" Shane was outraged.

"Your mere presence here is clearly an influence," Agent Finn countered. "And for some damn reason the judge in this matter thinks that I'm his personal errand boy. And my *boss* somehow agrees. Babysitting you all is not what I want to be doing, but it *is* what I'm required to do, so you'll have to defer to my opinion."

"He's just as much of an influence as I am!" Shane stood, pointing an accusing finger at Jason. "If I'm out, then he should be, too."

"At some point, he may get kicked out," Agent Finn conceded. "But not at the moment."

Angrily, Shane departed. The two Cambric guards followed in his wake.

After the door clicked shut, Jason got up from his chair and skirted the table. Nobody stopped him. He rushed towards her. Val could see him out of the corner of her eye.

With each step he took, panic ratcheted up inside her. He would know. If he touched her, Jason would know the truth. How she denied him a baby, but was soon going to have one with someone else. How her body responded to that someone else.

As soon as he neared, she shot to her feet and tried to move away. She shoved at the black chair, clutched at her clothes, ducked her head.

Her actions hit Jason like a ton of bricks. He stopped dead in his tracks. Arms going slack at his sides, his face drained of color. She could feel the unending hurt that rolled off of him.

"Easy." She heard Agent Finn say. Glancing up, she saw him hold a steadying hand in Jason's direction. "Go easy."

Jason's sharp intake of breath seemed magnified in the tight silence of the room. Still avoiding his eyes, Val stole glances of him in her peripheral vision. She could see him run his hands over his face once before taking a seat.

More than anything, she could *feel* him try to calm down. Call it instinct, or an old familiarity they had once shared. It hadn't really been so long ago that she was his wife. When did she start to not feel that way anymore? Like she didn't deserve him, or their son.

Her chest heaved at the thought of Jace. She couldn't breathe. Her heart ached and twisted deep in her chest. Squeezing her eyes shut, she pushed him down. Way down inside her until he wasn't hardly there at all. If she let herself miss him, then she'd spiral away. There'd be no coming back.

"This nurse is here to complete her examination from before," Agent Finn was still talking. "You need to answer her questions honestly. We are no longer at Cambric. There are no cameras to record you or people listening to what you say. Everything here is confidential. Cambric will never find out about it. Do you understand?"

"Yes." Val nodded.

The nurse brought her medical bag over and settled herself beside Val. She again took all the particulars, noting that Val had lost another five pounds. All the while, Jason sat directly behind her, a few chairs back. Val could feel his stare. It bored into the back of her head, making her in turns uncomfortable and sad.

Then the questions began again, but by the nurse this time.

"Have you been locked in a room by yourself for longer than twelve hours?"

"No."

"Have any meals been withheld from you?"

"No."

"Have you been forced into sexual relations with anyone?"

"No."

"Can you explain why you continue to lose weight?"

Val hesitated, thinking over her answer carefully. She had to give them some sort of response, because no answer at all would trigger further digging by Finn. At the same time, she didn't want to go into detail about her time with Charlie, not in front of Jason.

"I chose not to eat," Val offered finally.

"Why would you do that?"

Again, Val paused. Her mind whirled, trying hard to come up with a satisfactory, yet vague, response. Jason twisted in his position behind her, she could hear him. The squeak of the chair. The brush of fabric against leather.

Glancing over her shoulder, she saw him motioning to Finn, who again held up a hand. Jason went silent. They must have some sort of agreement, she realized. But she let herself linger in her appraisal of him a beat too long. Those arctic eyes swept back to lock with hers, the desperation ran clear in them.

Quickly, she looked away and Agent Finn took over the questioning.

"Have you been locked in a room with another person for any length of time?"

Val sighed, wringing her hands. She had forgotten just how thorough and astute Agent Finn was. His questioning sessions had often gone on for hours during the height of their original case together. She maneuvered her chair back to face him and finally brought her eyes to stare levelly into his.

"Yes," she admitted.

"Was the other person male?"

"Yes."

"How many hours would you estimate you were locked in the room with him?"

"Not hours. Days. Three days," she corrected. Jason sucked in a breath. "Then he came and went for another three, but I stayed."

"Was he a client?" Agent Finn asked. "Because you aren't supposed to be seeing clients by order of the court."

"He is not a client."

"Who is he?"

"Another captive."

"Can you explain to us what's going on?" Agent Finn coaxed as gently as possible, eyes fixed on hers. "Because the rest of us will never be able to help you, or anyone else, if someone doesn't step up and explain it. Will you be that person, Val?"

"I will." Val held Finn's gaze. "But only if *he's* not in here."

Agent Finn didn't respond immediately. He knew who she was talking about. And so did everyone else.

"Please." Jason jumped into the silence. Getting out of his chair, he closed the distance between them and crouched beside her. "I can take it. I can, I swear. Don't make me leave."

Tentatively, he reached out, ran his fingers through her hair, tugged gently at the ends. It was a reminder of their once easy connection. And a painful reminder at that.

Closing her eyes, she flashed to Shane and Ben, to Peter and Charlie, to all the men who had touched her and kissed her since she had vowed to belong only to Jason. She thought of the one who had made her want things, things she shouldn't want. She was a bad wife. A terrible person.

"Don't." Val pushed him away before stumbling out of the

chair. "Don't touch me. I can't be with you anymore; don't you understand that?"

"No." Jason shook his head, rising to his feet. "I don't understand."

Pacing away from him, Val sought escape but found none. Agent Finn hadn't released her, Shane was waiting just outside the door. Burying her face in her hands, Val faced the wall and leaned her forehead against it.

Sucking in oxygen, she squeezed her eyes shut. Just behind her, she could sense Jason's approach. He was slow, measured. His energy hovered and collected at her back.

Placing his hands gently on her arms, he rotated her around to face him, but she kept her face covered. Her skin tingled beneath his touch. She heard Finn issue a warning, then go silent as Jason pulled her hands away to carefully study her face.

Finally beaten, she let him get a long look. Eyes shining with guilt and heartache, she felt him cup her chin, run a thumb gently over her lips.

"I love you," he said simply. "No matter what you think you've done, or what they've done to you. I will never give up on you. I will never stop fighting to bring you home. To your *real* home. With me and our son. Tell us what's going on. Please, Val. Please."

"I'm in the breeding program," Val answered, and watched his face turn ashen.

CHAPTER 22

The moment she let the phrase fall from her lips, the room erupted in sound. The nurse scrawled notes and murmured to herself. Senior growled at the lawyers he was paying so much for. They answered back, flipping through papers.

All the while, Agent Finn sat resolutely silent in his chair, watching. Val was still backed up against a wall, with Jason's hands stroking reassuringly at her cheeks. He nodded to her, as if to say, see I'm still here. But she knew he didn't quite get it, and she feared it wouldn't take him much longer to get there.

"The son of a bitch can't sell her to clients, so he puts her in breeding?" Senior was furious, slapping his hand down on the table.

"I don't see how we missed that in the injunction." One attorney was saying, as the others scrambled for their phones. "It covers all forced sexual encounters."

"The breeding program wouldn't be covered under the

injunction if the sex was consensual." Agent Finn's voice was low, but steady.

All others fell instantly away.

"That's enough," Jason said, not taking his eyes off his wife.

"How are they getting your consent?" Agent Finn persisted. "Is that why you stopped eating?"

Val's mind flashed to Charlie, strung out and hungry, exhausted from running all night long. Closing her eyes briefly, she opened them again to the discerning stare of her husband. Jason was remembering things, too. Long ago things she had confessed to him about Cambric's effective punishments for Gabe and herself.

"You know him." Jason watched her expression. "Are they starving him?"

She nodded, eyes brimming uncontrolled.

"What's his name?"

She shook her head no, then gripped his wrists tightly in her hands.

"Why won't you tell me?" Jason asked almost to himself, she could see him thinking. "You're protecting him… from me. Have you slept with him, Val?"

"No." She whispered it, eyes pleading, she began to shake. "Not yet."

"Ah." Jason grimaced as understanding washed over him. "How long do you have?"

"I don't know," she choked. "I have to convince him."

"*Convince* him? What kind of sick game do they have you playing?"

"I don't want to cheat on you," she pleaded.

"Cheat?" He paused, thumbs still stroking the skin of her cheeks. "Have they got you wanting him? Is that it?"

He was so close, his face barely inches from hers, with his strong hands steadying either side of her face. Even though she wanted to, she couldn't look away. His intelligent eyes absorbed her own, and the miserable truth that lay there. Finally, she let go of his wrists, hands falling slack at her sides.

"No," he whispered. Wrapping his arms around her body, he pulled her tightly against him. "Don't you let you go. I'm not letting go."

Tilting her face up with his fingertips, he pressed his lips to hers, kissing softly. At first, she didn't respond. It hurt too badly. But he remained undaunted, continuing to apply his mouth to hers until she parted her lips for him and kissed back.

One hand shifted around her neck, his long fingers curling in her hair. The other hand worked its way around her body, holding her in close against him. The heat of love that flowed from him overwhelmed her senses. How could she have forgotten what this felt like?

"Do you want to have his baby?" He broke the kiss, whispering it.

"No." She was adamant, hands shooting up to grip the collar of his shirt.

He shifted then, ever so smoothly, creating just a hint of space between them. Val could hear the others talking in the background, they were arguing. Jason tugged on the front of her shirt where it tucked into her waist. Lifting the material, she felt him expose her skin. Then all of a sudden, a pinching sharp pain stabbed her. She gasped in surprise.

"Shhhh," Jason soothed, and the pain stopped. "No more babies, right?"

"No more babies," she repeated, realizing he had just injected her with another dose of birth control. "Thank you."

Laying her head on his chest, she exhaled slowly while he worked to tuck her shirt back in unnoticed. What a wretched miserable wreck her life had become. And for what?

The stress of it all came on and her knees buckled. Jason held her upright, but called out for help. The nurse got to them first and they eased Val down in a nearby chair.

"When's the last time you ate something?" The nurse asked, holding Val's wrist limply between her own fingers as she timed her pulse.

"This morning."

"And before that?"

"A few days."

"Let's get some food in here," Jason demanded.

One of the lawyers scurried out while the rest of them resumed their debate. How much of this could they report to the court? What effect would it have on Val in the meantime? Should they change their strategy? Admit to the Kelly Martin identity and argue that Jace was born to a non-captive?

The room went back and forth. The nurse returned to her notes. Jason hovered, face awash with concern. Agent Finn's expression was serious, unreadable.

When the lawyer returned with a sandwich, Shane and the security guards came back inside with him. Instantly the room boiled with renewed tension. Shane pointed out that the court's time limit had been reached, then demanded he resume custody of Val. As before, the dialogue escalated quickly. Both sides found themselves yelling and making threats.

Through it all, Val focused on the sandwich. It smelled of hot baked bread and turkey, there was even a hint of Swiss cheese in the air. Her mouth flooded with saliva. She yearned to unwrap it from its crinkling white paper.

Reaching her hands out, she had to lean up from her seat to just grasp the edge of the plate and pull it towards her along the table. Agent Finn was the only one who watched her now. His eyes were calculating, but reserved. Quickly, she unwrapped one side and took a massive bite. The flood of taste erupted over her tongue as she chewed, a soft moan escaped her mouth.

But one bite was all she got before Shane was grabbing her arm, yanking her up beside him. What happened next was a blur of motion.

The two security guards had entered the room after their boss, and one of them was still stuck behind an attorney. Shane had ranged out in front of them in his effort to get to Val, so when he grabbed her, he was at least three yards away from his normal hulking protection. It was as if Jason had been waiting all his life for this particular moment. He moved fast. Faster than Val could even blink, and slammed his fist directly into the center of Shane's face.

Val rocked back with the shared impact, until Shane's hand sprung open and released his grip. Then Jason was on top of him, smashing Shane into the ground, hitting him over and over. A look of pure satisfaction transformed his handsome face.

For a split second, Val stood over the pair of them in absolute shock. But then Cambric security was pushing past her, diving on the pile in an attempt to rescue Shane. Val tipped to one side as the police officer followed suit. Stumbling back, she glanced over her shoulder and looked directly into Agent Finn's face.

He grabbed her arm and hauled her hurriedly from the room. Down the corridor they went, out past the receptionist and into a bathroom. He released her then, and jogged to each stall, slamming open the doors to make certain they were empty. Taking his phone out of his pocket he placed it into a sink and turned on the water to flow over it.

"Finn?" Val blinked at him, wondering what was going on.

"I told you before that I couldn't help you." Finn dug around in his pocket and produced a thin black box, one that resembled a cell phone in every way, except that it wasn't one. "And I had to do my job returning you to Cambric."

"I know." Val nodded as Finn took her right forearm and pressed the box to her skin just above where the tracker lay.

"But if I have to watch that psycho put his hands on you one more time, then I might have to try to kill him myself."

"You let Jason do it," Val gaped. "You let him hit Shane."

"Hell yeah I did," Finn acknowledged, the black box beeped once and he shoved it back into his pocket.

"What are you doing? What is that?"

"I can't help you myself," Finn qualified. "But it turns out that I know a gal. We don't have much time. Just remember what I'm about to tell you, okay?"

"Okay."

"Be patient and trust the process. Can you do that?"

"Be patient?"

"And trust the process, Val."

"What did you do to my scanner? Will they know?"

"It will open doors and function just the same." Finn glanced to the door of the bathroom, then back to her. "But instead of turning cameras on, it turns them off, and there won't be any record that you were there."

"You've hacked it."

"Do *not* tell anyone about this. Got it?"

"Okay."

"No one."

"Alright!" Val twisted her fingers in worry. "I won't."

"And when you get where you're going," Finn said finally. "Tell Ava hi for me."

Ava? The name was a question forming on Val's lips, but before she could utter it, Agent Finn had retrieved his phone and was marching her back out the door.

Waiting at the end of the hall was Cambric security, and a very pissed off Shane. When they spotted Val, she could hear him growl. The sound had her trembling under Agent Finn's touch. His eyes darted to her once, then away.

"Where have you been?" Shane demanded, his face was swollen, dried blood was smeared beneath his nose.

"I removed her from harm's way, then she had to use the bathroom," Agent Finn explained, releasing his hand from her elbow.

"I want to press charges." Shane's left eye was a tiny slit, the skin had already begun to turn blue.

"That sort of thing involves a lot of paperwork."

"I don't care."

"Well, I'm sure we can get started on it here, but it could take a few hours. We'll have to order in some dinner."

Shane sneered at the implication. He understood what Agent Finn was trying to accomplish. Stall him long enough to feed Val. There was no way Shane was going to let that happen.

Turning to the two security guards, he instructed one to stay with him and the other to escort Val back to Cambric. He would either stay overnight in the city or call for another vehicle, depending. Making sure that Agent Finn overheard, he told the guard in charge not to stop for food.

"Straight back," Shane stated. "No stops."

"Yes, Sir."

The guard nodded his head before wrapping a massive paw around Val's arm and taking her away.

The drive back to Albany was a slow one, full of hunger both physical and emotional. Val slumped by herself in the backseat, absently watching the sunset through the thick window. The tint made everything darker, more purple, unnatural even.

And that was exactly how Val felt, unnatural, out of sorts. She rubbed at the place her tracker lay just beneath her skin. Catching herself, she tore her hand away, eyes darting to the front seat. But no one was paying any attention. The driver drove and the guard played on his phone.

Val had promised Agent Finn that she wouldn't tell a soul about his manipulation of the tiny device, but she knew in her heart she couldn't keep it from Charlie. As soon as they let her back in to see him, she would whisper her news in his ear.

If somehow, someway Val was going to get out of Cambric, then she had to take Charlie with her. She couldn't leave him there, not after everything that had gone on. Her blood picked up a bit at the thought of him, then regret came to follow, knowing she shouldn't feel that way. Pinching at the bridge of her nose, Val willed her mind blank, tired of fighting with herself and everyone else.

When they pulled into the front drive of Cambric, night had fallen. It was dark. There was no moon. The crowds that Val had seen gathered before were no longer there. Even earlier in the day, when they first left for the city, there hadn't been one protestor around. Val wondered if the gunfire from before had anything to do with it.

The driver pulled into the garage and parked in a designated slot. Her guard walked her as far as the door leading back to Cambric before passing her off to someone else. His shift was over and he was ready to go home.

Val held her forearm out for the new Cambric security, who happened to be a woman. She was short, but fit, with toned shoulders that were highlighted beneath her collared shirt. Glancing briefly at the electronic display of her reader, she took Val by the elbow and guided her down a hall and out into the courtyard. They crossed towards the low front building and beeped inside, then all the way back into Isolation. Val's stomach clenched with hunger and she trembled slightly with raw nerves.

"I think there's been some sort of mistake," Val said, as the guard motioned her inside the cell.

"Not a lot of mistakes around here." The guard muttered, pushing at Val's back firmly.

"I'm supposed to be in Breeding." Val stepped reluctantly into the room, then turned to face her guard.

"Take it up with the next shift, I'm done in another few hours."

"Please," Val pleaded. "May I have something to eat? They were supposed to start feeding me again."

"I'm sorry that's not on the reader."

"What about water? May I have a drink of water?"

Frowning, the guard shook her head no before swinging the door shut. Val's shoulders sagged in defeat. She had wanted to see Charlie, to tell him what had happened. She was sure there would be food again in their apartment, now that she had made a deal with Shane.

The weight of it all, the overwhelming blend of exhaustion and emotion was simply too much. She sat on the concrete floor in the middle of the room and cradled her head in her hands.

A minute later the door swung open again, but this time, Val didn't lift her gaze. Suddenly her neck was too weak and her head too heavy to bother. It was the female guard again. She cleared her throat and set something down on the floor before retreating back out and locking it.

When curiosity finally weaved its way into Val's mind, she straightened to find a single bottle of water and yellow bag of chips. The labels were ones she had seen many times on the outside, but they weren't brands stocked by Cambric.

Crawling over to them, Val twisted the cap off and chugged at the cool rush of liquid. No water had ever tasted quite so good. It was fresh and sweet, like a song that ran over her tongue instead of into her ears. About halfway through the bag of salty chips, Val realized what the guard had done. She had given Val this food out of her own lunch.

The small act of kindness was almost more than she could bear. When she finished with the meager meal, she took a few steps towards the thin mattress that was shoved into the corner. Collapsing down onto it, she fell into a fitful sleep.

"Get up."

The command was firm, but otherworldly. It snaked itself into Val's sleeping brain, stirring her mind to reach for wakefulness. She didn't want to wake up though, not yet. Her body was heavy, so heavy, and her thoughts were long and drawn out. But then someone was shoving at her shoulder, and the command came again, closer.

"Get up."

It was a man's voice, a deep one. The kind you would expect from someone large. When Val opened her eyes, she squinted up into a formidable figure. It was a different guard. The woman was gone. Her shift must have ended, Val thought.

Sitting up, Val felt dizzy, like she'd only been out a few hours, no more. Was it morning already?

"What's going on?" Val questioned, standing as he had indicated. "Are you moving me back to Breeding?"

"Let's go."

The guard took hold of Val's elbow and she stumbled

slightly while trying to step into the high heels from the day before. He took her out of Isolation, down the maze of corridors and back out into the courtyard. It was dark, so dark, and nearly pitch black without even a hint of moon in the sky. No one else was about, it was the dead of night still.

Val's stomach began to trip uncertainly, they never moved anyone at this hour. The only tales she had heard about night transfers were murmurs about the missing. Ben had said he witnessed it. Cambric security came for you while everyone else slept and the guard shift was low. They took you from your cell and you never returned.

Had Shane called in from the city? Had he finally had enough of her? Of the trouble she was causing? Was this his way of getting back at Jason for the attack?

Terror at what came next had Val yanking back her arm and struggling. The guard only tightened his grip on her and dragged her along faster. He held her wriggling forearm under the scanner, passed through the apartment buildings and down the back corridor that ran to the parking garage.

Val's pulse jumped and she cried out, causing him to clamp a hand heavily over her mouth. He carried her now, writhing against him until they slammed out a side door and onto that long strip of grass that bordered the high brick wall. It was the one where she had watched the lone rabbit eat. Where everything had seemed so peaceful.

Kicking out with her feet, she lost both of her shoes. The dewy cold wet of the lawn soaked into her stockings. There were no other guards around, all the lights from the surrounding buildings were off. The rolling door of the garage was locked down tight.

Heart bursting inside her chest, Val realized in that moment just how much she wanted to live. She didn't want to die here, at the hands of Cambric. They came to a stop at the imposing iron gate.

"Listen-" The guard hissed. "You have less than a minute to make it through the gate and into the tree line, then the camera starts recording again."

"What?" The shock of it had Val's body going slack. "You're not going to kill me?"

"You all freak out like this." The guard set her on her feet, then began pushing her through the bars of the gate. "You see that big tree right there? On the other side of the road? Run past it and keep on going until you come to another road, then stop. Wait there."

"You're letting me go?"

"Forty-five seconds."

"What about Charlie? I can't leave him here, please you have to go get him," Val pleaded.

"If this was him instead of you, would you want him to run or miss his chance?"

Val's heart ached but she was already on the free side of the fence, looking back into the face of the guard who offered her escape.

"Thirty seconds."

Squeezing her eyes shut for the briefest moment, she made her choice. She turned her back on the guard and ran.

As fast as she could go, she headed for the tree line. Her bare feet slapped over gravel, tearing holes in the bottoms of her stockings. The rocks stabbed at the souls of her feet, but it was like an afterthought, she barely felt the pain. Arms pumping, adrenaline shot into every inch of her body so that she tingled all over.

Crossing the two-lane highway, she leapt from the pavement back onto dirt. The trees were so close now that she could see the tops swaying slighting in the breeze. She tripped over a bush and stumbled, then shoved up and kept going.

Lungs burning, throat tight, she dove into the cover of an old growth forest. She ran past the tree the guard had pointed out. She ran and she ran and she did not stop. She couldn't stop. She wouldn't. Not for anything in the world.

CHAPTER 23

BY THE TIME SHE FOUND THE OTHER ROAD, A STABBING SHARP pain had erupted along her right side. Holding both hands to the spot on her waist, she wheezed, trying to suck in enough oxygen to get satisfaction.

She didn't know how far she had run, or for how long. The dark asphalt roadway had appeared out of nowhere. One minute she was dodging tree branches and jumping roots, the next her feet were jarring over the smooth surface. By the time her mind registered that she could stop, she had reached the middle of the deserted highway.

It was dark all around her, there were no street lights and no traffic. Cambric was positioned in a rural area, one surrounded by forest and large plots of privately owned land. Val's legs began to tremble, muscles twitching with overexertion. In the far off distance, the sound of a car motor rumbled its way towards her.

Limping lamely, Val made a feeble attempt to clear the

road. She didn't know who was coming, or what was going on. Maybe Cambric had been alerted to her release. Maybe they were coming for her.

Before she made it back to the safety of the trees, she was caught briefly in the sweep of headlights. Holding up a hand to stave off the blinding glare, she bit at her lip. Her knees throbbed, her feet ached, and her breath still came in too shallow gasps.

The car slowed. Eventually it came to a stop. The driver side window rolled down and a man hung his head out.

"You alright there, Miss?"

Val rotated to face him, but it was hard to see details in the flood of sudden light. Certainly, he could see her better than she could see him. The car itself was an older model sedan with four doors. The paint was dark in color, though she couldn't say whether it was navy blue or black. No words came to mind. She didn't know what to do next.

"I'd be happy to help get you where you need to go," the man continued. "Of course, that would mean you'd have to be patient with me. I'm an old timer."

Be patient. The instruction clanged like a bell in her head. That's what Agent Finn had told her. That she would have to be patient. It was code.

Nodding then, Val quickened her steps over to the car. She settled herself inside the front passenger seat and before she had even fastened her belt, the car pulled away.

"I wasn't sure at first because you aren't dressed in the same uniform as the rest."

The man slid a glance her way. His hands were gnarled from decades of hard use, the skin wrinkled and thin as they clutched at the oversized steering wheel. The silver hair on his head peeked out from under a blue ball cap. It was clean and appeared new except that she recognized the style as being quite old. His clothing was pressed and spotless. The car smelled of lemon, without a speck of dust anywhere.

Val's breathing began to even out, and the pain in her side melted into a persistent throb. She closed her eyes, leaning her head back against the leather rest. So much had happened, so much change in such a short span of time. The shock of it all numbed her senses.

"Most of you at least have shoes." The man leaned over to look down at Val's feet.

"I'm so sorry," Val said, realizing that her torn feet were leaving spots of blood and dirt all over the man's clean floor mat.

"Please, don't apologize." The man was cheerful. "We must've gotten you out just in time. I wasn't scheduled for another pick-up until next week."

"Pick-up?" Val's mind raced. "You've seen others? Other captives from Cambric?"

"Oh, yes." The man nodded, navigating the backroads with practiced care. "I've been driving for the underground for at least three years now. Keeps me young."

Val blinked, then thought about what he was saying. About picking up others, others who normally had shoes and wore uniforms. Then it dawned on her. He was talking about the missing captives. The ones that had disappeared in the night, never to return. They weren't being hauled off and killed, they were being snuck out.

"How many have there been? Where am I going? Who are

you?" The questions tumbled out of her, one on top of another.

"Slow down, Dear." The man patted at her hand gently. "It doesn't quite work like that. I'll drive you to a safe house where you'll get a warm meal and a change of clothes. They'll remove that tracking thing you all get, and then someone else takes over from there."

Val nodded, mind racing in a million directions at once. This wasn't one single rescue orchestrated by Agent Finn. This was an organized group that had moved hundreds of illegal captives without anyone finding out. Be patient, he had said, but there was something else.

Holding her breath, Val counted to four and worked to think back to the bathroom with Finn. *Be patient and trust the process.* The process of getting out. The process set up by unknown people for an ultimately unknown reason.

If Val let herself feel hope in that moment, it was only because she had come to trust Agent Finn. Throughout all of their dealings together, he had eventually worked to her benefit in the end. Underneath his hardline exterior that claimed only to see black and white, lay a man who saw the truth in its many shades of gray. She would do as he asked.

Without any more questions, she let the old man drive her on.

Val didn't know it at the time, but that night would be the first of many spent at the mercy of strangers. The underground, as they all called it, was actually a series of homes willing to hide and transport illegally freed captives. Each house was connected only by the knowledge of the one person delivering her and then the next one receiving her.

Some offered Val their names, and others only smiled, offering silence and rest instead. Val stayed in average-looking houses in sleepy towns and tiny apartments with not much room to spare. She stayed in a remote cabin with a family of ten, and in a suburban mansion with a lone woman who cooked a lavish meal.

They were all so very different from one another, yet all shared one common thread. Captivity in any form was abhorrent to them. So abhorrent, in fact, that they were willing to risk possible imprisonment and outrageous fines if caught harboring her.

When she asked them about this, for it was a question she often found on her lips, their eyes all clouded with equal fervor. Chins tipped up, a touch of pride was displayed. No human should be the possession of another, no matter what the cost. It was a risk they were all willing to take, and would continue to take, until the end came on. Whatever the end may be.

The route itself was winding and long. Some of her protectors preferred to drive her at night, while others took her across state lines with the music blaring and five kids yelling in the back of a minivan. No one ever stopped them. No police officer pulled them over, no border check searched the car.

These seemingly average, everyday people were actually brazen warriors. They had done this hundreds of times. They were bold and fearless risk-takers who battled the rising tide of laws and society in order to do what was right. Doing the right thing meant more to them than almost anything else.

Val was humbled to be among them. Humbled and ashamed at how little she had done with her own life these past four years. She could have been helping… instead of hiding. By the time she counted the eleventh house, she had crossed into no less than five states, working ever south and west.

Traveling now through the Blue Ridge Mountains, Val marveled at the peaks and valleys. A never-ending forest blanketed them all. It was so green at times, the towering pines lining the highway almost covered the sky. Then the road would take a sudden turn, and an opening would reveal the vast blue-tinged range that rolled out into the distance.

It was breath-taking. Just the earth and its natural undisturbed glory. They were growing more remote with each progressing stop, until finally Val found herself bumping along an old dirt road that clung desperately to a sharp mountainside.

Her driver was a young man, stout but soft-spoken. When he did talk, his drawl was slow, almost like he had to really consider each word before he let it roll out of his mouth. He wore a button-down plaid shirt and tan canvas vest. The weather had turned cool, so he offered her his over-sized jacket. She wore it now, one arm braced along the open window of his old green truck. The wind felt good whipping at her hair, tangling it, and she didn't care how she looked. There was nothing in the world like an open window.

"This ain't where I normally take you all," he said.

"Oh?" Val turned to appraise him, but saw nothing dark about him.

"Got specific words about you, though," he continued.

Grabbing the stick-shift, he shoved at the clutch with his foot and worked to slow them down.

"Should I be worried?"

"Nah," he gave his head a shake, but said no more.

They bumped steadily down the road until a fork appeared and they turned sharply left. Ahead of them, the trees cleared just a bit to reveal a rusty gate. It hung across the single lane, swaying slightly with the breeze. Val could hear the occasional clank of the chain latch as it came taut against the bracing pole of a barbed wire fence.

The young man came to a stop and hopped out, walking to open the gate just about as slowly as he talked. Val waited, eyes squinting as far as she could down the path, but it made another turn and she lost it amongst the trees.

When he got back in, they lurched forward only to repeat the entire process with the closing of the gate behind them. With the truck idling, it was hard to make out any other noise, though she swore she heard what sounded like running water somewhere off to her right. When they finally got moving again, Val's pulse jumped a bit with each new bump in the road.

Deciding that she needed more information, she turned on her driver and opened her mouth. Before she could speak, he pointed out the windshield.

"There," he said.

Shifting her head to look, Val gaped at the sprawling complex that unfolded before her. The land had been cleared in places. It was lush and smooth and green, with neat rows of corn and what appeared to be an orchard. On her left stretched a collection of low buildings that were tucked into the tree line. Off to the right was a large red barn and enormous old farmhouse. A wooden porch wrapped all the way around it.

As the truck drew closer, Val noted a collection of men and women walking casually in the open. They crisscrossed the grassy area that housed cows and sheep. A cow mooed. A few pigs grunted.

Leaning her head out the window, Val spied the edge of an enclosed pen. Several happy pink beasts paced lazily in the sunshine. Nearby, a man stood over a wooden trough and dumped a bucket of scraps over the side. The oinking increased. A smile tugged at the corners of Val's mouth, but then she looked closer. The man had a large rifle slung easily across his back.

Sitting back in her seat, Val's gaze swept the others. They all had guns. She blinked, then squinted. Yes. Every person, even the women, were armed. Some of them more obviously then others.

"What is this place?" Val whispered.

"Gonna have to ask him that." Her driver nodded towards the farmhouse.

Under the shade of the porch, stood a man. He had one shoulder braced casually against a wooden pillar, his legs crossed at the ankle. As the truck pulled to a stop in front of him, he kicked up to standing, but did not step down. Val stared up at him a moment, watching as he assessed her.

Though his skin was fair, his hair was dark, which made the intelligent gleam of his hazel eyes pop all the more. His mouth was drawn in a firm line and although he did not smile, he didn't look upset either. Val had been trained in the ways of men all her life and *this* man, whoever he was, owned everything she saw around her. In fact, she would wager he owned a whole lot more.

"Welcome." The man spoke but did not move from his stance on the porch.

In this way, he forced her to look up at him, a position that he liked, a position that he was used to. Her driver had already exited the pick-up but was strolling around to her side with his usual lack of speed. Val tilted her head to one side, giving the powerful man a final lingering look before she opened her own door and got out.

The wind whipped at her loose hair, swirling it around her face as she crested the steps and came to a stop before him. She had been given ill-fitting boots and a cheap pair of jeans. Her loose cotton t-shirt was comfortably hidden beneath the black canvas jacket the driver had lent her.

Giving the man a quiet smile, Val stared into his eyes, wondering what his reaction would be. Wondering what he wanted from her.

"Val. Or is it Kelly Martin? Maybe you prefer Kelly Riggs or even Val Riggs." He listed her names, then held out a hand. "I'm Clay Montgomery."

Glancing down at his offer of a shake, Val was momentarily at a loss. No one had ever listed her various identities out before. Just hearing all the names threw her off, made her mentally back up a step, caught her off guard. She wondered briefly at Mr. Montgomery's background, but then shook it off. Whoever he was, he was good. Like really, really good at reading people.

Composing her features deliberately, Val chose to fight his fire the only way she knew how. With equal heat.

"It's a pleasure to meet you," Val purred.

As she clasped his hand in her own, she let her eyes drift up his body. She started with his stomach and chest, then up over his mouth before finally settling on his eyes. Briefly, she nibbled on her bottom lip before pulling her hand away. To her surprise, he laughed. The sound was full and robust and without any malice whatsoever.

"You really are impressive," he chuckled. "You make a man's jacket and crappy jeans look like lingerie. Please, come in."

Stepping to one side, he gestured to the front door. It was painted a dark red. Nodding once, Val let herself be shown inside. They were in a parlor. Walnut hardwood floors ran the length of the narrow room. Glancing to the side, she noted a series of old-style chairs and an ornate wood sofa positioned to take in the view from a bank of bay windows. Straight ahead was another closed door.

Clay moved easily in front of her and pushed it open to reveal a massive living room. There was a staircase off to their right. Its steps were made up of the same walnut wood, but the railing and risers were all painted bright white. It was clean and appealing, with watercolors of rich farmland gracing the walls.

Leather recliners, brown couches, coffee tables, end tables, ornate lamps, and Persian rugs dominated the space. There was a flat screen television blaring out news and an empty granite fireplace with a black iron grate.

More men sat inside. Val saw their flash of interest as they spied her, but then with a measure of reserve, they glanced at Clay. He bobbed his head as he led her past, but said nothing. Before they'd made it halfway across the room, all eyes had refocused on the television.

Through a far doorway they entered a commercial size kitchen. Val gawked at the double wide stainless-steel oven and two hulking refrigerators. Granite counters swept around three walls, all clean and shining. An older woman hovered over an apron style sink, filling a pot with water.

"Hey, Connie." Clay paused, spreading his palms over the counter top. "Any chance we could get a couple of sandwiches or something?"

"Sure thing, Clay." Connie gave him a warm smile, her eyes shifting to take in Val. "You like ham?"

"Yes, Ma'am." Val bobbed her head before wondering about the pigs outside.

"Oh, please don't *Ma'am* me," Connie scolded. "Makes me feel old. Even though… I guess I am."

"Yes, Connie." Val kept her hands stuffed into the pockets of her jacket, though something about the woman made her want to reach out and squeeze her arm.

Clay withheld any comment and instead spun on his heel and headed out through yet another door. With Val on his heels, he cruised down a hall that bordered the back side of the house. Window after window stood open. Pale green curtains floated casually in a soft breeze.

Val tried to keep up with his purposeful stride but found herself staring out, mouth hanging slightly. The pasture fence wrapped around the side of the house, then disappeared into a mass of thick trees. Up the side of the mountain, the forest climbed.

Towering pines bursting with needles and flowing green leaves from trees Val didn't know the name of. They were so thick you couldn't see the ground, so thick you couldn't hardly make out their trunks or where one started and one stopped. Up and up, they stretched on forever. So imposing and beautiful that it stole her breath. This was a wondrously harsh and wild place.

Ahead of her Clay ducked into a room and finally came to a stop. It was an office of sorts, with a wide mahogany table and padded leather chairs. One wall was filled entirely with books, another with flat screen televisions, all of them switched off.

Behind the desk was a framed map of the entire country. At first glance it appeared to be filled with red dots, but upon closer inspection, Val realized they were actually push-pins. The moveable place markers were everywhere, though it was unclear what exactly they marked because they weren't major cities, or even cities at all.

Clay took a seat behind the desk and gestured for Val to sit opposite him. She complied, surveying the tidy organization that spanned its smooth surface. There was a closed laptop, a coffee mug filled with pens, and a series of manila folders laid out one on top of the other. With a sigh, Clay leaned back in his chair and let his eyes meet her own. She cocked her head to the side and let him look, keeping her face clear, but open.

"I'm sure you have questions," Clay began. "Why don't I start by answering some."

"What is this place?"

"This is a survivalist training center," Clay replied.

"A what?"

"Our members come here to learn basic skills for off-grid survival. Farming, animal care, butchering, tactical defense, stuff like that."

"Members? What members?"

"This facility is owned by the Constitutional Militia."

"I've never heard of it."

"That's a good thing." Clay shrugged. "The less eyes the better."

"And who are you? Someone important."

"I'm the President of the Militia." Clay smiled then. "Now it's my turn."

"Alright."

Val paused as the door to the office was pushed open and Connie came in. She set down two plates that overflowed with ham sandwiches and hot baked French Fries. Val's mouth salivated and before she had finished uttering the words *thank you*, her hands were gripping the flaky soft croissant. In between bites, she answered Clay's barrage of questions.

"What has your experience been like with the underground? Have you had any issues? Has anyone pressured you for anything? Made you uncomfortable?"

"No." Val blinked. "You run the underground? Why?"

"Ever heard of the Bill of Rights?"

"No." Val watched Clay's expression shift from momentary surprise to an accepting nod.

"Well, it's a document which is supposed to guarantee all people born in this country a few things: life, liberty and the pursuit of happiness. Captives don't really get the last two very much do they?"

"No."

"I'm sort of a stickler for freedom." Clay reached for a pen, rolled it absently between his fingers. "Our government has gotten bloated, corrupt. Did you know that half of the military are captives now? Half."

"Okay." Val wasn't sure where this was going.

"Can you imagine what would happen if they were all suddenly set free?"

"We would be left pretty vulnerable," Val considered, mind working as she watched Clay's calculating face.

"Not if there was another force ready to take their place."

"Your force." Val narrowed her eyes at him. "The men outside with all the guns. The ones who follow you."

Clay leaned back in his chair and lifted one arm, indicating the map just behind his head. Without turning to look at it, he explained that each pin was a holding that belonged to the Militia. A parcel of land, a business, an apartment building. Their membership was in the millions, trained, ready, like-minded.

They valued the Constitution, the Bill of Rights and were strict in their interpretation of freedom for all. Val listened to him talk, saw the passion that sparked in his eyes and the power that vibrated there, too. He had to be highly intelligent, patient and organized in order to have reached the height upon which he now sat. So what was his end game? And what did it have to do with her?

"Why are you telling me all of this?" Val asked.

"I want to show you something."

Pulling open a desk drawer, Clay grabbed up a remote control and flicked on one of the television screens. He clicked through a variety of options, then selected a video that had a picture of Jason frozen in the middle of speaking.

For the next ten minutes, Val watched a speech given by her husband. It had taken place some weeks ago, perhaps a month even. He stood in a perfectly pressed suit, hands gripping either side of a podium on a stage in front of an audience of thousands. Each time he paused for breath, the crowd thundered their applause, howling and yelling in agreement.

He spoke of ending the captive industry, he spoke of securing equal rights for all, he spoke of dreams, pure dreams, and making them into reality. Towards the end of the speech, the fervor of the crowd rose to the point of drowning him out. He stood there, staring out at them, nodding his head. The camera swept away from him then and panned out over the arena. It was filled to the brim with people.

Clay shut the television off and the screen faded to black.

"Your husband-" Clay shook his head a bit, a sly smile working at his mouth. "Has a certain something about him."

"You want Jason to join the Militia?" Val asked. "He's no soldier."

"No, he's not a soldier. He's a leader of men." Clay's eyes became fierce, she could feel the passion with which he spoke. "When he talks, people listen. Hundreds of thousands of people, from all sorts of backgrounds."

"What do you want from him?"

"There's a senate seat opening up in Texas," Clay explained. "He should run for office."

"Jason doesn't like politics."

"All the better," Clay reasoned. "He's an influencer, whether he likes it or not."

"And you want to use that influence?"

"If it's for the good of the people, then why not?"

"For the good of the people, but also for the good of you, right? It opens a place for you to assume power."

"Someone has to have the power, Val," Clay pointed out. "Why not someone willing to set you all free?"

CHAPTER 24

THAT NIGHT, VAL FOUND HERSELF IN YET ANOTHER STRANGE bed in a long line of unfamiliar surroundings. After the compound had finished a group dinner, she had been shown to her bedroom, which was situated on the second floor. Outside, the wind was whistling. Fall was coming, and with it, the promise of an icy winter.

Dinner itself had been subdued. Overflowing plates of spaghetti had been served family style on a series of long tables that ran the length of the back porch. There was hot baked bread slathered in garlic butter and fresh green salad dotted with cherry tomatoes. Propane heaters were positioned every so often. They provided a comforting warmth against the evening's chill.

Sitting amongst the Militia, Val noticed some of the trees in the yard had leaves just beginning to turn. The valley would soon be a symphony of reds, yellows and browns, excepting of course for the evergreens. Clay sat at the head of the table with the others ranging down either side.

Val settled in next to Connie, content just to listen to their banter in reserved silence. She still wasn't used to so much talking. Cambric didn't like a lot of talking.

But the free men, and women, they didn't share in her compulsion. Their talk was full of friendly joking, boisterous outbursts and the occasional stomping of boots. The pigs were getting plenty fat. Maybe Tony should stop feeding them so damn much. The cows needed another pasture cleared. Angela would ride one for twenty bucks and a fifth of whiskey. The chicken coop could use with some new wire. What, no volunteers?

Val's brow furrowed. They could eat what they wanted and say what they wanted and no one did anything about it. She had forgotten what that was like. And it was that small slice of remembering, that finally got to her.

Later that night, when she sat heavily on the edge of her queen-sized bed, Val felt the first crack. It split suddenly, like the seam in a pair of pants you had been testing for too long. Her careful veneer, the outward serenity that she had clothed herself in out of necessity. It shattered.

Shoulders trembling, uncontrollable sobs ripped themselves from her throat. For despite all of Clay's talk of freedom, when Val had asked him to call her husband, his answer had been a gentle, but firm, *no*.

This is a process, he had said. *You must be patient and trust it.*

All the buzz words from Agent Finn and the code words from the underground rolled out of Clay's smart mouth and into Val's completely captive ears. He assured her they would talk about it again, that eventually she would see Jason, and her son, too.

But the awful truth was, from where Val sat, she had been lifted out of Cambric's control and placed firmly in the hands of the Militia. She was a pawn still, like she had been her entire life. The worst part of all, she thought, was the throbbing hope that had filled her at arriving here. She believed she was within an inch of seeing Jason again. That would put her one plane ride away from reuniting with her son. But that was a lie. A false, ugly, hateful lie. She was nowhere near either of them. Nowhere at all.

Bordering on hysterical, Val fell back on the mattress and clutched at a pillow. Burying her face deep into it, she screamed and screamed until her throat felt raw and bruised from the work of it. The last thing she recalled before passing out, was the continued sound of her own anguished moaning.

The following morning, she woke at sunrise to the crow of a rooster. Lifting her aching head from the mattress, she rubbed at her sore eyes and tripped towards the windows. Outside, the first rays of yellow sunshine had begun to crest the eastern ridge of the valley. It was sorrowful and beautiful.

A grayish haze had settled amongst the buildings of the compound. Far below, men were already up and at their work. A pair strode together towards the red barn, heavy jackets protecting them against the early chill.

Inhaling, Val smelled the first tickling aromas of a country breakfast. Her stomach turned sour. Her appetite, along with her emotions, had gone off. The steady self-control she had once exercised now eluded her. Pushing her way into the attached bathroom, she sat heavily on the toilet seat and endured another round of crying.

At some point in the late-afternoon, Connie made her way up to the bedroom and rapped gently on the door. Val sat reclining on the floor, her back pressed up against the wall just below one slender window.

Earlier in the day, she had opened it wide. A tickle of air brushed over her hair as the sounds of the earth entered her room. All day she had listened to the lowing of the cows, the calling of the sheep and the grunting of the pigs. Once those sounds became familiar, her ears began to pick up bird song and the whisper of leaves.

"Val dear-" Connie lifted her voice. "Please come down. There's someone new here who would like to speak with you."

Not bothering to answer, Val felt only a vague curiosity. She had heard the rumble of a motor about two hours before and swiveling up on her knees had observed the arrival of a silver SUV. Its occupant, a single blonde female, strode directly under the protective cover of the porch and out of sight. Val didn't recognize the new woman, so had no real interest at the time, but Connie seemed a well-meaning person and Val felt an underlying obligation to respond.

"Alright," Val answered, and ducking her head Connie retreated back out her door.

Getting up, Val dusted at her t-shirt with shaky hands before running her fingers through her mass of hair. A bit unsteady on her feet, she tottered to the door and felt the twist of the old brass knob in her hand. It creaked as she opened it onto the narrow hallway, the farmhouse seemed filled with them.

The same walnut flooring from downstairs was repeated on the second level as well. Val's bare feet padded silently over the worn surface and down the stairs.

When she came to the front door, she was half tempted to shove out of it and never look back. But the truth was that even if they didn't try to stop her, she wouldn't last more than a mile in the North Carolina wilderness. She didn't know which direction to hike, or how far the nearest town was. Although she was tempted, Val had learned well from her experience with Cambric. She needed to remain quiet and complacent, wait for an opportunity to present itself, then be bold enough to take it.

Eyes darting about, she didn't see anyone in the front parlor. There were no telephones either. Deciding to make a quick investigation of the house, Val walked through the living room and headed for the kitchen. There were no phones, no electronic devices anywhere.

Lingering at the threshold of the kitchen, Val steadied herself against the doorframe and took in the scene. The blonde that had arrived earlier was standing over the stove looking down. She was all alone in the room, and appeared to be focused on cooking something, though her body blocked what it was.

She was shorter than Val, maybe five-foot-four or even five at the most, with a slender figure that seemed to thicken out around the middle. Humming to herself, the woman shifted, and her bright blue eyes caught hold of Val. Though her expression lit with surprise, the blonde did not cry out, instead she pressed her lips together purposefully and exhaled a huff of breath. Subconsciously, her hand stroked protectively over her belly. Val judged her to be about six months along.

"Hello, we haven't met." The blonde crossed the space and extended a hand. "I'm Ava Moore."

"Ava." Val frowned, recalling Finn's last words to her. "Agent Finn asked me to say hi for him."

"Did he?" Ava looked amused.

Just then the whistle of a boiling tea kettle began to blow. The sound climbed in intensity as Ava shifted to fetch it off of the stove. She didn't waddle quite yet, but it wouldn't be long.

"Would you like some tea?" Ava called over her shoulder.

Opening cupboards, she grabbed a box of green tea bags, then let her hand hover over a collection of mugs. Val's stomach was in knots. She hadn't eaten well, couldn't hardly sleep. At any moment a fresh set of tears loomed. In short, she was overwrought.

There was guilt at having abandoned Charlie and the others. Then there was anger at being held in place, forbidden from contacting her husband. And underneath it all there was a deep longing to see her son again. It was an ache that sucked at her very soul, threatening to drain her completely. Did she want tea? No, she didn't want any tea.

Not able to give an audible answer, Val crossed her arms over her stomach and stared. Glancing back briefly, Ava plucked down two thick white cups and set about preparing the hot liquid. Steam drifted slowly up as she worked. Silence hung in the room like a cloud.

"Here." Ava thrust one mug into Val's hands as she passed her. "There's a phone in my brother's office."

Eyebrows shooting up in surprise, Val followed the methodic pace of the other woman. Down the corridor they went, the same as the day before. The windows were once again open, admitting the late-afternoon breeze. It had been warm all day, but the sun had shifted in its position. Now that it dove for the western tip of the mountains, a coolness had begun.

Without knocking, Ava opened the door to Clay Montgomery's office and let Val inside. It was empty, but the once tidy space had been left cluttered. Papers were scattered in disarray, pens rolled on the desk top, one even sat on the floor. Grumbling to herself, Ava set about straightening the mess. She stacked and filed and cleaned until she eventually eased her bulk to sit in the wide leather office chair.

With a sigh, she gestured to a cell phone.

"We are not in the business of keeping mothers from their children," Ava said. "But before you pick up that phone, I would like to explain what will happen if you make that call today."

Val's hand shot out greedily towards the sleek cell phone, but then stopped mid-way. She leaned forward in her stiff wooden chair, elbow propped against the tabletop. Flicking her eyes to Ava, she wondered at the look of concern she saw there. Who was this woman that Agent Finn seemed to know? She had said this was her brother's office, could she mean Clay? Their last names didn't match, though.

Sitting back, Val let her gaze travel to Ava's hands as they cupped the warm mug. She was married, her ring finger glittered with a toss of diamonds. Giving a tight nod, Val decided to wait for her explanation.

"Finn wanted us to get you out almost the second he dropped you off," Ava began, sipping quietly. "I have to admit I'm the one who refused."

"I don't understand."

"The process of freeing captives is a very delicate one. More delicate than one might think. It took us years to infiltrate the security contractors, then months to develop a reliable escape plan."

"Us? You mean Clay? The Militia?"

"It was my brother's idea originally and the Militia helped in the beginning stages, but I run the operation. I use my own people, we have our own funding."

"Your brother is Clay Montgomery?"

"Yes." Ava laughed at the look on Val's face. "He's made a great first impression I see. He has a way of doing that."

Val resolved to remain silent on the subject. Clay hadn't done anything against her, save for preventing her from contacting her husband and son. Though his manner and way of talking made her feel pressured. Pressured to comply.

"When we select a captive to rescue, they have to meet certain criteria. They must be low-level, with no set clients or schedule. We prefer party or hourly captives because there are so many. It helps if they are at their lowest point. If they've been under discipline or in Isolation for an extended period of time, then they have little to no contact with other captives."

"Why?"

"The guard detail in Isolation does not work in the housing

sect and vice-versa. We want to take a captive that no one will miss."

"Are you telling me that Cambric doesn't know when they're missing captives? Don't they have a head count or something?"

"We eliminate the captive from the database. The Isolation guard thinks the captive has been returned to housing, and the housing guards are so overwhelmed by the sheer number of you all, that they forget the captive was ever under their section. Believe it or not, it has worked well in the past."

"But the captives knew, there were rumors of the missing."

"Yes." Ava smiled. "But did any of you ask Cambric about it?"

"No." Val frowned. "No, we were all too afraid. We thought it was them killing us."

"I'm sorry," Ava replied. "There's no way for us to correct the rumor and protect the operation."

Val flashed back to her time on the inside. She thought of Ben and how he had witnessed others taken while he was left behind. She remembered how he had wanted it all to end. The truth was, they would never have selected him. He was a trainer, with a schedule and a high-profile, he would be missed. Then Charlie and all of his hope. What were they doing to him right now? And Amber, and Mandy, and Gabe's boys and all the rest.

"Who's next?" Val asked suddenly. "Who is the next one you've selected? If you made an exception for me, can you do it again? Can you get Charlie out? Ben?"

"Slow down." Ava raised both hands in a calming motion. "No one at Cambric is next."

"What? I don't understand, didn't you just say-"

"We've taken the most high-profile captive there." Ava waited a beat to let that sink in. "The place is on lockdown. *You*… are definitely missed."

Val shoved away from the desk, causing her chair to clatter behind her onto a worn Persian rug. Hands covering her mouth, she paced to the bookcase. Then over to the wall of television screens.

What was Ava saying? That it was over? That rescuing her had cost countless others their chance at freedom? Throat tight, Val spun on her heel, eyes rolling around the room, unable to focus on anything. All at once, thoughts piled up in her head and began to tumble from her mouth.

"You can do it again, right? You can get more out. You can find a way. What can I do to help? Do you need more money? What can I do?"

"You can refrain from contacting your husband and son for just a few more months." Ava watched as a look of horror crossed Val's face.

"But they don't know I'm safe." Val stalked to the desk and clutched at the phone. Ava didn't try to stop her. "When Cambric reports that I'm missing-"

"Why would they *ever* do a thing like that?"

"Wha-" Val's mouth dropped.

"Cambric has not, nor will they ever report that they do not have custody of you." Ava motioned for Val to resume her seat. "They will investigate your disappearance and find absolutely nothing. Hopefully they won't find out there have been more captives taken.

Maybe they'll think you're dead, killed at the hands of

some reckless guard who then covered it up. It doesn't matter really. What matters is that things eventually calm down and return to normal. At that time we can start moving captives out again."

"I still don't understand why I can't call Jason."

"If Jason knows you are here, then he will come for you. He will try to get you out of the country, and we all know how well that worked last time. The court case involving you and your son is ongoing, so Cambric still technically holds the rights to one of you. I'm asking you to let the case resolve. Let things at Cambric die down. Let us resume the underground and then we can contact your husband."

"You're asking me to stay away from my son for months, possibly longer. How can I do that? I don't think I can do it."

Ava softened then, her look of earnest persuasion dissipating as Val continued to clutch at the cell phone. Then Ava told Val a story.

She explained that she herself had once been locked in a cage. She herself had once sacrificed months with her own son in order to keep him safe. It had been a difficult cross to bear, but ordinary people had to do it all the time.

Soldiers were shipped overseas, leaving their children behind. Parents split up and moved to different states, having to share custody over alternating months. It could be done, if you could organize your mind in the right way.

"I am not asking you to give up your son forever," Ava persuaded. "I'm asking you to give up a few months so that others like yourself have a chance at a lifetime of freedom. Your fellow captives need this from you. They need your sacrifice in order to live. Can you give it to them?"

Val's hands trembled. But then she slowly, deliberately, set the phone down on the desk. Tears brimmed from her eyes and her heart jerked in her chest. Demurely, she returned her hands to her lap.

How could she refuse? Jace was safe and loved by friends and family. Jumping from house to house on the underground, Val had been so moved by the willingness of people to risk their lives for her own. She had wanted to do more. She had wanted to help, too.

"I will wait." Val's voice cracked at first, but she swallowed hard and went on. "But I want something in return."

"What's that?" Ava's eyebrows raised.

"I want to be a part of the underground."

CHAPTER 25

In the wee hours of the morning, just before the roosters began to crow, Val's eyes would pop open and she'd suck in a sharp breath. Despite the chill that now crept over the valley, the narrow window in her room was thrown wide. It was so utterly silent at those times. All the night animals had returned to their dens and all the day animals hadn't yet woken.

Wrapping the heavy quilt from her bed around her body, Val crossed the floor on bare feet and stood watch. Dawn was approaching. It traced and touched at the once midnight sky, chasing away the stars that winked all night. Soft gray mist floated down the crevices of the mountain, sneaking and creeping to infiltrate the valley floor.

In the coming light, she could see the movement of the fog. It was beautiful. Across the pasture, the low buildings that housed so many constantly changing men were still dark. They wouldn't begin to move for another half hour or so. Val didn't know why her body woke at this time. She didn't know why she couldn't go back to sleep.

Witnessing the sunrise on an anonymous farm in the Blue Ridge, Val wondered how much longer she would need to do this. Again, she didn't know. Maybe it was the call of a new purpose. Maybe it was the far off pull of her family, or the nameless dreams that chased her from their hold back into the blinding reality of waking life.

It didn't really matter, she supposed. Her vigil was a consistent one.

After watching the sun crest the eastern sky, Val gently slid the window closed and made her way to the bathroom. She shed the quilt, tossing it on the nearby dresser before shutting herself inside and twisting on the shower faucet. Holding her fingers underneath it every so often, she waited for the water to warm before stepping in.

Connie thought Val was a touch crazy and often grumbled about her little window habit. Who sleeps with the window open in winter? There's snow on the ground, it makes the whole upstairs hard to keep warm, the complaints went on.

Val could've tried to explain it but the right words eluded her. How do you explain to a woman who has always had a choice, what it's like to not get one? How do you explain not having a window?

This morning would be no different. After Val's shower, she wrapped her hair in a towel and slipped into a pair of worn jeans and thick knit sweater. Her footsteps caused creaks on the old floor boards as she snuck down to the kitchen but Connie was already there. She had beaten her to it once again.

Standing over a hissing stove top, the woman pushed diced ham around in a sizzling pan.

"Good morning," Val offered.

"Can you start in on the eggs?" Connie eyed her a moment.

"Sure thing."

Half an hour later, Ava waddled in and the three women sat together at the small round table in the kitchen. Breakfast was made up of ham, eggs and English muffins slathered in homemade apple butter. As Val licked the sticky-sweet substance off her fingers, she endured yet another round of grumbling about her window.

"I've had to add another quilt to every bedroom upstairs," Connie scolded. "And the boys will have to cut more wood if this keeps up."

"I have a thing for open windows myself," Ava cut in. "Gives you something to crawl out of."

"Oh." Connie stopped mid-sentence.

Val too, flicked her eyes up in momentary surprise. She had almost forgotten about Ava's confinement. It was a powerful motivation for a life now spent in service to the underground. Though Ava had never been a legal captive, her time locked away had given her just the tiniest taste. After that, the three women's talk was more benign.

When breakfast was complete, Ava directed Val into the living room where the real work was set to begin. The order of the day was assembling "go bags" for freed captives. For the rest of the morning, the two women knelt on their hands and knees in the middle of chaos. Surrounding themselves with all the basic necessities for survival, they stuffed black backpacks until the zippers would barely close.

There were travel size toothbrushes, toothpaste, combs, shampoo, soap, clothing of various sizes, shoes, socks, underwear, and other similar items. Stacks of stuff covered the couches, chairs, and coffee table until they overflowed into piles that spread across the walnut floor. The idea was for the kits to be both inconspicuous and portable. The only outward difference between bags was a blue key chain for men and a red one for women.

During Val's first week at the farmhouse, Ava had introduced her to the general workings of the underground. After successfully traveling out of an agency, a captive could expect to eventually land in a group home. Once there, they were provided with intensive therapy, a new identity, an education and skills training. The exact individual needs varied depending on the type of captive that was saved.

A Corporate Captive or Domestic Level 1 had already worked in a particular profession. They had job skills and were often able to assimilate at a much faster rate. It was the D2s and anyone who had suffered abuse that had the most trouble.

On several occasions, Ava took Val to one of the halfway houses located a few hours' drive from the farm. Though she sat in on a few of the therapy sessions, Val felt uncomfortable sharing. Listening to the others talk was painful enough without having to relive her own experiences.

The Militia provided all the new identities while financial support came from a variety of private donors. A charity known as the Freed Captives Transition Fund provided the bulk of the funding. It was a name Val had heard before…

over a dinner table in the Maldives. It was the very charity Bee had given her settlement money to. In the end it was Bee's money that had gotten Val out. How she longed to tell her oldest friend. But she couldn't. She couldn't tell anyone.

"When do you think you'll be able to move the next captive from Cambric?" Val asked quietly, selecting a fresh pair of socks to go in one bag.

"It could be weeks, or even months," Ava replied. "The Agency fired all guard staff that worked the night you got out. Fortunately, that's as far as they went. We still have employees on the inside."

"How does that work? How many do you have?"

"We try to protect the guards involved as much as possible, even from each other." Ava paused as she zipped up a backpack, then grabbed for another. "There's a selection team that scouts the captives most available for extraction, and then another team that moves them out. The first set doesn't know about the other and vice versa."

"You lost an entire extraction team?"

"We lost one extraction team, but we have two more." Ava placed a hand on her protruding belly, sighing softly before continuing her work. "We keep them on different schedules, planning for this sort of thing. Of course, I never would have pulled a captive like you voluntarily."

"Why did you?"

"Finn." Ava shrugged. "He said if I didn't get you out, then he'd go in there himself. I couldn't let him risk it."

"How do you know him?" Val shifted back to rest and watch Ava's face. "Finn, I mean."

"Hmmm." Ava gave a soft smile. "You know the story I told you about how I was kept in that cage?"

"Yes."

"He was in there, too."

"Agent Finn was locked in a cage?"

"He was." Ava turned remorseful eyes on Val. "Giving you up to that Shane guy was one of the hardest things he's ever had to do. I just thought you should know."

"Thank you." Val returned to her work a few moments. Nibbling at her lip, she continued. "Can you get information from the inside? Can you check on how a captive is doing?"

"I suppose that I could."

"Can you check on a captive named Charlie for me?"

"I can." Ava paused to study her. "Is there something in particular I should know about him?"

"Agent Finn was in your cage, right?"

"Yes."

"Charlie was in mine."

"I see."

Ava reached for a tube of toothpaste. Val folded another shirt. Their packing resumed in silence.

But try as she might, Val was unable to keep Charlie from her thoughts. She hoped that with her absence, Cambric had returned him to his former status. She hoped he was back in his dorm, had regular meals in the cafeteria, was able to work as a trainer in the gym. The alternative scenario was just too hard to contemplate.

Shaking her head, Val made herself focus on the work

before her. There were still so many captives being rescued, it was hard not to be hopeful. Though the extraction network at Cambric was on pause, the underground remained fully functional throughout the rest of the agencies. They were successfully sneaking captives out of Havana, Lakeport, Beechwood Hall, Old Brulay, Ramsey House, Sion Hill, the list went on. Over the years the underground had infiltrated them all. Save only for the government's military program.

That evening, when the packs were all complete and dinner had been eaten, Val and Ava joined a handful of Militia in the living room. They were all lying about, digesting and watching the television.

Sitting on the edge of one leather couch, Val crossed her legs tidily as Ava heaved and shifted beside her. She scooted the coffee table closer and propped her feet up, then groaned and rolled up on one side. Val remembered the un-comfortability that came with those last few months. Stifling a chuckle, she knew Ava's belly would only expand more.

In front of them, the enormous flat screen television hung over a roaring stone fireplace. It flashed football statistics and game highlights that had all the men shouting insults and teasing one another in turn.

The Militia members currently in residence weren't locals to North Carolina. In fact, they came from a variety of states all across the nation. After all, the farmhouse was really a survivalist training center first. The point of their stay was to expand their abilities through hands on experience.

When they left here, these men would be better marksman and hunters. They would know which plants grew in which region during what time. They would know how to start a fire without matches, how to preserve meat without a refrigerator, and how to defend against predators, whether they be wild beasts or otherwise.

If they needed to, these men could take a group of ordinary people and live off the land for an undetermined amount of time. Val wasn't quite sure what they were all preparing for, but she was impressed by what they could do all the same.

Suddenly, the laughter from the sports highlights died away. Val heard Ava's sharp intake of breath and followed her line of sight up to the television. There, on the wide screen for everyone to see, was Jason. He was sitting opposite a news anchor. Both men were clad in expensive suits.

The anchor was talking, his hands clutching a sheet of paper as he introduced Jason and began a line of questioning. Her husband's face was serious but reserved. He looked like he was in complete control. Nothing like her visit with him inside Cambric and later at the courthouse. At those times, he had been on the very edge.

"I understand that Judge Allen has recently ordered your case proceedings sealed," the anchor stated.

"Yes, he has," Jason confirmed.

"It is widely believed that the outcome of your case will be a landmark decision, one upon which other similar cases will be based. Don't you believe that the public has a right to understand every detail of this process?"

"Unfortunately, I am subject to a gag order by the court and so cannot comment on that specifically. I can say that the final decision will be made public."

"At that time will the case be unsealed?"

"You will have to ask Judge Allen that."

"Before the gag order, you admitted that the captive Val was indeed Kelly Martin. The same woman to whom you are legally married."

"That is true."

"Is it also true that the child at the center of this lawsuit is actually your biological son by the same woman?"

"Yes."

"Then by law wouldn't he also be considered a captive? Having been born to one?"

"My son was born to a free woman's identity. Kelly Martin was never a captive."

"It's an interesting argument based off of a technicality. Do you think it will work?"

"Cases have been won and lost on technicalities. The strict rule of law is important to a successful judicial system. Judge Allen certainly runs his courtroom that way."

The anchor ducked his head in acceptance and shuffled through an assortment of papers that littered the table. Jason waited patiently, not looking into the camera, but instead focusing on the man across from him. Val's heart beat rapidly. It made her nervous to have them discussing Jace so publicly Hands gripping the leather seat of the sofa, she reminded herself that her son was still safely out of the country, or at least she prayed that he was.

"Mr. Riggs, let me ask you-" The anchor paused, swallowing. The next question wasn't one he appeared comfortable with. "How do you feel about having your wife sold to other men?"

"Do you have a wife?" Jason's voice was smooth and even, but the muscles in his jaw tightened as he spoke.

"I do."

"Children?"

"Yes, two."

"Describe how you would feel if she were being sold to other men. If you tell the world what that does to you first-" Jason waited a beat before continuing on. "Then I'll explain how I feel."

The anchor's eyes flicked to the camera once, then back down to his paper. He fidgeted a while, then tossed the paper to the ground and decided to move on.

"You have been an outspoken proponent of captive rights, even giving speeches calling for the outright dissolution of the entire industry. There have been rumors of you entering the political ring. Is that true?"

"I have no intention of going into politics." Jason managed a knowing smile. "But I would urge everyone who agrees with me to contact their Senator. Get your voice heard. Encourage them to vote for Bill S-2309, it has already been passed by the House."

"And by that you are referring to the anti-captive legislation that your family has been working on for the past several years. If passed, it calls for the immediate release of all captives, including those owned by the government itself. Some say it's a radical idea."

"The founding fathers had some pretty radical ideas for their time as well," Jason countered. "I think this is more in line with their original intention."

That comment drew a round of applause and shouts of affirmation from the Militia in the living room. Catching the sideways glances from some of the men, Val knew that they recognized her. At any other time, she may have felt vulnerable, but not with these people. She didn't know any group that valued privacy and keeping secrets more. And true to form, when the interview concluded, not one of them said a word.

That night, alone in her room once more, Val was plagued by anxiety. For the first time the truth about Jace was completely exposed. Now the whole world knew he was the child of a captive, and therefore, a captive himself. Legally, he belonged to Cambric. The realization frightened her beyond anything she had known. It was worse than Isolation. Worse than starving. It was worse than Shane and what they did to Charlie.

Pacing to the window, Val let the icy air sting her face until her body shook uncontrollably. The shivers were a natural reaction to an outside stress. Her body was too cold, much too cold, so her muscles jumped and vibrated in an attempt to keep warm.

Standing in place as long as she could, Val welcomed the physical pain. It made her thoughts go away. Once she finally returned to bed, she pulled the heavy blankets around her and let her exhausted body shake itself to sleep.

Over the next month, Val threw herself headlong into the reality that surrounded her. When she wasn't helping Ava with the underground, she assisted Connie around the farm. She used the skills she learned from living on Javier's ranch to help with cooking, cleaning and tending to the groups of Militia that moved through.

Physical exertion was the only thing that kept the worry about her son at bay, so Val threw herself into almost constant work. She mucked animal pens, fed the pigs, milked the cows, and tended the flock of sheep.

Even in the cold of winter, the compound grew its own food using a series of greenhouses. Val spent long days bent over rows of vegetables, weeding. She tended onions, peas and asparagus. Back in the kitchen, Connie taught her how to preserve all the food in jars.

Together they spent hours washing, cutting and preparing the food for long term storage. It was exhausting and often dirty work, but it was work, and it was the only thing that left Val feeling close to okay.

Ava's visits to the farm became fewer and farther between. She was getting large now, closer to her due date. Though she didn't say it, Val knew the father, whoever he was, probably wanted her at home with him. During Ava's last visit to the compound, she gave Val an update on Cambric. With that, came the painful news about Charlie.

After Val went missing, he had stopped eating. News of his apparent hunger strike then filtered through the walls at Cambric until more than half the captives stopped eating too. It took The Agency weeks to get the entire thing under control and by then Charlie had been heavily medicated. Despite the drugs, they were still having to forcibly tube feed him, even now.

When Ava stopped talking, Val rose to her feet and locked herself in the nearest bathroom. Dropping to her knees, she vomited repeatedly in the toilet. Charlie was starving because of her. Jace was in danger because of her. Jason still thought Cambric had her. How many more people would have to suffer so that Val could be free?

It suddenly seemed so very selfish and unnecessary. Part of her wanted to give up. Part of her wanted to go back to The Agency and put a stop to everything.

Ava rapped on the door, but Val failed to answer. Sitting back on the wooden floor, she drew her knees up to her chest and pressed her forehead down against them. Ava tried the handle. It was locked.

"Please come out, Val," Ava spoke quietly, fingertips drumming on the door.

"Call Cambric." Val cleared her throat. "Tell them where to come get me."

Through the closed door, Val heard Ava's sigh. Then footsteps walking away.

In the end though, Ava didn't call Cambric.

In the end, she called her brother.

Val didn't know where he came from or what he had been doing before, but within several hours Clay Montgomery was sitting on the floor outside her door. He didn't use a key to open the bathroom. He didn't dismantle the knob or kick in the door. He just quietly reasoned with her.

"Cambric will never let Charlie kill himself," he said. "They'll medicate and force feed him until he snaps out of it. He's got a client list and the whole breeding thing."

"It's not just him," Val's voice cracked. "They can get my son."

"Jace is still out of the country." Clay again. "I'm keeping an eye on things. They can't touch him."

"Other captives are suffering."

"Other captives are finding freedom." Clay slid a single sheet of paper beneath the door. "Here's a list of names. The underground is up and running inside Cambric again. *You* are making this happen… by staying here and staying quiet."

Unfolding from her ball on the floor, Val crawled over and read the names. There were three. Three more had been saved this month alone. And that was just from Cambric. Closing her eyes then, Val bit at her bottom lip. If she went back to Cambric, they would know she had escaped. It would jeopardize the whole underground and she just couldn't do that. Not now.

Shoving up from the floor, Val put her hand on the doorknob and opened it.

CHAPTER 26

A thin layer of snow was stuck to the ground. Val's breath came out in puffs, hovering just in front of her face as she hiked. Ahead of her, rays of sunlight pierced through the canopy of thick pines. Glancing up, she could see the backs of the other men. Rifles slung over their shoulders, their boots crunched almost imperceptibly in the mix of slush and dead leaves. The Militia's hunting party moved along slowly, placing their steps carefully on the slanting slope.

Deer season was coming to a close. It was mid-December now and this particular group had yet to take a single animal. Though Val had been reluctant to participate, Clay Montgomery had been insistent. And he wasn't a man you said no to. Not easily anyway.

She had eaten the meat provided to her over the past months, he reasoned. All of which was hunted and taken humanely. Clay believed in having an intimate relationship with one's own survival and it had become a tenant upon which the Militia was run. They never wasted the animals they took. All of the meat was eaten, the skin was processed and used or sold. He claimed the act of killing itself was an important lesson. And for some reason, Clay wanted Val to learn it.

It was Clay that hiked just in front of her now. The point position was taken by another man, though. Clay already knew how to take down deer and the others still needed to learn.

Looking down the slope, Val could barely make out glimpses of the compound. Through the tree trunks and array of branches, the red barn stuck out, its flashy color drawing the eye. When she had commented on the color, Clay had explained that they wanted the valley to blend in. Anyone flying over would see it as a well-tended homestead, not a place worthy of further inspection. Hide in plain sight, he had said. Sometimes that's the best place to be.

The group came to a stop at a rocky outcropping. A few of the men knelt down while one crawled on his belly to the edge and held a pair of binoculars to his eyes. While he swept the neighboring mountainside for signs of game, Clay pulled out his phone and checked his messages. Cell service was spotty up here, but Val watched him hold the sleek device to his ear and listen intently. A voicemail had come through at some point during their trek.

Her lungs burned as she stood still, hands braced against her hips. A damp sweat had collected across her brow and down her back. Beneath her heavy jacket, she could feel her thermal shirt cling to her skin. Brushing an errant hair from her face, Val noted the instant everything changed.

Clay's eyes caught a spark, then darted over to lock with hers, and held.

"We're going to have to leave you boys to it." Clay whispered to the man just ahead of him. "Val and I have some business back home."

"Alright, Clay." The man nodded, and the others bobbed their heads in acknowledgement.

"Bring home a big one," Clay added before turning to Val and motioning her on. "Verdict is in. We need to get to a TV."

All the way down, Val's stomach flipped inside her body. She felt at times high and others absolutely sick. Clay set a brutal pace, charging down the mountainside like a steamroller. The demands of the hike took all the oxygen from her lungs so there was no room for the million questions that zoomed through her head.

Did Cambric win? Or Jason? Could she contact him? Would the Militia continue to protect her? Or her son?

Where she was winded and panting, Clay was the picture of control. He walked with a purpose, like a man who knew these mountains well. He didn't pause to catch his breath, he didn't stop to check his direction.

Val struggled to keep up, even slipping once or twice on a slick patch of leaves and snow. At those times Clay looked over his shoulder but he did not stop. He did not turn back, nor offer to help her up. Clay treated Val like any other member of his Militia. He expected her to take care of herself. He valued strength and self-sufficiency.

Gritting her teeth, Val rose to the occasion. Deep inside, she didn't want to rely on him, not any more than she already did. Not even for a hand up off the hillside.

By the time they reached the valley floor, Val's heart was pounding and her legs felt weak. Despite an outside temperature that hovered around freezing, she shed her heavy jacket and carried it slung over her shoulder. Panting a few paces behind Clay, Val almost smiled when she noted his shoulders were heaving now, too. At least she wasn't the only one winded by their rapid descent.

When they crested the porch to the farmhouse, Connie met them at the front door. Reaching to take Val's jacket and Clay's pack, she stepped aside as they swept through the parlor and into the living room. He leaned his rifle against the wall before shrugging out of his own jacket, his attention fixed entirely on the television.

It was already on with the news channel blaring loudly. Val came to a stop next to Clay. She gripped a cramp in her side. He exhaled slowly. Two commentators sat talking at a desk. Behind them was a live feed of the courthouse steps. For now they were empty, save for a group of reporters and cameramen, but a news conference appeared imminent.

Along the bottom of the screen, bold words drifted by in ticker tape fashion. They were on a never-ending repeat. Val's legs gave out and she dropped to her knees.

Victory for Riggs family. Jace Riggs found to be the child of a free born identity. Conscription clause for former captive Val determined to be null and void.

CHAPTER 27

"Can I call him?" Val gasped it, looking up at the still towering figure of Clay Montgomery. "Can I call Jason?"

While Val had collapsed at the news, he had remained standing. Tossing her his phone, Clay cracked the tiniest of smiles. It was the first one he'd shown her in a long time. In the background, the television droned on. The court case was over. It had been judged in their favor. Jace was legally and completely free.

Val's hand trembled only slightly as she grasped the sleek cell phone in her hands. She no longer belonged to Cambric. Her son no longer belonged to Cambric. It was a miracle. A technicality. A long shot in a game that had always, always been determined in favor of the agencies. But even still, here it was.

Swiping her thumb across the screen, Val's eyes searched the display of tiny icons. She touched the one that had a picture of an old-style telephone on it and a keypad appeared.

That's when she hesitated. She didn't know Jason's phone number. She didn't know anyone's phone number come to think of it.

Vacantly, the phone slipped from her grasp and clattered against the hardwood flooring. Val rocked back onto her butt, her hands shooting out behind her. All these past months she had tortured herself, thinking about how easy it would be to simply contact her husband. She had held herself back. Talked herself down. And for what?

All those nights filled with guilt and second thoughts were wasted. They were wasted because that entire time Val had been unable to actually call him. Her own refusal all these years to get her own phone had resulted in a complete and utter dependence on other people. How could she have been so blind? How could she have been so naive and stupid?

"I don't know his number," Val admitted quietly, head down.

Slowly, Clay crouched down beside her and retrieved his fallen phone. Val didn't bother to look over at him. She didn't want to see the expression that crossed his face. Straightening up, he walked a few paces away and placed a call. She couldn't hear what he said.

But then the news anchors on the television were whispering and Val's ears pricked at the sound of a familiar name. Lifting her face to the box on the wall, she watched Jason step up to the podium. All murmuring died quickly away.

He did not look happy. His face had drawn lines of stress, his jawline was tight, his teeth clenched. If anything, he looked fierce, as fierce as she'd ever seen him.

"What can you tell us about the case?!"

"How are you feeling about your landmark win?!"

"Where is Val?!"

"Where is Jace?!"

"Can we expect a joint interview in the future?!"

The reporters shouted and tossed questions at him, one on top of the other. With measured reserve, Jason let them come on. He made no move to answer. He didn't gesture or call on anyone. For the longest time it seemed, he stood still amidst the chaos.

But then he was sliding a quick look off to one side. All at once Jason centered himself and opened his mouth to speak.

"Due to a non-disclosure agreement signed by all parties in this case, I am not at liberty to discuss any specifics. I *can* tell you that I expect my son to arrive back in the country shortly and I very much look forward to reuniting with him.

This has been a difficult experience for my entire family and we appreciate your understanding at this time as we ask for our privacy. I will reach out to you in the future to provide more information. Thank you."

Val blinked. The reporters blinked. This was not the statement anyone expected to receive. There would be no victory lap. No speech about freedom and winning the day.

As quickly as he had appeared at the podium, he left it. Though the cameras shifted in their attempt to chase him, Jason ducked into a waiting town car and pulled away from the curb. He was gone. It was over and he was gone.

"Hmmm." Clay ended his call and stood beside her once more, frowning at the screen. "He knows Cambric no longer has you, but he's made a deal and can't say anything about it."

"What do you mean? Were you able to get a hold of

anyone?" Val shoved up from the floor and reached for Clay's arm. He didn't shrug her off, but instead patted at her hand gently.

"I spoke with Finn, he's going to reach out to Jason right now. He was just waiting on approval from us."

"Did he mention anything? Is my son okay?"

"Everything that has been done here has been done for the benefit of you and your son. Jason will know that you're safe as soon as he answers Agent Finn's call. I'm sure it won't take him long to show up after that."

"Thank you." Val wiped furiously at tears as they began to fall down her cheeks. "For everything."

"You're welcome," Clay answered, then added. "I still want you to think seriously about what I said before. About Jason running for office. About making sure that legislation becomes law."

"I will," Val promised. "I will, Clay."

The next hour was agony. Val paced the living room. Connie wrung her hands. Clay reclined in one leather armchair, seemingly unperturbed as he absorbed the wild speculation that filled the commentary on television.

No one could wrap their heads around Jason's press conference. They played back snippets of his speeches, late-night interviews, and radio appearances. The man had been a bonafide media machine for the past six months but now went silent. On top of it, the secret contents of the non-disclosure agreement had everyone salivating.

When Clay's phone buzzed and he answered, Val held her breath. There was murmuring on the other end. Clay held up a single finger, then flicked his eyes to Val.

"No," he said. "He has to fly into Charlotte."

Val frowned. Clay listened to the talking on the other end.

"We can't risk having that sort of attention," he explained. "I'll have a driver pick him up. He's waited half a year to see her, he can wait another four hours and do this thing right."

Pushing her hair back from her face, Val paced another few steps before stopping. Clay gave a last series of instructions before ending the call. The Militia's priority was to keep the farmhouse under the radar. They would take extra precautions to make sure Jason wasn't followed while they brought him in.

"He knows you're safe." Clay caught Val's look. "You've got to be patient and tru-"

"And trust the process, I get it," she snapped.

"Why don't you go get cleaned up, Dear?" Connie cleared her throat. "After all, your husband is on the way."

Ducking her head, Val looked down at her clothes. Worn jeans, sweat stained thermal shirt, frazzled hair. She hadn't bathed the day before, had given up caring about that sort of thing. Connie was right, she could use a shower.

Pivoting on her heel, Val made for the stairs. Her thoughts jumped from Jason to Jace and back again. If her son was on his way back to the country right now, that meant she might be able to see him within twenty-four hours. Suddenly, she was in a rush. She took the steps two at a time, ran down the hall and shoved into her bedroom.

Closing the door behind her, she shed her dirty clothes and left them on the floor. As she made her way to the ensuite bath her hands shook. A part of her could hardly believe it was all over. Would they be going back to France? Maybe a place in the Maldives would be better. Somewhere without extradition, just in case. She'd have to talk to Bee and Gabe about it. And Jason of course.

But she wanted to still help the underground, too. She wanted to help get the rest of them out. And Charlie. Stepping into the shower, her knees felt weak. She forced herself to slow down. Inhale. Hold. Exhale.

Scrubbing at her body, Val took the time to shave and even condition her hair. She was going to see her family again. It was time to wash off the past. She wanted to start fresh. She wanted to feel new. By the time she was finished, Val was looking at a subdued version of herself once more in the bathroom mirror. Maybe her green eyes were a touch jaded, but they were free eyes.

Back downstairs, Val resumed her chronic pacing in the front parlor. Clay was nowhere in sight, probably back in his office, doing important Clay things. She looked out the windows and surveyed the far entrance to the valley, the one she herself had driven down not so very long ago.

Dusk was coming on strong now, giving an unearthly feel to the pastures dotted with snowfall. The hunting party hadn't returned. Shoot time was almost over.

Eventually, Connie made an appearance and convinced Val to sit and have a bite to eat.

"It won't do you any good if you faint at the sight of the man," Connie persuaded, setting a plate of cold chicken and apple slices in front of her. "You must eat something."

"You're right." Val picked over the food distractedly. "What time is it? How much longer do you think?"

"He'll get here soon enough. Now eat."

With one bare foot tapping a nervous beat beneath the table, Val made herself eat everything Connie offered. She drank deeply from her glass of water, ate all of the chicken and managed the apple in a series of purposeful bites. When she was done, she trailed Connie to the sink and cleaned her plate, then offered to assist with dinner. Shaking her head, Connie waved her back to the front of the house where Val resumed her vigil.

Night fell. The men returned empty handed from their hunt and Clay sat down beside her in the parlor. Feet propped up against a long window frame, they waited together in silence, watching the edge of the valley. Where was he? Had something happened? Val twisted the ends of her hair between her fingers, then returned her hands to her lap in an attempt at self-control.

"There." Clay pointed to the flash of far off headlights as they disappeared and reappeared through the trees.

Jumping to her feet, Val was out the front door with Clay walking calmly just behind. It was blistering cold outside but deadly calm. They stood on the porch and watched the progress of the vehicle. It wound its way towards them, eventually clearing the tree line and sweeping to the left along the dirt road that skirted the central pasture.

As the car rounded the final corner and slowed in its approach, Val leapt from the porch and ran forward. Before the vehicle came to a stop, the front passenger door burst open and Jason was stumbling out to meet her.

She threw herself at him. His hands circled her body. She clutched at his shoulders. He buried his face in her neck.

"I thought you were dead," he whispered. "They told me a guard killed you. I thought you were dead."

"I'm sorry." Val sobbed. "I'm so sorry."

"You've got to understand." Jason squeezed her against him, making her gasp. "We didn't know you were safe. We didn't know."

"I know." Val buried her face in his chest, inhaled his scent.

"They kept sending videos of you doing things with another man. Then the videos would stop. We didn't know what they were making you do. We didn't know."

Val grimaced, remembering the fake videos with Ben. Anyone watching would think they had completed each act in private. That was how she and Ben had structured them, in order to fool Cambric.

"Nothing happened." Val tried to pull back, to look Jason in the eye, but he wouldn't let her.

"You *have* to understand. We made the deal thinking they still had you."

"What are you talking about? Who's we?"

Jason's hands slid up to her shoulders. He loosened his grip, let his arctic eyes dart across her face. She could see him in the light from the farmhouse. Tentatively, he reached up and brushed one thumb across her lips. Squeezing his eyes shut, he took a sharp breath.

"He told me the two of you had a deal."

Jason paused then, opening his eyes wide.

"Who? What deal?"

"That night on the dock… you made a deal."

"No." Val shook her head, trying to back up a step, but he wouldn't let her.

"You *both* agreed. He would give you a chance to fix things. If it didn't work… then he would fix it himself."

"No." Val struggled. "No, Jason!"

"We thought they still had you. We weren't sure if we would win in court." Jason's words tumbled out as he fought to explain himself. "Cambric agreed not to argue their case. They agreed to a bench trial with Judge Allen. Without Cambric putting up a fight we all knew he would rule in our favor. Not only did it free Jace permanently and irrevocably, but it's now a case that others can cite. It can be used against all agencies in the future. Only… now I know why Cambric agreed to it."

"Why?" Val sobbed.

"It wasn't just that they wanted Gabe back. It was that they no longer had you to give. They played us."

"No!" Val screamed at him, screamed and beat her closed fists against his chest. "Tell me you didn't let him do it. Tell me you didn't give him over to them."

"I'm sorry." Jason pressed her against him, winding his arms around her sagging body. "Finn tried to talk us out of it, but he wouldn't say why. I've never wanted to take something back more in my life."

Her knees gave out. Her body went limp. Cambric had Gabe. Jason traded him back to Cambric and he was never, *ever* going to escape. The Agency would never let him out of their sight. What they had done to her wouldn't even begin to compare to what they would do to him.

"I wish I could take it back." Jason repeated, talking quietly into her hair. "I wish I could set him free."

"Oh-" Clay's voice sounded from the porch steps. "But there is *something* you can do."

Val twisted to watch his face in the dark. Jason followed her line of sight. The corner of Clay's mouth quirked a moment before settling into seriousness. His eyes glittered with calculation.

"Why don't you two come inside?" He resumed. "I think we've got a lot to talk about."

A word from the author:

Just so you know… Agent Finn has a story of his own to tell. Check out VANISH ME and find out just what he's been hiding.

Get Book Three in The Captive Series by clicking now on the following link… THE CAPTIVE RISING

Want to know when the next book is ready?

Sign up for an email notification here…

LK MAGILL NEWSLETTER

Join my ARC Team!

Click on the link - ARC TEAM - LK MAGILL

Reviews pretty, pretty please…

Each and every positive review makes a huge difference. Please leave one with the retailer from whom you purchased this book. I love hearing from you.

Websites:

www.lkmagill.com

Like me on Facebook:

https://fb.me/LKMagill1

Follow me on Instagram:

https://www.instagram.com/lk.magill.author
Check out my Amazon page:
http://amazon.com/author/lkmagill

ALSO BY LK MAGILL

Standalone novels:

VANISH ME

The Captive Series:

THE CAPTIVE BORN - Book One

THE CAPTIVE MISSING - Book Two

THE CAPTIVE RISING - Book Three

Outlasting Series:

OUTLASTING AFTER - Book One

CHASING TRUTH - Book Two

SURVIVING THE WALL - Book Three

BREAKING BEFORE - Book Four

TAKING TOMORROW - Book Five

FINDING FOREVER - Book Six

SNEAK PEEK

THE CAPTIVE RISING - BOOK THREE

Gabe

His palms were sweating now, the line along his brow, too. But it wasn't hot in the SUV. Nope. It was his nerves. His fucking nerves clutched at him, they wouldn't let go.

Swallowing, Gabe widened his eyes. He used to be better at this.

Outside the SUV's window, rain coated the highway. He could hear the drops falling, echoing against the metal roof, splattering across the hood and doors. It was a downpour. If the temperature in New York dipped just a few more degrees, then they might even get a flurry of snow.

Music from the speakers pumped with the violent undertones of a rap song. The Cambric driver bobbed his head in time with the beat, murmuring the slurred words quickly under his breath. An oversized guard was sitting shotgun and with a huff of disgust, he leaned up to the radio and switched the station.

"Hey man, what the hell?" The driver's hand shot out to change it back.

"I don't get paid enough to listen to that shit," the guard growled.

"Quiet," Shane spat. One word from him had both of the men falling silent.

Gabe's chest tightened. The asshole himself was seated in the back, right beside Gabe. He was wearing a gray suit and a lavender tie.

Stealing a quick glance at the prick, Gabe's teeth ground together inside of his head. They hadn't seen one another in years. Shane's face sported a short beard now. It was blonde, the color of his thinning hair. Even with those blue eyes of his locked on his cell phone, he still managed to look smug.

Evil piece of shit. *What did you do with Val? Where the hell is she?*

The questions pounded around like a drum beat inside Gabe's head. He was still reeling from the shock of it all. Their exchange at the courthouse had not gone as planned. Not even close.

Squeezing his eyes shut, Gabe reached up reflexively to loosen his own tie. It suddenly felt too tight around his neck so he tugged at the navy-blue knot with one finger.

Inhaling deeply, he paused before letting loose a shaky breath. The meeting today kept flashing through his mind. He couldn't wipe it away.

Jason had been tense, his shoulders tight beneath his black suit jacket. Gabe had been walking next to him, also wearing black, the color of mourning. It had seemed fitting that they both chose it.

"You sure you want to do this?" Jason tugged at Gabe's elbow, pulling him to a stop in the crowded hallway of the courthouse.

All around them, other people had continued to cruise by. Lawyers, plaintiffs, defendants, court clerks, janitors, secretaries, everyone. Jason's voice had dropped to a whisper, his arctic blue eyes zeroing in on Gabe.

Sucking in a breath, Gabe glanced down at the guy's hand. He was fidgeting with that silver wedding band of his. The ring Val had given to him. Gabe nodded his head as if to reassure himself that he was doing the right thing, then he glanced away.

"Yeah," he said quietly. "I'm sure."

"We can try to find another way..." Jason's voice wavered.

"No," Gabe cut him off. "This is the only sure way, and you know it."

Giving his head a quick shake now, Gabe opened his eyes. *The only sure way.* Hah. Neither of them had known how wrong they could possibly be.

"Don't get undressed yet, lover boy," Shane interrupted Gabe's thoughts as he glanced at the gold Rolex on his wrist. "We're almost there."

Gabe's insides flipped then, and he fought the flash of rage that surged through him at the sound of Shane's voice. Shit, he wanted to ruin the prick. He wanted to slam the guy's head against the window glass over and over until it shattered.

Shane had gone back on his end of the deal. He was supposed to give Val back. He was supposed to set Val free and stop fighting the court case over Jace. In exchange for those two things, Gabe had agreed to turn himself back over to Cambric.

The Agency would own him once more, but his conscience would be clear.

No more listening to Jace cry for his mommy at night. No more killing a bottle of Gin with Jason just to get the guy to stop asking about Cambric. He'd wanted to know about the breeding program, and Ben, and what you had to do to pass training.

Shit. Gabe just didn't have the heart to tell him, so he'd agreed to the deal. Easy right? Nope, like all things with Cambric, there was a catch.

Shane lost Val. She disappeared. The asshole had announced that tidy little fact the moment Jason and Gabe had settled into the meeting room at the courthouse.

Val was missing.

And to top it all off… if Gabe had changed his mind and decided *not* to turn himself in, then Cambric would keep pursuing Jace. Not only would they continue to fight the court case, but they'd also produce evidence that this illegal back-room deal was proposed by Jason himself. Which of course, was true.

And that wasn't even the sucker punch. Ready for it? Agent John *I'm A Complete Asshole* Finn was there to confirm it.

He *knew*.

Shane had contacted the FBI Agent the week before and had him do an internal investigation, which turned up (surprise, surprise) nothing. Finn knew that Cambric no longer had Val, and he hadn't told them.

And sure, Finn had tried to talk Gabe out of turning himself in, but he hadn't explained *why*. He'd kept his mouth shut. He'd betrayed them. Not for the first time, Gabe reminded himself, and released a slow breath through his nostrils.

Grumbling under his breath, the Cambric driver checked his blind spot before changing lanes. The SUV rocked with the abrupt movement as Gabe focused his attention out the rear window. Darkness was falling all around them now, as the rain continued to pelt down.

Clearing his throat, Shane stared pointedly at the side of Gabe's head. Gabe could feel the implication. Shane's order had yet to be obeyed.

Jaw ticking, Gabe worked to tighten his tie once more. Securing it as instructed, he smoothed his slick palms down the front of his jacket before returning them demurely to his sides.

He couldn't hit Shane.

He couldn't hit a free man, no matter how badly he craved it. It was against the law, not to mention he was a little outnumbered. Three to one to be exact.

Nope. Gabe would have to content himself with the knowledge that Jason had wrecked that smug face a few months ago. He would have to learn once more to live in dreams that danced inside his own head.

As the driver merged off the freeway, water splashed up from puddles that were steadily forming in low spots on the asphalt. Muddy rain coated the passenger side window for a moment before sliding slowly away.

Gabe blinked at the maze of roads and humanity rolling

by. This wasn't the way to Cambric. They should still be driving north.

"Where are we?" The question jumped from his mouth before he even thought about it. Four years as a free man would do that to you.

Shane's quick bark of laughter filled the small space. There was no way he would be answering to a captive. Involuntarily, Gabe's hands clenched themselves into fists. He had to work hard to release them.

All this time, Gabe had assumed he would be returning to The Agency's property in upstate. He figured he would be readmitted through intake, the way Val had been. And he figured he was pretty well prepared for that now, since it was the one thing Gabe had wanted out of Agent Finn… prior to his betrayal and all that.

Where was intake located? What had he seen them do to Val? Who had been there?

Of all the places Gabe had been inside Cambric, intake had never been one of them. It was an unknown that he'd wanted to learn about in an attempt to mentally prepare for it. The worst thing a male D2 could show at Cambric was fear.

But it had been a battle to get the information from Agent Finn. Gabe recalled their heated conversation. Jason was pissed, having been locked out of the room. It was just the two of them then, only Finn and Gabe. That's when the former had tried like hell to talk Gabe out of turning himself in.

Trust me, he'd said. *Don't go back in. Please, don't do it.*

Looking back now, Gabe wondered how long Agent Finn had known the truth. Those bastards at Cambric didn't have

Val. She was dead and buried somewhere, or worse, alive and in the possession of some rich psycho.

Gabe tried to wipe the dread from his thoughts. He tried like hell not to feel like his sacrifice was for nothing. After all, they still had the court case. Cambric folded just like they were supposed to and the Judge had ruled in Jace's favor.

Val's boy was now forever free, and other captives would someday be able to use his case to gain their freedom, too. At least Gabe hoped so.

Rocking to the left, Gabe's shoulder tapped against the passenger window as the SUV took a sharp right turn and then another left before merging onto a narrow two lane highway. Forest surrounded them, swallowing up the view on either side of the road. It was pitch black outside now, and the rain continued to pour down.

Occasionally, headlights approached them from the oncoming lane. Gabe held his eyes open as long as he could before he was forced to blink or look away. He liked the pain. He wanted to hurt.

He wanted to *do* something, to have some sort of control. Hell, he was half-tempted to slam his own head against the window glass right now.

Val was probably dead, or being hurt. And it was all his fault. His. Fault.

If he'd just gone back to Cambric to begin with, none of this would have happened. Jace would still have his mommy. Jason would still have his wife. And Bee…

God, the thought of her made Gabe's heart want to explode.

What would she do when she found out her best friend was

missing? As if Gabe leaving her like that hadn't been bad enough, now she wouldn't have Val either.

If he closed his eyes, he could still see Bee standing on their dock in the Maldives, her tear-stained cheeks, her red-rimmed eyes. The baby-blue dress she'd been wearing had picked up in the breeze, whipping around her tanned thighs as he'd turned the boat motor over and driven away.

Shit.

Gabe's eyes shot open now, and he bit hard on the inside of his cheek. So, what prevented him from head-butting the glass until he blacked out? Well, the answer was pretty simple really. It was hope. The most dangerous, toxic and addictive drug that any captive could possess.

Hope that Val was alive. Hope that the answers of what had happened to her lay somewhere inside of Cambric. Somewhere that Gabe was sure he would eventually end up.

It might take him months, maybe even years, but he would find out the truth. He would keep himself in check, if for nothing other than that.

The SUV slowed. An enormous razor-wire fence shot up before them and behind it stretched a collection of brick and concrete buildings that towered under metal light poles. What is this place?

Gabe's mouth hung open slightly. The sweat on his brow dried up. Suddenly, he was parched. His breath came out hot and dry.

Pulling to a stop alongside a guard shack, the SUV shifted into park. A thin man in a rainproof trench coat walked forward before leaning down to lay his wrists just inside the open driver side window. Water dripped from his dark cap.

The gold emblem that decorated its peaked front was familiar.

He was law enforcement of some sort, Gabe realized. He was a prison guard.

Gabe's lungs shriveled in his chest. He began to wheeze. Why the hell were they at a prison? Were they going to kill him? Torture him?

If he hadn't already sweated every drop of moisture out of his body, Gabe felt certain he would've pissed himself.

"It's well after visiting hours," the guard remarked.

"We hoped an exception could be made." The driver handed over a thick envelope. Rain pattered on the pavement.

Making slow work of opening the envelope, the guard thumbed through the stack of neat greenish bills. Gabe could almost smell the new mint off the money. He had felt the crispness of cash run against his fingers in his free life, so much cash. But what had his success bought him in the end? He still hadn't been able to avoid the inevitability of this path.

The guard said nothing. Tucking the soggy white envelope into his coat pocket, he simply backed away.

Up ahead, the imposing chainlink gate rolled slowly to the right and the SUV navigated through it. Darkened buildings fanned out all around them. Gabe squeezed his eyes shut, leaning back into the leather of the carseat.

He couldn't breathe. He couldn't breathe.

His heart was screaming at him, thumping harder and harder. His fingers gripped impulsively at the seatbelt where it crossed his lap. His brain was swimming. Don't pass out. Don't... pass...

His head must have lolled to one side because the punch

from Shane came hard against the center of his chest. Gabe coughed, then choked in air. His lungs began to work again and he fought the swirling feeling that caused darkness to flicker in his mind.

"Don't faint on me, you delicate piece of shit," Shane spat out the words, before shoving a selection of tiny pills into Gabe's palm.

Raising his eyebrows in surprise, Gabe blinked down at the familiar drugs. Red to get you high and blue for… well, to get you hard.

What the…?

Cold, sick, overwhelming dread tipped itself into Gabe's bloodstream and moved fast to overtake him. They weren't going to leave him here as a prisoner. They weren't going to put a bullet in his head and bury him out back.

This was a client trip.

Holy shit. They wanted him to fuck someone at this prison.

"We don't have all night, lover boy." Shane forced an open water bottle into Gabe's other hand. "She doesn't like to wait. You know that."

"*She?*" Gabe's whisper caught on his lips as his hands began to shake.

"Yeah, she." Shane smiled wryly, enjoying every second of this sort of torture. "You're owner, Sharon. You know, the one you stabbed in the back… she misses you."

www.ingramcontent.com/pod-product-compliance
Lightning Source LLC
Chambersburg PA
CBHW030626310726
48979CB00003B/907

* 9 7 8 1 9 5 0 9 2 8 0 4 0 *